Collected Nature Stories

Henry Williamson

Collected Nature Stories

Macdonald and Jane's · London

ISBN 0 356 02945 X

This edition first published in 1970 by
Macdonald and Jane's Publishers Limited,
Paulton House, 8 Shepherdess Walk, London, N1

Second impression, 1976

Made and printed in Great Britain by
Hazell Watson & Viney Ltd,
Aylesbury, Bucks

Contents

General Introduction

Within the covers of this book are almost all the short stories about birds, animals, and fish I wrote in my youth. With them are a few brief tales based on what I heard in village pubs, and elsewhere, about old people who lived, or had lived, in some of the villages of North Devon.

In those days each village had its pride, or rather conceit, based on ancient rivalries. Generally speaking, no village—to judge by the remarks at its inn—thought much of any adjacent village. "They'm a lot of bliddy rogues!" was often to be heard, as I sat on a bench, amidst rank tobacco smoke, hoarse laughter, political arguments in shouted voices, and Chaucerian gossip about neighbours.

Many of the fields around the villages were then, as today, down to pasture, called grazing. Most of the cottages were thatched, upon walls of cob. Water was from wells, sanitation by earth closet. I and another ex-service man occupied one of these cottages. We were known by some, notably a well-to-do farmer who had not gone to the war but remained at home to make money, as 'Jarmans', perhaps because we both wore our war-time khaki tunics, and had grown beards. Our enemy was a stout little man who used to ride a cob over his lands, which lay upon a headland lying some way westward into the Atlantic.

For me all this countryside was delightfully wild, including the occasional arrival of the horseman red-faced and raging at our joint presence upon the right-of-way above the cliffs of the headland, and passing by the verge of his crops of oats, barley, and swede turnips.

"You be bliddy Jarmans!" he cried. "I'll 'ave'ee for trespass into Town, ah, woan I, tho!"

Sometimes my poet companion, whose beard was tawny while mine was brown, would stand and regard the tubby fellow on a tubby horse. Then he would say slowly, "You bore me, little man!", and then, "As I was saying, Harry, when Father—', but I was already striding on ahead, not wanting to hear autobiographical details of his life when on extended leave from his flying duties in London among actors, actresses, and others of the gay night-life of the town in war-time. When not speaking of these adventures, which included forgery of his father's cheques, appearances in police courts, etc., (usually in a scoffing voice) he was reciting the poems of Swinburne; while I wanted to see the ravens, peregrine falcons, rock pipits, cormorants and other birds that lived in the air and upon the sea below.

The year was 1921; it was spring; the gulls were about to lay on the rocky ledges below the path, for—immemorial sign—the pale green stems of barley had arisen two inches out of the stony fields. As we drew near to the precipice at the end of our walk, where the land ended, I could see far Lundy on the horizon, and, to the north, the western coast of the Gower peninsula in South Wales lying under slow moving clouds drifting in from the Atlantic. To the eyes of youth, were it evening (and my friend happily addressing another audience in one or another of the village pubs) the clouds reflected the burning Valhalla in Wagner's *Götterdämmerung,* to which I had listened in the gallery of Covent Garden opera house the summer before, during the season of Sir Thomas Beecham's company. Almost every evening during the year of 1920 I went to listen to opera: a new world of the Imagination opening before one after five years in the Army.

I was the owner of a new motor-bicycle, bought with part of my gratuity on leaving the Service. It was a Brooklands Road Special Norton, with long-stroke racing engine and long nickel-plated exhaust pipe from which I had removed the silencer. It had lapped Brooklands motor-racing track at 73 miles an hour, and was my pride and joy. The engine-beat was music to my ears. There were no gears in those days. Propulsion was by a flexible rubber-and-canvas belt from the engine to a large v-shaped rim on the rear wheel. The pulley was a Phillipson, with a phosphor-bronze ring, which, touched by the sole of my left shoe, opened the outer flange of the pulley and thereby lowered the gear, thus enabling the driver to get away at speed. When well open, the pulley enabled one to get up a barbarously steep and very narrow lane near Lynton called Beggar's Roost, bestrewn in those days with lumps of shale and ironstone. At the steepest part the way up lay over the rock itself, where was a gradient of 1 in $3\frac{1}{2}$.

Before one lay Exmoor to the east; and northwards lay the Welsh mountains.

O, I loved my trusty Norton! Sometimes, in those early days, I took my red-bearded friend on the carrier behind me; but even then with mixed feelings, for often he was full of beer, which amplified an attitude of scorn and arrogance. Together we hared through the sunken lanes, on our way to the moors and the sea-shore. Our friendship, such as it was, soon ended. He had been told to leave his father's house near London, by an aged parent whose attitude towards one whom he described as his 'blackguard son' was as scornful as that of the son to the father—"Beer is for the young, father; bed is for the old. Why not go to bed, Father? You not only look very old and tired, but you are a very great bore, and must have been equally boring during all your Seven Ages, Father."

I, having been forbidden my father's house, stayed awhile with Mr. Warbeck and his upset son, Julian. One night we decided to go down to Devon, and work hard at our writing, and win fame together; Julian to continue his literary career with 'the finest translation of the love poems of Catullus ever rendered into English'.

It was soon evident to me that I had taken the place of 'Father' in our new relationship. Julian's scorn was inevitably directed upon me when he returned, night after night, after closing-time, from one or another of the two village pubs. There he stood, by the open door, flushed and arrogant: derisive of myself sitting at the table before the open hearth, writing *Dandelion Days*: he wrapped in an enormous bear-skin flying coat which he had worn while piloting a scout 'plane on the Western Front during 1918. Our quarrels reminded me of an early Charlie Chaplin film, when, one night, I felt so deranged at the glowering bear tormenting me with words that I got up with a scream (assumed) and fired my double-barrel gun past his head, aiming for the coal-house door in the corner of the kitchen (the only room downstairs).

The report clapped out the oil lamp; a clumsy bear pursued me up the short stairs, hindered by the coat; but before he could get up from all-fours, I pushed my bed between us as an obstacle. He hauled off the bedding, lumped it on his rusty second-hand half-crown bed in the adjoining small bedroom; and, lying upon the heap, composed himself to sleep, snoring.

This was too much! I tipped up the jangling bed, and jerked the iron frame on top of the heap. From this he struggled free, to pursue me down the stairs. There we wrestled, neither wanting to hurt the other, in a half-hearted way. I got on top of him. He burst into tears; and getting up slowly, made his apologies while I relit the lamp. Two ragged holes like big inkblots, one beside the other, now adorned my coal house door. Without further word he went upstairs.

I waited until he came down again, carrying a portmanteau which he had, without permission, removed from his father's house.

"Where are you going?"

"Back to Father."

"Father will be pleased!"

"You can sneer, Harry, but you don't know what I have to put up with, at home."

With these sorrowful words, Julian set off to walk to London, 200 miles away. After a while I followed him up the village street. He was sitting on the stone step of the pub. "Come old boy, let's make friends, shall we?"

I gave him one more night; he must leave the next day.

He left in the morning, but not for London. He found a lodging down the street with a sailor whose ship had been blown up at the battle of Jutland. On that occasion 'Sailor' and others had floated all one night, covered by black oil-fuel, before rescue. He was a dumb ox of a man, who spent three days drinking every month, until his pension slip, which arrived by post, was expended.

'Sailor' had one small room in his brother's cottage, where he was barely tolerated. Julian shared his bed. I heard that 'Sailor' complained that Julian was a 'drunken booger': to which Julian replied that it wasn't worth arguing with 'the lumpen proletariat'. I wrote a story about 'Sailor' some time after leaving my cottage, to get married; the curious will find it in *Tales of a Devon Village*, which does not come within the scope of this collection.

With some peace now, I put aside *Dandelion Days*, and began to write a story, based on a walk, during the winter of 1919/1920, to see a friend who lived near Dartmoor. Then another story about an old man, who had lived in the cottage before the war, and was the friend of a mouse. To my excitement this was accepted by the editor of 'The Royal Magazine', but with a condition.

I will accept The Mouse, but I trust the author will allow me to remove some of the provincialisms apparently in use among the lower orders in Devonshire. I like this story, speaking for myself, so I will buy it for £12/12/– but cannot guarantee to publish it as it stands.

*

It never appeared in the 'Royal'; but I received my twelve guineas.

Other stories written during the autumn and winter of 1921/22 went to 'The Strand Magazine', famous since the 'nineties for serialising the Sherlock Holmes stories. Mr. Greenhaugh Smith, the editor, refused all of mine. This did not surprise me. Most of its post-war stories were unreal, so it seemed to me; and I scorned them.

Then occurred something which confirmed the ideas which, to adapt a phrase in Shakespeare's *Hamlet*, 'hung on me like clouds'. The clouds condensed in gentle rain when I went to a performance, in a London theatre, of *Saint Joan*, by Bernard Shaw. The deeply moving play confirmed what I had already discovered for myself during the Great War: that tragedy arises not so much from mis-understanding, but un-understanding: that both antagonist and protagonist could be right, in their differing worlds, at the same time. All great poets (here used as a general term to include philosophy, painting, sculpture, novels, verse, etc.) were the lightbringers of humanity.

At school I had undergone a sort of classical education, or inculca-tion, which I had entirely rejected. Now, as my mind became clear, I saw how great a poet was Virgil, and his opening theme of com-passion, *Sunt lacrimae rerum, et mentem mortalia tangunt* ... 'My pages follow the tears of life, wherein human misery cuts the heart'.

Shakespeare, Hardy, Shelley, Conrad, Jefferies, Barbusse, Duhamel ... these and others were my constant companions of the mind as I walked alone by the sea and on the hills, and read at night before my cottage hearth by the light of a solitary candle.

The Peregrine's Saga
and other wild tales
(1921—1922)

Preface

These were published in book form in 1923, by Messrs. Collins, on the advice of J. D. Beresford, then the Reader for that firm. It was through 'J.D.' that Collins & Co. published my first novels—*The Beautiful Years, Dandelion Days, The Dream of Fair Women*—and my earliest collection of essays entitled *The Lone Swallows*. These 'titles' failed to sell. Indeed not one earned its advance royalty payment of £25.

When, a year or two later, I asked the publishers if they would advance £25 on the option of my next book, which was to conclude *The Flax of Dream*, they wrote to advise me that it was not their intention to exercise the option; that they were returning to me the copyrights of the five published books.

This gave me freedom to turn elsewhere; and soon afterwards another publisher wrote to me, saying that he had been hearing about my work from Walter de la Mare; and had I any manuscript for his consideration?

In due course, *Tarka the Otter* went to Messrs. Putnam.

Now to the short stories, written during the early days in Devon.

A Winter's Tale

One December afternoon, not long after the ending of the Great War, a young man of pensive and unshaven countenance, without a hat, wearing khaki breeches and puttees, with a coat made out of an Army blanket of fine tweed material which had been scrounged from a Dispersals Unit on the south coast of England just before demobilisation, and carrying on his back a shrapnel-torn infantry pack, might have been seen perambulating down Piccadilly towards the west.

He might have been seen, but it is more probable that no one saw him; for at the time a dense fog lay over London. It was a period of intense cold. Most of Europe was frozen, and the majority of its population was starved. The Treaty of Versailles had been signed a few months since, and that fact, or more particularly its repercussions in the family to which he had returned, at the age of twenty-four after five years' service in the Army, was one of the reasons why he was determined so resolutely to get post-war London, with its mental and physical fogs, as far as possible behind his back.

The young man said to himself as he strode through sulphurous yellow vapour that he had rejected the old European civilisation, based on war-mentality, for ever. With a feeling of freedom and a new life he walked through the rest of the day and all the following night and the next day, and five days later he had reached Exeter, more than a hundred and seventy miles from The Smoke, as now, from casual talk with other tramps, he had learned to call London. Leaving his lodging in darkness at five o'clock, on the seventh day he came to the eastern edge of Dartmoor.

That young man was myself. Never before had I experienced such a feeling of happiness and well-being; and in the sudden sense of power which the thought gave I broke into song. I felt I could walk for ever, and the thought of being able to sleep every night in a bed gave me, at the moment, an additional sense of joy. For the homeless winters of the recent war were still immediate in my mind.

My destination was a house in a coombe beyond Princetown, where I had been invited to spend Christmas by a friend I had known during the war.

It was Christmas Eve. I had telegraphed C--- that I would arrive before dinner. But having slacked off that day, I still had far to go. Exeter had been left before dawn and the route I now followed was the old coach road under Cotley Wood, up and down hills to the River Teign, through Bridford Wood, and so to Moreton Hampstead. There I had eaten a big meal, for it was very cold. A black north wind swept the rocky ground, every runner was frozen and the big rivers were edged with ice. I knew, of course, that to drink and eat amply would break the rhythm of walking, and now I was paying for it as I slogged on mile after mile, on that bare road which climbs up and up to more than a thousand feet above the sea and leads on through the incult moor.

I felt very much alone; I did not see a single bird. There was no food on that ice-bound place of granite where the wind screamed in rush and heather.

On my right as I walked I saw dark tors ranged one behind the other under the cold and heavy gloom of the sky. Could I last out to my friend's house? I began to feel pessimistic, that I was a worn-out scarecrow to the spearing wind and the revengeful Treaty of Versailles, negation of all that the positive old soldiers of all nations had learned upon the battlefield.

Higher and higher the road climbed, past Shapley Common and Birch Tor, my map marked by the hut circles and tumuli of the ancient men who were buried there.

At the Warren House Inn I rested, spreading my hands to the peat fire which had been burning continuously in the grate for more than a century. I drank two pints of beer for the sake of comrades left with the war, and for no other reason. I felt forlorn as I sat there, thinking of the past; and then, facing the wind again, walked downhill to the bridge over the East Dart. Onwards, over the Cherry Brook, and so to Two Bridges, where the West Dart ran dark brown and noisy among its plates of ice-armour and granite boulders white with spray-crusts and sharp with icicles. All these names I learned from my 1-inch Ordnance map.

A man in a bearskin flying-coat overtook me in an ancient

battleship-grey Mercedes-Benz car and stopped to offer a lift, seeing the army pack on my back. I nearly yielded, for my feet ached, and I longed for army friendship; but my mind was set to endure, as in the war upon the Western Front. Also I had a fixed mental picture of myself stumbling in through a nailed oak door into a vast hall and swaying with weariness before the flames of an open hearth.

So I walked on alone, and came, as afternoon began to darken, upon an appalling group of buildings within a square of high walls, which was the convict prison. Conscientious objectors had been held there during the war, but now, I supposed, another set of wretched men were imprisoned. It was a sickening sight, that prison, originally built to hold French soldiers captured from Napoleon. My walk began to seem meaningless thereafter. Was there any escape for men upon the earth?

Somehow I limped into Princetown. I went into another inn and looked at the map and reckoned I had walked twenty-six miles that day. Being damnably weary, I thought I would save several miles by turning left-handed up a lesser road to Tor Royal; and, by following a track beside the Devonport Leat, arrive at where the Abbot's Way joined a track by disused tin-mines. There I would be, according to the map, about a mile and a half from my destination. I visualised that great oak door opening, the welcome of voice and handclasp and the flames of an oak-wood fire, an armchair, a large whisky, drowsy talk, a soft bed into which I would crawl, half-tight, and sleep, sleep, sleep.

Now I must make the effort to leave the inn; my sweat was becoming chilly on shirt and breeches; so pulling myself up upon monstrous heavy boots, I hobbled into darkness and saw the constellation of Orion glittering over my right shoulder.

That walk on the track above the Devonport Leat seemed endless. My feet stumbled unexpectedly; I knew this for extreme fatigue: so one had lurched sideways, and occasionally fallen without sense of falling, when going out of flooded trenches on those everlasting wastes of water, shell-fire, and utter negation of life called the Somme and Ypres Salient.

I began to enjoy my present and voluntary fatigue: was I not FREE? I tried to imagine that far-away nightmare time: the light-handed feeling and the frozen boots knocking about: the fiery thunderous bursting shells in the waste-land: the never-ceasing crackle of musketry: the flares spilling in greenish-white pools of radiance behind the slow staggering shadows of exhausted and homeless men: the dead mules and horses, the wailing of Strombos horns .. *gas*!

And walking on mechanically as in that same world without horizon I was suddenly conscious of the constellation of Orion sliding up the sky in a peculiar manner. I had fallen over, and was lying on my back in fathomless contentment. What did it matter?

I lay there until the nails of my fingers began to throb, as though being prised by frost. I was imagining the flash of guns at night, and the dilating pallor of the flares. And then, as warmth began to leave my body, another set of thoughts entered my mind: I was alone on the moor, and if I didn't rouse myself, I might sleep into death, and perhaps find my comrades again, men of all armies of the Great War ...

Who was touching my face so lightly?

At last I managed to get to my feet and stand upright. All sound had gone from the world. A black gloom was closing about me, and with a kind of terror I saw the stars were darkening out. Was I ill, perhaps dying? Was I possessed by the dead, about to receive mystical revelation? I sought for a match, but my fingers were made of wood, and I poked half the matches out of the box before I was able to strike one end and hold its flames against the map. The match burned out in my fingers, but I felt nothing.

I must make an effort to move onwards; or go back. Should I go back to Princetown? No, walk on. The mysterious and unearthly presence was touching my right cheek again and again, as though my hair had suddenly grown long, but I could feel nothing there with my hand.

It was now so dark that I could not see. Standing still, I felt a minute cold touch on my neck, inside the open collar of my trench-coat. Another. Another. I seemed to be imagining many slight noises, not exactly tapping nor yet rustling, but a sort of gentle sighing all around me. Something cold and wet lodged on my eyelashes. With relief I knew it was snowing.

The relief was but momentary, for now indeed I might be lost altogether. What should I do? I must decide quickly.

I remained still, unable to make up my mind whether to return or to go forward. One section of my mind was set on going forward, the other said it would be wise to return. To this prudent section of my mind I addressed the suggestion that there was danger of falling into the leat—a channel of water running in its bed of granite blocks, perhaps to a distant reservoir—and if that happened I might be unable to get on my feet and crawl out and so would be drowned—

The rest of the walk seemed to be through another dimension of life. The ground before me would rise up and bump me, and yet I was walking on without realisation of how I had got to my feet again. Snow fell thickly, blindly, and I went on uncaring whether I dropped into any hidden hollow or mine-shaft. I came to a cross-track and, visualising the map, kept straight on. Then, to my immense exaltation, I heard a dog barking somewhere in front.

2

Unexpectedly a door opened and a light shone out. Oh, blessed relief! A man was shouting in a furious voice at the dog. I called out, but the door was shut. I groped a way to the door and knocked, and after a while it was opened about an inch, and I saw a woman's head against the lamp on the table within. To her cautious and reluctant questions as to what I wanted I asked if it would be possible to find accommodation in her farmhouse for the night? She hesitated a moment and then said no, and the door was shut again. I sat down in the porch and felt myself dissolving into sleep.

About half a minute later the door opened once more, wider this time, and the man who had shouted stood beside the woman. The man asked me where I came from and where I was going. I explained that I was going to spend Christmas nearby, and had come that way because I thought it was a short cut. Would there be any objection to my sleeping in the barn? I was used to sleeping in barns, particularly barns which had broken walls and no roofs. I would, of course, pay what was asked for the accommodation.

"I'll pay you whatever you ask," I repeated. "In advance, if you like."

As the farmer and his wife still seemed doubtful, I said bleakly, "Well, I am sorry to have disturbed you; but would you care to sell me some old sacks and a few sticks of wood, so that I can make myself a shelter and a fire behind a rock somewhere? I will give you ten shillings, or even a pound, which is more than my life is worth, anyway."

I opened my note-case and showed them money.

The woman asked me in and begged to be excused for a moment. Immediately I regretted what I felt to have been my rudeness and began to stammer out that I had come a long distance. The man invited me to sit by the fire, before going with his wife into another room; and, first carefully closing the door, talking to her in low earnest tones. The buzzing of voices came through the lime-flaky wall. When they came in again I noticed that the woman had a woe-begone face, with eyes as though she had been weeping. The man was a heavy type of farmer, with rough, dark moustache, beard and whiskers. He had large hands hanging loose by his side, and thick, protruding ears.

The woman explained that they would not wish anybody to be outside on a night like this, but if I didn't mind waiting a while she would see about getting a bedroom ready. Would I like some supper? There was some cold pork and some pickles, and some stewed prunes for afters, she said, and cheese. I thanked her, and seeing that she was preparing to lay the table in the little room adjoining the kitchen, begged to be allowed to remain by the fire.

I was ravenously hungry; the food produced a feeling of hilarity; and I talked about my journey with a volubility that diminished as I became more and more aware of a curious feeling of tension in the room. Once as I looked up I noticed that the woman was quietly crying to herself. The man sat on a milking-stool by the hearth, his boots on, but unlaced, his coat off and his big hands touching the uneven, rocky floor, staring into the fire. The woman asked to be excused again, and she went out, repeating that she would prepare the room, and would I please to sit by the fire and rest. The man, muttering to himself, followed her up the staircase, shutting the door behind him.

Left alone, I picked up a copy of the *News of the World,* noticing it was three weeks old, and idly glanced from page to page with their accounts of murders, adulteries, embezzlements, burglaries, forgeries, larcenies, seductions, abductions and football. Putting down the paper, which was without interest for me, I looked around for something else, but all I could find was a copy of the *Old Testament.*

The national literature of Great Britain, I thought, ironically.

The Bible lay open on the window-sill, and it may have been that I had disturbed their nightly reading. Perhaps that accounted for the reluctant reception? They were gone a long time. I stared about the room. The ceiling above carried many strange sounds, as though of heavy things being dragged about. I began to doze in the heat of the room, and then the staircase-door was opening, the woman descending with a handkerchief to her eyes. Behind her the man said,

"If you'll plaize to come this way, my dear, I'll show 'ee the room."

I followed him up the creaking staircase, lifting one leg painfully after the other, and struck by instant cold after the warmth of the kitchen. The farmer led the way into the room. It was square and dark, with a four-poster bed in the middle and heavy curtains over the windows. The cold gloom smothered the candlelight. In the corner was a large cupboard. "I'll be bringing 'ee th' monk in a minute, my dear," said the farmer.

"The monk?"

"Aiy, th' monk. 'Twall yett th' bade for 'ee, my dear," the hairy fellow muttered, as he clumped down the stairs again. A monk to heat the bed for me? I laughed hysterically, lolling on the bed. Sleeping with a monk? What a scream, old top! I said to myself, and cracked my fingers. But, by heaven, wasn't there a monastery nearby, or an order of Friars on Dartmoor? Perhaps monks were being billeted out on people, their monastery still commandeered by the military authorities? Damn it, it was beyond a joke, sharing a bed with a monk. I decided to sleep on the floor.

Silence, as I sat on the bed and waited. Like most other people, I considered myself sensitive to atmosphere. I had never been able to make up my mind about spiritualism. I had been to one spiritua-listic *séance*, I had begun to think I had undeveloped powers of mediumship: that under suitable conditions I would be able to cause spirit-materialisations. This feeling was, at that time, an illusion common among people whose emotions were distraught by the griefs and excitations of wartime.

3

While I was thinking about the possibility of possession by evil spirits, a strange sound made me start and my heart to beat violently in my ears. It came from the corner cupboard. Against instinctive fear, I found myself walking to the cupboard with a feeling that icicles were forming on my neck. I was standing before the cup-board, the door of the bedroom being open, when the woman slipped into the room, grasped the knob on the door of the cupboard, and with a smothered cry stood with her back against it.

"I thought I heard a sound in there," I said, while my eyelids felt thick and heavy. "As though something had fallen."

To my surprise and alarm the woman burst into tears and cried: "Tidden right for anyone to be sleeping yurr! I knew 'twoulden be right!"

I didn't know what to reply to that, or what I should do, and feeling the unreality of everything, I said nothing. Should I offer to leave the place and go outside and chance finding a barn or a bracken stack or somewhere I could wait for daylight? I flinched from the thought and continued standing there dully. I felt impatience, irritability, anger. It was absurd: I, a soldier with over five years' active service, to be in such a position. And to sleep with a monk! Damnation, I would . . .

The woman, muttering she must find the key, went out of the room.

Left alone, I examined the small casement window. The lower panes were clotted with snow. Opening one half of the casement, I saw large, heavy flakes falling thickly. If it continued all night it would be at least a foot deep by the morning; should the wind arise, drifts would gather, hiding ditches and mine-shafts, and there would be nothing by which to guide oneself. I would remain where I was, monk or no monk! But where was the ruddy fellow? In the cupboard? What a joke! If only I had a friend with me, and a flask of S.R.D. rum! This was a proper Christmas Eve, I told myself.

After all, perhaps the man and his wife had been quarrelling when I arrived and it was a lonely farm and possibly they were unused to anyone coming at all. I had disorganised the household. I would inquire how far he was from old C---'s place—that might reassure them. Then I had an idea that they might be concealing an escaped convict. Poor devil, I'd be the last to betray him!

When the man came up the stairs he was carrying an object like a copper pan filled with embers swinging inside an oaken frame. He lifted up the heavy quilt and blankets of the bed and put the object inside. " 'Twill remove the death-sweat," was his alarming comment. "Monk us calls'n—proper bade-warmer, zur."

"So that's the monk, is it?' I began to laugh and laugh, hysterically.

"Aiy. There be embers in the pan."

The woman came into the bedroom. Death-sweat—whatever was that? I wondered. Perhaps it was Dartmoor for cold, unaired sheets? Cheerful expression! I would certainly sleep in my clothes that night.

"Did 'ee bring the key?" said the woman in a low voice to the man.

"Yurr it be," he whispered, with a glance at me.

The woman turned round at once and apparently locked the door of the corner cupboard. This action rather amused me, sitting on the bed, because I could see that she had not inserted any key; indeed, the key she held in her hand looked like the large one I had noticed in the front door.

Obviously her intention was to prevent one from prying into the cupboard. I was a foreigner, of course: strangers to Dartmoor were always called foreigners. Probably in the cupboard was the farmer's best chapel-going suit and 1880 bowler hat, and he was afraid of having them 'won' by an unshaven ex-soldier. Damned amusing!

The cupboard reached to the ceiling and was quite six feet across.

"I hope you'll slape well, my dear, I do," said the farmer, as he followed his wife out of the room. The door remained open.

Left alone, I pulled back one of the curtains. Then I saw I was being watched by the woman beyond the open doorway. Her attitude made me ask if they had any objection to curtains being drawn.

She looked startled at the request, and gave an appealing look at her husband.

"The curtains should be drawn across by right," he muttered. "But perhaps 'tidden no odds if they'm drawn a little way during the night."

At these words, I began to feel a derisory attitude arising in me. Alone in a coombe of the moor, snowing steadily, and the curtains must be drawn for propriety's sake!

"Well, good night," I said, standing up. "Merry Christmas."

The man and woman exchanged glances. "Good night, my dear," said the man, and the door closed.

4

I began to wonder if I were dreaming it all: if physical fatigue were causing some sort of mental obscurity—that touch of phosgene gas, perhaps? I tested myself by closing my eyes, holding out my hands, one leg pointed out, and balancing on the other foot. I kept balance, and felt reassured, and then remembered how hot and swollen were my feet. It felt as if the darkness of the room was trying to obliterate the candle. The flame spluttered, as though choking.

I knew I would never sleep in that bed. I turned back the bed-clothes, took out the heating contraption and put it on the floor. I lugged off my boots, and was ready for bed. There was no water in the room, and it was pleasing that I need not bother to wash my hands or clean my teeth in ice-cold water.

So I blew out the light and lay on the bed in my trench coat, the lumpy coverlet over my legs.

After a few moments I knew I would never be able to sleep with those suffocating curtains across the windows. I lit the candle, which gave only an insignificant, confusing dazzle, and jerked back the curtains on their wooden rings and poles—dreadfully loud the noise. Candle out again; darkness pressing upon one. Far away I could hear the dull buzzing which was the farmer's voice. This went on for quite twenty minutes, and then there was silence. The room, and the house, became blackly still.

I could not sleep. I lay with eyes open and ears waiting to warn me of the slightest movement. The thought of not sleeping became grievance, then anguish. I relived scenes of knife-edge nervous misery during the war, the nights in a Pilckem Ridge crater-post without sleep. I began to curse the headmaster of my old school and then my father, who had called me a traitor to my country, because I had said the Germans were brave soldiers who also believed in a righteous cause. My father had left the room in white anger, after asking me to leave his house and not return. I had apologised, before leaving, with tears hidden: poor Father had believed all in the newspapers about 'the Huns'.

5

These searing thoughts were switched away into the dark recesses of my brain by a board creaking outside, followed by slow, soft noises, as of stocking'd feet coming warily along the passage. I heard a small click and knew that a hand had grasped the handle of the door. My hair stood up: I could feel it moving as the handle was slowly turned, and I knew by the feel of cold air about me that the door was open. How far open? I wondered, half expecting the hinges to squeak. My hair was now as a hedgehog's. I regulated my breath silently through my mouth in order to hear the least noise near me.

I prepared myself to roll over to avoid attack. My legs were tangled in the lumpy sodden quilt. I dared not move them.

Just as I was feeling that I could no longer refrain from screeching, I heard the noise of the key being taken from its hole, and the footfalls went away down the passage. I felt like laughing, for an absurd variation of a soldier's rhyme, *It was Christmas Day in the Workhouse*, came into my head. *I don't want your Christmas pudding*, I thought, wildly, as I felt for the box of matches beside the bed, took it silently, and, suddenly pushing it open, seized a match and struck it. I could see absolutely nothing. And as calmly as I could I lit the candle and waited for the flame to sink and to arise again from the wick. Then with an inner explosion of nervous energy I leapt out of bed, seized the candle, and walked towards the door, my jaw sticking out, the fist of my right hand clenched as I prepared myself to shout threateningly at whatever might be there.

The door was closed, but the key was gone.

Should I put the chair with its back against the door? Yes, I damned well would! Then I got back into bed. O hell! I began to feel angry again, that this foolishness was keeping me from sleep. Had I not lost enough sleep already, fighting for the fireside patriots who had profiteered from the war—farmers especially? Oh, the sleeplessness, the cold, the gangrenous battle-field dawns, the never-never-never-see-home-again hopelessness, at times longing for an arm or leg wound . . . the invincible fireside righteousness of the older stay-at-home generation who shivered with fear when a Zeppelin or Gotha flew over London and dropped a bomb or two; and here I was being denied sleep by the same occluded mentality which had caused the destruction of my generation in Europe. I lay raging, impotent and immobile, in the shut darkness of the horrible house.

I must have fallen asleep; for the next thing I knew was that I was intently listening to a sound like a groan, or a belch, or a dyspeptic rumble close to me. Someone else was in the room. Perhaps there really was a monk and the bed-warming thing had been a hasty excuse. A monk, a rascal monk, a Rasputin? Hiding there, perhaps! Or had I imagined it? I lay and listened. It came again, a bubbling groan, startlingly loud in the thick darkness of that room: and it came from the direction of the large corner cupboard. Someone was hiding in there!

I lay still, with hard-thudding heart.

An escaped convict? The weeping eyes of the wife—a relative, brother, perhaps—a deserter, hiding from the military authorities for years? Perhaps he got into the cupboard on hearing the knock on the front door and had not yet had a chance to get out. Perhaps he would turn nasty? If only I could get my boots and use them as weapons. But keep calm and think: why should anyone be shut in the room? Why not in *their* bedroom? Panic? It must be an escaped convict. When I had knocked at the door they had thought me to be a warder and told the convict to hide in the cupboard, an obvious place for their mentality; and the convict had not dared to leave it; and they had not risked bringing him out.

And that copy of the *News of the World,* which was three weeks old—was it kept because it contained an account, perhaps, of an escaped convict? Was the poor devil inside the cupboard? Memories of reading *The Hound of the Baskervilles* made it possible. A convict *had* recently escaped, I remembered. They were always escaping, and foul man-hunts ensued. Couldn't I reassure him that a soldier who knew what life was would not betray him?

6

I relit the candle and got off the bed and, whistling *Tipperary,* put on my boots. I would tap on the door of the cupboard and tell him that he need not be afraid, that I wouldn't give him away. As I crept over the floor, my boots making an enormous noise on the bare boards, I began to feel so scared that I dared not even tap on the panels. I stood still shivering and listening, and then I heard a noise at the other end of the house, in the direction of the farmer's bedroom: a door had opened: footfalls were coming along the passage.

Blast! It was happening all over again. I stood shivering before the corner cupboard, fascinated with fear. Oh, why had I put on my boots?

Dare I blow out the candle! I told myself I must not lose my head. I blew out the candle and stood still on the floor. I tried to control my imagination, which otherwise would have reduced me to anticipating someone leaping out of the darkness and bearing me down. I waited for the handle of the door to turn. I stood there for perhaps a minute. Footfalls went back along the passage. I heard the distant door close. After waiting and listening, I relit the candle.

All men have weak moments in their lives; all men feel fear on occasion, since fear is an instinct which stimulates to quicker action in attack and defence. But when no action follows a stimulus of fear the mind or will becomes temporarily paralysed. Unable to act, I sat in furious misery on the edge of the bed, not daring to do anything except sit still, not knowing what to do, while the candle burned down. When an inch only of stump was left, I said to myself that I didn't care what happened, and taking it up, walked across and knocked on the door of the cupboard and said in a voice higher in pitch than usual, "You can't be more uncomfortable in there than I am here. Why not come out, old soldier? I won't hurt you, and I promise I won't tell anybody about anything."

There was a dead silence.

"If you are there," I said in a voice not so strained, "do come out. I can't sleep in here, and I'm sure you can't in there. You can have the bed, and I'll doss down by the kitchen fire."

At any rate, I thought, I was beginning to build up from his cowardice. I intended to see it through. I returned across the room, coughed loudly, put the candle stump on the window-sill, where the little light it gave was not obscured by the bed posts; and, feeling a sort of cold prickle breaking out again over all my body, I walked across the floor with the intention of opening the cupboard door.

I grasped the handle of the cupboard with my left hand, while holding my right hand clenched ready lest the door should open before I was ready and the convict spring upon me. Taking a deep breath and only just able to prevent my teeth chattering by clenching them and breathing through spread nostrils, I pulled the door open.

Inside against the wall hung a few coats and dresses; but what I looked at immediately was a barrel smaller than one usually used for cider.

Realising that no one could spring out of the barrel without giving some warning, I went back for the candle, and returning again, raised the puny light to the level of the barrel-top and peered into it. The top was missing. The barrel was three parts full of liquid. As I peered I saw, in the liquid, the upturned face, sightless eyes and gaping mouth of an old bearded man.

A draught of icy air seemed to be blowing down my back. I walked away quickly from the cupboard and stood beside a chair, grasping it, and judging it was a weapon of defence should the farmer attack me. For the face of the corpse looked as though death had come by strangulation.

Listening intently, and hearing nothing, I tiptoed to the window and drew aside the curtains. The window must have looked out on the north, because most of it was wadded with snow.

Then I hastily blew out the candle, for the footfalls were coming along the passage again. I was beginning to know them now. A knock on the door, a voice saying, "Be 'ee all right in there, my dear? Can't 'ee sleep, tho'?"

"Yes, thank you. I'm just cold—I got frost-bitten feet in the war." I stood by the chair, grasping it firmly.

"Us heard 'ee walking about and us thought 'ee might be needing something."

"I was just walking about because I had cramp in my leg. What's the time, do you know?"

" 'Tes about six o'clock, my dear. Plaize tu say what time would 'ee be liking breakfast?"

"Oh, when you have it, thanks."

"Us be havin' a cup o' tea in a minute or two. My wife be kindlin' th' vire now, my dear."

I imagined the farmer with a billhook in his hand, crouching there. A double murder, body dismembered and burnt in the fire by sections. I wouldn't crash the chair down on him, but jab him in the belly with one leg, as though it were a bayonet.

"I'm afraid I disturbed you. I've been walking about most of the night. Very sorry. Cramp." I was shaking violently.

"Would 'ee care for me to rub in a li'l hembrycation, my dear? I've got a big bottle handy here for 'ee. It won't cost 'ee nought extra."

"Oh, please don't bother." Planning to give me a crack on the head with a bottle, was he? "My leg's much better now, thanks."

"Thank 'ee, zur." I heard the fellow walking away. Perhaps he was going to get a gun! O hell, why hadn't I accepted a lift in that pre-war Mercedes-Benz?

7

Looking under the bed for a better weapon than a chair, I discovered a coffin lying there, with loose lid on top. Immediately everything was plain. I felt sick with relief, and sat limply on the edge of the bed, yawning repeatedly and feeling grey and thin. Thank God the night was over. I realised it was Christmas Day, and determined to leave at once for the house under Ringmoor Down, to arrive there in time for breakfast.

Boots laced up, trench-coat belted, pack adjusted, feet clopping down the bare wooden stairs. "Won't 'ee stop for a cup of tea, won't 'ee, surnuff? 'Tes snowing thick, but the cold spell be broken, I vancy, sir," said the farmer's wife, who seemed almost cheerful.

"Yes, I will, thank you very much."

While the 'green' bacon was frying in the pan, I went outside, into snow falling large as goosefeathers, and talked with the farmer milking a cow by the light of an old brass lanthorn with horn windows instead of glass. I wanted to offer to buy the lanthorn, but didn't like to ask just then. Then I went for a walk, and when I returned the snow had ceased falling and the dawn was beginning to flush over the cold austere spaces of the moor, and the soft brilliance of the morning star diminishing in the east.

A wonderful Christmas morning, indeed! Peace on earth and kindness among men.

After breakfast I said goodbye to the farmer and the farmer's wife, who refused to accept any money for the night's lodging. The farmer went with me as far as the track, to point out the way. He said, as we parted, "Did 'ee find th'old chap in the' 'ogs-'ade, my dear? 'Tes my wife's father; he died ten days ago, poor old chap, and there was naught else to do, but put him to pickle, the ground being 'ard as iron. But this snow means a thaw, I fancy, and now 'a can go home."

I went on my journey, while full realisation came to me of what those two must have been feeling during that Christmas Eve and morning—the daughter's thoughts of her father all alone in his silence and helplessness, waiting for the frost to break, waiting for her dear one 'to go home'.

The Mouse

A dark thing, wretched and lowly, dragged itself among the frozen elm-leaves and the hardening mud. It knew by smell that if it could reach the wall in front, it would be safe. Its nose, nearly hidden by a ruby crust of blood, told that others of its kind had recently passed among the leaves and the mud on the way to the hole in the old cob wall. The lowly thing crept laboriously, because it was weak and its hind legs were bitten.

A weasel had been tracking the field mouse in a garden, and had caught it, biting its legs as it rustled desperately through a chink in the wall. The mouse had screamed, and the white apparition on the top of the wall bent a head downwards and detected with black round eyes the movement below.

Fortunately for the mouse—it was but chance, for nothing protected the wee parcel of life in the browny-red coat—the apparition gazed on the side it was not, thus seeing the weasel. It would have been quite as convenient for the barn owl to turn his head, without moving his body, and to peer down his back; indeed, a complete swivelling of the head was natural and easy to the bird with the fixed eyes. Chance was that it saw the moving weasel, that it slipped noiselessly down the wall and gripped the body with a taloned foot. The weasel chattered, and fixed its teeth in the foot just before the talons, instantly puncturing hair, skin and ribs, pierced the hunter's heart, and life sank away.

The scent of the creature dismayed the owl, who screeched, dropped it dying into a cabbage pulped by rain and bored by caterpillars, and flew up into the elms. The field mouse, which had gone into the garden in order to find food, lay quivering. Its beady eyes were wide with fear, its legs ached, its long ears drooped.

Some time later it stirred, and lifted its ears. Its smell, usually so keen and helpful, was dulled; it had to breathe through its mouth. It crawled forward, pausing often lest the terror return. It dragged itself over frozen mud craters and across brittle ice, coming at last to the wall. One desire the mouse had, to creep into its hole and lie still. Its tail was cold and stiffening, it could see but indistinctly; it must reach the hole where there would be no terror, no pain in its legs, and no noise to make its heart close in its throat.

At last the sanctuary was reached, and with stronger steps the mouse disappeared within, safe and so happy that it squeaked a welcome. Finding a dry nook it curled up, wrapped its head in its paws, and slept.

All the long January night the mouse was curled in the dusty corner. Quick patterings and dull thumpings passed near, but it did not wake. Greenish circles came with the patterings, and went out as the rats disappeared round the corner. Once the sleeper leapt sideways, bumping its head, and trembling at the grunts that seemed to envelop it. But the doe-rat had no young, so the mouse was not bitten.

2

Later a grey light came into the tunnel, and the mouse was awake, feeling hungry, and remembering nothing of the night's horror. It limped along in the dust till it came to an opening bigger than its body. A beam of light poured through this crack in the cottage wall and showed an animal hunched in a corner. The thing never moved, but remained as though it were eating something. No scent came from it, and the mouse crept nearer.

The thing remained in the same position, looking like a bullying rat; it had a tail, but no hair was on it: it had ears, but stiff and brittle: it had paws and legs and body, a head, but all furless, dried and inanimate. Although it appeared to hold food in its paws, there was no food there; while the teeth were long, yellow, and projecting in two curls—one upwards over its snout and the other downwards under its chin. The mouse trembled, wrinkled its nose, and bolted as fast as a broken hindfoot would permit.

It returned to the nook, and dozed, pain preventing sleep. It was startled by thunderous noises. To its surprise, this new terror was not greeted by the silence and stillness of all things, but by squeaks, thumpings, and swift patterings in the tunnel. The mouse knew that the thunder was therefore undirected to itself, and there being no hostile smell, it emerged and followed the rats.

Past the motionless object made grey and fearsome by the light it limped, passing many turnings, side-tunnels, and twistings. After a long and gradual descent it came to a round hole very white beyond. With caution the mouse approached the glare of day, trying to smell through the clotted blood on its nose. Immense noises came to the hole, but as large rats were running over the floor beyond there seemed no danger; and it must get to some unmolested place; why, it knew not, but it must.

The first thunderous noises had been made by an old man getting out of bed, and dressing. His dressing did not take long, for all he had to do was to insert his swollen feet into a pair of botched boots. When this was done he clumped away from the bed, an affair of rusty iron, single mouldy blanket, a dozen corn sacks, and a bag of straw. On the dry board littered with plaster and dust his boots shuffled and clumped, for the old man was bent nearly double by rheumatism. With the help of a stick grasped in a root-like hand he shuffled down the wooden stairs and entered the living room.

On the lime-ash floor his boots clanked, and hardly had he opened the door of the bodley—as the Devon hamlet folk called the kitchen range—to get his loaf and cheese, when three rats emerged from a hole, ran up the table leg, and waited among the grease stains near the one chair. George Miles put the bread and cheese on the table, drew up the chair with difficulty, and wheezily sat down. Meanwhile other rats had scampered out of the hole, and were climbing up his trousers, perching on his shoulders, his head; some, with the familiarity of a long friendship, began to wash their faces while waiting.

"Ullo midears," croaked the ancient, "my li'l boys come to zee granfer, hey! Bide awhile, midears, an' granfer wull give ee zum brakfust."

A palsied hand was inserted into a coat pocket, and a knife taken out. After many attempts to open the single blade he succeeded, and hacked a slice off the loaf, cutting it into pieces which he distributed among the scrambling rats. They seized them, squatted on hindlegs, and little noises of nibbling mingled with the harsh breathing of the old man. When all had been fed he cut himself a slice and then began his own meal; with hard gums he munched the bread and cheese, regarding the rats as he ate and sometimes stroking one.

Then his misty eyes saw a mouse wandering feebly over the floor. Although he was nearly blind, the old stonecracker could see that the mouse was hurt. Since early youth he had been accustomed to sit by the roadside, and always he had loved to watch the wild creatures of the hedges and ditches. Now he spoke to the hurt mouse, who crept nearer to him without any fear. He picked it up in his hand and watched it crouching there. Its bright beady eyes looked at him—small crawling rodent and ancient lonely man, living breathing things.

"Gordarn if ee bant a bootiful li'l boy," the ancient chuckled, "Don't reckons ah've zeen ee afore, maister. Ah'll be dalled if ee bant hungrisome, too. Well mi-boy, you'm welcome. Li'l Jearge ah'll call ee, because my name be Jearge. Gordarn, fancy a wild un coming to see Granfer Jearge."

For an hour the old man sat there with Li'l Jearge in his palm, telling him how pretty a mouse he was and how his li'l boy must stop along of him. Li'l Jearge ate some crumbs, then ceased eating because of sudden pain. In the horny palm of its patron's hand it crouched, its head leaning to one side, waiting.

3

Ponderous steps rang on the cobbles outside, and George Miles was glad that Uncle Joe was out and about. The footsteps drew up outside the door, and a voice said it was gude weather fur the time o' year. George Miles croaked for the door to be opened, and after some fumbling at the latch, the room became lighter, and all the rats were fled into their ancestral highways of the yard-thick cob wall, passing the mummified rat that had remained there while on the rafters above the single bedroom over a hundred broods of owlets had been raised; one brood being raised in a summer.

"Aiy, it be gude weather fur the time o' year, Granfer Jearge," said Uncle Joe, slowly. He called the other Granfer with the respect that all Devon men pay to age. Uncle Joe was seventy-seven, and that was not so old; whereas Granfer was nearly ninety, a very great age.

Uncle Joe wore a check cap given him by his reverence the parson ten years ago, only he wore the peak over his ear, pointing to the

sky, so that it no longer appeared to be a cap; rather did it resemble
a piece of rag thrown by someone out of a window and coming to
rest on his white head as he passed under it. His face was long and
pale, with a clipped beard; his eyes were like the blue petals of a
flower under thawing ice.

"Aiy, it be zeasonable weather, sure-nuff," mused Uncle Joe.
"I be going to look at my seedling tetties. Aiy. Aiy. Well, I be going.
Aiy."

He took nearly a minute to announce and corroborate this statement, said "Aiy" once again, mentioned that if the weather did not
change it would remain as it was, confirmed the prophecy with a
further aiy, and shuffled away to his potatoes.

All the while Granfer Jearge, who lived on an Old Age Pension,
whose wife was dead, whose children and grandchildren and great-
grandchildren were away in furrin parts—some reckoned to be as far
away as London—all the while Old Jearge nursed the mouse. It
was then, as he sat musing, that Li'l Jearge gave birth to her first
litter of six tinies.

Granfer Jearge borrowed from Uncle Joe a cardboard box, and
made a home for Li'l Jearge and her tinies. Even such a thing as a
cardboard box had to be begged, because in his own cottage Granfer
Jearge had no furniture save a chair with mildewed legs, a yellow
candle stuck in a champagne bottle with tarnished gold-foil, the
table, a battered bucket, and a clock. Jearge was proud of the bottle,
which the old squire returning from a shoot in a dogcart had jocularly
thrown at him (this was just before the failure to make his iron-
mining pay, and his death from alcoholic poisoning. That had
occurred twenty years ago; even so, Jearge thought of it as happening
last year, or yesterday).

The clock was, in his senile estimation, a most valuable one, and
worth quite ten shillings. So valuable did the old man consider it
that he never wound it up, in order to save wear and tear of the
works. These articles, with a holy picture of an ill-shaped woman
offering fruit to what looked like a waxen tailor's dummy, comprised
all his furniture. *Adam and Eve before the Fall* hung awry, and a
spider had found it convenient to attach a net to it. Some day,
Granfer told Uncle Joe, he would hold an auction and sell the
picture and the clock, when times were bad, as they would be if they
stopped his pension.

Several times every day the retired railway porter commented on
the weather, standing in the open doorway with his cap-peak pointing

to the sky where eventually he would go. One afternoon was so warm that Granfer Jearge pottered about his garden, and found a dead weasel in one of the cabbages. The location of the animal caused him to mutter many words to himself. Then Uncle Joe plodded by, and as usual, stopped.

"What do ee think I've found, Joo, in a cabbage?"

"What be ut?"

"A li'l dead fitchey."

"Have un been eating your cabbage, Granfer Jearge?"

"Noomye. Fitcheys eat mice and such things."

"Aiy. That be strange. Aiy. I do hear Bill Thorn be going to kill ees pig zoon. Aiy."

"Once 'a zeed a fitchey run away from a znake."

"Aiy. He do reckon the pig to vetch eighteen score. Aiy."

"One of them master girt znakes down by the mines, it were, zactly."

"They do zay pigsment wull a-come down tuppence zoon."

"Aiy."

"Aiy aiy."

Granfer Jearge slung the weasel over the wall, and went indoors. Later a small boy from a near cottage came and stared at him. The door remained open, for the sun was warm.

"Ullo, miboy!" greeted the ancient.

"Granfer Jar," murmured the child. Mud and jam were blended on his face and hands; he had reflective brown eyes and golden curls.

"Come yurr, midear," persuaded the ancient, "look what Granfer hev got."

He showed Ernie (for that was the name of the little tacker) the box, and Li'l Jearge within, content with her six tinies. Their eyes were now open, and so was the mouth of Ernie.

"Whatsat?" he inquired at last.

"Li'l Jearge, midear."

"It be yours, bant it? It bant mine, be it? Watsat?"

"Li'l mousie, midear."

"Be it yours?"

"Aiy."

"It bant mine, be it? It be yours, bant it? Where you get un to?"

"Her coomed in yurr."

"Her did?"

"Aiy."

"It be yours, bant it? It bant mine, be it?"

The monotonous child Ernie would probably have continued to emphasise his four-year-old knowledge of the law of *meum et tuum* till his mother shrilled for his return, had not Uncle Joe, who had been staring steadily at the sky, clumped along and interrupted.

"I didn't tell ee, did I, bout my seedling tetties? I reckon them to be growing too fast. Aiy."

He stared at Granfer Jearge uneasily.

"Aiy," he repeated.

4

The same uneasiness was shown on the following day, as though Uncle Joe knew something that Granfer Jearge did not. For Uncle Joe had heard that Farmer Goldsworthy intended to turn out the ancient, because his rent was two years overdue; and to do this Farmer Goldsworthy, so said rumour, had made application to the Union Guardians, so that Granfer Jearge should be put in 'the Grubber', or Workhouse.

And Granfer Jearge knew nothing of this, for everyone was afraid to tell him.

At the Nightcrow Inn, Brownie, a mason's mate with a black moustache and one gentle brown eye, a tender-hearted father of many children, lamented the decision of the Union Guardians that Granfer Jearge was an incapable.

"He wull veel it turrible, I do reckon." His voice had a natural rise and fall in speaking that gave the listeners a mournful sympathy for Granfer. "He'm having lived in the parish fur so long, and maaked up the roads roundabout."

When Farmer Goldsworthy took away Granfer Jearge's clock as part payment of the rent there was more talk in the village. The ancient appeared in the village street, tapping along with his stick and bent double, a corrugated chimney-hat without a top to it stuck on his head.

"He cried to lose ees clock," reported Brownie, "and did talk of going to get th' schoolmaster to write a letter on it to the Queen, darn me! Ho-ho-ho-ho-ho-ho! But it bant no laughing episode, noomye! It were his vather's afore him, and went most bootiful, it did, most loud-ticking clock in th' parish. Reckon poor old Jearge's heart wull be broke when he'm in thiccy Grubber."

The morning when the relieving officer came to warn him to prepare to move out, Granfer Jearge was thinking about eating, as a
great treat, the one cabbage remaining. The news made him sit down,
and for two hours he did not stir. Uncle Joe came and moped at
the door, but all Jearge could say was "hey?"

When he was young, George Miles had been by turn crowstarver,
carter's lad, kitchen boy, ploughboy, and eventually stonecracker. At
the age of twenty-three he had fallen in love with a maid, and
married. Till he was seventy, he never made more than eleven
shillings a week, and to earn that he worked six days a week from
early morn till after sunset. But he had been happy in his way, for
he had been able to pay all his small debts, and to have a glass of
ale when he wanted it. Two of his four children he had buried in
the churchyard, and over the green mounds the rooks cawed in their
colony. His two sons went off somewhere, and they may have
died; his grandchildren never came to see him: he owned no
property.

When his wife died Granfer Jearge continued to live on in the
cottage until all emotion had run from his withered heart, as the dust
spills from the core of a pollard oak whose last leaves have fallen
from it. But as an old tree can shelter much life—nuthatches, titmice, woodlice, an owl—so Granfer Jearge, reft of bud, leaf and fruit,
made friends with the despised things of the earth.

The rats were affectionate animals, and showed, in miniature, a
dog-like attitude towards him. They came when he called them, they
played on the table with one another, they paused at a strange noise
outside and bared their teeth as a dog will. Granfer Jearge delighted
to see them washing, and he never ceased to marvel at their clean
habits. They combed their whiskers, groomed themselves with paw
and tongue, washed their faces after each meal, and seldom
quarrelled.

Granfer was content, believing that until the Dear Lord called
him he would live at honest peace with everything—and then came
the officer with his dread news, like a woodman to fell the pollard
oak. Granfer wheezed his woe to Li'l Jearge. He were going into
the Grubber. It were a turrible disgrace. Man and boy he had paid
his way, and now to end in the Grubber. His brain repeated dully
the same thoughts: they were going to put him in the Grubber,
they were. For this he had toiled and toiled at stone-cracking, bringing up children, tending his pig and tettie-garden through all the
years; he had never spent his money at the Inn, as some had; he had

paid Varmer the rent reg'lar since he were wed except a bit recently —and now they were taking him away to the Grubber.

That night he made a bit of a fire, and lit the candle that he had been saving up for the future. Before the smoulder of furze-roots and driftwood he sat trembling, mouth open, with split blue lip fallen, staring with worn-out eyes at the rusted bodley. No one had baked in the oven for a dozen years; no hymn had been sung since Lou his wife had died; and now who would tend his mouse? He prayed the Dear Lord would be good, and take him that night to Lou up above the sky.

But in the morning Hope came to him. He would take Li'l Jearge with him into the Grubber!

5

The carrier came to the door, and asked if Granfer were ready.

"Aiy."

In a sack he carried his scanty wardrobe, and the chimney-pot hat was on his head.

"What be these, Granfer?" abruptly asked the carrier, pointing to the pile of sacks and the mouldy blanket.

"Thaccy be my proberty."

"Well, you won't want they things in Barum, noomye! Better be burnt, I reckon. And what's the bottle for?"

"That be a vall-uable bottle, midear, becass t'old zquire drowed un at me long ago."

"Aw, you be too old-fashioned, midear," replied the carrier. "Come along now, I be a busy man these days. You must look out for yourself these days, for no one else will help 'ee, you knows that, don't ee, Granfer?"

So from the cottage in which he had lived for nearly a century, to which he had taken a comely maid to wife, and reared his children, departed George Miles, stonecracker, with his picture, his bottle, and the box containing Li'l Jearge and her tinies. Slowly he dragged himself among the damp elm-leaves and the mud, tapping with his stick, his body curved like a sickle. He never turned to take a last glance at the thatched cottage, or the garden, or Uncle Joe watching silently while his cap-peak pointed to heaven. Housewives came to cottage doors and stared—Granfer Jearge were going into the

Grubber, he were. Poor old chap, some whispered, he wouldn't last long now.

But Granfer Jearge made no moan or spoke no word of any kind. Slower and slower his feet lagged. When he was hoisted up on the jingle-cart Ernie came by and said in his sweet, winsome voice:

"You be gwin away, Granfer Jearge? I bant be gwin away, be I? Tis you be gwin. It bant me, be ut?"

But Granfer on the seat made no sign that he had heard the voice of his dear little friend Ernie. His eyes were fixed with an unseeing stare, his mouth was open. Suddenly Ernie cried:

"Look, there ut be! Granfer's got that one! I ain't got that one! It be Granfer got that one!"

Granfer Jearge sat still, leaning on his stick. The box in his pocket had opened, and Li'l Jearge, tired of her tinies for a while, had climbed to his shoulder. The carrier knocked it off with a sharp and accurate blow of his hand, and Li'l Jearge fell on the road below. It was dazed, and while it hesitated a housewife put her foot on it, crushing out all life. Ernie began to cry, his small heart touched with pity.

One of the young mice showed itself above his pocket, and the carrier remarked that Granfer appeared to be a nest of vermin, poor old fellow. The lookers-on agreed that it was time for someone to take care of him. By the wall a cat was crouching, a thin black creature with high ears, existing on and allowed to exist because of rats, and as the small mice were shaken out of the box it bounded forward and ate all except one, a sharp little fellow, who nipped into a hole under a stone.

"Now us'll be off, Granfer," called genially the carrier. "A bootiful day fur a drive, and a bowl of hot zoup fur ee at Barum."

Uncle Joe scraped over the road, just to bid him a safe journey.

"Well, good-bye, Granfer Jearge," his voice quavered. "It wull keep fine, I reckon. My zeedling tetties by cuming on turrible fast. Aiy they be."

He paused, and spat; then stared at his old neighbour. "What, be feeling bad, Granfer?"

Now they were all looking at him. "My dear soul—" cried Uncle Joe, and the pipe dropped from his mouth.

Shortly afterwards Granfer Jearge was back in the cottage, and lying on the table, unmoving, like a disused sickle. Uncle Joe was trembling and muttering in his own house, the door shut fast. Ernie too was indoors and asking questions of his mother, who in a low voice was rapidly speaking to three neighbours.

A noise under the stairs, the tip-tip of claws on stone, a squeak, and the rats were out of their wall-castle, running up the table legs for food. On the accustomed figure they perched, combing their whiskers. An old doe rose on her hind legs, sniffing. Suddenly all were still.

Then they fled from the figure, and gathered together at the end of the table in a group, as though they were discussing something. They perched on their hind legs, and sniffed. It was very quiet in the cottage. First one, then another, then another, ran down the table leg, swiftly across the floor, and into the tunnel, passing the brown mummy with its curled teeth and hairless tail crouched in still attitude on the dust.

A Weed's Tale

A rook flying over a thatched cottage to its elm-top colony had in beak a stick, found in a near field. Something became dislodged from the stick, and fell. It was a small brown seed. A swallow caught it as it passed, but finding it uneatable, he dropped it, and it continued to fall until it came to rest on the cap of a grey-beard man who was smoking outside the cottage. For several moments it remained there, while the old cottager puffed his clay pipe.

He removed his cap to scratch his head, and the brown seed completed its journey to the earth. It fell behind the rusty iron scraper fixed beside the threshold. Nothing interfered with it during the months of summer and autumn, and when the New Year came it had been washed by rain into a crevice between the cobblestones, and the mud from the boots of the old man had buried it three and a quarter inches from the light.

The name of the countryman was Joseph Rush, generally known in the Devon village as Uncle Joe, a widower, and pensioned railway porter living the last years of his life after hard and faithful service at Bristol. He was seventy-one years of age, and he lived entirely alone, doing his own cooking, washing, gardening and housework. His mind was simple; he made the same remark about the weather, his garden and the topical murder, every day. The brown seed that was buried by the scraper was the seed of *Rumex sanguineus*, or Bloody-veined Dock, belonging to the Sorrel family, common weeds of the countryside.

An old man, a small boy and a weed, these are the characters of the story.

2

The sweet sunshine of a spring day gave a warmth to Uncle Joe's back that for a while made him content with life. He was kneeling on a sack, and laboriously digging up weeds and grass growing between the cobblestones of the path by his cottage. He gasped as he did so, because his joints were affected by rheumatism. The moisture from his mouth ran down the pipe and spluttered in the hot ashes of the bowl. Endeavouring to keep burning the few saturated threads of tobacco, he laid down the blunt knife, pressed them with a finger, and sucked with senile vigor. The bowl of the pipe was foul, and he sucked in an oily black drop of nicotine.

This misfortune made him rise slowly to a position nearly upright, and to spit with care, as far away as possible from his own cottage door, and in the direction of his neighbour's. A stone wall, enclosing the drang or passage-way between the cottages and the gardens hid from his uncertain sight a small boy who was coming round the corner. The boy's name was Ernie, and he was five years old. He had just finished his breakfast of fried bread, potatoes, the boiled stalk of a cabbage, with a cup of milk, and had scrambled down from table to see what Uncle Joe was doing. To his delight Uncle Joe spat almost on his, Ernie's, boot. The face of Ernie became animated; he pointed with tremendous excitement, and smiled with glee.

"You spitted like— like the mans I zeed— you spitted at me like the mans I zeed in a chollybanc—I zeed a chollybanc full of mans spitting, Uncle Joo! Did ee zee un, Uncle Joo? 'Twas me zeed un, warn't it? It warn't you zeed the mans in a chollybanc. It was me, warn't it?"

"Aiy," said Uncle Joe, laconically, spitting again, and looking up as a swift passed whistling by his door. The black bird turned and plunged into a nesting hole in the thatch.

"I zeed a chollybanc—" began Ernie, but the old man did not heed the excited reference to the charabanc from Ilfracombe that Ernie had seen the day before, when the young miners on holiday from Wales had spat at him.

"They birds be making a mess o' my thatch," he complained.

Swallows and martins were passing around and above the cottage, pursuing their insect prey. The male swallows twittered and warbled to their mates; sometimes a pair would perch on the angle of the

roof, wings folded over their backs, and slender tails like tuning-forks quivering as they told their love. Packs of swifts, unleashed and tameless, raced and wheeled in the air, coursing each other and giving shrill tongue. But Uncle Joe only lamented the dirty birds that plastered their mud cups above his windows, and who made the holes in the thatch. There was a noisy brood of starlings in the chimney stack that he would like to destroy. But he was too busy; and had no ladder.

He knelt down again, and continued his job of making the cobbles clean and tidy. Ernie watched him seriously, then hearing a sudden squeal he rushed away to watch the death of a pig in an adjoining farm-yard. The blunt knife of Uncle Joe scratched the stones and broke fibrous rootlets. Dandelions' roots were dug up, with tufts of grass, silverweed, lamb's tongue, chickweed, and daisies. Coming to the boot-scraper, he attacked the thick green stem of a dock. Its root went down deep under the cobbles, and in his anxiety to dig up all the root he jabbed the thumb of his left hand. Ernie came back a few minutes later nearly incoherent with a dramatic account of the pig's death.

"Uncle Joo! I zeed—I zeed—I zeed a pig tied by ees—by ees toofs to a door. Yaas, I zeed un— Uncle Joo! Varmer Golds'vy sticked un with a knife—and—and the blood coombed out turrible! You didn't zee un, did ee? 'Twas me zeed un, warn't it? He's deaded, Uncle Joo—he's—"

Uncle Joe grunted, and looked at his own blood on the twisted thumb.

"Gordam," said Ernie, when he saw it. "Look at thiccy blood, Uncle Joo! You be cut, bant you? It bant me, be it? It be you, bant it?"

"Aiy," commented Uncle Joe, in his thick, slow voice. "I cut myself praper. Aiy. Wull, I reckon I killed thaccy dirty weed by my szcraper! Thaccy weed has coombed up many years now. Aiy. Afore you was born. But I reckon he's finished now. Aiy."

He spoke to no one, for Ernie had run away and in his excited voice he was telling his mother that Uncle Joe's blood was as red as pig's blood.

3

But Uncle Joe had not killed the weed. Between the cold stones, in damp darkness, lay the mangled root.

Seven springs and summers had it started to build its tower towards the sky. Always its striving had been in vain. Seven years ago it had arrived beside the scraper, and no seeds had it been able to make. Seven immense strivings had ended in failure. During the first spring it had put down a tap-root, a feeler into the earth, its base of operations. For with the brown seed was a will, an unswervable determination. It worked patiently, thrusting a slow and minute tunnel with its root, feeling a way between the stones. It rested at midsummer, exhausted, till the following spring. Then the urge made it send upwards, out of its root, a green tower, builded slowly from materials sent from the base. The tower was broken early, and all work ceased. A third spring came; the root was now thicker, larger, and stored with a greater amount of nourishment. Undetected it ventured forth a green shoot, which was above the scraper when the swallows came back to their nests in the chimney. The swifts returned to their thatch-hole in May, and at the beginning of June the dock tower supported seventeen leaves, veined with crimson, and several hundreds of green seeds. They perished, burnt on the weed fire of Uncle Joe. Once more the sappy vitality of the dumb and gestureless root ebbed almost to nothingness. Yet it recovered, and when again the sun began to curve higher across the sky, work was begun once again. And once more its offspring was destroyed. A grub found the tap root, and started to eat it. When the seventh spring came half its heart was consumed, and rot had set in to the remainder. The old root was abandoned, and three fresh shoots sent out, to wind themselves among the cobblestones, and to draw in the richness percolating from the boot-scrapings after every rain. The old root became rotten: the tunnellings were abandoned by the grubs, because their own time was come for change, and they were asleep like mummies within black cases—unborn beetles. A chance thrust of a stick by Ernie pierced one of them, and it died; a thin rootlet near slowly absorbed the corpse, and changed it, somehow, into sap. The other ate a way out of its sheath, and became a beetle seeking a mate, but the wheels of a bread-cart in the road went over it almost immediately. After this the tap-root was not molested further by insects, but it had a

more insidious enemy to beat down, an enemy that arrived during
the eighth spring, just as the green expedition was beginning. This
enemy decimated all the new growth, shrivelling tender frame and
web, and pressing around the root itself, endeavouring to creep
into its very heart. Inoffensive worms, whose bodies were so sensitive
to the light, shrunk and writhed away, and died in their galleries.
All fruitfulness of the soil was poisoned, and many of the dock's
rootlets became withered and therefore useless. Paraffin.

4

Uncle Joe hated to waste good oil on a weed; but he hated the weed
more. Ernie came to see him while from the can he was pouring a
meagre stream with his shaky hand. The crystal liquid winked with
blue and red as it dribbled through sunlight to the stones.

"What be you doin', Uncle Joo?"

"Killing these yurr dalled weeds."

"What be you doin't that for Uncle Joo?"

"They do make thiccy drang dirty, midear."

"Do'm, Uncle Joo?"

"Aiy."

Ernie stared seriously for nearly a minute, and then he said:

"My daddy zays that he—that he like t'zee the grass grawin'
Uncle Joo. My daddy zays—he says that bare stones looks like graves
—yaas, my daddy zays that!"

The old man mumbled to himself.

"My daddy zays that there be plenty o' stone to zee in the'
Grubber, Uncle Joo. My daddy be right, bant he?"

This unexpected reference to the Grubber made Uncle Joe lay
down his knife, and rise on his knees. Finally he said to the child:

"Wull, maybe Daddy be c'rrect, Ernie. They do say that it be
turrible bleak in th' Grubber. Aiy. Turrible bleak. Poor old Granfer
Jearge, do 'ee mind old Granfer Jearge, Ernie?"

"Aiy," said Ernie. "You'm deaded that weed a'right, haven't ee,
Uncle Joo?"

Uncle Joe made no reply.

Ernie went away to play in the water by the stream, into which
he fell, receiving a beating from his mother soon afterwards. Into
the cottage he was dragged, howling that he would a-tell daddy,

when daddy coomed whoam. He sobbed, and moped for half an hour, then crept back to see what Uncle Joe was doing. The old man was still patiently uprooting the greenery that was striving to grow in the earth between the cobbles.

That summer no rain fell, and the brook became a trickle. In May, the potatoes, the cabbages, the lettuces, the onions, the beans and the peas absorbed the sunbeams and grew so quickly that all the hamlet folk were delighted.

No rain came. The blue sky smouldered, and the spirit of vegetation became listless. By the beginning of July the smoulder became a glow of fierce blue heat that scorched and destroyed. Finches and sparrows hopped about in the shimmering garden with beaks agape; there was no need for Uncle Joe to do any more weeding. He swept the drang about twice a week, gradually removing with stiff twigs of his besom the brown tufts of grass and weed.

Flies buzzed about him as he stood in the doorway, and flirted on the brilliant white walls of the cottage. The swifts were tireless in their coursing, and their cries in the burning sky were like the singing of green sticks thrown on a fire.

Uncle Joe's slow energy flagged in the heat, so that he rarely left the cottage, but stood and told every passer-by that rain was needed. At night he removed his trousers (in which usually he slept) and opened his windows two inches, owing to the heat. The interior of the house was dry and musty, and reeking with soiled clothes and worn carpets.

Hundreds of white cabbage butterflies passed flickering over the garden; the cabbages were eaten to skeletons by caterpillars.

Once Ernie, pale and languid and dirty of face, brought to Uncle Joe a grubby book, printed in large type and pointed to a figure, apparently unshaven and in night attire, reclining on a cumulus cloud.

" 'Tis mine, this one. Look, Uncle Joo. I got this one. Who be that now?"

Uncle Joe took the book and scanned the illustration.

"I can't say as how I know, midear. It bant your mother, now, be it?"

"That be God," replied Ernie. "I got this one. It be mine, it be. It bant yours, be ut? I got God. My daddy gimme um. Us was told to pray for rain in church last Zunday, so God will zend rain, won't un?"

Uncle Joe did not answer. He was afraid to talk in such a way about God. He left such answers to his reverence the parson, who only that morning had said that everything happened for the best, and that some inscrutable purpose had ordained the drought, with its maggot-mad sheep and stringy root-crops.

Four old people died owing to the heat, and were buried in the churchyard. Uncle Joe was no wicked atheist—noomye! Uncle Joe kept indoors, and read about murders and divorces in the ancient Sunday newspapers sent by his daughter in service at Bristol.

Every day the sun tore a fiercer silver rent in the hard blue sky. The fields were brown and hard. Three of the wells had dried up by August. Swarms of blowflies laid their eggs on sheep, some of which went mad, running about with flapping fleeces which shed maggots.

Uncle Joe, in company with his neighbours, moaned over the tragic loss of their little gardens. There were four wasps' nests in his roof somewhere. He grew much afraid of fire in the thatch, and gave up smoking his two ounces of weekly shag, opening the windows wide during sleep that he might be able to smell any burning. But the doleful noise of owls at night disturbed him, and he was irked by the twitter of martins feeding their young in the early morning above his window. He could not share in the joy of the wild birds. Childhood's drought had withered his mind's green tissue. He knocked down all the mud nests with a pole, and the nestlings fell to the cobbles below. Cats had several, but Ernie managed to catch ten, keeping them as pets. The little boy nursed them in his arms and spoke lovingly to them; but the unknowing pressure of clammy hands killed them. Ernie sobbed and spat on Uncle Joe's door, thrice, because Uncle Joe had knocked down the nests. And from his own threshold he shouted out, "Uncle Joo upside down! Ould Dawbake!" His mother laughed and scolded Ernie for calling anyone an old dawbake. Uncle Joe wagged his head and said, "Ah'll tell pliceman! Naughty young reskle, you!"

"Ould Dawbake," yelled Ernie, again and again, shrieking with laughter. Puny echoes seemed to come down from the sky, where the swifts were high, each like an eyelash. That night they started their yearly migration to Africa, but Uncle Joe did not notice the departure. He was interested only in the weather, in the topical murder, and in the weekly drawings of his pension. The earth only meant these things to him; and he had had firmly fixed in his brain since his schooldays the conviction that mankind was given hardships in this world in order to enable him to enjoy more the celestial harps and angelic songs of the next. At times he wondered why it was arranged that there should be a drought, but it would go no further than a vague wonder.

The earth rolled on in its orbit, giving to that part of the world hot day and starlit night, always rolling away light and darkness. One evening came a little cloud from over the ocean. It came at sunset and was seen by all in the village. The sun cast red-purple hues upon the vapour that followed in the track of the messenger. Everyone said that the rain was coming, and great was the rejoicing of young and old. In the evening fields the bullocks lowed their slow chorus and around them circled the swallows skimming low after winged insects. At eight o'clock Uncle Joe stood hands in pockets at his door and with contented puffs he watched the moon blotched in gold and red pushing like a fungus through the stones and mounds of the churchyard. He could hear the lowing of cattle, and the bleat of sheep from far away on the hills. The giant agaric pushed its head above the graves till it seemed to grow stalkless between two black elm trunks. Some minutes he passed staring at its unusual size and colour—he thought it beautiful—and then it was hidden by clouds. He went to bed.

5

But he did not sleep. With window wide open he lay in his mouldy bed. He was listening for the rain. Wood owls came to the elms and hooted, and the white owls floated over the garden to their young under the thatch of the cottage adjoining the dwelling of Ernie's parents, which had been empty since the death of old Granfer Jearge. Uncle Joe heard them as they came with rats and mice, for they made an unearthly cry, a witchlike screeching. "I be sweatin' a lot," he muttered, as though to a wife beside him. Clangorous through the sultry night fell the bell strokes of the clock in the tower of the church. Uncle Joe rolled over, and tried to sleep, then restlessly turned again. Sometimes he sat up and listened for the pattering of rain so long desired. Eleven clangs were beaten out by the metal tongue of the bronze bell, and at the last stroke Uncle Joe heaved himself out of the creaking bed, and shuffled across dry boards to the window. He fumbled in his coat pocket for matches, and struck one. Shakily he shielded the small flame and peered over the window ledge. Then he craned out his head, holding his face to the sky.

He remained sitting at the window for some minutes. The darkness grew thicker with heat. Suddenly his eyes were blinded by a lightning flash, accompanied by a hot hissing that seemed to sear his hair and beard. Instanteously there followed a burst of thunder that seemed to flatten the cottage. A hurricane of wind tore at the elms, whirling away most of the leaves already enfeebled by the long scorching months.

Rain fell violently till dawn, when the lower wind ceased; and for two days and nights the drops splashed straight. The brook swelled and ran over its stony side, flooding the three cottage floors. At first, Ernie was overjoyed at the sight of the water; but before it subsided he was entirely wearied out. Apple trees were stripped and ricks blown over. The seagulls had gone many miles inland twelve hours in advance of the storm.

The ebbing of the brown water left a deposit of mud over the cobbles of the drang, as well as over the cottage floors. Uncle Joe, scarcely able to move on account of rheumatic swelling of the joints, swept this away, or as much of it as he was able, with his besom, leaving a reddy brown pile of mud beside the door. This he intended for a top-dressing, or manure, of his garden.

It remained beside the scraper, because a week after the storm Uncle Joe was found, fully dressed but for his boots, dead in his bed. An inquest was held, an uneventful inquiry, that revealed the fact that Joseph Rush, widower, had died of natural causes. From Bristol came the daughter of the dead man to attend the burial in the churchyard. A grave site had already been purchased by Uncle Joe in his lifetime, and into this the mortal remains of the ex-railway porter was laid to rest, while the rooks cawed and flapped in the tree-tops above the few mourners.

6

That year was a good one for mushrooms, for the September sun shone throughout the month. Seeds of wild flowers burst their cases in the lanes and hedgerows. Larks sang again the songs of spring. On the thatch of the deserted cottage grasses and biting yellow stonecrop began to grow, and pennywort on the crumbling walls bought life with their thick green leaf-coins.

Nobody heeded the weeds that softened the stone harshness of the

drang. In the spring of the following year the rich soil beside the scraper was pierced by the leaf-enwrapped head of a dock. It grew rapidly, but not very high, as though the root was almost exhausted; only a few seeds were formed on its stalk. Ernie spied it one day, and snatched at the stalk. It was tough, but he twisted it away from the root. It so happened that friends of his (Babe, Tikey, Madge and Billy) were playing at soldiers in the churchyard, and these Ernie joined holding in his hand the stalk. The other children had twigs and sticks, but Ernie could not find one, so he held on to the weed, pretending it was a sword. Into the churchyard and among the leaning stones and grassy mounds it was borne, carelessly to be cast away a few moments later on a mound under the elm, and forgotten like Uncle Joe, who was buried there. Happily the children played, crying shrilly, until the sexton appeared, when they fled in joyous terror, pretending he was a bogey man.

The seasons passed, while the village folk worked and ate and talked and rested. In February the rooks returned to repair their old nests, and once again the cottagers heard from dawn till evening the familiar cawing. In March the first birds of passage were back; in April came the swallows; in May the swifts whistled round the church tower. The empty cottage became the home of many things. Rats made their nests in the walls, swallows builded in the chimneys, and the dishevelled thatch became a tangle of vegetation. Every crevice by the threshold had its green thing growing.

But no green shoot pushed up beside the scraper. The old dock's root was dead. During its span of life it had toiled to make seeds; and they were made. Now was come its time of rest, when it need toil no more in the earth that was of ancient scattered things.

The harvest that year gave even farmers contentment. Rain fell in the desired way in spring and early summer, swelling the sappy heads of corn; the sun in July and August ripened the golden berries. Cultivated wheat and despised weed, garden rose and dog-rose, all things flourished. In September the interior of the church was decorated for the harvest thanksgiving. The chants of field-workers mingled with the caws of rooks in the elms without, as they flapped and perched above the neglected grave of Uncle Joe, upon which were growing, as though in faithful and compassionate memory, a score of young plants of *Rumex sanguineus*.

Air Gipsies

The ploughshare, ripping a new furrow in the stubble, turned up something and left it there, with brown earth in the orbits of its eyes and mouth. The tawny-bearded ploughman cried *whoa!* to the pair of black horses, they ceased to strain at the swingles and patiently stood still. The human skull was picked up, and turned over in the ploughman's hands. He had heard of such things being found before; he remembered it being told that a battle had once been fought in the district. Several of the village children had brass coins discovered in like manner by the plough; they had been given them by their fathers, who had been unable to get ale for them in the inns.

Something in the nature of the man made him walk over to a corner of the field, and to wedge the skull in a fork of blackthorn standing stark and spiny in the October hedgerow. Before leaving it there, he hooked with a stick the earth from the broken dint in the brow, thus exposing the hole made centuries ago by the pistol ball of a Roundhead.

At night a rainy wind swished through the leafless hedge, and washed all earthy stains from the thing. A wet field vole climbed tediously upon it, and finding shelter within, the bedraggled creature slept there. After many weeks it had garnered a store of hawthorn peggles and acorns within this secure retreat, using the aperture of the nose as a peep hole before climbing out on its way to the humble path in the ditch below. The food was never needed, however, because a weasel caught the vole one afternoon, soon after the time of the first winter wheat-blade, and sucked its blood.

In March the blackthorns swelled, and put forth hundreds of buds. The sun blessed these, and they burst into white blossoms, which soon fell, and made white many webs of spiders. After came the green leaves, hiding the black spines of the hedge.

Then through the tangle of the hedge, slipping with silent rest-lessness, examining with bright eyes every leaf for grub or spider, came Sisisee, a little bird. She perched beside the yellow skull fixed in the thorns, with white flakes of blossom resting on its pate and where the teeth had been. Across the break in the forehead a baby gossamer spider had, with intuitive patience, spun its first frail web; with a quick hop and flutter the bird alighted on the skull, and took the spider neatly from its snare, leaving the web intact save for a small hole where the beak had pierced it.

The little bird called with hoarse sweetness, and paused to listen. Down the hedge came an answer. Her mate drew nearer to her with the same restless and tiny movements, now hanging upside down on a twig to see what insect was lurking under a leaf, now flitting to the hedge-bottom to seize a beetle. He came to his mate, perching beside her; their beaks touched and she murmured something to him. His whispered reply was so hurried that it seemed to the listening man lying still beside an embered fire that the male bird only said one thing by means of one uncertain note. But the voice of the long-tailed titmouse had many inflexions and expressions; the reedy twitter held tenderness and surprise, anxiety and speculation. He was considering the angle of the thorn-fork, and where the opening of the nest should be, in order that it be protected from wind and rain; the next instant an eye smaller than a black raindrop, very bright and shiny, was cocked skywards and had ascertained that the old bines of honeysuckle and goosegrass intertwined with matted twigs gave visual security from hawk and butcherbird.

Sisisee said his mate, tenderly. He sang an incoherent song, a song that meant very little, yet was a natural outlet for the love and desire in his heart. The sun was warm, his wings were strong, the eyes of his mate were beautiful, and so he sang or rather poured out his heart-trembled notes; she, too, was ripe for love, and pulsing with happiness. The pulse of the blood within her slender body deepened, shaking all her being, and she danced for joy, first on one leg, then on the other. Her tail feathers opened and closed; repeatedly the filmy membranes were drawn across her eyes; he danced as well, and sang. Upon the sorrowful human relic wedged among the thorns they tiptoed and bowed, knowing not of its disuse by the force that now made them dance, nor that it was the deserted storehouse of a dead vole, nor what it was at all, nor why it had been. Amid fallen petals and the straying sunbeams they looked at each other, making their sweet and faithful love.

2

After the marriage, love and work went hand-in-hand with happiness. First the cockbird, whose pied tail was longer than his grey and purplish-red body brought a fragment of moss in his black beak. This was placed in the fork beside the skull, at five o'clock of the April morning, while in the distant hazel copses nightingales, warblers and blackbirds were singing, and larks soared up to the paling stars. The titmice worked throughout the day of white clouds, blue sky, and windy sunshine, fetching moss, lichens, and grass fibres, which were felted together and bound by sheepswool. When the evening came they rested beside their work, perching side by side. Their eyes closed gradually; perhaps the cry of an owl would cause them to open again in alarm: there was no danger among the thick thorns, the eyes closed again, heads gradually dropped: with faint sighs they tucked them away in the feathers by the wing-shoulder, and slept peacefully.

In the May month the whitethorn blossomed, and the nest was nearly completed. It had its entrance in the side, and was nine inches long, shaped like an old-fashioned wooden ale bottle. Thousands of beak-loads had been used in its construction, each one woven into place with single hairs of sheepswool. The outside was completely grey, for the hen bird had covered it with lichen chipped off the apple trees in an orchard over a mile away. Beside the skull the nest was fixed; the one filled with rotting berries and earwigs, the other lined with hundreds of feathers, and, at the beginning of the third week in May, with eleven eggs. There was no nest more shapely in the hedge; none so tidy, no eggs so dearly loved or nestled over.

Every day the bearded man, passing down the hedge between the nettles and the green wheat, stopped in slow meditation and parted the branches. At first the mother bird, who while brooding had her long tail turned up with its tip resting over her eyes, left with a chirrup of agony, and circled round him, crying all the time. But realising that he meant no hurt to her treasures, she soon grew unafraid. Once the moucher went by with bundles of watercress slung on a stick. He flung these on the ground, and carefully put two fingers into the hole, feeling the eggs under her, and taking out one. This he held to the light, seeing that it was fresh, because the yolk inside made the shell, white and freckled with tiny spots, a yellowy pink. He pierced the egg with a thorn, and blew out the yolk, placing the shell in an empty matchbox. Before leaving he touched the smooth bone of the skull with caressing fingers. It was he who had placed it there in the winter; he had watched the mouse carrying its berries into store, unbeknown to the mouse; he had listened to the raptured whisperings of the titmice as they danced on the skull, and had come to love them, and to share in a peculiar way their joy and hope. The moucher was tall, and a young man, without friends or relatives; he lived throughout the year in a shelter built of turves and branches, and situated in the spinny of hornbeam and fir that grew on the ridge of the wheatfield.

Again he touched the skull, whispering to the nested bird, then picked up his stick of watercress, and continued his way down the hedge.

The father bird watched him go, flew to the hedge, and crept along three yards of thorn and branch to his wife. Eagerly she greeted him from among the warm feathers, as she cuddled the eggs between her thighs and under her wings. So intense was her love for them that her blood was much hotter than usual; her ardour flowed into the mites soon to form within the shells. He settled beside her, and they slept, to be awakened by a little face looking in at the doorway. The face resembled their own, but it was smaller, the cheeks were not so white, nor were the eyes happy.

The stranger whimpered her name, saying "Jea-Jea"; the mother slipped out of her nest and inspected her. She was a miserable bird, a longtailed titmouse who had been caught on her nest by village boys. Her tail had been clutched, but she herself had escaped, only to see her nest torn open and the eggs taken. She had had her fill of sorrow already, since her mate had not returned for a week, and she had been pining for him. He had been killed by a sparrow-hawk when the second egg had been laid; Jea had called and called, but never had he come. She had just laid the eighth egg when a great hand had clutched her, and raped her out of her home; she lost her tail, her nest, and her eggs. She slept a disconsolate night in the deserted nest of a wren, waking to face a weary and hopeless day. She fed herself, and called continually, wandering farther and farther away from the place of tragedy, and towards midday she heard a familiar voice. She crept through the green leaves, and came to the the green leaves, hiding the black spines of the hedge. skull.

Jea whimpered again; the father bird flitted from the nest and touched her beak; Jea crept into the nest, followed immediately by Sisisee. Widow and wife settled down together; and ten minutes afterwards another egg was in the nest. Jea laid five more, making a total of eighteen. The two hens were friendly, and the cockbird made no difference between them; he fed them as they brooded, and slept at night perched on their backs—there was not room otherwise.

3

The pink babies came out of their shells in due course, and then the three were busy. Jea's eyes were bright nowadays, and she was accustomed to movement without the balancing tail. She was never sad, because she had a short memory for past events. Besides, she had the babies to feed and tend; of herself she never thought; she was a mother.

They were often worried; indeed, their life was constantly one of furtive search for food, while many things caused them alarm and terror. Usually a kestrel was hanging in the wind somewhere over the wheatfield, and frequently he glided over the hedge. Sparrow-hawks came as well, flying with greater dash and suddenly appearing. Hedge-sparrows and chaffinches were taken by these birds, and once Jea was missed less than three inches by a terrible snatch of a taloned foot. She was so terrified that she fell into the ditch, her beak gaping and her throat a-throb: a minute later all was forgotten and she was dropping a stick-caterpillar (looking just like a twig) into one of the many mouths that yawned in the nest.

The following day a curious sound caused Jea to peer out of the nest, and glance down the hedge. It was an angry stuttering, the clacking of a bird perched on a spray, and staring at the sky. *Clack-clack, wakka-wakka, clack,* it cried. The bird sometimes shook its wings. Then a great bird in the sky called *peeou*, making a noise like the wail of a kitten. The sentinel on the hedge shrieked at the sailing bird, and a pair of carrion crows flew upward to it, calling harshly, and drove it away.

With rapid wingbeats the bird who had given the alarm at the passing of the big buzzard hawk flew towards Jea, detected the nest, and glanced inside. With a twitter of frenzy Jea dashed at him, but her ounce of weight, although it hit him in the chest, was disregarded by the intruder. Into the nest he thrust a head, seized in a beak bent like a rusty nail one squeaking baby, and bore it away. The period of the raid lasted three seconds. Jea dashed at the raider again and again, making weak pecks at him, and tearing away a feather each time. The red-backed shrike, or butcher bird, ignored her, and bore the dying mite to a long thorn on which were impaled several humble-bees, a red-admiral butterfly, a fledgeling greenfinch, and a dragonfly, from whose drooping body the sun-painted scarlet was already fading, since it was dead, and therefore of no further use as an agent of life.

Upon the crumpled gauze of shimmering wings the baby titmouse was fixed, its body pierced by the dark thorn. This was the larder of the butcher bird, and his own fledgelings would be fed from it.

4

The moucher came every day to the nest; he knew the nest of the butcher bird as well, and he loved equally the young of both; his peculiar mind, beginning to comprehend the natural scheme of life, gave pain to his heart as he pondered on the necessity of death to maintain life. One morning he came with a brown-eyed girl wearing her Sunday-best clothes of ill-fitting blue serge, patent leather shoes, and red tam-o'-shanter, and he showed her the home of the bottle-birds. He took the fluffy mites from their licheny cradle, and placed them in her hand. She stroked them with a rough forefinger; her eyes lifted to his with soft shyness. He looked at her, and made a movement as though to stroke her cheek, but turned away when her gaze was lowered to the nestlings again. The glance of the maid's brown eyes followed him lovingly when he was staring over the corn, with his back towards her, and he did not see how they were shining. In silence she went to his side, and gave him the little birds, which he placed, one by one, through the pistol hold of the skull, telling her as he did so that there were too many in the nest, and that two hens were mothering the li'l birdies.

Jea and Sisisee made no fuss over the division of the young; they were used to the visits of the man, and did not fear him. Human thought saved the double brood, for some of the young birds would otherwise have died by starvation and crushing; as it was, two of them were weakly, and had each a withered leg. For when they were little, and crushed beneath the others, a piece of horsehair had become twisted round their legs, and they had grown up joined together, each with a shrivelled leg. The moucher had put them inside the skull, seeing that they were deformed.

The leading forth from the cradle caused great excitement in the families. Parent birds called advice and alarm repeatedly; by evening they were exhausted. Two of the fledgelings were dead, but forgotten: they had been eaten by a dwarf owl and a grass snake. The dwarf owl was scarcely bigger than a thrush, a creature that flew by night and by day, that searched with its yellow-ringed eyes for frogs, nestlings, beetles, little rabbits and anything that flew, crawled, hopped, or walked. Its ancestors had been brought from Spain by a naturalist called Lord Lilford during the nineteenth century; now *Athene noctua* was devastating the English countryside. The little owls nested in hollow trees and in rabbit burrows, in old crow-nests and squirrel-dreys, anywhere and everywhere.

After eating the titmouse, it flew to a rearing field nearby, where were many pheasant coops. It seized a chick, and was hit by a lead bullet from the catapult of a small, thin, dark boy wearing a moleskin cap. This boy was so excited when he picked it up dead, that he began to tell an imaginary companion all about it. "Coolord," he exclaimed many times, "coolord, I aimed by instink and hit it. I took aim by instink. Coolord, you should have seen it fall! In-stinkively I took aim!"

But nothing avenged the death of the other bottle-tit, which a snake had fascinated as it quivered and squeaked on a twig.

The family wandered. Jea remained behind to tend the youngsters in the skull. They could not escape, entangled as they were. Once again human aid was given; the moucher took them out and cut off the useless limbs at the knee. The little things trembled, but the pain did not remain for long, and a week later they joined the gay family and began the summer wander through the countryside.

The family dwindled. Hawks and weasels, brown owls and sparrowhawks, and once a cat, took first one, then another. Every day brought something new, a change. The weeks slipped by, but the moucher remained to note the woods turn red and yellow and brown, the butcher birds migrate to southern lands, the swallows to desert barn and chimney, gossamer webs shimmering golden in the fields at sunset, fountains of gnats playing in the quiet autumnal air, the leaves scattered by winds and rains; still the family wandered by hedgerow and copse, orchard and forest. *Zee-zee, zee-zee,* the restless creatures called to each other, ever moving onwards, these

timid gipsies of the air.

At night they roosted in haystack or ivy. They awoke at dawn, when rime encrusted twig and bough and the white morning star shone softly over the great beechwood—life then was hard, and anxiety made them more restless. Sometimes they shivered in the frozen nights, half-starved and huddled together.

In their journeyings they passed several times their old home, now pulped and shapeless, and the yellow skull-roost, filled with dead leaves and withered berries. They visited the spinney in the middle of the brown wheatfield, searching the firs and stunted beeches in company with golden-crested wrens and fieldfares. The moucher saw the one-legged couple, and the sight cheered his loneliness, but the unheeding birds noticed him not. Jea grew her tail again, and at the New Year there were seven of them, including mother and father, three children, and Jikky Jikky Oneleg, the only surviving child of Jea.

When the coltsfoot and the celandines came, so long-desired by the young moucher in the spinney, the family of seven was still wandering. Jikky was small, and he had the sweetest voice. All day they talked and whispered: sometimes sudden joy would possess one of them. From the spinney came the crowstarving clappers and windborne cries of *hullo-a, hullo-a*, where the man was warning off rooks and daws from the spring-sown barley.

5

One morning as the party straggled in the wind across a field the sight of something above made them sink to the earth, there to cower and press themselves against the clods. A dark bird with thin wings bent backwards was slipping across the blue sky; he was made tiny by height, yet he passed over and beyond them in a few seconds. This was The Backbreaker, one of the Devon Chakcheks, a family haughtier and more feared than any other in the West Country. The Backbreaker glided at an altitude of two thousand feet, and his speed on this occasion was over seventy miles an hour.

The bottle-tits crouched to earth, watching. The Backbreaker made his half point at the centre of the spinney a mile away. He slid downwind at an angle of thirty degrees. Others had seen him as well —two kestrel hawks, also flat on the ground in a far corner of the

field—a pair of carrion crows silent and skulking in an oak tree—
the moucher who was standing by an oddmedodd—and, too late, a
ring dove circling about the spinney. The pigeon had been flying at
three hundred feet when Chak-chek was two miles distant, and three
thousand feet high. The wild dove was a swift flyer; but The Backbreaker could sweep through two miles in a minute with the wind
behind him. The half point changed to a stoop, and The Backbreaker
rushed down at him, headfirst. The pigeon heard too late the scream
of air in the tiercel's pinions. The Backbreaker was only two hundred
feet above him: the pigeon raced for the tree-tops, but he seemed
not to be moving: the dark thing hit him, burst away into the wind
hundreds of his feathers, clutched the headless dove, and was gone.

Silence. The crows were skulking, the moucher was gazing under
his hands, the kestrels made no movement, the titmice, the larks, the
finches, all remained still. Nothing more happened; but earthwards
danced the feathers, tossing in eddies of wind, floating and scattered
in the sunshine. One of the crows made a low remark, *krrok*, and
repeated it twice, *krrok, krrok*, but said no more; he had said all that
was necessary. The Backbreaker was gone.

The man stood for a while by the oddmedodd, then continued
to stuff straw into its loose sleeves. One of the kestrels rose into the
air, hovered, beat his wings, then flew away. Once more the normal
life of the wild went on, while nearer to earth danced the sunlit
feathers.

A lark began to sing again. Three of the titmice wing-jerked themselves towards the spinney. One of the feathers floated near Jea, and
she seized it in her beak. Her two companions, who were the be-
friending parents of the previous spring, flew after her. The cockbird
endeavoured to seize the feather from her, but she dipped, and the
pursued Jea swung round, bearing the feather in the opposite direction. He flew on, then turned, following with drumming wings that
beat so fast that his progress seemed more airily jerky than ever. He
called queezily to her, but she gave no heed. The two reached the
thorn hedge, and she hid herself, but he found her, so onwards she
went with her trophy.

Jikky Oneleg and the others had disappeared. Through the hazel
wands, hung with yellow catkins, travelled the three of an older
generation, Jea leading and bearing the feather. Sisisee took a leaf in
her beak, called to the cockbird, and flew away; but he did not follow
her, so she followed him. Sometimes she called to him, a plaintive
whisper, but his tweedle-dee was not for herself, but for Jea.

That night the three slept in the side of a corn-stack, undiscovered by the rats that throughout the darkness were tunnelling and squeaking below them. They roosted together on the following night, for the last time; Jea and the cockbird were in love, so the odd hen went her lonesome way. Being incomplete, she was not happy, and her wheedling cries sounded continually in the budding woods. She thought no more of her old mate; she was pining to be complete. From the hazel catkins the floss was blowing, such soft floss with which to line a nest. Day after day she called her despairful cries, until suddenly, as she was searching the barky cracks of an oak trunk for spiders, bright eyes looked at her from above, and a tender voice said *"Zee-zeelee! Jikky Jikky deedle, Sisisee!"*

She searched for awhile, then answered tremblingly, *"Sisisee, Jikky, deedle-deedle, Jikky!"*

He came to her, brimming with love, fluttering his wings, and dancing on his single leg. Once more she was made complete, and happily wandering in the sunny woods and fields. After a raptured marriage they made a nest in the thorn hedge, bringing off their brood in safety, and in summer the woods were filled with the tender cries of happy titmice children, very fond of Sisisee, their graceful mother, and of Jikky Jikky Oneleg, their father, smallest bottle bird, whom their mother had helped to hatch.

Wood Rogue

With mouth wide agape Raskil waved his stretched neck to his mother, shouting his loudest. A great red worm was dropped into his maw, and he gulped it down. Its weight made him subside, and he heaved about. But a low throaty noise from his father made him stretch up again, open his maw to the fullest extent, and yell. Four nestlings were with him, and they too, were famished; but Raskil was bigger and stronger than any of them, consequently he got most of the food, becoming still bigger and stronger. On this occasion his father, an old fellow with a white face, showed no discrimination whatever, with the result that the greedy Raskil swallowed another lob worm.

Raskil was ugly. His mouth was big, and when it was open, all the red-yellow throat was exposed. He was blind, but the skin-covered eyeballs bulged bluely from his black skin. Tufts of down seemed glued to the creature. His companion nestlings were equally unpleasant to look at. Yet to their parents they were most beautiful.

Raskil's father was considered by his neighbours and co-tenants to be a silly old fool. They had often said so. Nevertheless, when a few weeks previously they had all been busy building, they had benefited considerably by him. For Raskil's father was without guile, and that season's wife was very young; consequently with patient labour they had brought sticks snapped with their beaks from off the oak trees in the distant wood, borne them to the nest, pleached them into place, and flown away again, only to have the sneering neighbours fall upon the pile and "nick" (the term all rooks and all real boys employ as a euphemism for "steal") the good oak-twigs for themselves.

Raskil's father was perched near the nest in the tall beech tree, preening his dull breast feathers, when a vast outcry arose from the thousands of rooks nesting in the colony. Raskil's father—his name was Rdwurkr; Honest Rdwurkr, the neighbours called him—

Rdwurkr cocked his eye heavenwards and detected an unpleasant object, a horrible object. It was black as themselves, with immense wings and a scarifying beak. Moreover, the terror was coming down. Thousands of rooks protested. Out of black beaks into the sunshine was poured a great variety of oaths. The little boys watching on the ground below wondered "what was up".

"They sound angry, don't they, man?" said one of them, a dark thin child wearing a curious hat that he had made from the skins of moles, "do you think it's us they're cussing at?"

"I d'no," replied his friend, "I'm sure I d'no, Willie, old man."

"I hope they don't come for us. I wish I had my cattypult for protection." They seized some sticks, and stood ready for any assault on the part of the rooks. It was fine fun, they thought, to kid themselves like that. Unfortunately no rooks came, and so no valiant battle was fought.

For it was not the little boys below who were the cause of all the shouting. It was the monstrous black stranger. He descended to the tree-top, near the sleeping Raskil, and looked about him. The rooks in the beechwood colony were silent.

The creature was something like themselves, only magnified. He was as black as soot. He was mangy in spots. Black bristles grew near the base of his beak—four inches long, his fearful beak. Now he leaned forward, loosened his reasty wings, opened that awful beak, and a deep and solemn *kr-r-r-onk* came from him.

Cries of rage followed. Rdwurkr, flying distressfully above with his wife, swore and kaa-a-d. Hundreds of rooks took to the air at once; the wind from their wings set a-dancing all the dried leaves below. Rdwurkr knew what sort of thing it was. Many years before he had lived by the sea, where there were lonely cliffs and rocks. He recognized that worshipper of all the devils, Kronk the Raven— one of the most savage, unscrupulous, and devastating of birds.

Why Kronk had come so far inland to Rookhurst Forest, it is not possible to say. Perhaps it was because after a hundred years of sea-side life he wanted a holiday. For he had cracked his own egg exactly a century before. But, there he was, perched near the sleeping Raskil, unheedful of the clamour and outcry his presence had caused. With a flap of his lousy wings he rose, alighting on the twigs at the side of the nest. He peered at the mudded bowl in the centre; and as he leaned forward to extract a meal with his beak, Rdwurkr's wife flew blindly at him, there was a shriek of rage and distress, and with a bleeding broken wing she flopped downwards. Kronk's

beak had delivered a pickaxe blow at the elbow joint, and shattered it. The mother toppled from branch to branch, till she reached the ground, where she ran about until captured by two ecstatic and bewildered boys.

Kronk ate all the nestlings save Raskil. This infant slept peacefully during the rape of his brothers and sisters, his elaborate system of digestion hard at work on the dissolution of the lob worms. He merely slept and it so chanced that he escaped dissolution within the craw of Kronk.

This ghoul ate eleven nestlings and nine eggs, selected at random from various nests, then flew away. Where he went, neither Willie nor Jack ever knew. Probably he carried on his pillage and plunder as he wandered—duckling or partridge chick, baby rabbit or kitten, carrion or worm; all was food to Kronk. He ate his own fleas. He never returned, and the work of the colony went on as before, with its petty quarrels and corvine arguments.

The wheat rose higher in the surrounding fields; windflowers on the dead leaves below yielded their petals to the wind, and the bluebells pealed their passing. The time came when the apple orchards were beautiful with blossom 'falling showers of painted snow'—it was the second week of May in the West Country. Raskil grew up. Rdwurkr patiently filled his open maw till he was grown nearly as big as himself. During Raskil's growth, many kestrel hawks had been mobbed, many sneaking carrion crows driven away with communal oaths from the rookery; rain and sunshine passed over the land. Now came the time of a great fear for Raskil, indeed, the whole colony was to withstand the greatest tragedy of the year that very afternoon.

2

Some warning was given by the sinister approach of a dozen and more men. Immediately the adult rooks rose high in the air, and formed a great circle—an aerial cartwheel, spokeless and black. It revolved in silence; hundreds of eyes were looking downwards, hundreds of hearts palpitated within black breasts. For several minutes the black cart-wheel turned above the beechwood, while human figures at the base of the tall trees constantly showed tiny specks of white—their upturned faces. But the silent wheel broke into clamorous segments when the first rifle-crack reached the rooks' ears. The annual onslaught on the Rookhurst Forest colony had begun.

For many hours the agony of the nesting birds lasted. So distressed were some parents that they ventured quite near the homes they had so laboured to build, crying to their children to take wing and flee to the sanctuary of the sky. Several youngsters essayed to fly, but their efforts became mad flappings as they lost claw-clutch and fell asprawl upon lower branches nearer the dreaded noises and terrifying, upturned faces. Raskil was one of the first to abandon the nest from which twigs were snapped and sent flying upwards by the hissing cracks that caused him to gape with fear. He managed to reach a branch very near the top of the tree, but the hissing cracks followed him there. He yelled for Rdwurkr, yelling a hundred replies to the summonses to follow, but he was afraid to let go. Every time a crack tried to stab him (he thought it was the beak of an invisible enemy) he beat madly his wings. Soon his voice became a mere parched screaming.

Bullet after bullet from small-bore rifle passed by him, but the sportsman below, a rich retired bookmaker trying to metamorphose himself into a sporting squire, was not a good shot.

Raskil gasped and gasped for protection, but none came. Soon the sportsman grew tired of aiming at the same bird, and went away to other trees; and as he only hit three birds out of one hundred and forty-three shots he fired the remainder of his cartridges into the nests, on the chance of killing late broods. The last shot he reserved for Raskil, and to the satisfaction of the sportsman he hit him, sending him tumbling into the main fork of the tree.

Some hours later the rookery was strangely quiet. The human raiders had departed with their shoulder-sticks hung with young rooks, and the old birds had returned. Some sat apart, as though they were tired, or moulting; others huddled with ruffled feathers beside empty nests. Others fed nestlings as though nothing had happened —they had already forgotten their agony, and the living claimed all their energies. The huddled and seemingly moulted rooks also had forgotten their agony; their cradles were deserted, and they could not understand at all why nothing cried to them for food and for the comfort of warm wings. They just sat there. A few more imaginative hens were brooding on empty nests, with an appearance of melancholy content; to them the cock-birds came with food, and seeing the food the hens opened their beaks, cried like fledgelings, fluttered their wings, and were fed. The cock-birds departed for more food, and the hens continued to brood over vacant nests. But the old easy-going rookery noises were gone from the calm evening air. It was as though nightfall were come suddenly—the sun meant nothing to so many of them.

3

Raskil never returned to the nest. He had soon attracted Rdwurkr by his cries. Lying in the fork, while the humans were below, he had not moved or cried out. As soon as they were gone, he cried loudly for Rdwurkr, who came with joyful cries. Raskil perched on one foot. The other was drawn up in pain, for the hind toe had been shot away. Incessantly he cried for food. That night he slept soundly. His craw was full of chafer-grubs, wire-worms, thrushs' eggs, a piece of bacon rind, slugs, various beetles and worms, and a red rubber ring. The red rubber ring had been picked up by the clod-poll Rdwurkr, who thought it was a worm, whereas originally it had been on a beer-bottle.

During the days that followed, Raskil learned to fly, and followed Rdwurkr about in the fields for food. His father taught him to dig in the ground for wire-worms, which Raskil did for a day or two, but he soon grew tired of it, preferring to sit in the grass and watch the others work. Now and again he managed to sneak morsels from other young rooks. One afternoon he was sick, and vomited the red rubber ring. He was so greedy, however, that he swallowed it again; and for days that ring had a continuous up-and-down existence.

A fortnight after the rookery tragedy, Raskil found a nest of young larks in a field, and pecked at one. Their shrill chirping delighted him and he pecked again. He ate it, killed the others, and was eating them when Rdwurkr came up. Raskil resented his coming, and jabbed his beak at Rdwurkr, who flew away. Thenceforward Raskil lived by himself, and forgot that Rdwurkr existed.

He remained with the forest rooks, who deserted their colony soon after midsummer. The autumn was mild, and the October ploughing discussed by thousands of birds. Seagulls who had heard somehow of the yearly feast flew from the coast and joined the excited throng. Raskil had a fight with one over a chrysalis—at least, he tried to steal it from a herring-gull—and received one peck from the yellow beak of the stranger that made him avoid gulls in the future; but he profited by the encounter, for it taught him to be careful whenever he decided to filch, which was nearly always.

Snow fell in November, covering deep the downs and the plains. A black frost set in, lasting for months. During the time of starvation and cold, Raskil learned to kill small birds. He chased the little exhausted things until they dropped, then battered them with his beak. One day he saw a rook shivering on a leafless oak, and even as he flew to the tree it toppled sideways and fell on the snow. It flapped feebly one wing. Raskil did not recognise Rdwurkr, and he was famished. Later, when a starving rat, passing down the hedge, rushed over the snow as soon as it scented a meal, only scattered feathers, picked skeleton, and frozen blood-drops were left. The bones were cracked up that night by Fang-over-lip the fox, who buried some of the feathers—to such ignominious fare had he been reduced by his impoverished hunting ground.

By the end of the winter Raskil could hold his own in a fight with big hoody crows that came from Scandinavia. When the evil weather passed away before an insistent wind from the south-west in March, these hoody crows went back to their homes, but Raskil did not return to his. He was bored by the unceasing and unnecessary rook-noises of spring. Nor did he go digging in the fields for sprouting grain or wire-worms—he kept alone. He preferred to live away from noise that meant nothing but foolish reiteration that rooks loved one another. He took up with a female carrion crow, haunting a small copse of fir and elm in a large park, and near the garden of the house. He drove away two male carrion crows who had been hanging around and, in the last week of March, was accepted as her mate.

4

They chose a high and unscalable fir-tree for their breeding place. Raskil's mate taught him several things about observation posts; the first thing she did after allowing him to preen her glossy pinion feathers was to take him to five trees (all within three hundred yards of the unscalable fir) and show him sentinel branches that commanded a view for a long distance every way. The carrion crow was cunning, having been born so; for centuries everything had feared and hated the carrion crow. Raskil was not born cunning; he was amoral and with a natural propensity towards ruffianism and laziness. He learned quickly, and by the time four eggs were laid he was far more dangerous to old Bob Lewis, the keeper to Squire Tetley, than his mate had been or ever would be.

Two boys came one day to the fir-tree, and with the help of a new pair of climbing irons attempted to reach the nest. Willie tried first, but he had to give up owing to fear. Jack was not so imaginative as his friend, and managed to climb up the branchless bole and reach the nest. Then he lost his nerve, and only after a terrible ten minutes, and with the help of a passing man, did he manage to descend with four eggs unbroken in his cap held between teeth. All the while Raskil and his mate, after hoarse cries, were skulking in a beech-tree a quarter of a mile away. Afterwards they flew back to the nest, and the crow with a deep *crok-k-kr* told him that her treasures were gone. She still had another egg to lay, and Raskil aided her in the repairing of the old nest of a sparrow-hawk in the woods. Here the egg was deposited, but as she was shot a week later by Bob Lewis, who came upon her as she was eating a duckling stolen from the aviary or wire-netted game hatchery, this did not hatch but provided a meal for a jay, also of the crow family, and himself a grawbey.

So Raskil found himself alone once more, and he did not miss his mate very much. He went back to the rookery and tried to rob a nest or two, being driven away with oaths. This infuriated him, and he avoided rooks thenceforward.

Willie found the aged keeper sitting on a log in his rearing field one morning in May, and Bob told him about a bird that was giving him a lot of trouble.

"He'm that saucy, miboy, that he wull a-follow me in th' wood, just out of gunshot. A girt grawbey, dang un, taking all my eggs, Ah um."

Willie begged to be allowed to accompany the 'head-man' on his rounds the next morning, and Bob was delighted. Willie got up at half-past five, and met him at the aviary. The wild flowers that Bob had planted there in bygone years were sweetened with dew, and sleepy bees were passing to them through the golden haze of morning.

They climbed over a low wire fence, and entered the preserve of hazel wands and ashpoles. Wide paths of green-sward impressed by the marks of hob-nailed boots went round, and through, the trees. Willie was excited when they found a stoat caught in a gin; it chattered ragefully at them, and bared its teeth. Bob knocked it on the head, and tied a piece of string round its neck. As soon as he came

to one of the vermin-trees he hung it on a branch, among all its perished fellows.

"I wonder where the rook-grawbey is," asked Willie excitedly.

"Us'll see presently, shouldn't wonder."

They did see Raskil presently. But he saw them first, and flew away from the hen pheasant with whom he had been fighting for over an hour. He flew away with an egg in his beak, but he did not go far. He perched on the branch of the oak-tree to which were tied the corpses of the stoats, weasels, crows and hedgehogs, and holding up his beak, drank the egg.

Then he cawed defiance at the keeper, seeming to bow as he did so.

"Bob, Bob, look at the pheasant!"

Willie pointed at the sitting bird. Her right eye, which faced them, was broken and bleeding. Many of her neck feathers had been plucked out.

Bob tried to lift up the sitting bird, but she pecked at him. When he had got her, they saw that only seven of the brown eggs were left.

Raskil continued to sit on a bough of the gallows-tree, sixty yards away. Frequently he called a deep *karr-rr*, bowing each time. Bob swore at him, and Willie swore as well, using different words, more bloodthirsty words, like "hellfire" and "devilskin".

"Come wi' me," said Bob.

They walked away, leaving the hen-bird on the nest. When they had gone out of gunshot Raskil flew down and lunged at the pheasant with his beak. They fought until Raskil had banged her off the nest, then he seized an egg and flew back to the gallows-tree.

They walked down the path until they came to a small hut. Bob unlatched the door and peeping in Willie saw rusty gins, old coats, wooden pheasant traps, bags of shot (he wanted to nick a bag of shot, but thought it would be mean to nick it from Bob, who was so decent) and old boots. Bob took four sticks, a trap, and a piece of turf.

They returned to the pheasant's nest. Bob drove the four stakes into the ground in a small square. Upon the top he placed the piece of turf. From his pocket he took several addled eggs and laid them on the ground. To set the trap he stood on the rusty spring, so that the jaws fell open, and bending down with difficulty, he set the spade, or metal tongue, in position. Carefully he lifted up the iron death-dealer and placed it on the turf. Around it he put leaves and grasses, then the eggs, softly, one by one, in position. Seeing this, Raskil called *ka-r-r*, and bowed saucily several times from the gallows-tree.

They went away from the crude dummy of a nest. Raskil immediately flew down to it. He must have known that it was erected solely for his harm, for his destruction. Yet he flew down to it. The impulse in his nature that had made him, as a very young bird, prefer stealing to working, must now have dominated him absolutely. He possessed no instinctive cunning—only assimilative cleverness and a lust for destruction. Now that overcame and destroyed him. But he never lost his courage.

For when they came back two minutes later they found him, as the old keeper knew they would, caught in the trap. The serrated jaws springing up had smashed his thigh bones so completely that he was forced to lie on his side. Lying thus, and levering himself with his wings, he sought the unbroken eggs and shattered them. Little boy and aged man peered at the spectacle of a broken-bodied bird savagely wrecking what had lured him to death. With a black beak fouled by stinking yolk, Raskil made his last lunge at the stick that the compassionate guardian of the forest brought down on his neck so surely that his life was instantly ended.

5

In autumn the leaves fell from the hazel wands and the ashpoles, from the elderberries and the oaks, exposing against a drab sky the squirrel dreys and the birds' nests—deserted tokens of hope. Deprived of leafy protection, the forms of the year's failures were shown, hanging starkly and in silence. The flies that had buzzed about the wasted corpses were dead, and only moisture dripped upon them from the bare branches above. Some were green and mouldy, others were hairless and mummified. In places only a whiskered skull—grotesque caricature of life with its empty eye-sockets—hung grinning on a rotting string. Dishevelled crows dangled from other tiers, with sparrow-hawks and kestrels, hedgehogs, rats and poaching cats. This was the gallows-tree of the failures, of the wood rogues, of the beasts and birds unrepentant in life and in death.

When spring came again nothing visible remained of Raskil. His skeleton had fallen and broken up, his bones were hidden by grasses and by the tender sweet violets that grew at the base of the oak.

After two more springs had come and gone not even a bone remained. All were merged into earth which embraces with tranquillity the forms of those who, after toil and endeavour, are discarded by the spirit. Sun and wind and rain attend the inexplicable comings and goings of bud and leaf, of egg and bird, of babe and parent. After toil and endeavour there was equal rest for Rdwurkr and Raskil.

Aliens

A dandelion on the bank of the stream was bent as the creature's body passed over it, and an oily smear tarnished its disk, so disfiguring it that no bronze fly came to explore it for pollen, and eventually it withered without forming any seeds. A year ago a small brown speck had swung there under a silken parachute, but no bird had found it; one, indeed, had chased the rolling seed-bearer as it was blown over the sooty grasses, but the seed had already been released.

The creature passed on—a black rat, the last of its kind remaining in the south-east of London. For years it had lived by the banks of the Ravensbourne stream, that in a greasy brown mud bed meanders through an open space that once was a park, called the Recreation Ground, under an old brick archway bearing the road, passing tattered fences, dying trees, factories, timber yards, and sordid back-gardens, to turn a mill-wheel below which in olden time trout used to lie; and meeting the dead brook Quaggy by a railway station, together the poor streams flow through a land more desolate till they reach the Thames rushing with its load of filth to the sea for absolution.

Lewisham was once a quiet village—"lazy, lousy Loos'am" said George III, driving through its length early one morning, while the inhabitants yawned and scratched at their open doors. Through that village in olden time rumbled the Kentish fruit and vegetable carts on their way to the Old Kent Road and the Covent Garden Market. The Ravensbourne stream was once clear and its waters were pure, nourishing scarlet-finny droves of roach and dace; trout and grayling lurked in the pools wimpling by the roots of overhanging willow and oak. In spring the great gold goblets of the king-cups cast a thick lustre on the water, and later there came the forget-me-nots, the purple flag-lilies and the bulrushes, hiding moorhens and dabchicks. But when the surrounding cornfields were built upon, and row upon row of brick houses sprung up, all these things began to disappear. As the years went by the old manor houses were pulled down; everything was changed. As the human poor invaded what had been the country, so the wild creatures died out. Progress spread with the increase of chimneys, so did the smoke, which, mingling with the damp breath of Father Thames, sometimes swirled over the low-lying south-eastern suburbs, blotting out all things—little house and grimy tree, droning tramcar and heavy beer-lorry, sparrow and falling leaf—in The Smoke, as carters and tramps called London.

But this short chronicle does not deal principally with Lewisham and its pale-faced inhabitants, or with the Ravensbourne and its dead waters; rather are these things the background for the drama of Jack o' Rags, surely one of the strangest natures that civilization had distorted; of Slimey, the last black rat in the south-east of London; and of Splitail the last fish, if one excepts visiting eels, to be left alive, or rather, dead-and-alive, in the stream. Even that does not describe properly Splitail's condition, for he was an animated corpse. A pale blue fungus grew on his broken tail, on his sides, corrupting his red fins and dulling his eyes. Now Splitail was a big roach, over twelve inches long, and twenty ounces in weight. How he had managed to survive in the polluted waters was a mystery to the boy who sometimes wandered along the banks with a catapult, potting at sparrows and rats and an occasional water-vole. He was a boy who combined observation with dreaminess, a desire to hunt and trap (like a Red Indian) with a love of birds and animals. When he was ten he and his small sister went into the Rec, as the London County Council Park was called, with slices of mutton, some string, and two S-shaped meat-hooks. Through the planking of the imitation rustic bridges they let down their curious instruments for snaring fish, waiting so long for a bite that they were three hours late for tea. Phillip would have been wildly happy had he known that he had nearly caught something, for Slimey, swimming upstream, had smelt the meat and had a good meal.

This was the first encounter of the boy and the rat. Many times afterwards he saw him, and took pots at him, but he always missed. So time went on, and one day the boy saw the form of Splitail lighted by a slanting sunbeam as he waved his fins and tail, trout-wise, in the pool by the ancient alder near one of the rustic bridges. He told his friend, and the two made many expeditions to feed it with worms and bread-pills. It delighted them to think that in the river there was a fish still alive and known only to themselves, and Phillip wove many romances about it. He had a cousin called Willie far away in the country, who was awfully lucky, because he lived near a huge lake, among all kinds of rare birds and animals that Phillip had only heard about from his father, who had been born and brought up at Rookhurst. But now all that was done with; his father had to work in an office in the city; and he suffered, living in an alien and crowded suburb of London. He had no friends, and was becoming more bitter as the years went on.

2

The invasion of the brown rat into England centuries ago caused the extermination of the black rat, a smaller, less fierce animal, with a longer snout and tail. How Slimey came to the Ravensbourne rat-colony, whether he was born there, and why he was so big, are mysteries insoluble. He was a buck-rat, and a great fighter; his ears were torn and his tail was scarred; he had been the father of over a thousand rats, his right to paternity being gained by superior strength in many a fight with brown bucks. He cared nothing for the litters of which he was parent; happened he to approach a nest of one of them, probably because he was hungry, the doe which a little while since he had wooed invariably bit him, and he went away, because he never argued with a doe-rat, but suffered her biting remarks patiently.

After smirching the dandelion, merely because it so happened that it was in his way, he crept along a rat-run, leaving behind him the imprint of claws and the wet mark of his tail. Suddenly he stopped, remaining quite still. Just before him was a hawthorn bush, growing behind the fence that terminated the dreary vegetable gardens of the Lewisham Infirmary. He looked quickly across the stream, which at that place was about eighteen feet wide, but there was no human on the path beyond the railings. The sparrow in one of the lower twigs of the thorn had not seen him.

He crept forward with infinite slowness, moving carefully one foot before the other. With a noise of wings and shrill chirpings other sparrows flew to the bush, and started to squabble over something. Slimey was pleased, and slightly increased his forward movement.

The sparrow he was watching made the squabble into a personal quarrel with another cock-bird, and the two fell about six inches to a lower branch. Slimey took a swift run forward, leapt into the air, there was a squeak of alarm. The others forgot their squabble and flew away.

By the leg Slimey held the bird, which fluttered wildly its wings and pecked him twice on the nose, drawing a small bead of blood. The rat stood on the bird, and with a quick bite severed its neck. It shuddered and lay still.

Slimey dragged it into a near hole, turning out a neat little creature with a clean brown coat and a blunt nose—it was a harmless water-vole—and ate the sparrow. What he did not want he left, and when the timid vole returned it worked for a half-hour at the cleaning of its burrow, taking the feathers and the wings to make more comfortable its nest at the end of the hole.

Slimey ranged far in his hunting, some miles of bank being familiar to him. Sometimes it rained heavily, and the Ravensbourne quickly flooded, driving hundreds of rats out of their galleries. But having no home of his own he did not mind the floods, especially as wonderful foods sometimes came down with the swift water and the branches of trees—dead cats and dogs, drowned fowls, and once the brown-paper-wrapped corpse of a new-born baby.

Periods of sunshine, Slimey noticed, became periods of cold and frost; and these periods recurred at regular intervals. Also he was accustomed to the dread hooting of the brown owl that followed the death shriek of some hapless rat, for that was part of his life; but the sudden colossal bangs at night, and once or twice the crimson roar near him nearly killed him with fright. He noticed that the hum of the creatures in the sky was invariably followed by the colossal bangs, the sweeping of the sky with gigantic whiskers of light, and the frightened cries of humans who sometimes in the early night were lying on the banks in whispering couples. Once Slimey was caused by his heart to jump into the river. Something whined above him like one of the mosquitoes that haunted the river, only the whine grew louder and louder, increasing till it became a hiss of something that never before had he met, although once he had dreamed about it. With a gigantic *whoosh* it passed by him and hit the river, sending up a vast spurt of ooze. Slimey dived, and swam under water so far that he nearly drowned, not knowing that the nose-cap of the anti-Zeppelin shell had missed him by two yards, that it had missed Splitail by ten feet and Jack o' Rags, asleep in a disused swan's

nest, by fifty yards. Of the three, Jack o' Rags was the most alarmed; he rose from his bed and went under the railway footbridge, distant by four minutes' walk. In the morning he awoke, and went down to a Lewisham stable to help groom some light-draught horses.

3

The origin of Jack o' Rags, like the origin of Slimey, was a mystery; but whereas the human was a perpetual mystery to Lewisham, the animal was of interest only to Phillip; at least, it had been during his boyhood. Jack o' Rags was a short and sturdy man, with his head and face half hidden by an enormous cap worn back to front, from which sprouted hair resembling a bunch of over-ripe banana skins. The face itself, or that part of it visible, was not unlike an apple; an apple that has been thrown with violence against a wall and left there for a week in wet weather. The hue of Jack's round face was the hue of a pulpy apple; his voice was hoarser than that of the oldest rook nesting in the colony of the Infirmary grounds; he looked like the stump of a lightning-blasted tree to which rags had anciently been nailed; his feet were protected by big boots, completing the resemblance to a tree-stump in upright motion. Usually he hid his hands in his pockets as he slouched along.

Most of the boys of Lewisham called after him, and 'sauced' him; and those boys who did not 'sauce' him only refrained because they were timid, or because their mother repeatedly impressed upon them the knowledge of their genteel parenthood. Jack o' Rags would hurl curses at them, and they would jeer the more. Many Lewisham residents, meeting him in the High Street and elsewhere, swung away in a semicircle about him when they passed; he slouched along, and people made way for him. He was said to be an Old Etonian who had been brought low by gambling, racing, women, wine, song, and a wicked uncle; he was said to be the co-heir-in-chancery of a large estate, but having had a bitter quarrel with his step-sister, the co-heir, he refused to sign a paper that would make them both fabulously wealthy; he was said to have been a schoolmaster of the local grammar school driven mad by boys; he was said to be a musical genius crazed by the Saturday-night music of the Salvation Army bands. All the statements, rumours, misstatements, jokes, and remarks made about Jack o' Rags by Lewisham reflected directly upon the credulity and the intelligence of the Borough's population.

Jack lumbered along Lewisham High Street, annoyed by boys as flies annoy a horse. He replied to them with hoarse oaths and fist-shakes.

"Wait till I get you, you boys. Yerrse! Just you wait, yerrse!" Alfred, the ratcatcher, with Flo, his foxterrier-bitch, passed him on his way to ferret the Recreation Ground banks, and said good morning.

"Lend us a penny, maite. I'll pay yer back. Yerrse!"

Alfred gave the penny good-naturedly, and Jack o' Rags walked towards the Lewisham Obelisk. Outside a coffee-house he waited, till a fat man emerged with hunks of broken bread and a pint of tea in a receptacle made out of a rusty can that once had contained tinned fruit. It was Jack's special cup, and he would have no other.

Afterwards he went round to the Mews behind the Rat Trap, a pub near the mill, and asked in a hoarse voice how Kate was. Erb the tenant said that she was better, and advised him to go away.

"I don't want my mare lousy," he said; "you ain't washed yerself, Jack.'

"Garn!" shouted Jack, "I'm nert lousy. Nert me. Ner. Straight, I'm nert crummy."

So Erb allowed Jack to groom the mare, which he did lovingly, making a gentle whispering whistle with his lips all the time. The mare stood still sometimes turning soft eyes to regard her benefactor, and touching him with her nose. Jack refused to accept sixpence when he had cleaned out the middens and polished the harness.

"Giss a penny, maite. I don't want no other payment. Ner. Giss a penny ter pay back a bloke."

At midday he again was 'sauced' by boys, but that evening something worse than verbal abuse awaited him. He was seized by some half-drunk youths and taken into a stable near a coffee-stall, held down, and one half of his head cropped with horse-clippers, and one side of his face roughly shaved. Then they stripped off his clothes and threw water over him, while Jack cursed and swore and blas-phemed and protested in his hoarse and ruined voice.

Later on he went as usual to the coffee-stall with his tea-can, and got the scraps that the kindly proprietor always had for him with the hot dregs of one of the tea urns. The youths came insolently up to the shaded stall, telling everyone how drunk they were; and the stall-keeper told them sharply they ought to be ashamed of themselves. But, he supposed, the marks of their mothers' handslaps were still on certain parts of them, otherwise they would have been in the army. The discussion went on, abuse being given on both sides, and Jack cursing and muttering to himself until someone came up—a tall pale man in mufti. This individual asked for tea and the youths guffawed, but they were ignored. They began again to torment the miserable man, when the stranger said:

"Go away, you fellows. Be off, and behave yourselves. Leave the man alone."

"Be off! Be off!" they jeered. "Gorblime, wot a toff! Go awee, you fellars! Aye come from Hoxford Collidge, aye do!"

"Be off, be off!" warned the stranger.

Jack slouched away, and the youths followed, six or seven of them, and began pushing him.

"Wait till I git yer, you boys. Yerrse. I ain't done no harm to you."

Bill the coffee-stall proprietor related afterwards how the toff went swiftly after the youths, who, thinking that he would provide better sport for them, left Jack alone and crowded round the stranger.

"Lorlumme, mite, it would have warmed yer heart. 'Be off, you boys!' cried the toff, and one of them, the biggest, who fancied isself with the mitts, asked him who he thought he was, and squared up to im. Lorlumme, they didn't arf get a shock. The toff, quick as a flash, hit the bloke on the jaw, and dahn e went, then e hit another and then another. Dahn they went like skittles, and the others did a guy. Lorlumme, e didn't arf upand them! Then the toff orffered Jack a dollar, but Jack cursed at im, saying e put the blokes on to im! So the toff turned away and come back ere. E lived in these parts, and were an orficer on leave, by name of Maddison."

4

Alf the ratcatcher chuckled, and said that Jack was always like that. The next day Alf invited a few friends to see some sport with the rats he had caught, and in the backyard of the Rat Trap they gathered —all old men, too old to be in the army. Jack o' Rags was there, and Flo killed a dozen by neatly picking them up as they darted out of the wire cage, flinging them in the air, catching them by the back as they fell, and giving one shake that broke their life mechanism as a bomb shatters a dynamo. Alf had a big black rat, a fierce old monster that was too good to waste in the same manner, so he fetched Lop, the polecat-ferret, out of his musty hutch, and put him in a large box with Slimey. Flo he locked up in the stable, barking.

Lop was a young dog-ferret, and therefore without the skill that an older animal would have possessed. Slimey immediately went into a corner, reared himself in a crouching position, and waited. The men leaned over the box, watching Lop creeping nearer and nearer the corner, weaving his head right and left like a restless dray-horse in a stall. Slimey bared his fangs and began to cry. He made a noise like a child in a temper, and ground his teeth. Suddenly Lop darted forward, but Slimey anticipated it, leaping by him with a thud of his tail on the wood, and gashing Lop's shoulder as he passed.

"Lorlumme," muttered Bill, the coffee-stall man. Slimey waited in another corner. Lop approached with the same sinuous motion; Slimey cried with rage and fear. Lop's instinctive desire was to get the rat by the back of the neck, when he could kill it with ease. Slimey knew that, and relied upon his agility to leap aside as the ferret dashed at him, ripping a long red gash in his body every time. Lop got angry and chattered his rage; Slimey whined and grizzled in the corners; and the bottom of the box was imprinted with bloody footprints.

"The rat's too good for Lop," said Alf; "he'll kill 'im if we aren't keerful. Let Flo finish 'im."

He grabbed Lop, and left the rat in the box, and was taking the ferret to the stable when Jack o' Rags put his arm in the box. Slimey jumped up his arm, nipped his ear as he passed, and swift as a thrown stone went across the yard.

Blood streamed from Jack's ear-lobe, and he bellowed gruffly after the rat, "You wait till I get yer. Yerrse. I ain't done no harm to you."

He may have meant to release Slimey after his sporting fight; he may have been sorry for him. Anyhow, Slimey bit his benefactor, and got away, swarming up the wall near the mill and jumping into the Ravensbourne. A week later he was back near the old swan's nest in the Recreation Ground, living on sparrows, young rats, snails, beetles, worms and any edible morsel that the muddy waters brought down. Again and again he made attempts to catch Splitail, swimming under water like an otter, but the ancient fish avoided him.

Food got scarcer, and in the beginning of the year nineteen seventeen Slimey found that there was practically no floating food to be found in the water. The morning after a severe frost he found Splitail near a shallow mudbank, and lying on its side. Slimey walked over the mudbank, and seeing him the roach made a feeble attempt to reach deeper water. But it was dying, and the slow flaps it made told the rat that it was his at last. The blue-grey fungus was thick on its side, the metallic green of its back scales was gone, the fins and the tail were no longer red, but frayed and drab. Slimey dragged it to the mudbank and began to eat it. While he was doing so other rats came nearer, but dared not approach. When he was gorged he went away to sleep in a rotten willow near the swan's nest that was protected by hurdles, leaving the others to squeak and scurry over the corpse. Soon all that remained of Splitail was a backbone with tail attached, lying on the mudbank in the midst of claw-prints.

Jack o' Rags felt the pains of hunger and whistled. Alf the rat-catcher met him in the High Street one Sunday, also whistling.

"What're yer whistling for?" growled Jack; "yer ain't ungry, are yer? Lend us a copper, maite."

Alf gave him tuppence, and was paid back within a week. Jack was very particular about his debts. A water main burst in Lewisham in the frosty period, and at night Jack went near the coke-brazier of the gang. But they warned him away, saying that he did not wash. Jack cursed them, and went to Bill's coffee-stall with his can for tea. He whistled loudly, and Bill gave him some dry bread which he ate hungrily. Food queues in Lewisham was growing longer and longer, and people were talking about the submarine peril. Jack did not talk with anyone about it, but whistled louder than ever. The cold increased, and in the early morning he went to the gaudy advertisement hoardings, tearing down strips of paper which he took under the arch of the railway footbridge, wrapping himself up in them. Sometimes when he awoke he could not move for an hour, and his lips were too cold to be pursed for whistling.

5

He was lying one night in the swan's nest, when an owl came over his head and peered down. Jack did not see it, nor did Slimey, who was two feet away from his pocket. In that pocket Jack had half a loaf and some rancid pork given him by Bill the coffee-stall man, and he was musing about it, and how he would enjoy it in the morning. Slimey had smelt the rancid pork, and had crept nearer to the smell. The rat knew the old man, and did not fear him. He had stolen food out of his pocket before, when he had been asleep, and tonight the smell of the decaying meat delighted him.

Jack o' Rags did not stir, nor did the wood owl peering above with round black eyes. Nearer went the rat; a rimed branch creaked above, and he started in fear. The night was undisturbed by bombing airplanes or shunting of Woolwich ammunition trains in the distance. But when the owl launched itself downwards, having decided that the movement below was capable of being destroyed by itself, there was a long and terrible scream. The feathered feet gripped the black rat's body, but that body was so tough and big that the talons were unable to squeeze the heart into stillness. To the owl's surprise it was dragged along the ground, flapping its wings and snapping its beak with anger.

Harder and harder it gripped with its claws, more desperate were the struggles of Slimey, who was endeavouring to climb up the owl's front and tear the artery at the side of the neck. Attracted by the screams, a wandering cat ran forward, but seeing the owl and hearing the snap of its bill, the cat climbed a tree. Jack o' Rags was awakened by the struggle, since it was taking place on his body. He caught the owl and crushed its skull (an easy matter) in his fist; then he hit Slimey and broke all the rat's ribs. The owl died with slow flaps of broad wings, and when it was dead Jack spread its softness over his legs like a blanket.

The pale-faced inhabitants of Lewisham who were working for much money in Woolwich Arsenal, and had to be out as soon as it was light, were startled out of their apathy the next morning by the sight of Jack as he slouched along the pavement carrying a large bird, some sort of foreign hen, they imagined. Near the eating house Jack skinned the bird, which had a small body, and the rat, and boiled them together in his special can over the water-gang's coke fire. He boiled them for three hours, finding the owl very tough; but still, he managed to eat all of it. He did not whistle that day.

Thus the last fish in the stream and the last black rat in the south-east of London disappeared from the world of mortal things. The Ravensbourne still runs, and at night the blurs that are human creatures trudge the paths by the water. Sometimes they stop and speak to taller blurs that approach, and together the pairs go to places among the trees, secretly, rarely speaking. Human dereliction remains; but the bulrushes and waterfowl are no more; nor does the king-cup make its golden goblet in the spring. Beauty dies where man goes often. The swans have gone too, and the old nest has been burned with the dead leaves of an autumn. Jack o' Rags is no more, for in the hard winter of nineteen seventeen, just after the teeth of Slimey had pierced the flesh of Splitail, and the owl's talons had pierced the body of Slimey, they found him lying frozen in the old heap of sedges and sticks, his heart pierced by the black frost of that tragic year.

The Chronicle of Halbert and Znarr

A small, red-haired, ragged boy sat on a log among the nettles of the forbidden forest, and with a joy-trembled heart he saw the blue-bells. It was the first Sunday in May—a real sun-day for the ragged urchin who had come from the slums of the Waterloo Road to what he believed to be the real country. Only after many adventures had he reached his journey's end. He had set out with several of his friends—Jackie Slipper, Billy Smith, Tom Gown, and others—but owing to an encounter with Winking Wooldridge, the bullying paper boy at the Elephant and Castle pitch, the little barefoot band had been broken up amid howls and groans. For Winking Wooldridge, whose father was a prize-fighter with only one ear, was a bully and a hooligan, a big loutish boy of fifteen years, and he had given Tommy Gown a bleeding nose and kicked Jackie Slipper on the shins while he lay in the gutter on his back amongst orange-peel, hair-pins, road filth, and bits of paper. There had been no reason for Winking Wooldridge doing this; unless it was a purely business reason, since they all sold evening newspapers in the neighbourhood of the Elephant and Castle, that big valve of trams and traffic in the south-eastern heart of London, choked with beerhouses, gin-palaces, and bookmaking touts.

But Halbert had spat on Winking Wooldridge's back, and run away down the Old Kent Road. He wanted to reach the country and get an armful of bluebells. While rushing about on the cobbled street the night before with his bundle of papers, he had seen many tramloads of people laden with the magic blue flowers. That morning he got up early from his bed, made by himself out of clothes' props and wire netting, took a pocketful of cold potatoes, an onion, some cheese and a hunk of bread, and sneaked out of the room. In the bed his father was snoring away his beery breath, and his mother was sleeping with the baby pale against her black, curl-ragged hair, as far away from Dad as possible. Meg, the crippled sister, was huddled in the other bed, with Oobie, otherwise Hubert, the cat. This room was Halbert's home, and these living beings were Halbert's people. The address was No. 17 Arcady Street (adjoining the Board School playground), a big house with sooty bricks and rotten roof that sheltered twenty-three families similar to Halbert's.

Down the Old Kent Road Halbert had padded, outstripping other bands of migrants making for green fields and shady woods. Some carried jamjars and fishing nets, and little tins of worms and gentles. All were hurrying, but Halbert was faster than any. He got to Peckham Rye, where a dog nearly bit him, because Halbert went too near the chicken foot it had just discovered near a drain. Halbert swore at the mongrel, and hastened onwards. A stream of vehicles flowed past him. Ancient motor-cars wheezed and thumped, Ford trade-vans made their characteristic noise, barking rusty motor-cycles clanked and shuddered with old wicker side-cars attached by iron pipes to them, bicycles, tandems, horse-and-traps, tram-cars, omnibuses, and perambulators. All laden with men, women, and children, of all ages, shapes, sizes, deportments, habiliments and expressions. Only one idea these travellers had—to get into the country on this Sunday of the May month, when the sun had found its way to the hearts of all.

2

Halbert got to New Cross Gate, and was nearly run over by a long aluminium motor-car. He darted out of the way of one disked wheel, and was about to loosen his string of oaths at the driver, a young man without a hat, when he saw the driver's companion. A slim lady smiled at him, and Halbert smiled back, showing the three teeth in front that Winking Wooldridge had not yet knocked out. The aluminium car pulled up, and the lady beckoned to Halbert. Without any hesitation, Halbert rushed forward, with about nine other children who also scented coppers. But Halbert was first, and he said: "I beg yer pardon for nearly inkerveniencing yer as I did, ma'am."

"Oh, but it was our fault," replied the gracious lady.

Halbert, however, repeated:

"I am erfraid it was my keerless manner, ma'am. But I was thinking of the bluebells I shill git for me old cripple father."

Halbert was seated in the dickey seat a minute later, and the racing car was gliding with gruff coughs towards Lewisham. Halbert saw at least three people who knew him and he looked at them with a haughty stare. He imagined that they thought he was driving with his friends. In reality they imagined that he was being taken to the police station for sounding the horn, or stealing some of the rugs in the toff's motor. They jeered: "Whip be'hind, guv'nor!" Through Catford he went, telling the toff about his fights with Winking Wooldridge, and to the wide Bromley Road. They passed decrepit motor-cars overladen with family parties; they passed droves of bicycling youths and maidens; they passed full motor-buses and tram-cars. At Southend Village Pond Albert touched the driver's knee and said, in the politest voice he could manage:

"Thanks werry much, mister. A werry good ingine indeed. I bet it can do sixty mile a hower, mister!"

"It can do ninety," smiled the young man.

"Lorlumme!" gasped Halbert, "I thought we were travelling fast. Ere's the place I was making for. Thanks werry much, guv'nor."

"Haven't you any shoes or stockings?' asked the lady.

She spoke softly, and Halbert had a desire to tell a pathetic story about his crippled father, and how he himself supported many baby brothers and sisters by selling papers. Then the lady would be good for a shilling or two. Instead, he said:

"Yes, m'am, only it's nicer without them. We're quite rich reely, because pa's got the best fried-fish shop dahn our way." Halbert invented this in order to convince them of his social prestige in Arcady Street. Whereas pa did no work at all, unless touting in pubs and collecting betting slips for a syndicate of Jews could be called work. Halbert hastily added:

"Our jellied eels are better'n any in the Hold Kent Road."

"I'm sure they are."

"Not alf they ain't guvnor."

"What's your name?" inquired the lady.

"Halbert, ma'am."

"Halbert?"

"Yes'm. Ma and pa named me after a beautiful statyer in London —the Halbert Memorial."

They both laughed at the proud information, and the man offered the child a shilling, which he refused, saying: "That's all right, guv'nor."

"But why not take it?" urged the soft voice of the lady.

"That's all right,' muttered Halbert, doing so, and with a grin he hurried away.

3

At Southend Village there is a terminus of the London County Council tramways and a public-house called The Green Man. Some of the men leave outside wives and children, dressed in their Sunday-best, while they go into the crowded and murmurous bars. A few, indeed, are so happy at the thought of freedom and unrestraint in the country that they spend most of their time and money within, while listless wives come periodically to venture a suggested walk, and while the disappointed children cling to the iron railings that separate Southend Pond from the pavement, and watch wistfully the swans and moorhens passing to and fro on the muddy water. Often in past summers Halbert had been one of the waiting children, for usually when his father had come out he had gone straight to The Green Man and remained there till closing time, when he would come out and tell them how he had enjoyed himself.

To get to the forest Halbert went up Beckenham Lane and climbed swiftly over a wooden fence. Trespass was forbidden, so said a warning notice, but Halbert did not care. The only living thing that saw him as he went across the field to the trees bordering the railway line of the South-Eastern and Chatham Railway Company was a crow. The crow had a nest in the wood across the line, and it gave a low croak of warning. Halbert did not hear it; his own actions were rather crow-like as he slipped across the twin metalled and sleepered track—he was furtive, cunning, and ready to flee at the least alarm.

He jumped over an iron railing and was in the forbidden forest. At last he could see the bluebells. He began to dance, solemnly, silently. He touched the bark of an elderberry tree, and said: "Wot ho, mate, ain't this a bit of all-right?" He forgot his name, his parents, his daily struggle to sell papers at the Elephant and Castle, his fear of Winking Wooldridge. At last he was really living; the stains of a city environment were washed away by the wandering bluebell air. He climbed the elderberry tree and hung upside down, swinging his arms. His ragged coat flapped over his head and his shirt pulled away from his belt, so that his pale and skinny and grimy body was exposed to the thrust of a golden lance of sunlight. Soon he tired of this, and began feverishly to pick bluebells. Only when he had broken scores of stems did he learn the way to pull them, with a moist wrench, from the buried bulbs. These he abandoned with a shout, because he saw a small blue-green bird, with red on it, dart past him in a straight line, like a coloured stone shot from a catapult. "Gorblime, a small parrot," shrieked Halbert, casting away the flowers and running after the bird as it gave a shrill whistle. It was a kingfisher. Halbert pursuing the same line sprawled over several brambles, crossed a path, and came to a lake, partly surrounded by trees. Seeing some ladies and gentlemen, he collapsed behind a tree, shaded his eyes with his hands and regarded them. He felt himself to be a daring trespasser as he shivered with happiness. The ladies and gentlemen were apparently hitting stones with sticks, and walking after them. "We play that gaime dahn our street," thought Halbert.

The edge of the lake broke gently against a pebbly shore, and the wavelets gliding forward carried with them golden lines of light which were reflected on the sandy bottom. Sometimes Halbert saw fishes drift almost within seizing distance of his eager paws, fishes with red tails and fins and greenish backs. "If only I ad a nook," he groaned, "and a lovely fet worm."

4

It was at this moment that Halbert heard the hoarse exulting voice of Winking Wooldridge. He crouched like a mouse against the leafy mould and his heart beat against a stone.

Winking Wooldridge's voice was saying: "Blime, mate, this aren't alf a fine place. I've got four balls and a toff's clubs. He left them on a grassy eap, and went wiv is girl into a shed to see a swaller's nest, e said, really to spoon a bit, I expect. Lovely clubs, ain't they? I'll lay Uncle Ike will give a dollar for them."

Of what happened next Halbert remained uncertain. The face of Winking Wooldridge, with the cast in one eye and the lid that flickered, grinned through a bush. Halbert was up instantly, Winking Wooldridge after him with an oath. Simultaneously a man shouted, another one answered, a dog barked, and Winking Wooldridge was rushing one way with two friends and a mongrel dog, and Halbert another way among the trees.

The chase lasted several minutes. Halbert fell over roots and branches, doubled round trees, and plunged through bushes. His pursuer could not be shaken off. Halbert was swift, and so was the young man chasing him. Seeing that he could not gain on him, Halbert started to screech. By doing this he lost energy and his flight became weaker. He yelled his fear, and burst into tears, crying: "It warn't me, strite it warn't! Strite it warn't me! I swear by Christ it warn't me! It warn't me! It warn't me! It warn't me!"

The pursuer fell over, and Halbert took strength from the lengthening distance, and ceased to cry out. He dodged through the undergrowth and around tree boles until he saw a tall chestnut tree, easy to climb. He swarmed up and hid in the branching fork, which was low. He did not see a large black bird slip away from a smaller fork above him. Like a cat Halbert climbed until he was thirty feet from the ground and hidden in a kind of socket out of which spread several branches. While crouching thus his furtive eyes saw a nest of sticks by his left shoulder. Rising a little he peeped in. It had a deep hollow in the middle lined with grasses, pieces of string and torn paper. There were five greenish eggs nestling in the hollow, and even as he watched Halbert saw that one was chipped, and that something was sticking out. It was the beak of a young carrion crow. Halbert said, to the egg:

"Strike me pink if it ain't a blasted chicken, atching isself." He forgot about his danger. The beak of the bird was tapping away at the shell making the hole larger. High overhead the mother commenced to call with repeated anguish. The hatching crow soon became exhausted, and rested.

"So it's you, is it?" said the voice of the young toff in whose car Halbert had ridden.

Halbert began to whine at once.

"It warn't me, guv'nor, strite it warn't. Search me and see!" Halbert dramatically held open the flaps of his ragged coat. "I didn't take nuffing, sir."

There was a sound of barking in the distance, the whistle of an engine, and the clatter of a train on the permanent way, echoing among the trees.

"I saw you, my dear chap," said the young man pleasantly.

"No, sir, yer saw someone else. I was fishing, sir. I wouldn't inkernvenience any gent's game, guvnor, swelp me bob, I wouldn't!"

"Come down from that tree, there's a good fellow. You might fall, you know."

"Not me, guv'nor."

"Then I'll fetch you down."

"I'll spit on yer, if yer do!" cried a terrified Halbert. "I'll chuck a branch on yer nob! I'll rotten-egg yer! Naw than, don't yer try, guv'nor! I'll chuck meself to me death, strite I will!"

"Well, I suppose it isn't your fault that you're a thief," the young man said half to himself.

"No, sir, that's right, sir. Mind yer, I *have* pinched, but never from a pal. And you're a sort of pal, ain't yer, kind of like a pal, since this morning?"

No attempt was made to climb after him. The young man sauntered away, Halbert remained in the tree. He suspected a trap. His terror returned when he saw a brown dog and another man with the toff.

"Oh, gord! a blood-ound," he whispered as the spaniel looked up and growled.

"Yes, sir," the other man, fat and in shirt sleeves was saying, "they escaped just in front o' the train. They can thank their lucky stars they wasn't runned over like a mongrel dog they ad with them."

"My, is poor old Minnie dead, guv'nor?" asked Halbert. "My gord! and him the finest cat fighter sarth of the river."

"Shut up!" called the fat man.

"Keep yer hair on, Arbuckle!" jeered Halbert.

They could not get him down from the tree until the lady came with the information that the clubs had been found in a ditch, and that someone had said that the thief had a cropped black head, whereas Halbert's hair was the colour of carrots and very, very shaggy.

"Of course it wasn't that child, John," she said, and Halbert began to descend. When he got to the ground he was, to his satisfaction, sniffing and crying.

"I've got a weak art," he grizzled, "and I've lost me dinner onion aht of me pocket. But I'll come quiet to the flycops."

The blue-eyed fair-haired girl was so distressed by the misjudgment of the slum-waif and the weepy announcement of the loss of the dinner onion, that she invited Halbert to call upon her at an address in London, giving him a card, which he put in his pocket.

She had been married only a few months, and her young woman-hood, blossoming naturally in love, made her tender to all weak and small things. In giving her card to the little boy, she desired desperately to do something to help him, and already had a wild desire to find employment for him in her household.

Halbert forgot about the card almost immediately because she also invited him to share her own luncheon. Halbert became chirpy and dried his tears. They gave him some sandwiches from a basket under a shady oak, resting on a cool lawn by the lake side, the like of which Halbert had only dreamed about. He was gaily telling lies about his life to them when he remembered the card, and taking it from his pocket, glanced at it. Immediately his high spirits went, and he became furtive and subdued. He dared not speak any more, and feeling awkward in the presence of white napkins, he went away into the wood and ate his sandwiches slowly, to make them last. Several times he muttered to himself, "My Gord, Halbert, you was dining wiv Royalty!" Afterwards he lit the fag end of a cigarette and went back to the chestnut tree, climbing up and taking the five eggs. One bird was nearly hatched, and he pulled off the shell till it lay damp and limp in his hand.

The idea of having it as a pet overjoyed him, but when it raised a weak neck and opened its mouth for food, he realized that it was too young, and that it would die. So when later in the afternoon he found a thrush's nest with two nestlings, he put the 'blasted chicken' in with them, marking the spot so that he might be able to find it the following Sunday. Halbert did not see on the ground below the nest two broken eggs and a dead nestling, nor did he know that one of the living nestlings was a baby cuckoo, and that it had heaved out all except its companion. Thus in one nest were a baby thrush, a baby cuckoo, and a baby carrion crow—all blind and crying for food.

But Halbert did not return for a month, owing to various circum-stances, which included his father's being 'in trouble' for that period. And when the father came out of prison he celebrated his return by getting drunk and bashing everybody he met in No. 17 Arcady Street, including two policemen who came in hasty response to female screams, so back he went again to Wormwood Scrubs, where he remained during the strange sojourn of Znarr, the carrion crow, at No. 17 Arcady Street.

5

Znarr, as has been recorded, began his eggy existence in the nest of his mother, a carrion crow, but being abstracted by a small boy continued his life in the nest of a song thrush. Naturally Znarr was very weak after the shell had been peeled off him, and he sank back between the other two nestlings. His sleep was interrupted by one of them endeavouring to heave him out of the nest. The creature that did this had a slight hollow in its naked back, useful to hold eggs in, and a sensitive skin covering the hollow that it could not bear to be touched. On previous occasions eggs and nestlings had touched it, and now they were either broken or dead on the ground below. For the creature was a young cuckoo, and it was endeavouring to get rid of Znarr.

The efforts to shift Znarr soon exhausted the blind infanticide. All that morning it had tried, without success, to shift the other thrush. It managed to get Znarr upon his back, but once Znarr was there he remained, thus getting a warm seat and all the food brought by the pair of thrushes. Periodically he heard a sound, shot up his black beak, opened his enormous gape, and cried aloud his name: "Znarr! Znarr! Znarr!" The result was the same every time he called his name. Something dropped into his mouth, something soft and luscious that was gulped down (often it bulged in his neck as it slid lower) followed by "Znarr! Znarr! Znarr!"

The cuckoo and the thrush beside him poked up necks and heads as well, but Znarr was stronger and bigger than them, so they had none, and the thrush quickly perished. Znarr trampled it under foot, and four days later the cuckoo died of starvation. Eventually the corpses of the baby cuckoo and thrush were pushed by Znarr's strong legs through the foundations of the nest, with its damp mud-and-grass bottom.

Thereafter Znarr found his perch insecure and awkward. Feathers, black feathers, sprouted on his wings and on his back, but his stomach was red and bare for a long time with the irritation of straddling across the broken nest. His beak was long and black, his cries raucous and unceasing as black bristles sprouted by his nostrils. All day and every day the pair of thrushes brought slugs and snails and worms and grubs for Znarr, but the more they brought the more Znarr wanted. Sometimes it happened that his craw was choked sufficiently to cause the raucous voice to be stilled, and then Znarr's head flopped down and he slept, with an uneasily proud mother thrush brooding over him. Her own rest was fitful, since the terrible baby sometimes stirred in his sleep, and his heavings tossed her sideways and anyhow. Nevertheless she was proud, and did not mind a head bald of feathers, since Znarr scraped them off it in his eagerness to swallow.

To her tunnelled chamber in a sand pit the kingfisher took silver dace and roach for her children, passing every time within a few feet of Znarr. Flies came and settled on him, he learned to snap them in his beak. Once a mouse, fancying an egg to suck, climbed to the nest, and before her astonishment ended Znarr had swallowed her. He was very big and heavy when at midsummer the nightingale was silent, and the bluebells had seed-pods. And on the first day in July, having broken the nest completely, he took to the ground and followed the foster-mother, who was feeding a lob-worm to her terrible charge when Znarr, in his hunger, got her head stuck in his throat.

The thrush lay still when at last they were separated; and Znarr began to strike the body with his beak. When he tasted blood he finished off the wretched thrush; and was half-asleep upon the ground under a bush when Halbert saw him there; and shrilling a cry of triumph, caught Znarr and held his flapping wings while the black beak struck at his hands.

Znarr on the homeward journey became dejected and sick. Everywhere were grinding roars and terrible eyes. His captor tied his wings with a handkerchief, and wrapped him up in a newspaper. The tram-car was filled with poor people going back to their homes in the south-eastern districts of London. These people had drooping wild flowers stuck in their buttonholes and blouses, and the children chattered eagerly about the wonderful times they had had.

"I found a bird's nest full of feavvers!"

"Garn, that's nuffing! I found a pond full of fishes and frogs, and a fat old man chased us, didn't e, young Bertie?"

"Yuss, and we id in a ollow tree, where there was undreds of spiders, and we weren't ketched neither, was we?"

"My farver's boozed, so mum's come away wivout im. Silly fool to get boozed, when e can roll on the grass and ketch frogs, ain't e?"

6

Albert the liveried pantry boy had become Halbert the urchin for the Sunday, since he had been given a day off by Mr. Simpson, the old butler who ruled Albert with severity. Albert had left the servants' entrance in Upper Brook Street in a bowler hat and dark suit; he had gone to his home at No. 17 Acrcady Street, arriving there breathless owing to a chase by a howling band led by that ragged hooligan Winking Wooldridge; he had changed into his country clothes, otherwise his newsboy shirt, trousers and coat, taken grub in pocket, and gone to the woods joyfully with barefoot steps.

The arrival at the Elephant and Castle made Znarr nearly sick with fear. His beak and head stuck through the newspaper. The crowds waiting for tram-cars, the grind and throb of motor-buses made Znarr quiet with fear. And only when he was inside No. 17 Arcady Street did his aggressive spirit return.

'Whatever 'ave yer got, young Halbert?" inquired Meg, the cripple sister, who was nursing the pale baby by an open window that gave a view of the brick wall of another house, and a row of chimney-pots.

'A Hafrican parrit, brought back by Sir John from Injer when 'e was capting of a battleship at Pompey. Only it kicked up such a terrible rarr, wot wiv wisslin', scritchin', and swearin' somethin' crool, just like they doos in the navy, that I was arst by 'er Laidyship ter find a nice 'ome for it. So I brought it 'ome for ter sing yer ter sleep, wot oh!"

"Well, she might 'ave given you its cage." said his mother.

Znarr gave out a harsh cry, and emerged from the newspaper, hopping and flapping to the table.

"Why, it's a common crow, Halbert, you little liar! My, ain't it fierce. It won't pick out baby's eyes, will it? Oo, go away!" she shouted at Znarr.

Thus, inauspiciously, began Znarr's town life. Albert went back to Upper Brook Street, leaving him in his sister's care. Znarr sulked, and slept that night in a box. In the morning he pecked and thumped with his beak. He escaped, and skulked in the corners of the room and under the bed. At first Meg's mother, who had been born in Kent, said that she would not have the dirty thing in her house, but when after two days of starvation Znarr took food from her and hopped after her, she came to like it. "Reminds me of my

childhood," she told Meg, "afore I came to this 'ere pauper's life. Many a time I've eaten young crows in a pie after the farmers had shot them, with a carrot or two and a bit o' bacon. Now that there crow's lucky, I do believe. Have you noticed how baby's sleepin' better after 'er bottle instead of 'ollering? My, ain't the sky a lovely blue, Meg? Young Halbert's struck it lucky riding with the gentry in a swell car all day in the country!"

It hardly need be said that Halbert was not accurate to his mother in his accounts of the duties he had to perform. But she believed him to be a wonder ever since he had won a prize at school for the spelling-bee at the age of nine.

7

Znarr soon learned to fly. He ventured outside on the landing, and waged continual war with various lean cats. He killed and ate sparrows. He flew to window ledges and peered into rooms, often stealing. Yet every one in the neighbourhood liked him. Meg became very proud, owing to the fame that came to her as the owner of Znarr. He haunted the chimney-pots, calling: "Znarr! Znarr! Znarr!" He was well fed, and in August he was observed to perch on a lamp-post near the Elephant and Castle. Winking Wooldridge saw him, and flung a potato that made Znarr jump with alarm; thereafter he became suspiciously shy of small boys. Day after day he left the window on the fourth floor of No. 17, and commenced his usual wandering, returning at night.

There was one cat that Znarr hated more than the others. It was a dingy yellow, and usually sat above a dustbin in Angel Alley. Znarr called whenever he saw it, and one day, flying over the garden, he saw a movement inside the tiles of a broken shed. He alighted near and peered through the opening. Something twisted, mewing as it did so. He merely thought that it would be good fun to peck it, and so the kitten was abstracted. He carried it in his beak to the window-sill, and two taps of his beak killed it. He skinned it and swallowed it, returning for another.

The cat's name was Alice, and her nominal owner was the mother of Winking Wooldridge, who took in shopkeepers' and publicans' washing. That night she told her son that the crow had killed two of her kittens, and pecked the ear of Alice. Winking Wooldridge said that Znarr should pay for it, and threw a stone that went through the window and missed the head of the baby by three inches. Halbert was told of it when he returned on the following Sunday, and swore vengeance on Winking Wooldridge. He encountered him the same afternoon, when he had Znarr with him, in an adjoining area called Angel Court. He ran away, pursued by Winking Wooldridge, who caught him quickly. Halbert was wearing his natty little bowler hat, given him by the butler, and this the elder boy stamped upon, swearing as he did so and saying that he would learn Halbert to be a toff. Then he held the head of Halbert under his left arm and pounded the face with his right fist. The blood poured from Halbert's nose, and he bellowed, attracting a crowd of gossiping mothers and pale children. Winking Wooldridge did not cease to pummel Halbert for over a minute. Then he dropped him suddenly and seized Znarr who was quietly perched on a wall.

Winking Wooldridge did not realize that a carrion crow was a dangerous bird to tackle. He meant to wring its neck with his hands, but Znarr avoided the clutch with a quick hop; Halbert rushed with a cry upon his adversary. Winking Wooldridge gave him a swinging blow with his foot in the stomach, and Halbert fell. Turning from Halbert he made another grab at Znarr and succeeded in grasping his claw. Znarr cawed harshly, and beat his wings in the face of Winking Wooldridge, who drew the crow towards him, and was intending to twist the head off, when Znarr made a swift movement with his beak. The muscles of a powerful neck gave that beak a considerable piercing power, and the first fighting instinct of a crow is to blind its enemy.

Thus was the strange scrap in Angel Court abruptly concluded. Winking Wooldridge gave a frightful scream, clasped his eyes, and lay down beside Halbert, who was choking for want of breath, and on the verge of sickness. Men and women and silent children formed a circle around.

8

There had been many fights before in Angel Court, but none of them had resembled this one. Some had been high comedy, even farce, as when a drunken Italian attempting to slash with a razor his companion, also drunk, had succeeded only in cutting his braces, so that his trousers fell down and he fell over with his companion, and had fallen asleep. There had been several stabbing affrays, and at least one dustbin murder within the memory of Halbert. Eyes had been smashed by drink-inflamed bullies, but never before had the sight of an eye been destroyed by a bird. That night it was discussed in all the Elephant and Castle pubs, and the tale became so distorted as it passed over the tongues of children that Znarr was said to have flown from the sky and gobbled up two fox terriers.

Winking Wooldridge went away to hospital, and Znarr became outlawed. Mothers in the district ceased to threaten naughty children by reference to bogeys and dustmen, and adopted instead a ghastly reference to the baby-snatching bird. The police were rumoured (among the smaller boys) to be armed with revolvers, and one bold urchin declared that Government traps had been secretly set at night on all the chimney-pots. Halbert for a long time was fearful lest he be sent to the dreaded Industrial School for bringing a wild bird to London.

Znarr was never caught. He enjoyed his outlawry, and wandered far among the forests of the chimney-pots. For a time he was observed to be in the district of Bermondsey, walking the tannery yards in that place of little old houses and ancient red tiles. He wandered Citywards, and for over two hours one afternoon was to be seen perched upon the brazen flame-tongues that crown the top of the Fire of London Monument, near London Bridge. Early in the morning he found much food in the neighbouring fish market; Covent Garden he knew well. He became one of London's winged scavengers, and used to roost with pigeons in the branches of a plane tree in the Temple Gardens, near King's Bench Walk. The throb and hum of Fleet Street at night eventually drove him away, and after stealing a bun he saw through the open window of Tiger's Apex House by Charing Cross, and thus robbing a lady typist of her tea, he wandered back to Arcady Street by way of Highgate, Muswell Hill, the Edgware Road, and the Tower Bridge.

He was seen by Halbert as that young man returned gleefully to the street for which he had been pining. Halbert's probationary term was ended, and with it his position as pantry boy at No. 9d Upper Brook Street. The butler gravely reported to his mistress that he was incorrigible; Halbert left, and was glad to leave. When the novelty of strange food had gone he had been dissatisfied, and longed to return to his pitch at the Elephant and Castle, to his free life of selling newspapers. So he went back, with a pound note in the pocket of his neat suit, and a parcel of food under his arm, "for mum, Meg, the chicken, and the baiby." He saw Znarr flying lazily above No. 17 Arcady Street, cawing; he watched him circle higher and higher, till he became like a flake of soot in the smoky sky. Znarr then disappeared, flying in a southerly direction. Perhaps the call of the woods, now that the leaves were beginning to fall and the wandering spirit was possessing bird and beast, had come to him, even as it had come to the slum-child Halbert. Znarr faded away in the sky, leaving Halbert standing at the street corner with his parcel.

So after an adventurous time Halbert returned to his pitch at the Elephant and Castle; never again did he see his benefactors. If he saw Znarr during his rambles in the bluebell woods he did not recognize him. Thus do earthly friendships slip away with the months and the years. But one friend Halbert made, and that was Winking Wooldridge, who recovered quickly, although he lost for ever the sight of one eye, and with it the odious nickname of Winking. He is now considered a light-weight of promise, and the fight fans that hang about the Blackfriars Ring expect great things of him when he is older. They call him Lord Nelson; but to his mate Halbert he is Oratio.

Mewliboy

Sipsitew the willow wren was there when Mewliboy was born. Sipsitew heard wailing cries in the wind and rain, and was terrified. She was crouching over her babies, who were as small as daisy buds, in the nest on the bank which had a grass roof and a feather floor. Blackthorns and brambles grew on the top of the bank, with young plants of cowflop and hemlock and ground-ivy, and the nest was hidden among them.

When the cries ceased she spoke to her mate perched on a crooked thorn above her in the under-voice that song birds use in the night after alarm, or when waking in the dawn.

The cries came from near the thistle that was rising from the field in a spiny green star, and were followed by the clank of iron on stone and the beating of wings, growing feeble and more feeble until the cries were choked in a sigh, which the wind bore away with other sighs of the night. Every passing of the wind set two old branches in the thorny maze talking in their dry squeaking voices. They were like two old women in a dark little house; they were always together, and whenever they were troubled, they talked. Squeak, squeak, squeak, while the rain from the Atlantic fell in the valley, and the wind shrilled in the thorn brake, and cried *Who? Who?* in the cracks of a pollard willow where Ie, the treecreeper, had a nest of twigs and fibres and feathers. The willow wands growing out of the top with ferns were thrown about; the gate in the corner of the field was shaken. In a lull the creak of pines and the leaf-murmur of oaks growing on the opposite hillside came with the rush of the stream below the wood. Sipsitew slept again, with drops of rain on her back unfelt, for she was warmed by the air-layer between feathers and skin.

The next noise to wake her was a sharp snapping *clenk* coming

before the puny screaming which choked itself silent in the throat of that which had screamed. Immediately from the earth under her came the sound of feet thumped in alarmed impotence. She was accustomed to these small cries, and slept again.

An hour before dawn the valley was quieter, a dwindling wind followed the grey clouds, and the stars shone above the cornfield. There were other noises which the willow wren heard: rats running in the wheat, sniffing and searching for food; the movements of worms —those soil-makers moving in their galleries and pushing out their heads to seize and draw underground rotting leaf and sapless stalk; and once Swagdagger the stoat sneezing. White owls winnowed down the hedge, sinking to catch mice, and the brown owl hooted as he flew from tree to tree in the fir-plantation. Higher up the hedge an old grey boar-badger with black bearlike claws was pulling out a nest of rabbits from a hole in the ground. Old Nog the heron flying to his next fishing post by the stream cried *Krark!* harshly.

Again the wailing cry and the flapping of wings. Across the valley a scream seemed to answer, and to bound back again to a point fifty yards away from the place of flapping and the clanking of iron, thence to rebound all the way up the bank of earth and stone and to jump into the distance. At many points on the starlit darkness of earth were awakenings from the stupor of pain which had thickened mental faculties, and struggles were renewed, while leg-bones grated at fractures. One by one the cries were choked by the grassy froth in throat and windpipe.

2

The darkness lagged, the old cries became feeble, they ceased entirely, but new ones arose, and when dawn came in the east many rabbits were in the gins set by man. There was also a hedgehog, and two rats; and by the thistle, held by its yellow legs which the iron teeth of the trap had broken just below the knees, was a dark-brown bird. Her wings spanned four feet. She was Wheeoo the buzzard hawk of Spreycombe Wood. She sprawled in the corn beside the ungrown spear-thistle, the twelve feathers of her tail spread like a fan. They were dead-leaf colour, barred with lighter shades, and dull white at the tips. There were yellow rings round the pupils of her eyes, and yellow skin above her eyelids and at the base of her hooded beak, which was open. Wheeoo heaved in thick breathing, and had partially disgorged her crop. Since the evening of the day before she had been in the rabbit gin. She lay still as a golden breath came in the sky beyond the eastern end of the wooded valley.

Softly the wind lifted a short feather on her back, the same wind that carried a honey-fly to its joyful laze on the dandelion growing on the pollard willow. It stirred the greyish fur of a doe rabbit with twisted and torn hindleg, crouching in a muddy patch worn by the dance of three legs in the night so dark and terrible. It trembled the five-coloured tapered badger hair fixed in the mud by the print of the bean-shaped pad, or ball, of its foot—the badger who had dug out and eaten the third litter of the doe.

Warmed by the beams of the sun the air fled upwards to buoy the breast of a lark singing in the sky. A quarter of a mile away a bird was soaring above the valley. *Wheeoo* he cried, and again *Wheeoo*. His mate had not been near the eyrie in the pinetree when he had flown there before sunrise, and he was lonely. He passed over the field of growing corn where the rabbits were bunched in the gins. He saw a movement. With wings upheld above him, with clawed feet hanging and head bent to gaze below, he drifted in a slow slant down the sky. At four hundred feet he hung in the wind, with wings arched and bent backwards. His eyes stared at the thing in the corn. *Whee-oo, Whee-oo, Whee-oo* he cried, each cry ending in a wistful downstroke of sound.

He dropped to twenty feet, flapping heavily. Three birds were perched near his mate, a pair of jackdaws and a magpie. They flew some yards away, and sat uneasily on the thorn bushes, where a chaffinch, three titmice, and a wren were scolding her. The buzzard flew round her, afraid to alight on the ground.

For many minutes he swept and circled above his mate, beating his wings like an owl, uneasily and clumsily. The three magpies often chattered, and the daws called, *jank, jank*. A bird with a white patch on its rump heard the noises in the near fir-plantation, and with loping flight came over to see what the cries meant. Seeing the buzzard, he raised his crest and made a noise like the tearing of linen. This noise brought three other jays, which screamed continually at the trapped hawk. One of the pies saw a rabbit in a gin, and fluttered to it, but did not touch it, though its eyes were so large and round in its head. The pie had the cunning of her tribe, and dared not go near the gin.

Krok-krok-rr sounded in the sky, and the jays, the daws, and the pies—all the crow family—looked up. Scarl the Baseborn, the carrion crow, sidled and scrambled down to join them. He was an old and persistent enemy of the buzzards of Spreycombe Wood. He gloated in the sight of the fallen hawk, who made no sign that she had heard the cry of mate or enemy.

Scarl flopped from the bank and hopped to her. The buzzard cried as he rushed at him. Scarl got out of his way, cawing harshly. They fought in the air, hawk trying to grasp with yellow feet, crow endeavouring to remain above and to peck with his beak. While they were fighting, the daws and the pies walked nearer to the luscious thing they had seen in the corn by the hen buzzard's tail.

3

But, solemn and slow in the height of the sky, came a deep-throated *Krr-r-r-r-ronk*. The fighting birds fell apart. Lazily the croaker floated above the field, and in his own unhurried time, came down, rolling and tumbling sideways on big black wings. The buzzard went up to meet him, but the newcomer merely moved to one side and continued his rolling fall. When the hawk spread his taloned feet and rushed down, the stranger turned over and looked at him. He glanced up his beak, which was black, very thick at the base, and which ended in a point that had split many skulls of animals. For he was Kronk the raven, the King of the Crows, and therefore of all birds, and so old that he had pecked out the eyes of things that once had been called blackguards by rich men, because they had stolen sheep for their starving children. Kronk's beak-glance was enough; the buzzard rolled out of his way.

Kronk landed and perched on his right leg. Between the second and third toe of his left leg was a scaly piece of skin, which during his flight from the headland had been irritating him. Many times he had tried to pull it off with his beak, thrusting his head between his shanks to do so, and tumbling in the air. Now that he was on land he remembered it, and stretching out his left leg he snipped it off, and afterwards he cleaned his claws. His attitude was one of brazen indifference to the buzzard flapping and mewing round his head, to the inquisitive hoppings of daw and jay, the tail-dipping magpie, and the ragamuffin crow on the thorn. He eyed each toe, turning his foot first one way, then another. Satisfied, he lowered his leg, shook himself, but stopped the feather-shake to look pointedly at the buz-

zard. The look was accompanied by a stab of his beak at the hawk,
for the miserable bird had swooped down to attack him with his
claws. Again the buzzard checked in time.

Kronk shook his malodorous feathers, with a sudden bounding
hop he arrived behind the spread-winged hen buzzard, desiring to
take that which had been coveted by the others. Thereupon Wheeoo
rose up in a fury of flapping and reared backwards, dragging the gin
and chain, which held her by the silver-purple sinews. She tried to
strike the face of Kronk with her feet, but her legs were held by
three and a half pounds of steel and iron pegged to the ground.
Kronk opened his beak to seize what had attracted him from the air
—but the magpie chattered a new cry. At once Kronk turned. Scarl
the crow slipped thief-like off the thorn, and vanished below the
bank. Daw and jay and pie flew up and away. The buzzard beat
heavily into the air. Kronk muttered in his throat a noise like
blar-r-st, and hopped down the slope of the field to get the wind
under his wings.

He had seen an enemy.

4

A man was coming down beside the bank, walking with a slight roll.
He was the trapper, a pensioned A.B. from the Royal Navy who
purchased the trapping rights of the farm by giving free to the farmer
his services as a labourer for six weeks every year. He carried a sack,
in which were gins, a hammer, and dead rabbits taken that morning.
A sieve was tied to the leather belt he wore round his middle. He
was turning a quid of tobacco in his cheek, for he was unmarried.

Coming to a sprung gin, he threw off the sack from his shoulder.
He squirted brown saliva from his pursed lips, and seized the head
of the animal in his left hand. With the sole of his right foot he
pressed the steel spring, so that the jaws fell open. He lifted the
rabbit free, and when the pressure of his foot was removed, the teeth
of the gin snapped up again. The rabbit kicked and shuddered, but
clasping hindfeet in one hand and head in the other, the trapper
wristed, or broke with a twisting pull, the animal's neck. One more
article of food for the market where women went to buy food. He
tilled the gin before another hole, hammering the iron peg into the
ground, and setting the jaws by contracting the spring with the
powerful thumb and fingers of his right hand, and fitting the tag of

the tongue into the notch of the catch with his left. Carefully he laid it on the earth outside the bury, and shovelling earth into the sieve, scattered it over the gin, which was soon hidden under the damp dark soil, ready for the step of another rabbit.

He passed down the bank, coming over a slight rise, and immediately saw a raven and other birds fly up from the corner of the field. He swore, because usually the presence of any of the Crow family meant a mangled rabbit, with battered head and broken entrails. He did not see the crow, as Scarl the Baseborn was too cunning to allow himself to be seen, because he did not want to be detected as the bird who had picked out the eyes of more than two score and ten rabbits.

When the trapper came to the gin he had tilled in the open (which was an unlawful act, but he had set four traps there to catch a rabbit-stealing badger whose regular nightly path had lain that way) he was surprised to see a buzzard caught by both legs. There was an egg beside her in the corn, and he knew thereby that it was a hen bird, whose nest in the wood he had been observing with an idea of taking a young bird for a pet. He stared at it for some time, wondering what to do, whether to hit the bird on the head with a stick, or to take it and tame it. He decided to tame it. When he went near the bird, she rose up and tried to strike his tattooed hand.

"Steady on, old gel," he said, "or I shall have to dot you one. No, I don't want yer egg, I've had me breakfast."

The bird made it impossible for him to release her with his hands, so he emptied the sack and threw it over her, first removing the egg. He squeezed the spring, taking the yellow legs out of the open teeth. She flapped so violently that she escaped, leaving the sack in his other hand.

"Sink me sideways!" he exclaimed, gazing at her as she flew away in unsteady flight, her legs hanging loosely. He rolled the quid twice with his tongue, and screwing up his lips, spat violently out of the corner of his mouth.

5

Wheeoo flew wildly across the valley, followed by Scarl the Baseborn and the egg-sucking female who skulked through life in his company. This pair of carrion crows pestered every hawk they saw (except

Chakchek the Backbreaker) because they had a nest of young crows half a mile away in a holly tree, and because they were impudent, quarrelsome, and faithful by nature. Wheeoo did not try to avoid them as usual, but flew into the wood, where they left her to look for pigeon-squabs, or nestlings, in the larches. She struck many branches with her wings, often tumbling near the ground. She passed a pine where her nest was, but flew out of the other side of the wood, and over the top of the hill. Her mate saw her from where he was soaring, and called to her, and after flying together for several minutes he persuaded her to return to the eyrie.

The eyrie had been used by buzzards for more than twelve years. It was a dark pile of sticks and rootlets four feet high, and about five feet wide, flat on the top. The base was covered with green moss, and the centre of it was damp and rotten. Below the pile, hidden by cowflops (which some call fox-gloves) was an ancient barrow, or grave, where the bones of thousands of rats and moles and rabbits were crumbling. There were grass-snake skins as well, the hollow teeth of vipers, and the skulls of kittens.

Three weeks before, Wheeoo had jumped on the pile with a cow-flop in her beak, the buds of whose flowers were not then turned pink. She had brought during the days that followed several larch twigs, some sheeps-wool, and a piece of paper. Thus was Buzzard Castle set in order and repair for the season's residence. The first egg was heavily blotched with brown, the markings of the second were lighter, and the last egg of her clutch, which was laid on a thistle in the cornfield, was marked hardly at all on its rough grey-white surface.

Now she fell on her nest with spread wings when she tried to alight on the branch above it, and lay on her breastbone. She did not understand why she was unable to perch. For a while she lay and panted while her mate watched her from above.

A moment later he saw her settle to brood on the two eggs, and she remained in the nest until past noon, when she roused herself off the nest with the elbows of her wings, and dived into the air below. The eyrie was built on a flat bough and against two vertical branches so firmly that not even the most violent winter gales had shifted it. It was thirty feet from the steep slope immediately below, and after falling thirteen feet the weight of her body was less than the resistance on her wings, and she glided. Then out of the trees she soared unsteadily in the valley breezes, and began to rise to her mate. She was hungry, and in flat spirals they soared away from the valley, coming to the heather hill where rabbits and pipits had their homes.

They hovered a hundred yards apart, hanging head to wind, with wings bent back. At once Wheeoo observed a movement, and slid lower to scrutinise it. A baby rabbit was nibbling the grass. She dropped to it, and clutched. It ran away, and flying after it, she clutched again. Her feet, clenched in a stiffening bunch, did not obey her brain, and so her prey escaped. The reason was beyond her intelligence.

When her mate caught a rat she flew to where he was standing with it on a lichened stone, and cried for food, as she had cried when a nestling. With one stroke of his hooked beak he ripped it open from head to tail, and pulled it to pieces, swallowing the head and larger portions himself, and appeasing her screams with smaller bits and entrails. He also gave her the tail, which she refused, but she ate the feet gladly.

6

Wheeoo did not languish and die in the days that followed, as she might have done in a different season, because the desire to brood was more intense than personal anguish. Fifteen and a half of the seventeen hours of daylight were spent on the eggs. She became skilful in alighting on the edge of the eyrie, standing upright on the stumps (which gave her pain) and falling on the tips of her wings, which she drew in to elbow herself forward. Her mate fed her, bringing his prey to the pine tree and tearing it up for her. Mice and small birds she swallowed whole. He also brought her beetles and wood lice, snakes and moles. Once he saw an adder basking on a hot stone, and grasped it by the head. It lashed with its tail so violently that he flew high into the sky, where Scarl the Baseborn saw and pursued him. The viper swung him out of his steadiness, for it was more than two feet long. *Wheeoo* wailed the hawk. *Krok-k-kr* chuckled the carrion crow, pestering at his tail and trying to pull out his feathers. The hawk suddenly dropped the snake when Scarl was below him, so that it fell across his wings and made him squawk with fear. It did not bite him but such was Scarl's nature that he dived away, and in silence flew back to his holly tree.

The mate of Wheeoo did not heed the viper, which whizzed into the yellow blooms of a gorse bush and died in the sun it loved. He soared till he was hardly to be seen by the trapper watching him from the window of a cottage in the clearing of a larch plantation over the heather hill. But the bird could see the Wyandottes on the edge of the clearing scratching the earth; he saw even the head movement of a crowing cock. He wheeled above before drifting away to the down by the sea, descending to perch on a wall. The wall was made of shillets of rock and earth, and stonecrop grew with cowflops on the side away from the sea wind. Only green and black and orange lichens, that thrive where others perish, grew on the western side.

The wall, which was crumbling, had been built by a farmer to keep away brake ferns, brambles, and heather from spreading to the field. Oats were sown there, but they were choked with spurrey and nettle, ragwort, tansy, and dock. Many rabbits, dwellers in the wall, nibbled the corn. They did so much damage that gins were tilled throughout the year, for every young doe on an average had thirty offspring a year. All the does were young, for none lived to be old. And when the buzzard sailed back to Spreycombe Wood ten minutes later, there was one less to spoil the food of man. The hawk had waited until it came out of its hole, and gripped it in its talons. That night Swagdagger the stoat found six baby rabbits growing cold in a grassy nest in the wall, and slew them with six bites.

7

Some time later, when the second egg was hatched in Buzzard Castle, Wheeoo glided down to the clearing to catch a chicken. She still tried to hunt. The dried bundles of her feet clicked together as she flew. Every hen cried out to her chicks that an enemy was coming, and scores of little chickens ran to cover, and crouched still. Rosecomb, a broody Wyandotte, puffed out her feathers, and almost filled the barren entrance to the coop in her terror of clucking. She was the more alarmed because one of her thirteen eggs was well on the way to hatching. She had been listening to its cheeping all that morning and afternoon. It was an egg larger and more rotund than any of the other dozen eggs of her sitting. Within was the cheeper, very tired after chipping a ring round the large end of the shell with the horn on his upper mandible.

It is not known how or why the cheeper came to be in that shell; even the sun does not know. All that is known is that his mother laid the makings of him in the corn, covered by a shell: that two dark specks came in the albumen, and to the specks came red lines, which were linked blood-vessels breathing air that came through the pores of the shell, and that these joining up with others had slowly threaded their way beside wings and lungs and heart and neck, making the shape and form of a reptile, which had been the shape of the cheeper's ancestors ages and ages ago, before feathers were known. After three weeks the hens' eggs hatched, so the trapper put the egg, with the cheeper still growing, under a hen with a later sitting, and she was called Rose-comb.

The reptile shape changed into a bird, with legs trussed up over its shoulders, and the two dark specks grew larger, for they were the eyes of the cheeper. In the weeks of incubation he passed from development to development, and changes within the round egg happened in a day that had happened to his ancestors only after a thousand generations on the round earth. He burst into the airspace of his cell, and mewed—tens of thousands of years in swamp and jungle had passed away before a voice had come into his family. From a glairy liquid and a yolk bag the cheeper had appeared, and this was rather clever of the Quill Spirit, aided by the Star-dwarf whom some called the Sun.

The cheeper's adventures started early. When he had cracked his shell, he drew his first real breath, which made him so tired that he went to sleep, digesting the last of the yolk in the bag, which in future was to serve him as a belly. He was soon strengthened, and with a last heave and wriggle broke the shell. The top he pushed away from his pate, and the other he sat in, and went to sleep again, his head lolling over the rim.

It was not very long before he woke and pushed up, opening his beak. This exhausted him so much that he sank into the shell and rested. After a little slumber he awoke and waggled an open beak more persistently, touching the white under-feathers of his foster-mother. While he mewed, Rose-comb sat unmoving. The cheeper collapsed for another sleep.

When he awoke from his nap he demanded food once again. Rose-comb sat still, but his waggling head tickled her so persistently that she rose off the eggs and examined some broken meal for him to eat. She picked up pieces in her beak and dropped them again, which was to tell him to eat. The cheeper continued to wag his head and to mew, but became so tired that he suddenly sagged, and slept.

He was next awakened by the angry Rose-comb, who was pecking a tattooed hand thrust under the lifted door of the coop.

"Nah then, less of it, old gal," the trapper said, good-naturedly. "It ain't one of your Wyndicotts, and a hawk can't feed itself even if you was to cluck your head off with instrooctions."

The cheeper was almost naked, his eyelids were gummed together, and his belly was a lovely yellow like a waistcoat that had slipped down. The trapper took him indoors and fed him on tiny pieces of rabbit flesh. He put him in a woollen glove, but the baby got slowly colder. The glove was laid on the settle by the fire, while he brewed a pot of tea and boiled an egg for himself. Afterwards he tried to feed the cheeper, but the baby would not lift up its head.

"Sink me sideways if you ain't goin' west," he muttered, and a few minutes later set out to walk over the hill. He crossed the valley and the stream, and trudged to the eyrie in the pine-tree, which he knew was not forsaken because he had watched the old birds soaring above it. Wheeoo slipped off the nest when he was underneath it, and he heard the clicking noise of her withered swinging feet.

"Nah then, Mewliboy," said the sailor, "I'm going to give yer back to yer Ma for a spell."

The tree was not easy to swarm, since the bark was smooth and the bole was two feet thick. He gathered a number of rotten branches and made a heap against the higher side, but it was no help. He spat resolutely and took off his coat; rolled his two shirtsleeves— thus removing the only clothing they possessed from the figures of two fat blue women holding the White Ensign above their heads— put Mewliboy under his hat, and began to swarm up with hands and knees.

While he was climbing, the cock buzzard and Wheeoo, whose weight was diminished by a third since her agony, glided and flapped in the windless valley, not daring to venture near. The old A.B. reached the fork twenty feet above the ground, where he rested.

From the fork a round reddish branch curved outwards and up-wards, and it was upon a lesser branch growing horizontally from this one that Buzzard Castle had been founded and raised. The trapper swarmed up, and straddled across the foundation branch, and squirted luxuriously on to the whitened cowflops below. He found the torn body of a rabbit in the vast nest, with many rats' tails, shards of beetles, and cast up pellets of indigestible bones and fur.

Sleeping on each other in the slight depression in the centre were two nestlings. He removed his hat and tumbled out a lukewarm Mewliboy, and to recognize him again, he nipped off the claw of the middle toe of his right foot. Afterwards he turned him over and tickled his yellow tummy, and then leaned far across and dropped him on the other two, who awoke and waved open beaks for food.

8

Wheeoo flew back a quarter of an hour after she had watched the trapper leave the wood. She had learnt to pick up beetles in her beak, hovering, when the wind was strong enough, to find them. The feathers of her breastbone were gone from the skin, which was sore and bare, as were the elbow joints of her wings from continual use in thrusting the body forward.

The white down on Mewliboy's body grew very fluffy, and at the end of a week many joints of rat and vole and rabbit had made him three times as heavy as he had been in the trapper's palm. He began to explore the eyrie, and to have fights with his two sisters for the prey which his father brought and tore up.

His father was worried because he could not secure enough food for mate and nestlings. Wheeoo brought the few beetles and lizards she caught to her young ones, but her instincts of feeding them before herself did not extend to the prey brought by her mate, and whenever he came to the eyrie when she was there, Wheeoo behaved like a fourth nestling, and, being the strongest, usually managed to get most of the mouthfuls. So he flew to Buckland Wood, some miles away, where lived Jale, the young hen buzzard without nest or mate, and brought her back to hunt for his children.

She came and stared at them, and then flapped away to soar above the heather hill. From the very moment of her arrival she adopted Wheeoo and the nestlings, bringing many snakes for them while the father passed most of the day soaring in the sky. She fed Wheeoo, who followed her wherever she went, mewing to her as though Jale were her mother.

When Mewliboy and his sisters were a fortnight old the eyrie was foul with rotting bones and rats' tails. At three weeks most of the feathers had come, and only a little down remained. They were more quarrelsome than ever, and the dozens of flies that buzzed about the eyrie helped to make them savage. Once when Scarl the Baseborn was bold enough to fly to the eyrie, Mewliboy struck at him with a foot and drove him away.

Sometimes Jale brought a spray of beechleaves in her mouth to decorate the nest, but the young ones snatched it from her and tugged away among themselves until they realized that leaves were not good to eat.

When Mewliboy was a month old there were not many places on the eyrie-branch that he and his sisters had not perched upon. Wheeoo could not perch, and so she had to remain in Buzzard Castle, amid the tormenting flies, until she could bear them no more, and sailed away in the valley, calling the children to follow her. They were afraid, and told her so with wailing voices. Jale also called them, and ceased to bring food to them.

One afternoon came when they had had no food since the previous evening, Mewliboy was so famished that he forgot his fear for a moment, and flapped off his perch. At once fear returned, and with a cry to Wheeoo—whom he loved more than Jale or his father— he fell. The dreaded ground rushed upon him, and he felt much the same as one of his ancestors had felt when first it had flown. He clutched an oak sapling, clinging with his feet upside down for many minutes, and when he let go he fell into the cowflops, safe but frightened. He slept there.

Another night he slept by himself fifty yards away from Buzzard Castle, on a low branch of a beech tree beside the stream, to which he had hopped and walked and flapped and scrambled. He awoke at dawn, and mewed for Wheeoo, but the jays discovered him and returned, hour after hour, to annoy him.

When he could bear the hunger and thirst no longer he launched himself off the branch. He was in an agony of fear, but he flew. The ground and trees passed below and beside him in a curious way. A feeling of the wildest joy pushed away the fear in his breast when he held his wings and glided. He turned, but lost flying speed and fell: quick beats of his wings brought him up again. He flew over the brook and fence of wire-netting, clogged with beech leaves, erected on the farther side to prevent rabbits from ruining the field.

There was a white house among the trees across the valley, and towards this he flew, why, he did not know. Every beat took him farther from Buzzard Castle, and although he was frightened, he flew on, not daring to do anything else. He opened his beak to mew to Wheeoo, but he had no voice.

Mewliboy flew on. He dared not turn or alight on the ground. He flew straight into the house, no more able to stop than the wall was able to move. And Mewliboy being the lesser in bulk, stopped. He fell stunned to a flower-bed below, to the amazement of a

gardener, who was carefully replanting for the fifth time a root of jasmine, dug up by Dabster the puppy hound, who, hidden behind a rhododendron bush, was watching for him to go away, so that he might dig it up again.

But when Mewliboy tumbled beside the gardener, Dabster was so alarmed that he ran away to the stable buildings, where he ate the food of the ducks who had waddled to cover when they saw Wheeoo soaring above, crying for Mewliboy.

9

The gardener was a friend of the trapper, who had told him about the bird he had found in the trap, and the hatching of the egg under Rose-comb, and how he had nipped off a claw in order to recognize the bird again when he should return to take it. Only that morning he had heard the cries of the young birds when he visited his gins, and had determined to climb the eyrie in the evening after work. When he came to the kitchen for his dinner at one o'clock (for in addition to his trapping he looked after the electric light plant in the engine-room beside the coach-house) he was met by the gardener who with many mysterious nods and winks took him to his potting shed and pointed silently to a box with a big log on top of it. On being invited to look underneath, the trapper saw the buzzard and throughout dinner (which he ate most skilfully off the end of his knife, without once cutting his mouth) the gardener gave him an infinite number of unvaried accounts of Mewliboy's arrival, and how he had kicked and bit and clutched and flapped, while one of the old birds called for him in the sky.

So Mewliboy was taken to the trapper's cottage again, and put in an open-air cage of wire-netting and boxes, against the eastern wall, with the branch of a tree inside to perch upon. For food he was given young rabbits which were too small for the market. At night the cage was covered with sacks.

Rose-comb, sedately clucking and scratching with ten white chicks, saw him one morning, and rushed away most hurriedly. Mewliboy, of course, did not recognize her, and she could not possibly have known that the terrible enemy hitting the wire-meshes with its wings was the thing to whose cheeping within the shell she had listened so gladly.

Mewliboy was given rats to eat, and in the manner of the buzzards he ripped them open with one stroke of his hooked beak. The tips of his flight feathers became broken by constant beating in so small a space. He tried to break the wire, to push his head through a mesh; hundreds of times every day he cried *Wheeoo, Wheeoo*. At the end of a week he was still trying to escape. In the valley the other buzzards were soaring every evening, often in tiers, the cock bird highest of all. Whenever Mewliboy heard them calling to one another, he would beat his wings to be free, and wail again, desperately, *Wheeoo, Whee-ee-i-oo*.

The trapper never forgot to feed him and Mewliboy lost his fear of the human. Week after week of lovely summer weather passed away, and still Spreycombe Wood was the home of Wheeoo and the others. Jale remained with them, and fed her, but neither the cock-bird nor her daughters would give her of their catch.

Indeed, the two young hen-buzzards had always been ferocious and savage to her, even in the nest, except when their crops were full. At least once a day Wheeoo came down the valley alone and called Mewliboy and always he answered. Once he was looking through the front of his cage at a covey of partridges flying downhill about a hundred yards away. He began to hop and cry in tremendous excitement, for looking upwards he had perceived a speck of a bird sweeping down faster than anything he had ever seen.

Distinctly he heard the hiss of wind in its closed wings, and it was slanting down at such a rate upon the partridges that they seemed not to be moving: and their speed was forty-eight miles an hour. *Wheeoo, Wheeoo*, cried Mewliboy, as Chakchek the Back-breaker (a remote cousin of his) swooped down in a steep curve like the blade of a reaping hook, which was also the shape of his talons.

Mewliboy heard the thud of the peregrine falcon striking a partridge, saw its head fall, watched The Backbreaker clutch its body and climb steeply with it·to fly to Bone ledge in the precipice where the land broke and the sea moved. Still watching with his head pressed against the meshes Mewliboy heard a deep *kronk, kronk, kronk* remote in the sky, for the raven was calling his wife, with whom he had come inland when he had observed Chakchek flying towards the mainland. For half a century Kronk and his wife had waited above the return raiding-route of the Chakcheks, patrolling at five thousand feet. Mewliboy saw them descending upon The Back-breaker from opposite directions; he saw Kronk diving at the falcon and watched the body of the partridge falling and the dive of the hen raven to take it in her beak. Then Kronk harried the falcon, offering him his beak to fall upon whenever the peregrine stooped, but The Backbreaker swerved and swooped upon the other raven. With a cry she dropped the partridge, and rolled to impale the falcon.

When The Backbreaker plunged again to seize it, Kronk had got it. Abruptly the falcon broke off the fight and climbed to eight thousand feet, to sweep away in a south-easterly direction. He had seen the pigeons flying above the town by the tidal river nine miles away.

Mewliboy tried desperately to break his cage every day, but the summer went slowly without freedom for him. Never a day went by without Wheeoo calling to him, but she dared not come down. Then came a time when the days were as long as the nights, and the leaves of the trees were torn away by the gales which rushed up and over the valley.

10

One of his sisters was shot by a gamekeeper, and the other was driven away by Jale. She and the cock bird went inland and Wheeoo was left to fend for herself. She had learnt to walk a few steps on the stumps of her legs, from which the useless feet were fallen, but she could catch nothing except lizards and beetles on the ground, and these were hard to find, now that summer was ended.

She tried to tear rabbits in the gins, but without feet to hold them she could get hardly a mouthful. She became thin and bedraggled, like the corpse of her daughter nailed to the keeper's gibbet, and called so plaintively that one morning the trapper, making up his mind simultaneously with a large ejection of tobacco-juice, released Mewliboy with the remark, "Sink me sideways, if I don't believe it's yer old Ma a-calling yer to feed her." So Mewliboy flew up, crying *Whee-i-oo!* in his joy. He came back later for food, and the delighted man threw him a rabbit, which he bore away. For days he returned, and since Wheeoo became stronger and less bedraggled he must have fed her.

The gales blew themselves out, and as the sun went down like fire beyond the valley, the ex-sailor used to stand on his threshold and watch mother and son rise from their feeding, and beat into the

sunset wind that flowed over the valley. In the airs below the trees
their wings seemed clumsy and heavy, and often when they stopped
beating them, and attempted to glide, they seemed clogged with
earth and were a graceless support to the body. Slowly they flapped
upwards, until they broke through the stagnant airs and reached
the soft south wind stroking the tops of the pines and the oaks. A
wild and plaintive *Wheeoo* fell from Mewliboy's beak. The wind
buoyed his breast, his wings lifted him. At the southern end of each
loop he turned into the wind and pressed against it, flapping broad
pinions, and his white-barred underside was lit by the light of the
sun breaking into the sea. He beat the air three or four times at
the turn, then went with the wind. When he had gained soaring speed
he wheeled at a steep angle to face the south, and was borne up
easily to a higher plane.

He glided with Wheeoo while an unearthly air took them up, up,
up, serenely as they traced their winged arcs. *Wheeoo!* cried Mewliboy, from three thousand feet, and joyfully she answered. Sipsitew,
the willow wren, with his mate and children, heard them as the
little birds took their last beakfuls of water from the stream before
setting out for their winter home in Africa.

Wheeoo! Wheeoo! Wheeoo!—high and unseen, until the western
fire died, and the fields grew dark as the woods, and Altair the star
of all the falcons flickered gold wings as it flew in eternal watchful-
ness.

Bluemantle

It was for this that the long road in the air had been traversed. A sunlight sweeter than any in the south, and the water-sparkle of the brooklet coiling through sandhills to the sea. The aerial wayfarer followed its course, soaring and diving as he took the midges, and when he came to the sands he turned and sped back, singing his sun-song. So gentle was the song of Bluemantle the swallow, so sweet and gentle as the timid bird passed to and fro. There was no happier bird in Devon than Bluemantle as he flew over the marshes behind the dunes that April day.

Bluemantle had a mate. She was like himself, graceful and slim, but her wings were not such a rich blue, nor were her throat and chin so warmly brown. She loved to hear the song that her love sang to her and to the sunlight; they cherished one another, and both helped to make the nest on a beam of a tumbledown cattle shed in a field. Patiently throughout the days the pair flew to a stone by the side of the stream, where forget-me-nots grew every year, and mixed their mortar of red mud and dried grasses. Beakfuls were taken to the beam, and added to the shallow cup. Hundreds of journeys Bluemantle made every day to the flowery pool, until the time came when no more mortar was needed.

He went instead to the farmyard, and sought snowy feathers that were shed by the farmer's fantail pigeons. In his black beak he bore them to the beam, and so effortless was each flight that he looked like a big blue feather drifting after a small white one. Scores of feathers were borne in this manner, and lovingly interwoven with grass and lambs' wool taken from brambles growing on the low ground behind the sandhills.

The mate of Bluemantle waited to lay her eggs and often the two sat on the beam and twittered their joy. Then one morning

a fragile egg rested cold among the white feathers, and the next morning there were two, the morning after there were three, then four, then five—all cold among the white feathers, pale eggs with brown and red speckles. She waited a day before beginning to brood over them, and thereafter they were not allowed to be uncovered for long, lest the precious heat go and the things within die.

Long days in the cattle-shippen were made glorious by their twittered thoughts. Often Bluemantle took her place on the nest, while she rushed away to turn and slip and roll in the sunshine above the green water-meadows. Yet all this labour came to naught, because a small boy entered the shippen one afternoon, and took away the five eggs in his hat. Bluemantle cried wildly in his pain, but it availed nothing. The treasures were gone.

Bluemantle and his love pined for many days, but the sun, which gives hope to the brave, changed sorrow into love. When the wild roses came on the hedges, and the wandering voice of the cuckoo fell into ruin, they decided to make another nest. Still the forget-me-nots grew by the pool by whose edge the red mortar was mixed before being taken aloft to the invisible scaffolding of heaven. They had finished the new nest in the shed, so dear to Bluemantle because he had been born there the year before, when another boy came and put his finger into the cup. Disappointed at its emptiness, he tore it down, while once again Bluemantle cried *spink-spink-spink-spink*, in his anguish.

They quitted the cattle-shippen for ever, and went to a cottage standing by itself in a corner of a field near the village. Tall grasses grew out of the thatch, with sprays of oats and belled spires of penny-wort. The cottage had been condemned ever since an old man had died in it, unfriended and alone, two years before. Unlatched windows swung and clattered at every windiblore, the sparrows and starlings had tunnelled into the eaves. A great blackened chimney tun gaped at the sky, and down this Bluemantle flew, discovering a ledge made by the dislodgment of a stone several feet from the top.

Here at night the two birds slept, awaking with the dawn and preening their wing feathers while yet the stars were bright in the square above them. Once a white owl, tired after the night's hunting, appeared suddenly above, and with curious sideway movements of his head peered down. The swallows moved not even the nictitating membrane over their eyes. The dreaded white face, with the round black eyes, caused their hearts to throb and flutter for many moments, but at last the owl spread his white-and-gold wings and with a wild screech floated away.

Other sounds alarmed the timid birds. Rats scampered in the cottage, and seemed to be gnawing all night. Frequently the owl perched on the stone-work above. Once there were two for quite a long time, and when they flew away something fell down the chimney and ceased with a thud below. It was a dead rat, whose corpse was eaten by the cottage rats in the night.

The swallows built their nest in the chimney. It was not so carefully made as the first nest had been, nor were the feathers of white. The lining consisted of seven feathers, they came from the breast of two sparrows quarrelling in the roadway. The quarrel was stopped by a sparrow-hawk that came without warning over the hedge, seized one, and took it away shrieking pitifully. Bluemantle caught two feathers as they were in the air, and came back for the others afterwards, when only two small glistening red specks in the midst of the foot-marked dust told of the quarrel and its ending.

Three eggs were laid at the end of August, and both birds danced with silent ecstasy when in the middle of September a faint *cheep cheep* was heard through one of the shells. Little tappings, feeble knocks, came sometimes. Bluemantle spoke to the baby who so wanted to be born, and shortly afterwards the shell cracked and a naked morsel with an opened beak, tumbled out. Its name was Wip.

2

Thereafter Bluemantle, bright of eye, had a joyful task of bringing flies and thunder midges from the sun-plashy upper air. They were not so numerous as they had been, and so more effort was required to obtain a mouthful, but still Bluemantle sang as he fled carelessly adown lane and hedgerow, over meadow and sedges. By the stream other swallows were often gathered together, clinging to the stately mace-reeds that swayed to the wind while the great brown heads were yet unburst. They talked eagerly among themselves, these swallows in congregation, and Bluemantle felt distress in his heart. The families of these others were grown, the young launched upon their airy life; the nesting work of the year was done, and now they waited for the return to Africa.

The mornings were chilly, and the insects did not fly up from hedge and grass till the sun had swung some way up the sky. Blue-mantle wandered farther for food for the three chimney nestlings. They grew slowly, and he sang less; he was so earnest. As the days went on he felt more and more a restlessness, and as this increased so did his desire to teach his young to fly. One dawn there was a frost, and he cried his agony aloud, and when it was heard by the flocked swallows, they rose and wheeled over the stream. Some brought midges and flies to the broken chimney tun, where the pair received them and took them down to Wip and his two sisters.

Day succeeded day. From grey quills the pinion feathers sprouted and smoothed themselves, each filament in its place. Their breasts and backs became covered with featherlets which replaced some of the down of babyhood. Bluemantle and his mate, restless and worried, did not eat enough to appease their own hunger.

Every morn now the sun seemed larger when it came above the hills in a fume of frosted gold, and the meadow grasses were often white with rime. More excited grew the swallows among the mace-reeds. They were awaiting the tribal sign, given and appearing no man knows how, that would urge them climb the sky to their airlines, older than any Eastern caravan route, to follow them to the southern sun. By this inward urge all claims and instincts were dominated. Young birds forgot the parents who had so lovingly reared them, taught them to fly, and guarded their early adventurings into the romantic realms of the sky. Old birds forgot their young, and into their hearts came dread as some dim memory of drenching vapours and monstrous seas to be passed stirred in their minds. The gathered swallows twittered encouragement one to another, and rose for no seen reason all at once, then returned to roost. Every hour stranger swallows joined them, all eager and animated by the remorseless inward urge to quit. Bluemantle and his mate would fly among them to return to the chimney where their young called for them. They begged them to fly, but the fledgelings were too small to leave the familiar shelter.

An aged man passing down the lane by the cottage was the sole human spectator of the swallows' agony. Hearing strange whimpering noises, he stopped, shaded filmy eyes with his hand, and stared. The parent birds were uttering cries so strained with anguish and despair that he guessed at once the tragic turmoil within the loving breasts. For very many years he had watched for the coming of the swallows; they had shared the joy and the sorrow of this aged man.

"Ah, my little birdies," he mumbled to himself, "you were too late wi' the laying. And now your hearts be breaking."

That evening the ruddy setting sun stained as though with wine the combers of the Atlantic crashing and seething white upon the beach. The call had come—the call of life. With shrill cries, as though of farewell to all that was beloved and cherished, the assembled swallows cast themselves from the mace-reeds and climbed the worn steps of the sky. Wip and his trembling sisters heard the cries as they huddled on the sooty edge of the chimney. In vain the deserted fledgelings cried to them. Higher and higher climbed the wayfarers, a long smoke-trail of birds under the evening sky, passing over the coastline to join the hosts hurrying in silence to the far south. Bluemantle and his mate, with never a backward look, flew steadily with them. The sun went down, and the stars, travellers themselves, came to cheer them.

So they flew in the night. For life has its claim even as death has its toll; and perhaps in a happier summer Bluemantle would come back to the sparkle and the murmur of the brook coiling through sandhills to the sea.

The Meal

Walking over the winter stubble to the small gravel pit in a corner of the field, the boots of the two young men took on four clogs of clay. One man carried a sack and crowbar; the other carried a pick-axe and a spade. They were going to dig out a fox whose earth was in the gravel-pit, put it into a sack, and present it to the pack with which they hunted.

The gravel pit was disused. Three small thorns grew among the dead grasses that covered the slight hollow, with brown spires of sorrel, with sapless thistles and the hollow, fragile skeleton of wild carrot and cow-parsley. Withered creepers of goose-grass were tangled with the thorns; and a ruinous bird's-nest in one held rotting berries —the deserted storehouse of a field mouse.

Some of the deeper depressions in the pit were filled with water. Several rabbit runs led through the dead grasses, but there were no buries. The only hole in the gravel sides was larger than that made by rabbits. It was between eight and nine inches across, and some fresh gravel was before it with an appearance of having been pressed down. One of the men knelt before the hole, examining the ground. He looked for half a minute, and beckoned his companion to kneel beside him. There was a smell like hops being dried in an oast-house, tainting the air. The kneeling men again looked at the prick of claws and the mark of pads leading one way—into the earth. They went to a dyke to cut a long willow wand.

The earth had two tunnels, the right one being short, and the left being long. At the end of the long tunnel a fox was lying, curled up, throat resting on his soft brush. He was stiff and tired, having run many miles the day before across ploughlands and dykes, along lanes and down hedges, with hound-music ever following. He was an old fox, and had been run many times before, but this time scent had lain thickly, and he had known it. Often he had flopped down in a furrow to ease his thudding heart, but always the hounds had pursued him.

Then another fox got up in the middle of a ploughed field as he ran past, and the fresh dog laid a scent stronger than that of the exhausted animal, who came to the gravel pit in the stubble field and listened. He knew that the pack was running the new line, and although several riders galloped across the field fifty yards from the pit, he did not worry. That night he crept from the pit and fed upon mice which he snapped in hedge-ditches, worms, and a rabbit taken from a gin. He slunk home at dawn, dug for awhile, and crept into the earth, which he had extended several feet.

Reynard awoke and with cocked ears listened to the noises of human voices coming down the tunnel. They ceased, and he lay still. Shortly afterwards something came towards him, scraping the gravel, rapidly. He bared his fangs, and pressed his body tightly against the sand of the dug cavern. It came to him and touched him, but he did not snap at it, knowing that it was a stick. The stick was jerked backwards and forwards many times, but the point never touched the fox. It was withdrawn, and the earth thumped again and again while gravel fell into the tunnel and the dim light of day went out.

After three hours the noises of digging ceased, and the fox waited. He waited for a long time before creeping forward. He came to the loose gravel, and sniffed. He scraped with his claws, and listened. There was no sound except the mournful wailing of the dwarf owl which just before dark came out from a pollard oak in the hedge. The cry was dulled and faint.

All night the fox scraped sand and pebbles, making a new tunnel to the air. The way to the old exit had been blocked by a stout sack filled with gravel and dumped over the hole. A tiny air space allowed just enough air to enter where with broken claws he scraped, and with sweaty jaws he tore at hard flints and pebbles. Often he ceased, and lay panting in the tunnel; and thus the long night passed away. He was hungry and thirsty, but ceased work when daylight came.

In the afternoon the two young men returned, heaved away the sack, and examined the hole. One of them said that the fox had been trying to dig his way out; the other expressed the opinion that everything was as they had left it. He agreed that a smell of fox came up as he kneeled by the entrance, but he declared that scent would lay for days and weeks in a confined space, especially if it were gravel.

But he helped his friend with pick, spade and shovel, and after some hours' work they had excavated three more feet of the tunnel.

The red sun was sinking below the level Essex ploughlands when they ceased work, thirsty and tired. Again the willow wand was pushed down, and the stop of the tunnel prodded and touched. All the while the fox pressed himself against the farther wall of the cavern, watching with wide eyes the stick, as though in terror lest it touch him. It was withdrawn, and outside the men examined the end. Of course, no fox was there, declared the doubting one, because no tawny hair was stuck to the damp sand on the stick.

But the other persisted that Reynard was at home. How about the prints of his pads, he asked, that were so clearly leading inwards, when first they had examined the earth. How about the strong scent that had come from the tunnel? He believed that the fox was there; and he had promised the huntsman to bag a fox for him.

He had shot a rabbit that afternoon as they were walking to the gravel pit. He suggested that they should place it inside the tunnel, and leave the filled sack over the hole. Then if it were eaten on the following morning, or disturbed in any way, they would know that a fox was within.

He skinned the rabbit, to make it the more tempting to a starving fox, and, having blocked the hole, they went away, while the dwarf owl on the oak made in the dusk its plaintive cry.

They went hunting the next day, so did not go near the earth. That night there was a frost, and when they returned later the following afternoon the filled sack, in shadow all day, was white with rime. The shallow greenish water in the depression was covered with a thin film of ice. They cracked it with their boots, enjoying the sharp brittle noises of splitting. Nothing had been to the pit; everything was the same. There was the skin of the rabbit, flung on a thorn; the willow wand, the untrodden heap of gravel, the stubs of their cigarettes. They pulled away the sack, and the rabbit was seen, just as it had been left. They drew it out. There was not a mark on it.

They did no more digging, but sat on the edge of the pit, making occasional remarks. They agreed that the untouched rabbit was absolutely conclusive evidence that no living fox was within. He could not have escaped, since there was but one entrance or exit to the earth, and that had been blocked. The prints had led far down and inwards, and certainly no fox would come out of his earth backwards, and expose himself to a possible enemy. Therefore, they argued logically, a dead fox was within. He had either been suffocated, or

had starved to death before the rabbit had been left for him—a period of two days and a night. They felt remorse and shame, and decided to tell no one that they had tortured a poor brute of a fox by leaving it without water, air, or food.

They emptied the sack of gravel, slung the dead rabbit into the pool of greenish water, put tools on shoulders and walked away. Over the furrowed field of heavy clay the red winter sun was casting a purple tinge, and the dwarf owl started its petulant hooting.

Their feet in the stubble made a faint flipping sound as they walked across the next field. The dwarf owl wailed for some minutes, then flew to his hunting. Partridges roosting circlewise in the middle of the stubble-field ceased to call *cher-wick, cher-wick*. Through the wands of the willows shone the new moon, like an ancient hunting horn of gold hung on mouldered tapestry of ploughland mist. Night came to the earth.

3

In slow succession several sounds were made in the pit. Wheezy breathing, a pebble rolled against another. The dry trickle of gravel. Water being lapped. An animal shaking itself. The crunching and cracking of bones.

The curved silver moon wavered in the pool, by the shadow of a lean fox eating the rabbit with the eagerness of an animal that had been hungry four days and three nights.

Unknown

There was no sun in the dark continent of the evening sky. Overhead rainclouds were gathered like swart impis on the plains of heaven, massed for war by the drumbeats of the western wind. The air lying in the fields was hot and thick, restless with flies; not a leaf was moving in the hedges. Some hours since, the seagulls had gathered in a great flock, calling mournfully as they wheeled inland, like the remote ghosts of drowned seamen that were said to haunt the rocky coast.

I was in a sunken lane, and some way from the village. A rumble of thunder rolling far away over Exmoor caused me to move on. Before me on the road a round drop hit the dust. Another fell, and another; the leaves of docks growing by the hedge were being tapped again and again. My spaniel frisked, for he sensed an end of the torturing, glaring drought.

Drop after drop pattered on the lane, on the hedges, on my hands, on my head—splashing road dust from my boots. The wind was dead, a fanatic whose work was done. The clouds hung above, motionless and menacing, impis a-sweat to massacre the earth.

An assegai of lightning was flung from a cloud, a hissing silver-gold shock to the earth. Instantly with the thunder the dust was no more, and little spirts of rain leaping from its wet surface. The rain soaked me instantly. I ran down the hill in my sopped clothes, while the spaniel, looking thin in his wet coat, ran joyously by my side, leaping up at me.

At the bottom of the hill stood a forsaken cottage, a yard or two back from the lane. A broken gate ended the weedy path, and a padlock secured the gate. I vaulted over, while the dog pushed through the low hedge.

The porch was hung with the withering bines of jasmine whose ancient leaves were drifted upon the broken stone by the threshold. A percussion-cap gun leaned in one of the alcoved seats, with flakes of rust below it. Dusty cobwebs were tacked to it, for the cottage had been empty a long time. The rain was rushing down the pathway in a hurried stream, lashed as though by swan-shot. I noticed something white in the grass, and stepped out to pick it up. It was the skull of a dog, with some of the teeth fallen from the long narrow jaw—a greyhound or lurcher, perhaps.

When after an hour the rain still fell, I thought I would explore the cottage. The door was locked, but a broken pane I had passed would enable me to reach the hasp and so open the casement. Streams of water pouring from the rotten thatch beat a tattoo upon my shoulders as I struggled into the kitchen. My dog absolutely refused to enter by the window. I coaxed and scolded, but he would not approach. He whined and was abject; he whimpered dog's talk to me, seemingly frightened. So I got out and flung him in, trembling.

It was a desolate room. There are thousands of such cottages in the remote country, habitations built centuries ago by farm labourers when they married. Cowdung, mud, straw, and stones, all mixed together, formed the thick walls. Crude material, this cob, but it endures as long as bricks and mortar. When it crumbles, sand-like trickles run from crevices, exposing the wattles dry and rotten, and drilled by insects. Rats and mice have their passages within, and at night their noises of scuttle and scamper mingle with their squeaks. Beetles and cockroaches hide by day in the floor cracks, emerging in the hour of darkness for their food quests.

The cottage in which I had taken sanctuary was very old. The final processes of decay had, I thought, begun a long time ago. By the feeble illumination of a candle-stump the ceiling took on grotesque shadows; the laths hung down like ribs, the plaster gaped. Fires of past ages had blackened the walls, made sooty the cobwebs; rat-holes were everywhere. The dog kept close to me.

The torrent of rain had ceased a little with the lightning, but the steady hissing warned me that no abatement could be expected for hours. It was chilly, the dog shivered at my feet as I sat on a log stool. There was the cold and musty smell that goes with old places. Doubtless the cottage was condemned, its owner awaiting a favourable time to rebuild. There could be no harm, I thought, in making a fire on the open hearth. Looking around for fuel, I found only small charred fragments of sticks lying damply amidst fallen mortar and soot. I had some old letters, and with these tried to start a blaze.

After lighting half my matches, I had induced only a melancholy fume to wander up the chimney. Rain came down and extinguished it.

While I was thus occupied, the dog lay curled on the floor, his eyes wide and always watching me. Then thinking that there might be in the bedroom upstairs some fuel more accept-able to flame, I went up the ladder-like staircase, guided by the wavering gleam of the candle. He followed with a whimper. The room was even more desolate than that which I had just left. Mildewed newspaper sheets were gummed to the walls and the bursted ceiling, doubtless the efforts of the last tenant to repair his wretched home. Here, too, like broken ribs the laths leaned down. I seized one and pulled, and with a small roar one half of the ceiling crashed to the floor. A rat emerged from the fusty heap and darted into its hole. I urged my spaniel to seize it, but he did not move. He whined at my feet, wagging his tail, trying to tell me something.

With an armful of trailing laths I went downstairs, broke them up and lit a fire. This time a pale flame rose from the pile and spread its pallid radiance round the room. By means of continual fanning, ruddy flames danced on the walls, and with them a small cheeriness.

The fire sank, and was built up anew, only to sink again. Outside the rain continued. I lay down for a cold sleep.

2

What I remember next is not definite in my mind, even as in retro-spect I try to form some coherent sequence. The moon shone wanly in at the window, a moon wasted by vapour drifting low down. My dog was pressed against my side, and shaking. Of the change from slumber to that state of mind known as wide-awake I was instantly aware. I was filled with a mournful feeling, a reason for which I did not know, as though having witnessed a tragedy slow and inevitable. And yet no emotion was called up in me; my own self was so completely dominated that my thoughts and feelings were, as it were, regarded in a dream. Only I remember wondering why the spaniel was terrified—a fear so profound obsessed him that he did not even growl in protection of his master.

For how long this feeling was with me I am unable to say. I lay still, staring into the pallid gloom: the rain drip-dripped from the fringe of thatch, a wind stirred the withered bines of jasmine, and mumbled in the chimney. The dog trembled and clawed at my coat, as though in an endeavour to get behind me.

Then I thought I saw a grey thing, low on the floor, move in the darkness. It changed, seeming to divide into several parts, that moved away and drew together, and moved away again.

A cold shiver, as at contact of icy fingers, thrilled my back and twitched my hair. I believed that any moment something would tear my throat. Fear wrapped me in clammy folds. I heard a sound of pads on the lime-ash floor, very close to my head. I tried to scream, but to my terror no sound would come from my mouth. I tried to run away, but my legs were as though broken; I pulled myself by my hands, but made no progress. I continued to scream, noiselessly, impotently. The spaniel, with a wild howl, leapt at the window and crashed through the glass and the rotten wood frame.

I had been dreaming.

I knew that with an intense relief. I had been screaming in my dream. Yet my dog was gone; the casement shattered. I got outside. The rainclouds had been blown away, and the night was starry. How friendly appeared the light of those winking suns! There was Aldebaran low down, and Capella; Vega high above, and the constellation of Lyra. I had known them since boyhood, and they were my friends. But there was no moon.

I walked down the lane, calling my dog. From out of gloom somewhere he appeared, whining with joy, and fawning round me. This state of excitement lasted for a long time, until we reached the hamlet.

In answer to my thumps, the landlord of the inn came down, and asked through the closed door what I might want. I explained that I wanted a bed, and he opened the door. He looked at me by the light of a candle held high to see my face.

We went into the kitchen, and he began to light in the bodley a fire of dried sticks and furze roots. He began to spread a cloth upon the table, so that I might have a meal, but I begged him not to trouble, saying that I was not hungry. In the grate the sticks crackled, and from the worn firebars came cheerful gleams. It was an old inn, and draughty: the flame of the candle on the table was bent many ways. Seeing that I shivered, he suggested that I drank some hot rum and water, and I invited him to have a glass with me. The water was heated in a beer-warmer, a small V-shaped pot in which the labourer heats his beer before going to his work on dark winter mornings.

After two glasses of rum apiece, I lost my feeling of dread, but the mournful sadness remained. Gazing at the fire in the dim-litten room, I saw many rays of light glistening like golden thistle-seed wheels through my eyelids, half-closed, trembling, and moistened with tears. For the landlord told me about the last tenant of the lonely cottage, a man nearly a hundred years of age, who had lived with six dogs most faithful to him. They were mongrels, two of them being lurchers that poached rabbits for him throughout the year. He lived the ordinary life of the labourer grown too old to work, with children married and gone away and wife dead and buried. He tilled his garden, gathered sticks for next day's fire, and bought his food every Friday evening at the village shop, when he had drawn the blessed Old Age Pension of five shillings a week. He drank a pint of beer every Friday night at the inn, sitting quiet in a corner in his best black clothes, a worn red muffler round his neck and a rusty bowler on his head. And one Friday he did not turn up at the post office, nor at the inn for his pint of small ale. The following morning the constable went to the cottage and knocked at the door. From within came the barking of dogs, not robust or loud, but hoarse and feeble. The door was locked. He peered through the window-space, noticing that the marks of muddy pads were dried on the sill and the ledge within. It had not rained for five days. He saw three dogs in the room, who snarled and barked at him. He attempted to climb in through the window, but they rushed at him with bared teeth.

An hour later he returned with the landlord of the inn, who was the only able-bodied man in the village not working. They guessed what had happened and were apprehensive. Poisoned meat was flung to the three dogs, who devoured it, only to fall in convulsions. Only then were the men able to climb through the window, to pass the dying mongrels. The fur of rabbits was scattered on the floor, and the feathers of a partridge. They went through the door and up the stairs, where two dogs snarled at them. These were poisoned in the same manner. The sixth dog was already dead, and lying as stiff as the figure of his master on the floor. It was a fox-terrier and had died of a broken heart, no doubt refusing to eat the food brought to it by the three dogs which for many days had been guarding the door downstairs.

In due course the dead were buried; the old man in consecrated ground, and his faithful dogs in the garden. It had happened many years before. The cottage was allowed to fall into ruin, as it was not worth repairing.

3

The next morning, in sweet fresh air, I continued my journey. I could not forget my experience of the previous night, nor that bleached skull in the long grass. I felt that I had seen something that was beyond the pale of mortal endeavour. Through what medium it had been seen by me, I worried my mind to determine. If it had once happened, why should not my mind be able to sense the old emotion? The idea was no more wonderful than the idea of memory. In the world of imagination all things were possible: time did not exist. If I could think forward to when the world and its physical life would be dead, like its sister planet the moon, I could search backwards in my mind to the time of lifeless molten lava bursting through space with its bands of gases burning bright and roaring around it. Of what importance was the world of matter, regarded in the light of dream and imagination—of the soul? I walked on, pondering in the sweet air, while a wren sang in a blackberry bramble.

When later I was going across Dartmoor, I visited a white witch —who charms away warts, abscesses, and can heal most marvellously —a good friend of mine, who smiled and said that both the living and the dead have their own detachable doubles, intangible, which are ghosts. Afterwards as I sat within the Lydford Gorge, while the water thundered in white foam and shook all other sounds from the air, I pondered what knowledge of these things had been lost with the civilizations that had passed; civilizations of whose existence we know only by a tile, a vase, a mummy. While the solid glassy fall of water carved the stone, I strayed backwards through cycles of summers, among the wild moormen in their hut circles, the wolves and the bears; further and further back, to the age of tree-ferns and eyeless monsters, long before them when vegetation crept out of the sea and fastened on the land, and animal life-to-be stirred in the slime. Where was I then? Was there a burning love in my heart, as there is now? Have I been all the time, in a hundred different forms, each one evolving higher to the godhead of perfection, to discarnate, timeless omniexistence?

But the rude music of the water took my mind from pondering. I would be thoughtless as the swallows casting their lines of song in the sunlight, as the brown otter in the pool below, as the dipper perching on the mossy stone that made in the stream a resting eddy for the trout. Poor wraiths of the dead, if such they be, I would leave them to rest in their quiet places; the wildflower on the bank, the glitter and music of running water, the sad-sweet song of the woodlark, the lizard on the hot sunstone—the thoughts these gave were enough to fill my days.

The Old Stag
and other hunting stories
(1921—1924)

Preface

During the autumn following the departure of my odd friend, Julian, I settled down to steady writing. For relaxation—and also for 'copy', I travelled astride the Norton to various meets of foxhounds on Exmoor, and as far away south to Dartmoor and North Cornwall, to ride hired mounts costing 30/– a day. Sometimes I took a pillion passenger on the carrier of my bike, to which was strapped a small cushion. My guest was a sporting young woman of 18 years; today, nearly fifty years later, she is the seasoned Master of a pack hunting country west of Exmoor.

I had hunted during the war, when stationed at Grantham, while undergoing a transport course of the Machine Gun Corps, which had been formed in 1915, to be ready for the battle of the Somme.

It may be that the group of stories which now follow are inferior to the preceding earliest group. The hunting stories were in no wise written to please editors. They took hold of me so that they appeared to write themselves. Magazines such as Pearson's, Royal, Nash's, Strand, Cassell's, Blue Magazine and Red Magazine were flourishing in the mid-'twenties. One editor, I recollect, took me to task about them when I called upon him at his office in Henrietta Street, off the Strand, during the winter of 1924, when I was writing the early chapters of *The Pathway*.

The editor began by declaring that I was 'wasting a talent by writing for the restricted animal-story market'.

I protested that I could write only what I saw, and felt. This was not altogether true. One story, 'T'Chackamma', had been suggested by a crude pen-and-ink sketch of African baboons being attacked by dogs on the lower slopes of a mountain. I imagined all of the incidents in this story; but some native expressions were copies from a review, in Middleton Murry's *The Adelphi*, of Miss Pauline Smith's book, *The Little Karoo*—much praised by Arnold Bennett among other writers. I hasten to add that my 'description' of farming, and particularly of the Boer farmer in my story, was of impure imagination; and as such, possibly ridiculous; unreal.

"But surely in your village and round about are many happy people, who still believe in romance and clean, healthy living," the Editor's voice was postulating. "Well then, why not write about *them*? Why waste ink and paper, why burn the midnight oil writing about animals? Most of the stories you have written I have seen—and I have, against my better judgment, published several. Now, I am seriously concerned for you, my boy," he went on, waggling the editorial pencil at me. "People have enough troubles of their own to want to read about such things as nature red in tooth and claw. You have told me that you hope to get married, if you can earn enough to support a wife. Very well. You should write only what people want to read: stories of romance that will bring pleasure into their own humdrum lives. I repeat, my dear boy, that I am *really* disturbed by your persistence in choosing such depressing subjects. You may reply that what you write of animals' and birds' lives is true, and I can well believe it."

"But—"

" 'But me no buts'—remember your Hamlet? Well, it seems I am wasting my breath. I am sorry you can't see how I am trying to help you. I feel it is a tragedy—a waste of a real talent."

It was of course kindly meant, and he knew his public. He had published several of the hunting stories, among them 'Stumberleap', the story of the last run of an old Exmoor stag. Even so, he had deleted the phrase *soiling pit* from my text, declaring it was not necessary to "include cloacal details".

"I'm afraid I don't know what that word means."

"You use a sanitary term—*soiling pit*. It's not very nice, is it? That is why I cut it out."

"May I explain, sir?"

"If you must—"

"A soiling pit is a shallow watery plash where turf, or peat, has been cut. It derives from a Norman-French word *assouler*—to wash off scent. It was brought into England with the Norman Conquest, and is still used on Exmoor."

"Well, my readers easily would have mistaken it for something else, such as the soil cart which no doubt is still in nocturnal use in backward Devon villages."

"Earth pails are normally emptied by every cottager in daylight on his cabbage patch. To prevent soil-erosion. The Roman Empire fell because the fertility of Roman soil was 'squandered through sewers to the sea', as a German chemist declared in a book called—"

The editor shook his head. "Well, I can see that my words fall on stony ground."

"That's why earth pails are emptied on the slatey soil of many Devon villages—"

"In my opinion, you have a kink."

As I went to the door he said, "It really is a tragedy! You, with your uncommon gift of language, feel you must persist in writing of sordid things, and thereby deliberately restrict your reading public."

Spring brought its early flowers to the banks above the sunken lanes through which, daily with my spaniel, I walked to the higher grazing fields, where arose rich shining grass, said in the village to fatten bullocks. Sometimes I went farther afield on the Norton, spaniel sitting on petrol tank with the protection of my arms as I lay extended between saddle and low, wide handlebars.

Yellow celandines gave way to primroses blooming in such luxuriance that they made a continuous blur of milky moonlight as we sinuated through the lanes, once horse-drawn sled-tracks worn to the rocks, later to be grooved deeper by the iron-hooped wheels of small, sturdy carts called 'butts'. Winter rains falling upon the seaboard country washed away detritus of shale and ironstone, I reflected.

Suddenly the drifting cumulus lifted, blue sky appeared—out shone the sun, larks arose, and what joy it was to be alive, and soon one was to be married to one who also loved wild places, and the flowers and birds as I did!

All I had in the bank was £5 when the wedding was but three days away. Then, two days before I was to go across Bideford bridge to the little Saxon Church above the estuary of the Torridge, a telegram lying below the round hole in the cottage door, by which my cats and dog entered, and left . . .

It was from my literary agent in London. Two stories had been accepted for $500 each in the U.S.A.: 'Stumberleap' in *The Saturday Evening Post;* 'The Rape of the Pale Pink Pyjamas' in *Collier's*

Weekly, provided the author would allow the world *Flight* to be substituted for *Rape* in the title.

A thousand dollars! Two hundred pounds!!

Off went a telegram to my betrothed with the glad news; and when I got back from a quart of beer in the village pub that evening there lay upon the lime-ash floor of Skirr Cottage, Pie, my little black and white cat, keeping warm an orange envelope which had been brought up by old 'Muggy', the crab, mushroom, watercress and telegram man from the telegraph office in Cryde village by the sea.

HURRAY it said.

When the volume of *The Old Stag* was published in 1926, one critic declared that the ending of Stumberleap, the stag which escaped its enemies by swimming across the Bristol Channel to Wales, was impossible in real life. A day or two after the *critique* there appeared in *The Daily Mail* a letter from the Earl of Dunraven, whose estate lay in South Wales. The writer declared that there used to live in one of his woods a red deer from Exmoor, which was so old that it had ceased to grow an annual head of horn. Lord Dunraven went on to say that it had always been held locally that the stag had crossed the wide estuary to escape from hounds swimming after it in the waves. The stag had probably rested on one of the sandbanks exposed at low tide in the Channel.

Then I looked in a book written by Richard Jefferies, and published in 1884. *Red Deer* is a beautiful work. The author, for his health's sake (he died three years later) spent much of the time out-of-doors, on the high moor which he describes with a skill superior to my own. He accompanied the harbourer of the Devon and Somerset Hunt, and learned much from his companion, who knew where warrantable stags harboured in the wooded coombes, and led the huntsman there on the day appointed for the chase.

A hunted stag ... often makes for the sea, and swims straight out, followed by the hounds, leaving the hunters on the beach. So common is this, that the hounds, when hunting is not going on, are taken for exercise to the sea-shore, not only for a bath, but that they may be used to it. Stags swim splendidly for long distances, and can generally beat the hounds in the water. They have a great advantage over hounds— they can rest and float. They are so buoyant that they can cease striking with their hoofs and yet remain with their heads above the surface. Floating like this, they rest and gather strength, while a hound must continue using his feet, or drown.

Though the waves be high, the stag breasts them easily, and some-times swims so far as to be scarcely visible. After a while the hounds generally return to the beach if they find they cannot head the stag and turn him. Once now and then a hound overtaxes himself, or is buffetted too much by the waves, and sinks, but not often. The stags usually take to the sea in the neighbourhood of Porlock Weir, and the boatmen are always on the watch when they know the hunt is up.

Four or five fishermen are dispatched for the stag, and they row after him, helping any hounds they may see getting exhausted into the boat. They throw a rope round the stag's antlers, and draw him on board, and immediately tie his legs. A stag seems an awkward animal to get into a boat, but they manage it without much difficulty, and bring him ashore to be killed. The huntsman, as before observed, always kills, that he may be sure that it is a warrantable deer of proper age; if it proves not to be mature, the stag is let go. Stags have been lost at sea, and their bodies washed ashore at Cardiff or Swansea, on the opposite coast, drowned after a lone combat with the waves.

The chapter, from which the above quotation is taken, ends with the following sentence.

Norman-French may still be continually traced in hunting terms; the word 'soil' for instance, which is said of a stag bathing, was anciently written *soule*.

Stumberleap

When I was a little boy at school, I was indifferent to nearly all my lessons, including Geography. I remember the drawing of maps (but not the maps) and the putting-in of capes, rivers, bays, and mountains; the dull lists of towns and places I had to learn by heart; and what things, usually of commerce, the places were 'noted for'. It was dreary work, for usually I was thinking of other things —of how, if they would choose me for the team, I would kick a goal for my House, amid cheers, as the whistle blew; of a steam engine or an electric motor in a catalogue; of a raft to be made of boxes and provisioned by free samples, and steered by a compass out of a Christmas party cracker, with which I should set out on an exploration (I didn't know where); but most often I thought of the wild animals and birds—especially the birds—of the fields and woods I knew. And any reference I found, in any of the lesson books, to a bird or an animal—it must be an English one!—how my mind took hold of it, and dreamed on it, as a green weed takes hold and dreams on a brick wall in the smoke of London. There was, I remember, but one green and living plant in all the waste of the big Geography book we 'did lessons from', and that was a paragraph against a map of south-western England, which said that Exmoor was 'noted for' the wild red deer, because it was the only place in all England and Wales where the red deer had survived in their old wild ways. I think I used to hunt a red stag every Geography lesson, with a bow and arrow; I was a mighty hunter, although really my arms were very thin, and I was no good at boxing. And now I am more or less grown up: and perhaps in some school a little boy dreams of the wild red deer which Exmoor is 'noted for'; and here is a story of a stag for him, which is as true as my small knowledge of Stumber-leap can make it. It is not a quarter as good as the proper *Story of a Red Deer,* which Sir John Fortescue told me he wrote during a fortnight's holiday to please a small boy; but Sir John was bred in the country of the deer, and saw them as a child on his native moor, while I saw them only in the Geography book.

Now if the dull Geography book is still in misuse, which I hope is not so, it will be wrong, for it said that the red deer roam wild in but one part of England and Wales, on the high and tameless tract called Exmoor; whereas in Wales is a wooded hill overlooking the Severn Sea, and in the wood lives a wild stag who sometimes gazes across many miles of water to the dim blue moor of his birth. That book will be right again one day, perhaps before it can be corrected; for a stag's life is as a tree's, whose lost branches measure its years; and the last antlers have grown and dropped from the stag's head. He is a solitary, and this is his story.

The hound Deadlock nearly died in the last chase of the stag, but eleven thorns fastened his wound until I brought him to the farmhouse, where he grew well within a fortnight. But his pace was gone from him; and he was drafted to the otter hunters who walk in the valleys.

First I must tell you a little about the life of 'the girt old stag of Stumberleap Wood', as he was called by the farmer. Several times I saw him, before the stag-hunting season, once in the Badgeworthy valley in June, when his coat was glowing ruddy-gold, for he was fat with young corn and roots plundered from moorland farms.

And during the rutting season I saw him coming down from the hills before an October gale, driving a herd of hinds. Three young male deer followed the herd, and sometimes one would approach too near a hind, when Stumberleap would charge back and the young deer would race away. The old stag was gaunt with sinew and muscle, in shape of body not unlike a donkey, but taller; the hair of his flanks was shaggy with mud, and he was thin with so much travelling and fighting. They say on the moor that at such a time a stag's blood is black and poisonous, and that he eats nothing for weeks. The grey gale fell upon the valley, the oaks shuddered in the rainy wind, and as I crouched under a rock Stumberleap was seen against the sky. His head was thrown back as he roared a challenge to any other stag that might be in the goyal. Then bending his neck he dug his antlers into the boggy ground and tore up grasses and sods, which the wind flung away. Again he bellowed. So brazen was the

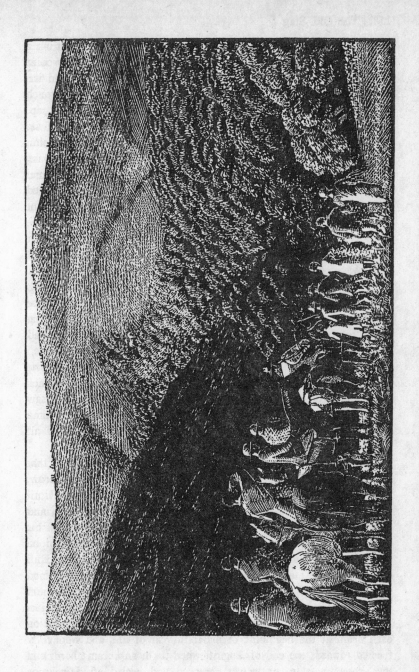

note above the wind that terror entered into me, and fearing lest when he crossed my scent he might charge back and drive the brow-point through my body into the trunk which sheltered me, I climbed the tree. The bark was rough with lichen, and I scrambled along a branch in order to watch as another bellow had answered Stumberleap. Immediately he roared back, and trotted forward, and, while I sat on the creaking bough, a strange stag came forward to meet him. The points of the stranger's antlers made the outline of a crown, whereas Stumberleap's was a forked head. Both stags jumped round feinting for an opening to stab and point. While the gale passed over the sombre moor they thrust and drew back to watch, but suddenly Stumberleap leapt up, and plunged down his head, and the horns clashed. With fury they wrestled and swayed, breaking the soft leaf-mould at the hill's edge with their slot, until the crown-headed stag (who for three days and nights had hardly eaten or slept, for every breeze that drew across his nostrils had made him more feverish to travel and seek the hinds of his rivals) was so buffeted that he was thrown down the slope. Again the antlers clashed, and a young hind stole back from the herd and butted him in the flank. She had been conquered by Stumberleap, and loved him. The stranger seemed to lose strength, and after a minute he backed away and ran into the undergrowth. Stumberleap threw up his head, stretched his thick neck, and bellowed; then rose on his hind legs and sniffed. I saw the instant alertness in the fine eyes of the head upheld. He scented man. The deer were gone, and the rain and the wind blurred all things in my sight.

Stumberleap must have been hunted many times before that October, as he had possessed all his rights—the points called brow, bay, and tray—some years previously, at the age of five years. Until his sixth year he was not called a stag, but a male red deer, and as such not warrantable or worthy of being chased. Every April his antlers began to grow, and every following March they dropped off, and then Stumberleap hid himself in a wood, and avoided all deer; the horns started to grow again soon afterwards, when blood and nerves rushed up the two beams (which were soft and tender, and gave him pain when anything touched them) and formed the points known as 'brow, bay, tray, and three-point-top'. Six points came on each beam at the beginning of his sixth year of life, and were fully formed towards the end of August, when the horn became hard, and the protecting skin, or 'velvet', cracked and peeled off. His horns itched, and Stumberleap travelled to the fir-trees growing on the high ground above the sea, and rubbed his antlers against trunks and branches to ease the itch. Many of these trees were dead, the bark having been ringed by stags in former summers, so that the sap could not rise, and they withered.

He grew bigger with the years, and took only the best food—he sought the buds of the ash and beech in March, and crunched the leaves of the ivy. In the early summer he roamed far into the green valleys below the heather moor, and wherever he went he pillaged crops, orchards, and gardens, exercising the rights of his race which roamed there thousands of years before the soil was tilled and sown by man. For the red deer were of more ancient lineage than any other creatures on Exmoor. Many races of the chief hunter, man, had lived there, and the red deer had remained. Their instincts were uncorrupt, and came pure from the earth-spirit, which had given them fleetness and grace, and a pride of race that prevented them mating with the tame fallow deer of the parks. Exmoor is a true child of her mother the earth, and her abiding pride is the tall red deer.

And now, in the twentieth century, while another human civilization was decaying, some of the farmers made straw-stuffed dummies in their own image, and placed them in the beech-hedges guarding the root crops, to frighten the wild red deer! Stumberleap ignored the oddmedodds as he walked down the rows, biting a turnip, often pulling it up and throwing it over his shoulder, to tear off the juicy flake between his teeth. Sometimes he and other stags would ruin a whole field in a night, but the hinds were not so destructive, for their necks were not so strong, nor were they so impatient. Cornfields he 'used', tearing mouthfuls of the golden ears, while the hinds wasted hardly a berry. To keep out the wild red deer the farmers put wires on the stone banks, fixed with tarred stakes, but Stumberleap easily leapt over the obstacles, although they kept out the hinds, which preferred to scramble up a bank or through a beech-tree hedge.

But most of all Stumberleap liked the acorns which fell from the oaks in autumn. He swallowed them without munching, as many as he could find. He bolted apples until his paunch was filled. At seven years of age the points of his antlers were thirteen, and in his fifteenth year he carried fifteen points, and three offers (which were little knobs on the beam, as though points had offered to grow there). His head was an 'imperial', or, as the harbourer described him, he was 'brow, bay, tray, five p'n-tap, four p'n-tap'. Five top-points on one beam, four on the other.

Many of his sons had been killed, but Stumberleap lived, because he was cunning and knew the waters. He lived through so many seasons that no one knew his age; but one morning in September, when the brown heather-bells of the commons were dry and honey-less, and a golden haze brimmed the goyals and lay lightly on the hills, he was dozing under his favourite oak-tree, unaware that a keen-eyed man had seen that his slot on the deer-path led into Stumberleap Wood, and not out again.

2

The man was the harbourer. He was the huntsman's secret agent. He had not seen the stag for a week, yet he knew where he had been, where he had drunk, and what he had eaten. Indeed, he did not need to see the stag, for he could read easily his comings and goings. His nose and eyes were almost as keen as a wild animal's, and his clothes were the hues of the moor.

He knew 'the girt old stag of Stumberleap Wood' by his slot, or hoof-print. A hind's slot was smaller, and had only a slight cleft between the two halves of the hoof, whereas that of a matured stag was square, the halves were longer and more pointed. For the last three sunrisings the harbourer had gone to the soiling-pit of Stumberleap—where every dawn before going home the stag went to drink and bathe—and 'made good' his slot.

In July the stag had returned to Stumberleap Wood, and the harbourer had seen in a goyal several trunks of rowan-tree and alder with their bark ringed, the work of a stag with itching antlers, desiring to rub off the velvet from the new hardening horn. During August he had come occasionally to the soiling-pit, which was made by the cutting of turf during previous summers. The water looked black with old dead heather roots. He read the slot of stag, hind, staggart, pricket, or calf as easily as he knew trees by their leaves.

September came, and a meet was fixed at Stumberleap Farm, a mile away and below the wood, built on the ridge which rose between two valleys, called the Globe. The day before the meet the harbourer did not go near the wood, but he went to the soiling-pit in the early morning and slurred with his boot all slot imprints. At sunrise next morning he saw the fresh slot of 'the girt old stag of Stumberleap Wood', with those of a staggart, or young male deer. Then he walked to a young ash-tree on the way from the pit to the wood. The tree was a perpetual cripple. Not only were its four sapling-trunks gnawn, but all its younger branches, which had striven to grow, were maimed. And every May its leaf-shoots were cut. The harbourer glanced at one new spray, and turned back downhill. He had seen what he wanted—stag's teeth had hastily torn at one spray in passing: he had not been hungry: therefore he had torn it when going to his layer, or bed, after the night's feeding.

The harbourer hurried to the farmhouse, where with the grooms he ate a hearty breakfast of eggs, bacon, hog's-pudding, and fried bread, washed down with a quart of mulled ale. Afterwards the ease of legs drying before a fire, while he waited for huntsman and tufters.

3

Stumberleap Farm was a long stone building roofed with slate. Bright yellow lichens spread in patches over the walls and roof. Starlings sang upon the great square chimney tuns, in the cracks of which grew ferns of wall-rue and hart's tongue. On the top of each tun two slabs of shale were mortared in the form of a triangle, to cut the winds which in winter would pour down the chimneys. Beeches and pines surrounded the cluster of house, barns, and shippen. One of the beech-trees was hollow and had held the nest of a brown owl every spring for half a century. On a thick branch parallel with the ground a rope swing was tied, and the farm children played here, swinging from the same branch from which, it has been said, their great-great-great-great-grandfather was hanged after a raid by the robbers of Hoccombe-goyal.*

In one of the stable buildings six hunters had been in stall for more than an hour. Now, at ten o'clock in the morning, grooms in shirt-sleeves and unhitched braces were finally polishing bits and stirrup irons, and unrolling bandages from tails and cannons. There was the clack and stamp of shoes on the brick floor. These were the spare mounts of the Master and the two hunt servants. In the stall of another building stood a clipped Exmoor pony, with old grass-champ on its dull nickel bit, carrying a saddle with irons and buckles rusted by the moor mists of many seasons. It had been born on the

* Mistakenly (some declare) called Doone Valley.

moor, and driven with its dam into Bampton Pony Fair fifteen Septembers since, and purchased by the farmer for a guinea. The farmer had carried it away under his arm, squealing and kicking, but since its fifth year it had carried him many thousands of miles, and eaten many apples from the paunches of stags for whom the mort blast had sounded.

At half-past ten, the time of the meet, over a hundred people had come to the farm. Hunters neighed, men and women smiled and chatted, moved about greeting friends; pink and black and tweed coats made gay colour in the field behind the farm. The sun of a fair September morning dropped its gold into the dewy freshness of the valley. In blinding spikes and splashes of light it moved up the southern sky, above the sombre moor whose summit undulated with the four curves of Dunkery's cloud-high crest. Seen from the Globe, the moor's outline against blue space was like the back of a monster petrified in the fires of earth's creation, showing black bristles singed almost to the roots; westwards the last paw-stroke of the dying monster had made claw-rips in the steep slope of Lucott Ridge.

The people on Dunkery Beacon, tiny as singed bristles, saw the horsemen waiting on the Globe a mile and a half below them. Black and scarlet specks moved by the farm, near one of the barns in which, pacing restlessly the clean straw, sitting moodily on haunches, throwing up heads and occasionally 'singing', the hounds were shut. Five couple of tufters had already gone with the huntsman and his whipper-in. Already they were approaching Stumberleap, and while the mournful 'singing' of a hound made the male starlings on the roof listen in order to imitate, the harbourer took the huntsman to the path where that morning the stag had entered the wood after his night's feeding. The tufters were old hounds, wise and trusty, and their job was to make Stumberleap break covert. The trees grew in the sides of the goyal, which diminished in depth and width until it ended half-way up the great slope, grown with heather and whortleberry, which stretched up to the crest. The watchers on the Globe saw a red speck on a grey horse cantering through the bracken along the farther edge of the wooded goyal. This was the whipper-in, who was to watch where the stag would run. Then they heard the horn faintly singing. So did the stag, where he lay in dread of the return of a fly whose wing-whirr he had just heard— a red-bearded bot-fly that was circling with almost inaudible flight above his head, ready to dart into his nostril, and squirt a drop of fluid containing tiny maggots, which would hook themselves to the skin before he could sneeze out their parent. When he heard the horn he pressed his chin on the ground, and waited. He knew what the horn meant.

A hound whimpered in the wood, but the stag did not move. He listened. The bot-fly settled on the long shaggy hairs of his upper neck, and washed its silvery face; for Stumberleap was not breathing. The stag heard the voice of the huntsman and the more abrupt cries of the whipper-in farther away. Then a hound threw its tongue, and jumped forward, followed by other tufters. Stumberleap jumped up and one of his top-points furrowed the bark of a branch above his thrown-up head. One hound made as if to run in upon him, but stopped, remembering.

When the huntsman came up he encouraged hounds with horn and voice, and the ten tongues clamoured about him. Stumberleap kicked at one, and drew from it a yelp of pain. The others pressed upon him, he sank slightly upon his haunches, quivered as he pressed all his strength into his muscles, and sprang over hounds and away among the trees. *Forrards!* cried the huntsman, and at the sound the harbourer, waiting at the edge of the wood, cantered to a place where it was possible to observe the going away.

Stumberleap, however, did not mean to leave the wood. With a clattering of horn against twigs and small branches he ran swiftly to the bed of the staggart. This male deer, four years old, bore only six points on his antlers. Since the previous winter he had followed Stumberleap wherever he went, feeding with him, soiling in the same pit, and lying near him by day. Now the old stag came to him and he sprang up, but would not leave his layer. Stumberleap reared up on his hind legs, then plunged down his head, and his antlers rattled against the antlers of the staggart. For a few seconds only they fought, and then the staggart, overmastered by his sire and terrified by the approaching clamour, turned and ran away. The tufters running the line of Stumberleap came to the bed, hesitated, and catching scent on the wind, pursued the staggart.

The huntsman heard him crashing through the bushes, and stood up in his stirrups to get a better view. He did not think that it was the stag, and a glance told him that hounds were pursuing the wrong deer. He called, and the whipper-in galloped along the ferny edge of the wood, crying the name of hounds as the wrist-power of his curling thong cracked off the lash into the air. They were called off, and the huntsman took them back to the stag. They roused him and drove him up the wood, but he returned again, and for more

than an hour he refused to leave. He was trying to wind another deer, in order to force it to run for him. He found none, and at last, followed everywhere and unable to shake off pursuit, he made for the bracken outside the wood. Short repeated notes of the horn twanged through the trees, and at this signal the whipper-in cantered forward to a place whence he could observe. Hardly had he checked when Stumberleap broke out of the wood, and in a lurching canter set off over the heather. On the crest he stopped, looked back for a moment, and was gone.

Without delay the huntsman returned to Stumberleap Farm, and the prolonged notes of his horn echoed in the goyals. At once the groups of men and horses around the stone buildings began to agitate. Farmers mounted their moor ponies, taller and sleeker hunters capered and whinnied, bowler-hatted grooms in black coats cross-braced with spare stirrup-leathers held bridles and threw up into saddles ladies in habits of brown, grey, and blue. Girths were finally inspected and reins laid flat on necks—"Steady, old mare, steady!" Pedestrians dodged dancing hoofs, and the farm wife looked on, bidding her children keep close to the threshold. Mournful singing of hounds changed to eager chorus as the rain-rotted wooden doors of the barn were pulled open, and the 'girt dogs' immediately pushed through. The pack trotted under ash-trees and the gold-blotched shade was transferred to heads and backs, tiger-like. A cowman, whose face, arms, and collarless neck were brown as old leather, said to the farmer's wife: "The girt old zstag of Zstumberleap Wood be zsparking now, a' reckons," which meant that the stag was away, fleet as the brilliant pinewood spark that shoots out of the hearth and vanishes.

The cowman was not entirely right. When the pack was laid on to the line from Stumberleap Wood the stag was three miles away, travelling easy and untroubled on his native moor, slanting up the goyal-sides with the ease of clouds in the blue sky over him, the halves of his slot spreading wide at each thrust.

4

He determined to cross the moor to the pool in the water he knew so well. He traversed a common where the wiry stems of ling and bell-heather grew with furze and bushes of whortleberry. Behind him was silence. He ran at the biggest furze bushes, gauging height and length and scarcely checking before rising up and over with the ease of tense strength, clearing the spikes with forelegs tucked back; so faultless his eye that not a spike was touched by foreslot polished and black. He hoped by the jumps to break the line of his scent. A light landing, and on again, over the common to a goyal, a deep narrow groove in whose turfy sides boulders were embedded, on which lizards and vipers were basking. His passing made them hide, and he went down until he came to the shady bottom where a small stream tumbled and bubbled over a clear brown stony bed. He lay in a pool, lapping the cold water, and then rolled, kicking his legs and tapping the stones with his antlers. He rejoiced in the soiling, then rose and shook himself, listened, and went in a slant up the coombeside. At the edge he met the sun again, and fled swiftly, while the blackcock crouched at the terse thuds of his feet. Sheep with curled horns stared at him, soon to be left far behind. The ground rose steadily to the line of the sky more than two miles away, but there was another coombe between, into which he descended. He ran in shallow water up to the stream's end among rushes and red-withering grass and rusty-filmed bog-water, where a curlew flapped up crying with bubbly sweetness, *cur-leek, cur-leek*. He never paused, but ran over tussocks of coarse grass and wild cotton plant to the summit, just under which was a bank of stone and earth six feet high. There was a slight break near a gate, but he avoided it, and choosing the highest part, slowed to a trot, tautened sinew and muscle, pressed his hind legs under him, and jumped. Miles away one of the watchers on the Beacon saw through glasses a speck rise out of darkness into a mist of light, and vanish again.

Stumberleap was now travelling over the high ground where in some years the winter snows lie beyond April, it is so high and cold under the sky. He turned south, and cantered down the long rough tawny slope until he came to where the sparse heather rooted itself in a soil of dry grains which once were rock. Its stems were blackened by the summer sun, and twisted with the struggle to hold the life-water. Whitish lumps of hard marble-like stone lay in

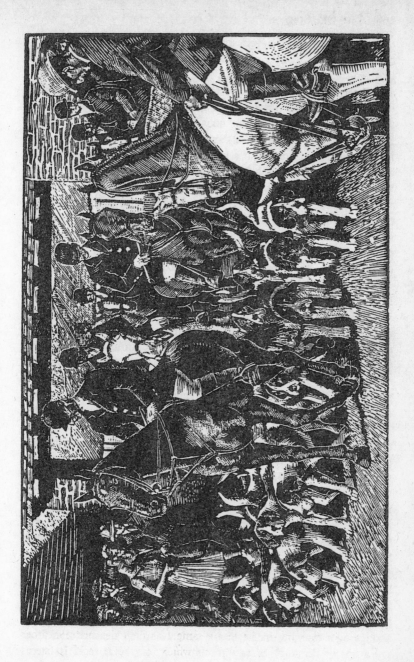

the sandy patches; the everlasting wind would one day make them dust. Across the treeless place he ran, over patches of scree shining like sun-sores, and going down into a goyal where grew thorns grey and hoary as though with hair, for everywhere the lichens clung to their branches. The thorns grew close, and Stumberleap knew it would be hard going for the hounds—whose feet were not horny like his own slot—and that the thorns would wound nose and pad. For half a mile he ran the bed of a stream, on the banks of which bracken grew under ash and holly-trees. Again he drank and soiled, afterwards lurching down the water while trout darted zigzag from his shape to hide in still caves under the brown boulders. Leaving the water before a footbridge made of a thrown tree, he climbed the steep side of the goyal again, bursting through bushes to delay pursuit, and crossed a further goyal. Loping up to high ground once more, he looked back before trotting on at slackening pace.

He disturbed a herd of deer which was resting with heads to leeward. Some of the hinds had calves with them, and when they saw Stumberleap they sprang out of the gorse and bracken and ran away, knowing that he was being hunted. Stumberleap tried to mingle with them, but was shunned. For half an hour he followed the herd, then turning away he made for the retreat where always before he had hid unseen. He ran in a loop of many miles. The sun of the afternoon was hotter in the goyals than at noon, and the air was thickening.

A motor coach was making a cloud of dust less than a quarter of a mile away as Stumberleap crossed a road. The driver stopped, and the people in it stood up and gazed. They decided to wait and watch the hunt go by, but after ten minutes, when no one appeared, the coach drove on. It had gone a mile along the narrow lumpy road when they met the huntsman, and by their timely information the pack was saved twelve miles of the loop, and laid on again where the stag had crossed the road. Huntsman and whip mounted second horses. The long-drawn file of hounds ran silently. Behind them a string of riders coiled over miles of moorland. Some horses had been bogged, others had gone lame, or lost their way, or were dead-beat. Sixteen and a half couple of hounds loped into the heather. They ran mute, without fatigue, without haste. And Stumberleap, topping a ridge by a tumulus, half a league distant as the blackcock flies (but a league by running) heard the thin echo of the horn. His heart pounded, his tongue dripped.

And the hounds ran on, mute and inevitable as the hours that passed. The sun of September became an orb of larger and duller gold rolling down to the sea, which could be seen grey and remote from the breezy hill. The wind had changed, and now was blowing from the south-west, from the headland dark blue beyond the remote sea. Above the headland, and travelling in ponderous silence towards the moor, was a black and ragged cloud, and others came after it, bringing the friendly deluge that washes scent from earth and air. Stumberleap knew that the south-west gale was coming. His sinews and muscles had lost their tension, no longer did he fly five-barred gates and banks. But he was nearing the refuge which had saved him many times before. He descended another goyal, and entering the stream at the bottom, drank and soiled, and rose refreshed. Upon the opposite bank he leapt, bounded along beside the water for a hundred yards, suddenly sprang sideways into the stream again, and ran on down. Trees grew here, and magpies scolded as he passed. For two miles he ran the bed of the stream, until he came to a pool near the ruined hut-circle of a primitive tribe. Into the pool he sank all but his head, and waited in the shadow of a rowan-tree that grew over it. So still was he that a pair of grey thrushes flew to the tree and began to swallow the scarlet berries. About fifty yards away a man was lying so still that neither thrushes nor stag knew he was there. The man never moved. The water made its music, the winged hum of flies sounded under the oaks, and all was quiet for a time.

5

From where I lay I could see the reflection of ripples gliding on his ears and antlers. For hours I had loitered in that sweet shady place, lying on my back and watching the flakes of sky between the oak leaves, waiting for Stumberleap. He had hidden there before. After a while, far above me on the sunlit height of the hill, I heard the thin gleaming note of the horn. The stag heard it also, for his head moved, and a ripple spread across the dark pool. Later the voice of either whip or huntsman floated down, and I knew that the hounds were coming to the stream. Minute after minute passed. A jay flew to drink, and his smoke-grey eye saw the larger brown eye of the stag; he screeched to other jays because the staring eye was unusual and might be dangerous. Two jays came at once, and perched on the lower branches of the rowan-tree, leaned forward and screeched. I showed myself. A jay saw me, warned his friends with a quicker note, and the three flew away. Again I lay down, and the minutes passed, until near me a voice said: *Hold up, you!* to a horse slipping on its haunches down the incline. Sound carries far in the coombes on a still day, and the wind was above the coombe. Hearing the voice, Stumberleap bent back his head, so that all of him was concealed by the water except his nose and the brow and bay points of his antlers. The ripples from the movement had hardly worn away, when a black-and-white hound named Deadlock ran down the bank with nose to ground, followed by other hounds. The pack had divided, and were casting down the banks to find where the stag had quit the water.

Last of all came a straggler, who nosed about among the dead bracken, and seeing me came and placed a thick white paw on my coat. He was a young hound, and I imagined by his callow look that it was his first season, possibly his first chase. I spoke to him, and he struck me with his paw, while his stern wagged like a flag. Again he struck my coat, so droll a look on his face that I knew he was begging for food. Where he had learnt to beg, in what household his puppyhood had been so pleasantly passed, I do not know. I gave him a biscuit, and after eating it he pressed his muzzle on my knee and gazed into my face with limpid eyes, the whites of which were of that tint of blue usually seen in the young eyes of the higher mammals, and most beautiful in children.

When the whipper-in trotted past on sweating mare I ordered the hound, in the usual phrase used to a rioter to 'get on to him', which was altogether a despicable betrayal of the creature's trust. The whip rated Credulous, and stung his hindquarters with his lash, so that the young hound yelped and ran away.

For half an hour Stumberleap lay in the pool, only his nose above water. Hounds had gone downstream a mile and a half; and two horsemen had followed after them. When it was quiet the jays flew back to the rowan-tree and peered at him, for his head was no longer held under the water. I heard them screaming as I returned upstream, and so did the huntsman, who was posted on the hill above. The harsh cries of the jays continued hardly without interval.

The huntsman rode down, and saw Stumberleap. He blew short notes on the horn, and I heard the whip's high voice recalling hounds. Good-bye, Stumberleap, I thought; you've had a very pleasant life, and all things have to die, and if it hadn't been for the hunt you

would probably have been shot or trapped before you were a month old. The pack pressed upon him, and Stumberleap swam downstream to shallower water where he might use his horns, but other hounds were there, baying in triumph and seeking to pull him down by the legs. Against the high bank, which the winter floods had carved, he stood at bay, the tragic head held high and ready to rip hound or man who dared go near. But no hound dared run within the slashing area of his antlers. I saw the huntsman loosen the long knife in its sheath under his left arm, before he walked into the water with two men, to wade across the stream. The current pressed against them, soaking red coat-tails and white breeches, and filling black top-boots. The two men hoped to get behind the stag with the looped thongs to hold back the head for the huntsman's quick stab in the throat; and the spirit of Stumberleap would roam the shining hills beyond the quest of stars.

Water dropped from the rough hairs of the stag's neck, but his eyes did not flinch. They strained down at the hounds. The two men felt their way step by step over the slippery stones to the opposite bank, fixing their sight on the eyes staring down. With loops ready to cast they edged nearer the stag, while the huntsman approached in front, to hold its gaze. Several hounds swam between him, and Guardsman bared his teeth to seize a knee. A couple named Darnel and Prudence swam with Guardsman, and then another couple. The whipper-in called them back, while the two men patiently climbed on hands and knees up the bank, one on either flank. They meant to twist their thongs round the top points which almost touched his back. Now they were off their knees, and crouching; step by step they moved, until one made a sudden grab for the beam. He shouted to the other man, who had grasped the other antler and was about to put all his weight on it when with a movement of great power and swiftness, Stumberleap plunged his head between his forefeet, hurling both men into the water. Without pausing he flung up his head, rose on hind legs, and struck down at the huntsman, missing him with his slot, but knocking him over with a glancing blow of his shoulder. Then he was across the stream, and through the oaks, the jays screeching at stag, hounds, and men.

Down the valley echoed the full-throated music of the pack. Hounds scrambled out of the water and pursued. Huntsman picked himself up, and his screaming cheer went after them. He floundered to the bank and remounted.

Another rider appeared, with battered hat, on a horse whose

flanks were covered with flattened froth. Wearily man and beast forded the stream and followed up the hill at a walk. Then came a riderless horse, that had rid itself of saddle. It was not sweating—its rider must have been lost hours ago. Should I ... ? The rolling music diminished as the pack reached the wooded crest and went on over the hill. The horse did not run from me. I patted its neck, felt its withers; it waited quietly. I scrambled on its back, pressed my calves in, and off we cantered, up through the trees, across a heathery common, past stone hut-circles around which wild cattle were staring, for Stumberleap had gone among them in order to destroy scent. The sunshine dulled, clouds covered the sun. The south-west wind made a running hiss in the heather and whortleberry bushes. After a mile he had gained a lead of five hundred yards, but after two miles he ran not so fast. Down another goyal side and a brake of furze; he sprang into its centre, causing a hind who had been drowsing there with her calf to press her chin on the ground. The stag lay down, and panted. With her nose the hind nuzzled the calf, which lay silently beside her. She heard hounds, and telling her little one to follow, she ran out of the brake and down the coombe. Deadlock led the pack (with the exception of the deserter Credulous) after the fresh scent, while the hind, who bore no protecting antlers on her smaller head, repeatedly glanced back at her pursuers. The legs of the calf went so fast during the first mile that very soon he grew tired, and the hind stopped, placed her head under his ribs, and tossed him several feet into a patch of bracken wherein he immediately settled himself and lay still. The hind ran on, and the pack followed her scent up the coombeside, passing the calf who held his breath and never moved. She ran swifter than Stumberleap had ever run, and returned in a wide circle to a point near the furze brake out of which he had turned her. Twice she ran to meet the hounds, swinging round and away again when they were almost upon her. Or she may have known that it was not yet the season of hind-hunting, and that the red-coat on horseback, viewing her, would protect her. She overran her starting point, describing roughly the figure 6 inverted, and seeing the huntsman, doubled back along the shank of the figure and stopped at the bushes where Stumberleap was resting. Then the huntsman knew that the stag was lying low in the brake. He and the whipper-in stopped hounds off the hind; Deadlock alone had to be lashed. Several times before a stag had been found in that covert. Hounds were capped into it. *Tally Ho! Yoi, yoi, then, pull'm down, yoi, yoi!*

Deadlock alone barred his way, and as the hound leapt at him, Stumberleap lowered his head and one of the uplashing points ripped him open, and with a howl the hound began to twist in a spiral, and lick his wound. Stumberleap leapt over him and crashed away through the bushes. The wind was rising, an ondrifting pallor made trees and hill-lines hard and distinct. Clouds massy and black were closing upon the moor, and before them wheeled a flock of gulls that had come from the sea. Their forlorn cries came sadly from the heights. Already the headland behind them was invisible, and half the sea of Bideford Bay was blurred in the driven grey slats of the storm. Hounds needed neither cap nor cheer nor horn. Up the goyal side went Stumberleap, not slanting up in his easy long-striding lurch, but straight up the steep side with a slow and heavy action. He staggered over the skyline, a long file of silent hounds pursuing him. Over the common from which the coast of Wales could be seen across the Severn Sea; over the road bridge under which lay the narrow gauge railway to Lynton, down the road for half a mile, over heath again and down a thread of water to a river. Hounds making the distance smaller, the hounds which had run nearly fifty miles and were still going. Moisture running from his eyes made them smaller; blood sometimes blackened his sight. His heart was throwing his legs about, the storm was still afar, although the clouds were above, and a great moaning was coming across the moor. A whirling greyness was between the four remaining horsemen and the pack, and the weary rider in the battered hat had been blown from the saddle by the gale which was hurling itself across Woolhanger.

Down the stony bed of the shallow river ran Stumberleap, past an inn, before which a group of people stood, watching the dark of the travelling storm, and the hard grey precipice-edges of the thunder clouds. A flash which stilled speech, a waiting for the reverberation, someone counting *one—two—three—four* . . a voice asking suddenly *What was that?* The baying of hounds! The man who was counting the seconds to calculate the distance of the lightning had counted *seven* when thunder broke upon them. Nearly two miles away. When the last stupendous tumbling of sound had ceased, they listened. They had motored to the meet on the Globe that morning, and the last they had seen of the chase were the tiny figures on horseback toiling up by the five clawmarks in the slope rising to Lucott moor. Yes, that was a hound! Six and a half hours from the lay on at Stumberleap Wood! Listen. Only a straying seagull wailing as the

wind hurled it overhead, while the gale tore at the trees on the hill, and then the storm crashed upon them—*boom*, the wind screamed around the Hunters Inn, and the rain instantly beat down the swirling dust cloud.

The sea was less than a mile away. The river flowed below a towering cleave, tameless and unclimbable, its sides grey and smooth with loose flakes of shale. All things in the cleave were hidden as the hounds of the storm bayed across the sky. The wind's thong whirled, the lash of the lightning cracked, the hills resounded with the hoofs of the thunder. Far behind on the moor the horsemen rode in a bluish mist of ground lightning which flicked and swished about them, seeming to curl in lashes of light about the huntsman's horn; icy thorns of driven rain pricked necks and ears; horses swung and swirled as though in a flood.

Fed by a hundred torrents, the river rose many feet, and when the storm ceased an hour later a muddy stain was spread in the sea at its mouth. Beyond the stain, swimming in the rolling waves, was Stumberleap, and after him, fifteen and a half couple of stag-hounds.

6

Just before dawn the bracken ceased to shake; the wind betook itself off the moor when a golden scarecrow rose in the east. Seeing the scarecrow the puppy-hound Credulous, who all night had been shivering miserably in the wet bracken because of the nearness of the hind, threw up his head and bayed. This mournful noise made more fearful the hind who, all the night, had been shivering miserably because the nearness of Credulous had prevented her from returning to her calf. The little creature had been quiet in the bracken ever since she had tossed him there. Credulous tottered towards the golden scarecrow, which was the waning moon, and blundered upon the calf, who was cold and frightened. Credulous was so very pleased to find himself no longer alone that he licked its soft head, whined to it, struck it with his paw, and curled himself up beside it. He slept for several hours. When he left the calf it was reluctantly to follow a human voice. So the hind had her calf again, and Credulous had breakfast with me in a farmhouse where Deadlock twitched in sleep because of the stitches in the skin of his belly.

A fortnight later he was well and back at kennels, among the remaining twenty-four couples. Fifteen days previously nearly thirty couple of hounds had lain at night on the straw-strewn zinc benches above the red-tiled floors, and eaten cold porridge and chopped horseflesh once a day. The pack that had chased the old stag of Stumberleap Wood never ate again in the kennel yard; indeed, when the carcasses of these hounds were eventually washed by the tides into Cardiff harbour, fish were eating them.

The Trapper's Mates

For generations the jackdaws that goister round the battlements of d'Essantville Castle have watched hounds leaving kennels four days a week in soft weather from November to April. The little viscounts of the house are blooded almost before they can walk; and they can ride long before they have learnt to talk (alternatively with the beautiful West Country dialect) the peculiar slang which, changing with every generation, is curiously called King's English; and they die before they learn to spell, but that is nothing to do with the way they hunt the fox. The first thing a future Master learns after his Nanny has buttoned the fawn-coloured cloth gaiters up his baby legs, and set him in the wicker basket-chair on the back of a Shetland pony, is that the fox is hunted *as a gentleman*.

The term is both actual and metaphorical. The fox is permitted to live during eight months of the year under the patronage of the great landowner. Any extravagances of taste which would bring an ordinary man before the magistrates—such as the killing of another man's hens—is tolerated. The fox's gentlemen friends will pay the cost, and he goes free. Like all gentlemen, however, he has his obligations. Certain things are expected of him. He must show sport when called upon by his Lordship's huntsman to do so any time during the daylight, Sundays and Christmas Day excepted, between the beginning of November and the end of March. If, after a long hard chase, he can run no more, but grows stiff, so that hounds catch him and break him up, he is a 'good fox'. If he skulks in woods, if he won't run, if he hides behind badgers in the deep earths, or otherwise tries to avoid his obligations, he is a 'bad fox'. But what can be said of a fox who behaved as though the hunt existed only for his own pleasure? A fox who, if a meet was fixed at Lashingcot Brake, would probably be there; as he attended the meets at Doves

178

Moor, Skilgate, Five Cross Ways, Smoky House, Hibbert's Folly, and Hanging Woman Spinney? That is what the bobtailed fox was wont to do. Naturally, he had a right to be in those places, and at any time, the hunt secretary told me, after my first day's hunting with the d'Essantville pack; but this fox had the damned impertinence to appear when another fox was being chased, and deliberately to draw hounds—unless the whipper-in happened to be well up with them—after himself. And when this fox had had, apparently, all the selfish enjoyment he wanted, he disappeared. Time after time he spoiled the huntin', declared the secretary, interfering with the hounds' legitimate desire for blood, leading them after himself, and vanishing at a certain field, just inside the western boundary of the d'Essantville country, called Cockabells. There was a League for the Prohibition of Cruel Huntin', Fishin' and Shootin', but what about one for the Prevention of Cruelty to Hounds, what?

I concluded that the secretary placed me among what he despised as the 'sentimentalizing public', and that his light humour was a kindness to one who had been publicly roared at by the Master.

You may imagine how this fox interested me as a writer. How could he know when the hounds were meeting at these places? I spoke to many people about him. To some followers, particularly among the young and unworldly-wise, I gathered that he was a creature of charm and mystery, whose continued existence was regarded with affection and delight; to others, he was a bore and a nuisance, to be gotten rid of as quickly as possible—in the only way in which a fox should die, it must be understood. The reader may be able to decide which of the two types possesses the better mind for the governing of our great people. And if this makes you snort (as his Lordship snorted at me) the snort is your answer, and you will be unable to enjoy the story of this extraordinary fox, whose early history I learned after the first time I hunted him, when I was reclining, as flat as I could get, in an arm-chair in the parlour of an inn called The Moon in the Mere.

It was my third glass of bullace wine, and it appeared to me then to be the funniest thing I had seen, the wrath and snort on the Master's face because I had said that surely the fox deserved his life after such a fine run. Outside the winter sky was dull, before me a fire of beech logs burned, warming the soles of my boots from which ruddy steam arose as the mud dried on spur and leather. Delightful to stretch one's legs after the chase, holding one's fourth glass of bullace wine, while 'baccy smoke strays past the nostrils from the bowl of the old briar pipe held loosely in teeth and resting on crumpled stock. Blackie in stall wisped and feeding, a ten-mile hack home in the dark, a bath, change, and food afterwards. Lolling in the chair I watched the sluggish ruby flame flickering in my bullace wine—I swear that the best sloe-gin in the West Country is made by the landlord of The Moon in the Mere.

2

I was about to call for a pint of ale when a man entered, and sat heavily on the settle, after bidding me good evening. Seeing my kit, he asked me if I had been out with his Lordship's hounds. I recognized him as a pig-farmer, a member of the Long White Lop-eared Pig Society, and a prize-winner at the last show. He was a big red-faced man, jovial like one of his clean beasts, of whom he was very fond and proud. I had noticed him during the run that morning, for he rode a piebald gelding seventeen hands high that carried him with magnificent ease. "And I'm no ladybird neither, am I?" And he confessed after a sorrowful tipping of the pewter pot, that he rode at 'twelve score'—two hundred and forty pounds. "Too much, too much," he sighed. "But they say a man takes after the things he has most to do with. Ah, well. Lordlord, another pint for me, and a pint for this gentleman."

"Yes, sir, I'll bring a lamp in a moment, gentlemen."

I asked the farmer if he knew why the fox had a tag instead of a brush. Perhaps he had been caught in a trap?

"No, it wasn't a trap," he said, leaning forward to stare at one of his boots. The girth of the leg seemed to depress him. He tapped it with the handle of his whip.

"Chopped by a hound?" I suggested, when I had allowed him enough time to consider his enormous calf.

"No, one of my boars bit it off when he was a cub. He disappeared afterwards."

The grandfather clock ticked on. The drinks were brought, and when we had proposed and drunk each other's health, I ventured to ask him more questions; and he told me the circumstances of the cub's birth, and its early life history; and the pictures which his facts made in my mind, I will try and make in words as now follow.

Bobtail's mother was the littlest vixen that ever leapt from shelf to shelf in the disused apple-cellar of George Cog, the gamekeeper. Indeed, she was so small that she was able to hide up the flue when they came to bag the foxes.

The country of the d'Essantville Hunt had many deep earths, both of badger and fox. When hounds drew the thick North Side wood there was never a screaming *Gone Away*! The foxes knew too much to break covert. They slunk about the wood, dozens of them. They preyed on the game birds in the coverts to such an extent that it was necessary to destroy them. Many were shot and trapped by George Cog, but more ran free; and the hunt agent made a bargain with the keeper, which was that he would pay the keeper half a guinea for every runnable fox or vixen dug out and handed over to him.

In turn the keeper made a bargain with Tom Cockerlegg, an elderly unmarried man, who earned his living by wiring and trapping rabbits in the winter, the right of which he bought from several farmers by working for them in the summer without wages. Tom Cockerlegg agreed to receive from the keeper five shillings for every uninjured fox or vixen brought to the apple cellar by the cottage in the wood.

There are hunting men in the d'Essantville country, and his Lordship is one of the most emphatic, who declare that a fox has no sense of fear, because its limited intelligence cannot formulate the idea of death: that the terror of annihilation, of ceasing to be, is unknown by animals. But there are many fears, and the greatest fear of a wild animal is when it is trapped or caged. One evening there were nine foxes in the confined darkness of the apple cellar. All night they sat on their haunches with restless sweeping of brushes, leaping upon the mildewed shelves, pacing the floor of trodden earth and cow dung. The smallest noise from outside quieted every movement. Ears were cocked, brushes stilled, breathing ceased, noses quivered. In one corner sat Fang-over-lip, a dog-fox with points of long upper canines showing over closed mouth. He was the most cunning fox in the West Country, the most experienced, and therefore he felt fear more than the others.

When footfalls of men sounded afar, he sprang up and leapt on the lowest shelf. A key was put into the padlock, and turned. The lock was lifted off the staple, the door opened a few inches, and the keeper looked in.

The rank taint of warm foxes, like hops drying in an outhouse, made him spit. Behind him stood Tom Cockerlegg, the trapper, with lantern, sacks, string, and thorning gloves. Cockerlegg spoke to a grey sheepdog, his constant companion. "Lie down, you." She sat down outside, obediently. Both men entered, and shut the door. The eye-pupils of the foxes were pale green slits glowing in the lantern light. Lips writhed back from teeth in silent snarls. They waited. Neither of the men lost his stolidity. While George Cog held the lantern and a sack Tom Cockerlegg grasped the brush of the nearest fox. It struggled and twisted and kicked while it was being pushed and shaken into the sack, which was tied up.

The keeper missed the ninth fox, and peering with the lantern he saw the white tag of her brush up the flue. She had scrambled there in terror. He pulled the brush, but could not shift her. He felt for her leg, lifted the pad off the stonework, and jerked. She yelped, and fell on the floor, trying to bite and lick the pain in the joint which was dislocated. Later in the morning the kennelman drove up with a cart, and she was slung up with the others and taken a journey made painful with jolts. The journey ended at the kennels, where several hounds were singing while they waited for the two whippers-in who exercised them in the summer. Soon the corn would be cut in the fields, and woodland cub-hunting begin. The little vixen was only a cub, and she was spared a worry in the dewy morning, for Charlie Tarr gave her to the pig-farmer, who bound and bathed the injured limb, and made it sound again. He tended her with regular care and after a few weeks she grew tame and friendly, answering to the name of Judy. She slept at night in the garden, wearing a dog-collar to which a chain was hooked. During the day he unfastened the chain, and she used to go into the house and curl up by the fire. Like many countrymen, the farmer rarely listened to the songs of birds wild in their native air, but the twitters of a goldfinch, caught and caged, his property, gave him pleasure. He had one in his sitting-room, and, during the many hours that Judy played before the fire, or leapt upon his lap, the bird was filled with terror. The vixen watched it continually, and people coming to see him on business or in friendship were usually treated to the sight of the finch falling off its perch in a temporary paralysis of fright—the sweetest singers are always the most nervous.

It was a green winter that year, and one night in January, as he was getting into bed, the breeder of long white lop-eared pigs heard Judy hooting. The cry was unmistakable. Three barks, higher in tone than a terrier's: sharper, shorter, and linked. He listened again, but it was not repeated, and soon he fell asleep. The next night was lit by the moon, and he heard Judy screaming again. For some minutes he watched at the window, for he had heard the answer of a dog-fox. He saw nothing. The next morning he moved the kennel nearer the house, and in the moonlight of the third night a lean grey thing stole down the orchard, and disappeared in the black shadow of an apple tree. This was Fang-over-lip, who sat there a long time. He moved sufficiently to keep the shadow always upon himself. He sat there so long that the farmer grew tired of watching, and went to bed.

Fang-over-lip came soon after owl-light the next night, but he did not linger in any shadows, although the nearness of the house made him uneasy. As he crept nearer his nose sought the smells of danger. He sat outside Judy's kennel, but she would not come out. She lay down in the straw of the kennel, watching him. He suddenly fled, alarmed by the sight of the farmer moving at the window. He must have returned again, for the next morning when the farmer took her a bowl of food, he found plover's feathers in the kennel. Judy slept all that day; and the goldfinch twittered to the birds seen through the window. Early the next night Judy was outside the kennel, and calling Fang-over-lip. The farmer did not see him return, but in the morning he found one of his own hen's feet in the kennel.

"The cheek of it! Would you believe it, sir, but that fox had left my fowls alone until the night of his final visit!"

Clicketting time was long past when the daffodils peered in their beauty from the grass under the apple-trees. When the first white wild violets bloomed in the hedge, the farmer took a ferreting spade and dug a hole in the gravel pit in the meadow, and Judy scratched it deeper. One day he took off her dog-collar, patted her affectionately, and turned her loose. Two days afterwards she scraped at the kitchen door, and jumped up at him licking his hand. He knew that she was asking for food, and gave her a basin of porridge, with cream in it, which she ate hungrily. A cooked rabbit was next given her, she cracked it up, gave him a sly look, and with a sweep of her brush ran back to her cubs in the gravel pit.

Regularly she came for food, and for the first fortnight she returned after a meal. Then she began to loiter and even to curl herself by the fire, watching the goldfinch that could not accustom itself to her bright hard eyes. After the third week she seemed inclined to spend all day away from the cubs, and the farmer had to put her out of doors, bidding her return and nourish them. And one morning while she was eating he saw five cubs sitting in the long grass below the bank, where nettles grew over the wilted white violets. They were dark brown and furry, and their blue eyes peered at their mother. The farmer went slowly to them, and four turned into the nettles and hid themselves. One remained, and tried to bite the hand that picked it up. It was carried to the scullery and given bread and milk, it began to bite that instead of a hand.

Again the next morning the five cubs sat in a row before the nettles, wondering where their mother had gone. When the bold cub saw the farmer, it ran unsteadily to him, and was fed on porridge. On the third morning while the mother and cub were eating and the pig-farmer was inside the house, a lumbering white animal trotted round the corner of the wall, so frightening Judy that she made off. The alarming animal was a boar, and at the scent of fox it snorted angrily. The cub went into a rabbit hole underneath a holly tree, but the boar bit the bone of his tail as he scrambled down. When the farmer returned the pig was goaded to its sty. Judy did not return that day, and when the next morning she did not come for her breakfast the farmer went to the gravel pit and dug out the earth. "It was empty, sir."

3

My companion in the fire-comforted parlour of The Moon in the Mere had aroused my curiosity about the disappearance of the vixen when the door opened and a hand came into the room. Then a squeaky voice begged his honour's pardon, and the hand was withdrawn. I saw a single eye beyond it, in the gloom, staring straight like an owl's eye. After a moment the hand returned, an earthy hand, knobbed and thick. The finger-nail of the index finger was half an inch longer than the others, a repulsive pale length of chipped horn. Then came a felt hat, the band of which was rotted to tatters, and a face. The shaggy hair, the thick eyebrows and the tangled moustache were like autumn bracken. The man wore a celluloid collar, worn and flaked, but I could see that when new it had been a striped affair of black and white and red lines. The man peered about until the wandering eyes fixed on me, then he squeaked again: "I beg your honour's pardon." I hastened to tell him that we were not having a private talk, and begged him to come by the hearth. He sat on the settle, and fingered a short clay pipe. His coat was faded to the hues of bark and earth and lichen, so were his trousers. After a wondering scrutiny of my form in the chair he said:

"I beg your honour to excuse me, but have you had good sport, your honour?"

"Your friend the bobtailed fox, Tom," replied the farmer. Brackenbrows scowled.

"Wait till I catch that there beggar," he squeaked, staring at the ashes in his pipe bowl. "I'll give he a knock on the head, won't I now?"

He tried to light the ashes in his pipe, and shook his head when the match went out. Promptly he took the tobacco pouch I offered him. Perhaps he was waiting for someone, for he pulled out a large brass watch from his pocket, levered open the back with the nail, and continued to fill his pipe while holding the watch in the same hand.

"This be Tom Cockerlegg," explained the pig-farmer. "He doesn't seem over fond of Bobtail. For why," he added with a chuckle, "I can't imagine."

It was a curious sight, an angry and violent expression in the large, hairy weather-roughed face of the trapper contrasted with the puling pipe of the squeaky voice. He stared at me while he declared that Bobtail followed him as he used his long net on windy moonlit nights, less than two hundred yards away. He would hear the cry of a caught rabbit, but before Bess or he could get there, the "varx would have'n out of the net."

"Bess here, her baint no good to catch'n," squeaked the wild man of the rabbit buries, pointing with the horrible nail of his lumpy forefinger. How many tons of earth and iron had the trapper handled? "Her's runned after un many times."

"Bobtail's too fast without a brush," said the massive member of the Long White Lop-eared Pig Society.

"Darnee, if Bess baint no good, they varx dogs baint no good neither!" retorted Cockerlegg. He began to laugh, an absurd and feeble cackling, while he continued to fill his pipe. It seemed to take him a long time. He saw me looking at it, and returned the pouch promptly. It was half empty, and it had been full. The farmer winked at me, and said:

"What be time, Tom Cockerlegg?"

"It baint closing time yet, midear," replied Tom, and fixed his owlish eyes on my pint pot.

"Will you have a drink?" I asked, when the watch had gone back into its pocket.

"Thank you, your honour," he replied immediately, and knocked loudly on the table for the landlord, who came, and returned with a quart of beer, which Tom had ordered almost before the door was opened.

Bess the sheepdog was a beautiful animal. She had long woolly grey hair, a noble head with contemplative eyes. She leaned against the trapper's legs, and he pushed her away with a hobnailed boot. I patted my knee, but she would not come to me, preferring to sit by the foot that had spurned her. She regarded her master's face with grave and watchful patience.

I wanted to hear what had become of the cub under the holly tree.

"You were saying just now that the earth in the gravel pit was deserted after the scare Judy had from the boar? Did she ever come back for food?"

The pig-farmer shook his head.

"What happened to the cubs?"

"They must have died without the mother. Two days afterwards she was found in a gin set by a rat-run in a cornfield. Died of lock-jaw. Tom found her, and brought her to me. I've got her stuffed in a glass case: we put it on a table opposite the goldfinch. And you'll hardly believe this, but it's as true as I'm sitting here. The constant sight of a stuffed fox killed my singing bird. It died of fright, did that bird. I was very fond of it, too, as I'd had it from the nest. You'd hardly believe it, eh?"

I said something, but not what I thought. These good country folk, unimaginative . . . sad little sun-singer beating the bars.

Presently I asked: "Then is Bobtail the cub grown up, the cub that had hidden under the holly tree?"

"Ah, now you're asking me one. You see, not knowing that Judy was dead, I didn't bother to dig it out, thinking that she would call it out in the evening. Perhaps she did call it out, and with the others went on the prowl—but I don't know, they were too small. Tiny creatures, like kittens, they were."

"Barbt'l baint much like a kitten to-day!" said the trapper in squeaking fury. "Wait till I clitch on to he!"

That ten-mile hack home awaited me. I arose, and stretched my legs. Cockerlegg was peering at me through the dry ferns of his eyebrows as though I were a being far superior to his humble self.

But he was only waiting to borrow my lighted match.

In the stable, Blackie, the soft-mouthed, greeted me with a whinney, and the groom unstrapped the rug. We set out for home. There were stars shining in the water of the ditches, and the wind passed in the darkness.

4

Three days afterwards I walked and trotted Blackie to the meet at Smoky House, a thatched inn at the joining of three roads. Charlie Tarr the huntsman was going to draw Scythe Wood. His Lordship was heard to exclaim to a friend that it *ought* to be a good scenting day, but of course, one could never tell. The keen blue eye of the Master had noted that no hound had rolled on the wayside grass, or bitten a blade. No gossamer floated on the air, and no spider webs were yet spun on the hedges. The paving stones of the courtyard had shown sweat that morning, the air was clear and light, and, most significant of all, hounds had smelled strongly as they trotted out of kennels. There was no wind.

Nimrod was out to-day, the pad of his near fore-paw healed. It had been cut by a broken glass bottle on Pippacott Common. He was the best hound in the country. His puppies were famous in the Quorn and the Pytchley, the V.W.H. and the Duke of Beaufort's. An American sportsman had offered five thousand dollars for him, but no money would buy Nimrod. His head was light and dignified, he had a long, clean neck, without looseness or throatiness, his ears were set low and close to the head. His muscular back was straight and wide, his chest was deep, his shoulders long and sloping, his forelegs white and straight as mushroom stalks, his feet round and cat-like. Strong and straight hocks for tireless running, a stern carried gaily upwards, and a tongue true as its music. Three young hounds were licking his head as he stood on the triangle of sward before the inn, watching the eyes of the huntsman.

While I was looking at the faces above the gleaming coats of horses around me, I heard a squeaky voice saying: "Good morning, your Lordship's honour, and I hope you'm very well, midear." Turning round, I saw Tom Cockerlegg grab his tattered hat from off his head, and with the horny finger touch his brow to the Master above him.

"Mornin', Tam, mornin'," replied the Master, as he fingered his bristly moustache. He was a short fierce tubby little man, and his intimate friends called him 'Seal'.

The horny finger beckoned. The Master leant over.

"If your Lordship's honour will excuse me, but please to listen, my Lord, there be a turrible lively varx (fox) in Smoky Wood, a monster girt varx I can't abear, for it steals all my rabbuts, my Lord, and I were so near to un last dimmity (twilight) I could have dapped un on the head, surenuff, if your Lordship's honour will excuse me telling of ee."

"Us'll r-r-roll'n over for ee, one day!" cried the Seal on horse-back, in a hearty voice. "Don't ee worry, midear."

Tom had taken his Lordship birdnesting when he was a boy, and they were good friends. Then the trapper beckoned, the Master leaned down again, and Tom whispered: "Yurr, you! Yurr! Has your Lordship's honour a bit o' baccy? I haven't had a smoke for a week and more. Too poor, my Lord, 'tis Bobtail, my Lord, taking all my rabbuts."

Out came the pipe, and the big brass watch. Now I knew why the fingernail was kept so long. Cunningly it levered open the back of the watch; and his Lordship's tobacco, the expensive John Cotton, was pushed and rammed with amazing speed into the watch, which was empty of works, and but a hollow box.

"Thank ee, my Lord, thank ee, midear," said Tom, giving back the oilskin pouch to the Master, and looking at the face of the watch. "It be half-past ten o'clock a'ready, my Lord!" and he hurried away to the van of the rabbit agent, which was collecting rabbits from farm and cottage to take them to the station.

Huntsman Charlie blew a note on his horn. Whipper-in called names of hounds. We moved off down one of the roads, and up a lane.

"Follow me," said the pig-farmer.

5

Just before eleven o'clock Nimrod entered Scythe Wood at the north-eastern end, followed by Thunderer, Doomsday, Firefly, Solway, Duchess, and Guardsman. The pig-farmer and I waited behind a cattle shed from where we could observe a gap in the western point of the Scythe, by a lightning-burned stump of an ash-tree. "The best place," he said. "If a fox is at home, he'll leave at this end. We must keep pretty quiet."

"Do you think Bobtail is here?" I asked.

"Tom Cockerlegg says he saw him last night, coming out."

I had to soothe Blackie, for the cries of huntsman and whip could be heard faintly in the wood. Immediately the pigeons flew out of the oaks. We waited. The last pigeon had clattered out and the wood had been silent for about a minute, when a jay started to scream in the querulous and sustained manner which I recognized as the call to other birds when man is not the enemy. My companion looked at me significantly. "Quiet, Blackie, quiet," I whispered, pulling the ears of the restless horse. A family of long-tailed tits flitted down the hedge, hanging upside down to search the bud coverings for insects, and calling to each other with tiny cries which made a gossamer-link of sound in the winter morning. The jay kept up its scolding. Was a fox on his pads? A dead stick snapped in the woods, and I could hear a hound going through the undergrowth.

I whispered, "Have you any idea how the fox seems to know where hounds will meet?"

He shrugged his shoulders, meaning that he didn't know.

"Shsh!" he warned.

A hound whimpered in the wood. A blackbird scuttled away down the hedge, and dived into the leafy ditch.

"That was Nimrod speaking. Hark!"

Other hounds were whimpering.

"That's Bobtail. I know the line he'll take to get to Cockabells. He'll run the bottoms, where it's thick stuff, and boggy, and take a sweep round through Pippacott Wood, and come out by Turbeville Common. You follow me."

He whispered this rapidly. Nimrod spoke again.

"Don't make a sound. He'll be out and away in a flash."

Blackie stood still. Sometimes his withers shivered. He who had been striving to shake the bits from his mouth, and half-playfully to rid himself of the irksome girths, saddle, and, perhaps, the two-legged encumbrance astride his back, now was taut from ears to cannons. A centaur stood under the hazels. Nimrod threw his tongue, the horn sang in the trees, the thrilling clamour of a find sent the blood faster. I felt light as the sunlight.

A brown leaf moved on the bank, and I was looking into the

mask of a fox eight feet away from me. It looked boldly at me without the least fear, and I had the extraordinary thought that the
mind behind the glance was equal with my own. But whereas my
knees trembled with excitement, the fox was calm, and a little
amused. Then it turned to look over its shoulder and listen to the
hounds. I saw its eyes a moment later and they were laughing.
Yes, as a dog laughs in play with its master. The yellow eyes laughed,
and blinked; and then it was gone, but not before I had time to
notice that a leather collar, with brass studs on it, was fastened round
its neck.

There was no time to wonder. The pig-farmer let out a series
of bellowing tallies. Hound music filled the wood. Then, among
the trees, *Ton-ton-ton-tavern, Ton-ton-ton-tavern, Ton-ton-ton-ton-
ton-ton-tavern!* The hill on our left turned back a faint echo of the
Gone Away. Horsemen waiting on the higher ground moved down at a
canter. The pack broke through the undergrowth, and streamed over
the bank by the burnt ash, led by Nimrod. He jumped from the
bank, his larger pads slurring the track of Bobtail. Blackie reared
and neighed as I held him back. Hounds dropped over the bank.
Blackie danced, pranced, and fought for his head. "Quiet, Blackie,
quiet! Let hounds go first."

When the last hound had left the wood, Charlie came over, his
chestnut climbing like a cat and changing feet as it jumped. "It's
Bobtail!" yelled the farmer, and added the weight of his "Yoi, yoi,
on little dogs", to the marvellous and screaming cheer of Charlie
Tarr. Blackie shot forward at a gallop—too much spirit for your
heart, my dear, you must be held at a canter. He shook his head,
the clods flew behind us, the hounds streamed before us, and two
fields away went Bobtail. Hounds ran like a string of black and
brown and white beads which had broken, but not scattered.

6

Bobtail leapt up the farther bank as Nimrod leapt down into the
stubble of the field called Broadwall. He was going at nearly his
fastest pace, but he did not fear. As he ran, many smells crossed his
way. The smell of flat-poll cabbages, whose outer leaves were decaying, lay like an air-covering all around the field. Mingled in this still
layer were the smells of rats, of tar, and of men. Squeezing under a

gate he came into a field where two men were putting down tar into the holes of rats. A terrier was watching the hole, with bent head. Bobtail ran quietly down the hedge, and then up, through a row of flat-polls a few yards south of the ratters. As he passed them they heard the hounds, and stood upright. Bobtail got to the opposite hedge without being seen, and he gained a field while the pace slackened among the cabbages, for the hounds were confused by the smell of tar, and, possibly, by the yapping of the terrier struggling in the arms of her master. Nimrod took them on, and down the next field to the impassable bottom, where among thorns, bracken, brambles, and marsh rushes, we could not follow.

I followed the pig-farmer and the huntsman. We went through gates and down lanes and over meadows, splashing through watery gaps which the hooves of the field far behind would soon beat into yellow mud. We crossed the main road, and cantered across several fields, coming to a small track green with sward in a rough heathland of gorse and heather. This was an old Roman road, which was used now only by carters. Here we waited, and dismounted in order to save our horses as much as possible for what was coming.

The beams of the sun were not yet warm enough to dry the dew from the sere heads of the carline thistles, and scent would be thick for their following. I was lighting a cigarette when the tongueing of the pack floated up from below the common. Almost immediately I saw Bobtail again. He was racing across a stubble field about half a mile away. The huntsman vaulted into the saddle, and was galloping downhill before I could get my left foot into the iron. Blackie stamped and snorted, and was off at a canter and then a gallop while I was lying across his back. Somehow I got my seat, and with flying irons we thudded down the swarded track. A brook ran over stones at the bottom, and this we hurtled over, and turned right-handed round a big awthorn that clawed face, hat, boots, and coat.

Other riders appeared over the brow of the common, and got between the pig-farmer and myself. The mud of their hooves fell on my face. The pack was running without a straggler—as Charlie said afterwards, you could almost have laid a rug over them as they crossed a root-field, and covered all except the muzzle of Nimrod and the flag of Juniper. They swam the wimpling waters of the Fawley brook, and crashed through a bottom and over a field where a white Minorca was kicking a crazy dance beside its head. (Another claim for the Hunt agent.) Bobtail ran the lane for six hundred yards, past a cottage where a woman was hanging out washing on the hedge, along a ditch and through a row of elms, and so to the soft brown earth of the Big Wheatfield. As he raced up the southern hedge a fox rose and slunk away from his bed in the centre; and in the northern hedge he sat and watched the hunt go by; and when the last horseman had gone he stole back to his bed, and slept, for he was Fang-over-lip.

Bobtail ran on, Nimrod three hundred yards behind him, and Juniper three hundred and eighty. Five of us galloping across Hangman's Marsh half a mile behind—huntsman, whip, pig-farmer, a girl riding astride, and I—and the Master cantering on the verge of the high road over and below the ridge a mile behind, at the head of a straggling cavalcade of fifty men and women.

It was a glorious chase. Charlie Tarr led, then the pig-farmer, then the whipper-in, the girl, and I came last. Through a gate, over more stubble, driving up three partridges with a whirr of wings into the air. A great bullfinch; I rammed my hat down on my ears. Steady, Black, old boy! Two were over, and then the whip's chestnut refused.

He forced its head round, swung back again, banged his heels into its muddy flanks; it turned away, he cried curtly, held its head straight, and clapped his boots against its flanks. I saw its muscles ridge and tighten. The man held its head straight to the tall black ragged hedge, it gathered itself together, its forelegs threw themselves up, it seemed to hang still, then crash; he was through. The hound-music was far away. Then the girl was over—her horse down on its knees. It stumbled, recovered, blundered. Somehow she pulled up its head, and cantered away over the stubble. It was my turn. Give Blackie his head, I thought hotly, he knows his job and needs no spur. A tremendous bullfinch, dark and thick and thorny, and I'm tall, and that branch of the crab-apple tree will smack my forehead, and perhaps catch my chin, and that will be the end of me, unless I'm dragged a mile or so first. Lord, I'm a funk. He who hesitates at the take-off is assuredly lost! Grip with the calves, tuck the toes in, and give Blackie his head. 'Ware that branch! Up! Reins across withers, throw yourself on his neck . . . My eyes closed themselves, before the sudden-big thorns—crash, rip bang! My topper was gone, but not my neck, thank God, and Blackie was sinking to his knees, so very gently, it seemed, and the grass rose slowly as I curled off his neck and rolled clear. A nice toss. Dear old Blackieboy, I think

I cried, as I picked myself up, and took the iron off my boot. Quaking and hot and happy, I fixed the strap along the safety-bar under the saddle-flap, hopped round on my right toes with my left leg up, and foot through iron, muttering, "Stand, you swine, stand!" to the excited and high-stepping hunter. He stood still for a moment, I threw myself across the saddle, and he hurled himself round and was off at a gallop. I had to shake free my left foot while leaning on the seat of the saddle, while nearer and nearer the ditch and low whitethorn hedge of the next field approached. The easy and smooth motion of the gallop enabled me to throw my leg over and get my seat just before we rose in the air and the loose swinging irons clanged dully against my boots. On, and on! I was only one field behind Charlie's holly-red coat. Blackie's heart and wind were splendid, and I shouted a sort of song to the beat of his hoofs. Lord, I was happy. Soon the ground sloped up, and over another hedge was Luckett's field, rising to the skyline. In this expanse of harrowed clods and flints stood an object wearing a broken bowler, a ragged tarpaulin, and split trousers. It barred the fox's way with open arms. Or it may have been welcoming him. It had a whitey-green face fixed in a ghastly grin. A clay pipe was in its mouth. Its head was sprouting through the crown of its hat in a thick yellow green curl. Its only companion hung upside down beside it, tied by a leg to a stick. Like itself, this companion was eyeless. It was a dead rook, beside a scarecrow. As Bobtail fled past, he disturbed three dying flies which had been sitting for warmth on the paper-white face of the shot bird. Straight the fox ran, through Crow-starvers Spinney on the ridge, and down the right-of-way to a field called Chowles Park. Over another field, in view of a cottage out of which ran half a dozen children.

'Marm! Marm!" one was still shouting to his mother as I passed. "Yurr be the varx-dogs! Come yurr, marm, come yurr to once, marm!"

Mother had been salting-in half a pig, and she hurried to the threshold with salt on her raw hands and dragging Parson's wife's old brogue shoes on her smaller feet. She faded out of the tail of my eye. I could see the fox running along a hedge three fields in front. About two hundred yards separated Nimrod's nose and Bob-tail's tag. Five and a half miles behind was Scythe Wood, where twenty-three minutes previously the notes of the Gone Away had glanced among the trees. Bobtail was about half a mile from Cocka-bells. Over a bank and into a by-lane, a scramble up another bank,

and down into Latten's Close, a grazing field. Nice going. Quarter
of a mile more, and then the chase would end. I urged Blackie on,
hoping to be near enough to see where the fox concealed himself.
I saw him nip over a bank, a tiny brownish object that disappeared
at once.

The pack poured over a few moments later.

There was one more field. Nimrod threw his tongue and led them
on, for he knew that unless he caught Bobtail in the next field, he
would lose him. The hound's sense of smell was keener than his
sight, and by this sense alone had he pursued Bobtail, covering the
level ground at twenty miles an hour, tongue flacking and flakes of
froth flying. Behind him thirty-five throats made a blended har-
mony as of bells in a tower brought down off their stays together.
Bobtail leapt between two elms on the last bank, and dropped down.
Twenty seconds later Nimrod followed, and after came Nemesis and
Starlight, Solway and Thunderer, Firefly, Neptune, and the milk-
white Chloe. They ran about fifty yards into the field called Cockabells, and hesitated, sniffing the air. Some ran with noses to the
ground, some straggled. Nimrod roved round the field, mute and
eager, but not with the stride of two minutes before. He ran as in
a maze. There was a certain area of the field, roughly defined by the
reluctance of all hounds to enter it, which seemed to hold confusion.
And then a hoarse long screeching cry was heard over the sunken
lane, and the huntsman cantering over Latten's Close saw a ragged
dark hat held by a great earthy paw waved above the plashed ash-
sapling hedge.

"Oi-oo-aa-aa-yaa-yaaoiegh!"

The effort must have torn the throat strings out of the viewer's
throat. The huntsman's horn spoke to the hounds. Up went their
feathery sterns. Crack! crack! the lash of Whip's thong a few
moments later. The pig-farmer, his big red face streaked with mud-
splashes running down to his chin in sweat, hooked the iron gate-
fastener off its staple with the stag's horn handle of his whip and
swung open the five-bars for the pack to pass. Led by huntsmen,
they trotted down the sunken lane, to where Tom Cockerlegg was
standing, ragged hat on ragged head. He was grinning. His grey
sheepdog sat on a sack high up the bank. He held a sieve in one
hand, for he was about to scatter earth over a gin he had tilled at
the opening of a rabbit bury. Big leather pads, like the armour of a
gigantic brown beetle, were tied round his knees; the bones of which
would have rotted seasons before if he had not always worn them.

"Have ee got 'n?" he asked.

"Which way did'n go, Tam?" cried the huntsman, abruptly.

"Oo, I can't say for sure, Charlie. I seed un rinning in Cockabells, and t'was alla'could do to hold Bess back from sparking after un. But they varx dogs don't welcome shipdogs (sheepdogs), and so a'gave Bess a dapp, and told'n tu lie down." A look of earnestness came into his face as he asked: "Have ee killed Bobtail at last, Charlie?"

"If ee didden view un, then why the devil did ee holle', ye old vule (fool), you?" shouted Charlie, in a rage, wheeling round his horse.

"Woll, Charlie, woll," said the trapper, blinking like a bewildered owl. "I didden see no huntsman and I were just sparking on the varx dogs, Charlie!"

7

Charlie muttered something about the trapper being mazed as a vuz-peg. Hounds were taken back to the field. Here stood one tree, the Icicle Oak, a sapless ruin many centuries old, hollow, and half its bark shed. It stood in the centre of the area of confusion. Its five remaining branches, all dead, stretched to the sky like the charred wrists and hand of a giant thrust up through the turf. It had not dropped an acorn for a hundred years. Again Nimrod cast round the field, followed by the bewildered and listless pack. The bobtailed fox had vanished, exactly as in other years.

The four long-drawn notes of the recall, a melancholy sound, for it meant no more excitement at bullfinches and over banks, floated out of Charlie's horn. The pressure against the corner of his mouth, where the mouthpiece was held, wrinkled his forehead, on which three thorn-rips showed red. The whip's voice calling hounds could be heard across the field in the air so still that not one woodpecker's tinder fragment, hanging on spider-thread from the dry bark, shook or spun.

The hounds sat down, rolled, licked veteran heads, growled, and yawned. In twos and threes the field cantered up on sweating horses. The Master had taken a toss in the Fawley Brook, and was covered with weed. He and the rest of the field had thought that a fox out of Scythe Wood would run another direction. Under the Icicle

Oak many dismounted, handing reins to grooms, while sandwich boxes were opened, and saddle flasks taken out of leather cases.

I heard the huntsman telling the Master and Secretary about the collar round the neck of the fox. "Wha?" barked the Seal immediately, and enquired the name of the man who had seen it. Charlie said my name. His Lordship exclaimed: "Pooh, that writin' fellar! He will be shakin' hands with the fox next, or writing that he has. Same thing, perhaps!"

Then he realized that I was near. He laughed, and said in a hearty bantering voice: "It's time you got a pair of spectacles, young fellar! Have some port."

I thanked him, and took the long parsnip-shaped glass flask. As I was turning the silver stopper, I watched the dismounted huntsman kicking with the toe of his boot one of the big yellow fungi that grew in the hollow of the oak, near its base. For years the tough growths had clung there, each as big as a saddle, but thicker. As I looked idly at Charlie's cap, something glinted in the weak winter sunlight. A drop of moisture fell on his boot, and ran a couple of inches down the black leather of the calf, where the stirrup leather had worn a smooth mark. Charlie sniffed, and drew his hand across his nose. But the drop had not fallen from it, for when I held back my head and tipped the flask between my teeth, I saw the head of the fox looking out of a hole near the top of the tree. I choked over my mouthful of wine, and kept my eyes on the ground, dreading to hear the shout that must surely follow my stupid gasp and stare. Then I realized I was pouring away the Master's wine, and hastily righted the flask, secured the stopper, and returned it with thanks. A moment later I realized that no one had noticed anything about me. I moved away, two feelings strong in me—elation at the honour of being invited to drink from the Master's flask, and dread at the thought of discovery, with immediate death, for Bobtail.

About twenty yards from the tree I stopped, and slowly lifted my gaze to where he was sitting, calm and at ease. He seemed to have found a natural seat within the tree, from where he could watch the men and women below him. His ears were cocked, as though listening to what was being said. He looked from one face to another, and at the hounds. His tongue hung over his teeth but there was too much noise—the jingle of bits, voices, laughter, caw of rooks overhead—for his panting to be heard.

While I was covertly watching him, I realized that someone was

trying to persuade the huntsman to try a terrier at the base of the hollow tree. It was the girl who had ridden before me during the run. Charlie grinned, and shook his head: "He baint there, Miss." I walked near to hear exactly what would be said when the famous, or infamous, Bobtail was caught at last. But why had not Charlie thought of the tree before? It was an obvious place, and had occurred to me the first time I saw it.

"Yurr, Vic!" said the huntsman, cracking second finger and thumb for the terrier, which had been carried during the chase in a leather satchel slung on a groom's chest.

Hounds sometimes walked up to the tree, to leave it again with expressions of disgust on their faces that all who are accustomed to any dogs recognize at once. The older hounds sat about thirty yards away, by the whipper-in, the terrier with him. Victor ran to Charlie Tarr. The terrier was patted, spoken to in a fierce low blood-thirsty tone, held by the ribs, and its nose shoved into the hole. Immediately it refused. Charlie called it back. It refused again, and ran away.

"No varx there, Miss!" laughed Charlie, while Bobtail looked down at him, with bright eyes. "It's my own opinion, Miss, that he runs himself out of scent just about hereabouts, and goes on, but the scent ends at this field. Scent is carried most in the brush, and that there li'l tag don't carry very much to begin with."

8

The Master now decided to draw Gardebone Wood, and with the pack trotting at Charlie's heels, and preceded by about a hundred motor cars, the Hunt moved off. Tom Cockerlegg stood and held open the gate. In his squeaky voice he asked Charlie why the mask of Bobtail was not hanging at his saddle.

"A' coudden hear no rattle o' worrying, or dogs barking, but ye've got un, surenuff?"

Charlie did not answer. The Hunt passed through the gate, a little girl on a pony led by a groom trotting in the rear. I turned off to the right, wanting to see the end. I hid myself round a corner, and dismounted, holding Blackie's reins while he pulled at the grass.

When the last shoe had ceased to clack in the lane, the trapper climbed the steep bank to the field. I watched Bess the sheepdog with him. At a squeak from him she ran away to the Icicle Oak. Tom was carrying a hammer in his right hand. I slung the reins on a stub of a cut hazel stole and walked to where man and dog were waiting by the cold growths of the fungi. I hurried, in a rage at the thought of the fox being hit with the hammer, and, in its tired state, worried by the sheepdog. When I reached the tree the tag of the fox showed as it climbed down hindfirst. I was amazed, and then I remembered the collar.

"Fetch un," whispered Tom, and Bess seized the tag, and pulled it, very gently. Bobtail came into daylight and licked the hand of Tom, who took off the collar and fastened it round the neck of Bess, where it had been when first I had met man and dog in the parlour of The Moon in the Mere. I watched the sheepdog playing with the fox, which she had loved, said Tom, ever since he had put the little dark brown cub with her own litter of puppies, years before, when the trapper had found it whimpering and shivering in the dewy grass behind the pig-breeder's orchard.

"He's been a good mate to me, your honour, and can snick a rabbut smarter nor a lurcher dog will. And he's smart enough to know that they varx-dogs can't abear the stink of Granfer's Saddles as us calls they girt toadstools."

That was why hounds had faltered. The taint of the fungi must have lain in a belt far around the tree, and overpowered the scent of the fox as soon as he entered it. It had lain warm and still in the windless morning.

"Yurr, Bob, shake hands wi' his honour, for a gennulman will stand by a friendship when his hand be to it."

The fox held up his slender paw, and I shook it, and then Bess held up hers, and looked at me with her grave and beautiful eyes. Afterwards dog and fox played together, bounding and rolling and running. I took out my pipe. Owlish eyes behind hair watched me, and the high squeaky voice said:

"Yurr, smoke a pipe of my baccy, midear. 'Tis grand to burn, surenuff!"

It pleased me to think that he considered me his friend to the extent of revealing his secret store; but to my surprise he did not hand me the watch, but an old cocoa tin, filled with various tobaccos, mostly shag, including what looked like a chopped-up cigar. When I had filled my pipe (intending to tap it out again as soon as I was out of his sight) the cunning old fellow took out the brass watch, exclaimed that it was time to get back to work, and walked away over the hoof-marked turf, squeaking with laughter, to his gins in the sunken lane.

Zoë

She would have died, like the weaker dog-whelp, if Captain Horton-Wickham had not been sitting that spring evening at his usual haunt by the pool above the waterslide, where yellow kingcups and pale cuckoo flowers grew at the grassy margin of the river. He was sitting, chin on hand, in an attitude of meditation, listening, perhaps, to the song of a willow wren in an alder that leaned over the pool when a shot rang out, and the bird jumped on a twig. A hundred yards up the river, unseen by himself, an animal rolled over. The shot had torn a furrow in her side, and the water was stained red as it flowed under her brown body. She cried to her mate who was hunting eels with her. The dying otter swung listlessly her brown rudder, paddled feebly to get to her cubs in the drain holt, and was borne away in the current.

Sir Godfrey Crawdelhook, the man who had shot the otter, walked downstream to the slide, where he might be able to recover the body. In the May evening he observed a stranger sitting on the bank.

"Good evening," he said shortly, staring at him.

"Good evening," replied the other curtly, as he scrambled to his feet with the aid of two sticks. He was thin and tall and haggard of face.

"I don't know who you are," said Sir Godfrey, with the direct challenging air of a man who cares nothing for the feelings of others, "Or what you are doing here. Who are you, and where do you come from?"

"I am living in the village," said Captain Horton-Wickham very distinctly; he turned his back on the other, and began to limp away. He limped because his spine was injured. A machine-gun bullet at Bullecourt had caused a wound that resulted in his being bedridden for two years.

He knew he was being stared at angrily, and he limped on, but a curious noise made him pause and look round. The old man was standing beside the weir, battering something with the butt of his gun. Captain Horton-Wickham watched him, till he seized what was obviously a dead otter by its rudder, lifted it dripping from the river, and dragged it to the bank, saying: "She'll take no more of my trout!"

"That otter has cubs," replied the other man.

"I'm very glad to hear it. They will starve to death."

The invalid looked steadily at him, while he gripped two trembling sticks. His blue eyes seemed to stand out as though with hate or pain.

"Go away, leave my water!" cried the old man irritably. "Clear off before I push you, sticks and all, into the river!"

If a friend of Captain Horton-Wickham had been present, he would have felt, among other emotions, distress for him. He began to shake all over, but with an effort of control forced down his feelings, and hobbled away, his heart thumping in his ears. A white hate burned in his head, and he went homewards with difficulty. At home, the feeling passed, leaving him faint and tired. The next morning he felt calmer, and set out to rescue the otter cubs in the holt, the position of which he had known for several days. It was near the pool where so often he had sat at evening.

2

The little whelp made a whimpering, mewing sound. It was caused by the pain of hunger. Bitten pieces of trout and eels lay around it; beside it was a dead whelp.

Something shuffled along the drain, and the little whelp cried out. A warmness surrounded it; it pressed with tiny clawed pads into the hair of the warmness, and sought with its mouth that which it could not find. Later it was quiet. More eels were brought in the jaws of the dog-otter; but the whelp could eat nothing. The dog was distressed; he could not understand the absence of his mate. Vainly had he been whistling for her; all night he had travelled, but her scent vanished at the slide. The cries of the whelp caused him to bring many more fish to it during the night.

He was away in a holt a mile downstream just after dawn, and remained there during the day when two men arrived at the drain. One of them started to dig at the other's direction.

"It doesn't matter if you crack the pipe," said Captain Horton-Wickham. "I know they must be here, because I've spurred the bitch going up dozens of times."

"I minds the time when Sir Godfrey were fined for shooting his mare. A working man would have got two years in jail for that!"

Abner spat on his horny hands, seized the pick, and began to dig. After two hours' work, the pipe was exposed.

It was a little over three months since the invalid had come to the village of Corse Barton, with one man-servant. That he was a crock every one knew. Beyond that they knew nothing. He was about forty years of age. If he was married, his wife never came to Corse Barton. Few letters arrived for him. The 'gennulman' was always playing his gramophone, or standing about in his garden. Abner's wife came to his cottage in the morning, cooked, cleared up, and waited upon him; he was invariably courteous and considerate; she pitied him, but he discouraged all sympathy or talk about himself.

The man-servant, who had been his soldier-servant in the war, never said a word about him.

Abner wondered what the Captain wanted with the cubs, but he did not like to ask. He cracked the yellow pipe, of Marland clay, and inserted the end of the pick into a small hole, using it as a lever. A shard, or fragment, flew upwards, and he knelt down and put his arm into the hole, pulling forth a trout.

'The gennulman' asked to be permitted to examine the cavity and Abner crawled aside. Captain Horton-Wickham rolled still higher his sleeve, exposing the wasted white length of an arm, and felt down the drain. Something sucked his fingers, and he drew forth a tiny grey-brown animal.

"Got them," he cried, triumphantly. "Fancy hitting the right spot right away! There's a pint for you, Abner, to-night at the Fox-hunter."

"Thank ee, zir," said Abner, satisfied.

The next cub was dead. Captain Horton-Wickham stroked its soft fur.

"Poor little fellow," he said, "died of starvation. But your sister is all right, aren't you, my pretty?'

The pretty was about eight inches long, with a flat head and beady eyes sunk into brown fur; she had white whiskers and flat ears, webbed pads, or feet, a rudder—or tail—brown like a tiny bulrush head. Languidly she explored the fingers of her rescuer.

"She'm hungrisome, Captain," said Abner.

"Where can I borrow an infant's bottle?" asked the other. "Or failing that, do you know of an old cat that's had kittens lately?"

"There be one at the Foxhunter, Captain. A turrible old grimalkin, her be. Her kittens be drowned, so her might give th' cub a dapp on the 'ade."

"Let's try," suggested the Captain. "Forrard to the Foxhunter. You can have your pint and Zoë—I shall call her Zoë—can be introduced to the turrible old grimalkin."

At the first sight of Teeter one realized that the adjectival description was correct. She was turrible—the Devonian dialect is more expressive than the conventional. Teeter had had more fights with dogs, female cats, stoats, had had more adventures with trap and gin, than any other feline in Corse Barton. One ear was so torn that it resembled a piece of frayed string; the other was depressed. She had one forepaw—and one stump—the result of a night spent in gnawing the limb held in a trap. One of her eyes was whally, the other was inscrutable. She sat on the window-sill outside the Foxhunter, content in the sunshine.

Captain Horton-Wickham and Abner approached. She did not move. They came to her, and held the whelp near her nose. She did not move. They placed the crawling thing on the ground. She did not even look at it.

The two men entered the inn, and spoke to the landlord. "Darn me, what 'ave ee there?" he asked, "a fitchey?"

They replied that it was not a weasel, but an otter whelp.

"What are you going to drink, landlord?"

"Thank ee, zur, I'll have a pint."

"Three pints then, landlord."

The landlord's wife came into the bar, and they explained how Zoë had been rescued. She was dubious at the idea of Teeter acting as a foster-mother to it; but went and brought the battered cat into the bar, and placed it on the floor beside the whelp.

Teeter, as before, disregarded Zoë entirely. Feebly the whelp struggled towards the warmth that she sensed. Teeter sniffed at it, and her stringy ear twitched. She took one step forward, a jerky movement owing to the single foreleg, and examined the strange thing. Then with a low growl she prepared to smack it with a paw, shifting the weight of her body on to the stump with a swift movement. Uncertainly she gave it a soft blow on the head. Zoë mewed.

Teeter paused, and Zoë mewed again. Then she made a chirruping sound, low in her throat, and went nearer. Zoë wriggled towards her, whimpering. Teeter licked the tiny animal's face; she lay beside it and purred. A hoarse sort of purring it was, but it never ceased; a purr of love, of maternal protection. She adored the whelp, and rarely left it afterwards, and people looked in to see the unusual spectacle of a fat little otter cub scampering over the floor with a battered old cat. Sometimes the lean, shaky figure of Captain Horton-Wickham was seen in the riverside town of Barum, carrying under his coat the bonny cub, usually on a Friday, which was market day. Always he carried in his pocket a feed-bottle of milk, to which he added hot water: Zoë imbibed with an eagerness that amused all beholders, pressing with her pads against the glass, her eyes beady and bright, her whiskers spruce. Wherever her master went, she went too; they were very attached to each other. Some men shook their heads and said that the otter would grow up fierce and wild; that the Captain would lose her in the autumn.

"She'll never leave me," he would say. "We're too attached to each other, aren't we, Zoë?"

3

A large garden surrounded his cottage, and Zoë had the run of it. The scent of apple bloom in the valley was borne with the songs of goldfinches unceasing from the first light till the golden rim of the hills was dulled; the blossom fell, the finch song became a reedy twittering as their young were hatched. Captain Horton-Wickham, in the intervals of the most intolerable pain, was usually among his garden flowers. Zoë ran over them, but he did not chide her; instead he, with the help of Abner, erected wire-netting along the borders of the beds. Under an old apple-tree, in the holes of which were nesting a pair of starlings, a pair of blue-tits, and a pair of redstarts, was Zoë's home; an inverted box attached to a net-protected run. During her hours of imprisonment Zoë slept in the box, emerging as she heard the footfalls of her master.

She was fed upon cooked fish and soaked dog biscuits for breakfast and supper, and for her mid-day meal she shared with her master. If he had roast beef, batter pudding, potatoes, and samphire, Zoë had roast beef, batter pudding, potatoes, and samphire. Unlike a dog or a fox, she chewed thoroughly, never bolting her food. Her canine teeth were long and white and curved inwards; with these she would have pierced and held an eel in the wild state. She was intensely shy of all human beings with the exception of her master, and would run with great swiftness to a shed at the bottom of the garden when anyone walked up the path. Upon one occasion she chattered with rage and disappeared into her sanctuary, and the very young man who had come to visit Captain Horton-Wickham explained that it must have been the smell of hounds about him.

"I'm the Master of the Barton Otter Hounds," he said, with an air of punctilio, "and I've just called round to see you. It has been of great interest to us to hear about your success in taming an otter. You do chase our friend *Lutra vulgaris*, don't you?"

"I'm afraid not," said Captain Horton-Wickham.

"Oh, I thought perhaps you did," casually replied the other, looking at the otter masks and pads mounted on oak shields on the wall, and several rudders tied with red ribands. "By jove, that's a big dog's head! Now it's no use you hiding your light under a bushel, sir! Southern Counties! And I see a hunting horn as well." But a peculiar look on the other's face made him stop awkwardly. "I say, I beg your pardon, sir. But I thought you must be joking when I saw these masks through the window. But surely—"

"Since the war," interrupted Captain Horton-Wickham, in a discouraging voice, "I'm afraid my memory for small details is very bad."

"I'm sorry you're crocked," stammered the other, "but if you would care—"

"Thank you," said Captain Horton-Wickham. "It is kind of you to have called. But I do not hunt; I have only time and energy to attend to my garden while I wait for my spine to go altogether. I say, have a drink, won't you? I've only got beer and whisky, I'm afraid."

The young man had a drink, made a few conventional remarks, and went away, feeling humiliated and angry at his reception, and yet sorry for the lonely man.

When the visitor had gone, Captain Horton-Wickham whistled Zoë and turned the hose upon her. She raced about, and dived into a zinc bath, swirling round in it, then lying on her back and clutching at the sun-laden jet with her paws, trying to bite it. Sometimes she hid underneath the water in the bath, blowing up a burst of bubbles, then began again the ecstatic clutching of the jet. And over the edge of the bath she slipped while the stream of water pursued her; such fun it was for her. Teeter wandered into the garden, announced by the scolding chorus of small birds, and tried to wash her face, but Zoë was in a playful mood and chased her old foster-mother into the apple-tree, whose occupants swore at her. At length the turrible grimalkin cleared off, and Zoë retired to the woodshed.

At the bottom of the garden the river ran, and during July boulders were bleached and exposed that hitherto had been the lurking place of trout. Zoë was so tame and obedient to her master's whistle that he often took her to the water, particularly to a deep pool into which she dived and where she could disport herself. As the weeks passed and she always returned in the evening, her master grew confident in his belief that she would never desert him.

Otherwise—

4

One evening, however, she did not return. He was agitated, and went to the river, repeatedly whistling and calling her. She never came, and after midnight he went back to the house, weary and disconsolate, and sat up till three o'clock playing the gramophone, and repeating his favourite records of *Tristan and Isolde*. When the dawn light made grey the room he went out into the cold morning and whistled again; but there was no Zoë. That afternoon he fell asleep in the orchard, and awoke in the twilight, his first thought being of Zoë. Abner's wife seemed nervous about his unwillingness to eat, but the man-servant said that he was often like that, and told her not to get the wind up; still, she worried. She would have worried still more had she known that the man-servant had hidden 'thik Captain's' revolver that evening.

There seemed to be some connection between the stray Zoë, the pool by the waterslide, Wagner's opera of *Tristan and Isolde,* and a photograph that sometimes Captain Horton-Wickham took from a drawer in his desk. The set of records had been purchased before the war, in Milan, and it was the orchestra of the Milan Opera Company that played. To the perfect phrasing of the prelude he would listen, to the interweaving of the three themes, those of love, of delirium, and of death. On the third day of Zoë's

absence, Abner's wife was alarmed, for he looked so ill and haggard. She made an omelet, and he was just sitting down when against the low window-pane there was a slight bump. He turned his head: there came the noise as of padded claws scraped against glass. It was Zoë, whistling him.

"Zoë," he cried, jumping up, "Zoë, my dear, Zoë! Tuckatuck, tuckatuck, where are you?"

Tuckatuck came from outside, and he flung up the sash of the window. Zoë stood there whimpering. She was changed. One eye was a red glaze of blood; one paw was bitten through; her coat, once so smooth, was dishevelled and irregular.

"Zoë, how have you been hurt?" asked Captain Horton-Wickham. "Oh, Zoë, what a sad return."

"*Tuckatuck,*" she whimpered.

He lifted her inside, and gave her the omelet, which she ate ravenously, and then fell asleep on his lap. Abner's wife made another omelet, and no sooner had she gone out of the room than Zoë woke up and sniffed; so the second omelet went the way of the first.

That night Zoë slept in a cushioned chair beside Captain Horton-Wickham's bed, the pain and exhaustion temporarily fled. The full round moon of the summer night discovered her curled form on the cushion. Sometimes she stirred in the moonlight uneasily. Perhaps some terror of that fight with the otter still lingered in her brain, for the thing that caused Zoë's woeful condition was the spouse of the dressing-gown her master heard the dog otter's whistle. Zoë had been shy and yet bold (but only in her mind) and had frisked among the spear-grasses and rushes of the river bank. Presistently the dog had whistled and coaxed, and at last she had followed; a handsome dog he was. But her happiness did not last long; perhaps some human scent still lingered on her coat; and the otter of her own sex that she met was jealous.

Zoë tried to bite the creature who was savaging her, but she never had a chance. In pain she dragged herself through shallow and over alder-hung rock till she came to the recollected pool, and the joyous scent of her master. Ten minutes afterwards she had eaten two omelets; she had many more in the weeks that went by; and though one eye was gone, the other eye seemed sufficient for her. She grew amazingly, and lost nearly every trace of her mauling.

Then one night as he wandered in the orchard in sleeping suit and dressing-gown her master heard the dog otter's whistle. Zoë was shut up in the coal-house. He did not know that the otter hounds had killed the dog's mate four days after Zoë's fight with her. He shut Zoë up in the coal-house, with a nice basket lined with sweet straw in which she might sleep at night till the danger was past. But Zoë did not sleep at night. She dug right under the foundations of the cottage, emerging through a flower-bed. In the morning she was gone; nor did she ever return to the garden; but she returned to her master, the only human creature she trusted; and her return fell out in the most woeful manner.

The dog had decided to quit the river and go to the dykes of the Santon Mires, fringed with rush and sedge seldom molested by bay of hound; only solitary herons stood on the banks with beaks held ready for rat or eel. Eels were there, thousands of them, for the yearly migration to the Atlantic had begun. It was here that the handsome young dog brought Zoë, his mate.

5

It was here, too, that the Barton Otter Hunt held their last bye-meet of the year; a cowman had seen the otters in the duckponds one day, and had earned half a crown by telling the kennel-huntsman.

It was a good field, and many half-a-crown caps were taken by the honorary treasurer, standing by the gate with his grey pot-hat in his hand, and a dutiful smile on his face. The local photographer had been avoided by some ladies and gentlemen, and welcomed (inwardly) by others. It was holiday time, and many boys and girls were out with their parents. Captain Horton-Wickham was there, standing apart; he had practically no friends, and the few people who had called were discouraged by his aloof manner, which in reality hid an extreme sensibility, and therefore a capacity for suffering, which may have been caused by ill-health.

Seeing him standing apart and alone, the Master went over to him and said in a cheery voice of impersonal cordiality, "I'm glad to see you out with us after all, sir. I only hope we shall be able to give you good sport. How's the pet? Going strong, I hope?"

"She's gone," replied the other, "and I'm living in fear that you fellows will kill her. That's why I'm here."

Soon afterwards one of the hounds, Fanciboy, spoke; somebody on the bank tallied, and the hunt began. From the start it was a wild hunt, over land and through water. Never had an otter behaved so curiously. Then it was realized that there were two otters.

Sometimes the Master ordered a stickle, or barrier of members of the field to stand on planks across the muddy dykes, and to stir the water with their iron-shod poles in order to prevent the hunted from going that way. Once they hunted the dog into a drain under a bank, and to drive him forth they banged at the turf, in order to create in his mind the illusion that they were digging. So out he slipped, under the legs of a hound called Molly; whereat Molly howled and 'music' rolled from the throats of the twelve couple.

"There he goes!" shouted a ragged, dirty man, pointing to a chain of bubbles rising to the surface of the water; and the scramble was on once more. Men in blue coats and white breeches got soaked in the sport; some of the younger ladies, with silver-mounted pads in hats, got wet as well; and one, the youngest and prettiest of them all, a red-haired girl called Diana Shelley, fell into the water. A young man jumped in after her, and they crawled out black with mud.

Small boys eagerly followed hounds, confusing them with shouts and noises, while Diana and her friends were laughing and joking at her saturated clothes. The huntsman was yelling, " 'Ware riot, Harper! Come, Fanciboy! Get-on-to-'im, Rufus!" and cracked his lash. The otters were marked in a holt under a hollow bank. Captain Horton-Wickham, limping along alone behind the merry people felt very ill. The hand pressing on the heavy stick was trembling. A man had just joined the field, and someone had called his attention to him by the greeting, "'Hullo, Nigger! I didn't know you were home. How's India?"

Captain Nicholas Crawdelhook was the elder son of Sir Godfrey of that ilk.

Hounds wearied the otters out, exhausted them physically and nervously; and finally marked them under a licheny stone cattle-bridge. The dog fought with them, and 'painted' the muzzles of several hounds. Perhaps he hoped to slip away while Zoë was escaping by the broken marsh-drain that led along the bank and emptied into a creek. Anyhow, Zoë crept away, while hounds were tearing at the body of the dog-otter and snarling at the worry. Captain Horton-Wickham, standing fifty yards away from the kill, and wondering when he would crumple up, saw the head of Zoë thrust itself over the sea-wall.

Zoë had fled the approach of all men, except one, the man whom she had known since whelphood, the man whom she, in her own way, loved. She saw a hostile form, and drew back; and then the scent she knew so well was wafted to her nostrils, and the hunted creature yearned to achieve safety by following it.

She came in her distress towards the loved scent. She was tired, and her nose and beady eye only were exposed as she swam the dyke. "Go away—go away," almost moaned the man on the bank. "Go down to the sea, you idiot! Go away!" he cried. He started to hobble from her sight, groaning at the misfortune. Down the grassy wall ran Zoë, through the rustling sedges, and across the meadow to him.

She gave a low cry of *tuckatuck,* the love-cry. Muttering his despair, Captain Horton-Wickham led her away. He knew that there was the greatest danger, for himself and for Zoë. Reason was of no use; the only thing he might do was to lead her away, and to trust in chance to avoid the hounds finding her scent.

After a minute had dragged away, hope began to rise in his heart. With the aid of sticks the anguished cripple was hobbling across the water-meadow, with Zoë running in front, and returning to him in the strangest and most unexpected manner. He had gone three hundred yards when the throbbing of his heart caused him to stop, to lean forward, supported by the sticks. It was at this moment that Hemlock, who had been whimpering in the rushes upstream, stern a-feather, spoke: immediately the pack gave tongue, and pursued in the wake of the old hound.

Captain Horton-Wickham must have realized the danger. He must have known that pack-law was as uncertain as mob-law. The Master blew the recall on his horn—four long blasts linked together. It availed nothing. The Whip lashed the air—*Crack!—Crack!—* shouting "'Ware riot, Chimer! Helmsman! Hold up, Tuneful!" *Crack,—Crack:* it availed nothing. The field stood still, staring at the disastrous spectacle of twelve couple of hounds in full cry on a breast-high scent across the water-meadow. The spectators saw the hounds reach the tall figure as he stood holding the otter in his arms.

Round the still figure, as incoming waves surround a children's castle on the seashore, the pack surged, worrying. Huntsman and Master were running to the rescue; several men swore; little Diana Shelley covered her face with her hands and sank to her knees; someone kept repeating—it was a man's voice—"Oh, I say —I say—I say." They heard a sudden report, saw the tall figure sink

beneath the onslaught . . . and the brown body of Zoë being tossed on a score of muzzles.

6

Young Howard de Wychehalse, late of the Coldstream Guards, and Master of the Barton Otter Hunt, was having tea with his friends at Wildernesse that afternoon, and he was wretched and depressed.

"You know, Mrs Ogilvie," he was saying, "I feel that I can never hunt again. Apart from the disgrace of hounds turning like that on a man, the hounds that I thought I knew so well"—he had been an honorary whipper-in for some seasons of his boyhood—"I feel that I am responsible for the poor fellow's death. We ought never to have held the bye-meet so near his place, when his otter was loose."

"Of course you are not to blame, dear boy," said Mrs Ogilvie, in sympathetic tones; "how can you say that? Did he not commit suicide! Did he not bring a loaded revolver with him for that reason?"

"They say," went on Howard in a low voice, "that he brought it to kill 'Nigger' Crawdelhook, but I don't believe it. 'Nigger' says that Horton-Wickham was an acting Brigadier in France, when 'Nigger' was one of his battalion commanders, and that he was Master of the Southern Counties before the War. No wonder he was so stiff with me when I, like a young puppy, went to him and practically suggested that it would be so good for his health if he came out and had a few days' hunting with us, instead of moping around by himself!"

"But you were only being kind," said Mrs. Ogilvie. "Of course, we know he was somewhat odd, but why should he have wanted to kill Major Crawdelhook?"

"Well, it's rather awkward to tell you," replied Howard, glancing at Mary, who, with wistful eyes, was regarding the speaker, "for, you see, Captain Horton-Wickham used to be married, and his wife —well, they say that Major Crawdelhook used to—know her rather well. In fact, after Wickham was hit so badly his wife went off with him. Her name," murmured Howard, frowning a little, and looking out of the window, "was apparently Zoë."

The Five Lives
of the Isle of Wight Parson

Since the Romans, proud and civilized and decadent, ate their dishes made of the tongues of nightingales snared in the hazel brakes of Vectis, the Isle of Wight has been a famous fragment of the earth. Rising out of the Channel four miles off the southern coast of England, the diamond-shaped island covers Portsmouth—the Admiralty base British sailors call 'Pompey'—and gives to Southampton docks those double tides which, lapsing and flowing east and west along its northern seaboard by Spithead and Solent, have made the port great.

For most men the printed name has some sort of association. It may be the white sails of the Royal Yacht Squadron, recollected, perhaps, only from the picture-newspapers; or the hollow roar of the swift and dreaded race that tears its way between isle and mainland, shifting course with every tide, and marked as by shark's teeth on its broken wave-tops. Some will be reminded of Keats and the goldfinches; others of the green rose which was seen first in the village of Bonchurch, growing in a graveyard. Queen Victoria and the Royal Family at Osborne, Tennyson, Swinburne—the Isle holds many tales of the illustrious dead; but one tale of the living there is that is scarcely known: the tale of the Isle of Wight Parson who, in the afternoon of July the Eleventh, some years after the Great War, was tarred and feathered, while tied to the corpse of his brother.

It was one of many persecutions for which sailors of unknown ships were partly responsible. There was, it may be remembered, some correspondence in the principal London papers, and a leading article in *The Times*. Individual members of both Houses—prominently the Viscount Grey of Fallodon—were anxious for an international agreement to prevent such cruelty; but the Governments of Europe were much too busy thinking about the Red Menace, War Debts, the re-arming of Europe, and other phenomena of obsolescent thought, to worry about the case of an Isle of Wight Parson.

I knew old Phalacrocorax well. This, by the way, is his correct surname, and not, as the ignorant may suppose, if they have read so far, a fictitious one. Phalacrocorax is a grand and crisp name, like walking on a beach of shells—the educated will know the Greek derivation of the family name, $\varphi\alpha\lambda\alpha\chi\rho\acute{o}\xi$ and $\chi\acute{o}\rho\alpha\xi$—but the Parson's appearance did not remind me of the beach by Morte Hoe when first I brought him home after his ordeal. His head, entirely hairless, was long and narrow, and his nostrils were so small, a natural defect, that he was forced to breathe through his mouth, which was devoid of teeth. He lived with me for several weeks, and I grew to be fond of him, and so did my dog; but the cat fled from him. There were times, I must admit, when I too preferred him at a distance, as when the air was moist and the wind in the south, my nose not liking him then as much as my anthropomorphic intuition.

I brought him to the village during the darkness and quiet of night, but in the morning the sound of his complaining voice brought children, passing down the street to school, to the threshold. The postman looked in also, with the farmer who lives opposite, and the gardener at the Rectory. The gardener told the Rector of the Parish Church, who came hurrying round.

"They tell me something dreadful about an Isle of Wight Parson," he began, and stopped, with his eyes fixed behind the settle, where on a heap of straw the wretched creature was hiding. After some moments of staring the Rector cried:

"But he has got a piece of iron stuck in his throat!"

I told him how it had got there. He screwed up his face in horror, and after some moments of imagining how it would feel if it were in his own throat, he said earnestly:

"Do you know, my dear boy, I think it would be for the best if you were to knock him on the head, and bury him. I should do it by night if I were you, when no little children would be about to see you."

I told him that I had only just dug him out of a grave, where he had been buried alive. The Rector wrinkled his brow in pity, and murmured in a placid voice: "It is very sad to think that men can be so cruel in England. Do I know the men or man, I wonder; but do not tell me if you would rather not."

"I don't mind telling you," I replied. "It was Bill Crang."

"Oh!" said the Rector, raising his eyebrows in a facial gesture which was meant to convey complete understanding. "Ah!" he added, and pursed his lips, and frowned, and nodded his head several times, slowly to himself, before looking at me and smiling a peculiar smile. That smile was meant to show his hopeless thoughts about William Crang, the Chapel preacher, for of course the Rector could not speak against anyone in the parish.

When I told him the whole story of the Isle of Wight Parson, he asked me to write it for the Parish Magazine. I did so, but it troubled the good priest. He returned it to me, and deeply regretted that he could not publish it for several reasons, one being that it would fill about six issues of his 2-page monthly sheet; another (the chief) reason that he thought people would be offended by some of my critical remarks. I assured him that they were not meant to be critical: that I had no dogmatic bias: that my description of Bill Crang was the mere truth.

"I do not doubt your sincerity, my dear boy," he said, in his kind way, placing a hand on my shoulder, "but I am certain that few people will understand your remarks about the Bible."

"They are true," I protested, "with reference to the type of mind, the common type, such as Bill Crang possesses. I like Bill personally. He's all right, except for his ideas! And I read the Bible more often than you, who see me in your church about twice a year, may suspect. At the same time, Sir, I cannot believe that, ethnographically speaking, our Island Race, of mixed Brythonic, Celtic, Roman, Saxon, Norman and whatnot other races came originally disguised as the Lost Tribes of Israel. As for the New Testament, I am upheld by the radiance of the Man who inspired it, by the divine spirit so infinitely beyond the comprehension of the little minds which would interpret Him. Bill Crang's every wooden utterance is a voiceless cry for Barabbas."

The Rector smiled patiently and sadly. I knew that he thought I was all right, except for my ideas.

He said, "Well, my dear boy—" and went away.

I was left with the Isle of Wight Parson.

2

As Bill Crang was directly responsible for most of the persecution, I must explain what sort of a man he was. I know nothing about the village chapel, except what I have heard through partly open windows while loitering outside in summer; and the quality of the sermons on each occasion did not fill me with eagerness to gaze upon the features of the teacher inside. So I declined the various invitations of Bill Crang to go with him on Sunday afternoons to his place of exhibitionism. The fellow was always trying to save my soul from some devil or other with whom he had had, apparently, an intimate acquaintance in his youth. Once, angered by what he called my " 'orribly 'eathenish attitood"—because I said that Jehovah, the jealous god of an extinct tribe, was the equivalent of an idol—he refused to sail me over the estuary, declaring that he didden want no thunderbolt o' vengeance dropped through his boat, which was not insured.

"It will sink by itself before long, so why should you think an all-seeing Providence would be so stupid as to use the force of gravity and a fragment of a ruined planet to destroy your old tub?" I shouted after him, as he shoved off.

Marooned among the sandhills, I slept in a ferny hollow, and when at dawn I saw the sun's tide flooding the eastern estuary of heaven, how glad I was that I had not gone home! The dew was on the mosses, and the bog pimpernels, tiny and numerous as pink raindrops at my feet, were waking out of their petals to steal heaven's gold breath for their seeds. Larks sang high above the white vapour that hid the distant grazing marsh, and all but the horned heads of cattle. My spaniel and I ran shouting to the sea. Soon I stood on the broken shells of the strand, naked in the beams of the sun and the spray of the waves, alone with the sandpipers who are pure in spirit as man's starry thoughts. I ran for a plunge, and they sped down the estuary. One behind the other the green translucent breakers rose for the foamy fall, seven of them regular and fish-shaped, and followed by three great combers which reared and curled and roared over my head, flinging the coloured sun-dogs behind me. I worked my slow way through the surf, to be lifted gently by the seven that came after, but the next great trio beat me under. I gasped into sunlight, amid water that was quiet, and rested afloat while an old bull seal looked at me with his grey filmy eyes. So near was he that I could see the water blown from his nostrils as he breathed. He filled his lungs and rolled under a wave, for he was hunting a run of salmon which had come over the bar with the tide.

I swam to the shore, finding my spaniel on my clothes with a young rabbit he had caught. There was driftwood for a fire, and when we had eaten our meal, and he had gone after the next, I wandered on a spit of shingle, where above the line of dry brittle sea-weed left by the highest spring-tide the ring-plover lay their eggs, so like pebbles and shells that even the carrion crows often miss them. The tide ebbed. Smoke had been rising from the chimneys of the village over the water for some time when I saw an open boat drifting down derelict upon the sandbank in mid-estuary. The sand-bank was bare, except for a black, as though gowned figure, standing motionless by the waterside, near the upjutting fluke of the anchor that held the mooring chain of the buoy. The figure was that of the Isle of Wight Parson, who had not moved for more than an hour. Many times had I watched him on the sandbank as the tide ebbed, usually at the same place, turned towards the east, his mouth open and standing in a cruciform attitude which was so familiar to the fishermen of the estuary.

The open boat turned slowly as it drifted. It was tarred, with white gunwales, and the number of its owner's salmon licence painted white on its bows. The figures were legible through my glass. It was Bill Crang's boat, and as I looked I realized the danger to the Parson. I stood and watched, while the ring-plover ran over the shingle near me, suddenly pausing as though changed to stone. Their wistful faint piping passed over sand and stick and shell of that desolate place, one calling another in its quiet distress. I was near their young.

How could I tell the Parson of his danger? Already in my mind I could see the red tinge of summer wavelets lapsing from the sand-bank, after the shot had broken him, and his body lay in the bright water, one with its shadow. Death! When the moving sun-shadow is stilled, and one is, perchance, already a shade! Why should this poor Isle of Wight parson be persecuted, when really he did no harm, except to take some of the fish that the fishermen of the estuary deemed it their own right to catch?

I wanted to warn him by shouting, but I had not the courage of my desire. The boat was drifting nearer to the ridge of sand on which he stood. An empty boat, apparently, moving with the ebb; but I knew that Bill Crang was lying under the gunwales with a loaded gun beside him. There was no wind, the waters of sea and river were slackening, the buoy marking the ridge end was spinning quite slowly. Through my glass I could see the red of rust and the green of weed on the riveted iron plates of the great sea-top, which every tide whipped into a rolling spin. A gull was perching on the stem, its yellow eye fixed on the drifting salmon boat. The gull uttered an angry yakker, for it had flown over the boat and seen the enemy.

No suspicion came to the solitary figure standing where the wavelets carried their stolen sun-threads to the shallows, to be yielded on the sand. The Parson was dozing after his meal, his head thrown back, with three fishtails sticking out of his open mouth. The sand near his feet was pitted irregularly by the salt water which had dripped from him.

Nearer and nearer drifted the open boat. In less than a minute it would be within gunshot of the Parson. Others were watching across the water, but without the same feelings for the safety of that insignificant black figure. The death of a Parson affected the fishermen smoking on the quay about as much as the death of a bass or a salmon.

When the Parson saw the gun, and Bill's fist and arm, and then his head as he took aim over the gunwale, he jumped. The Parson's voice was naturally deep and rather hoarse, but now it was buried under a load of half-digested fish. Even then, his strangled cries were borne over the water to where I stood watching him within the circle of my glass. He tried to throw up his dinner, which was so heavy that it hindered him. He waddled through the shallows to reach deeper waters, uttering shrieks and groans and gurglings, but before he could reach deep water Bill Crang fired, and the Parson fell on his side.

I watched the fisherman wading after the body, saw him pick it up, and carry it with the head trailing in the water to where his boat was nosing the sandbank with its iron shoe. He heaved it over the stern, pushed the boat afloat, and with easy dip of oars drifted down to me.

Bill and I talked, and it was then he tried to persuade me to go to the Chapel on the following afternoon. I said, to have fun with him, that I heard he was about to become a Catholic.

"There's none of them sort in 'Eaven," he warned me solemnly, and started to tell me why. How he talked! And how that very solemn Anglo-Saxon quoted those old Semitic polygamists! He knew the Old Testament by heart. Everything he believed literally. His mind would never change. While he was quoting the wrathful phrases which were meaningless under the sweet blue sky as the bloody sacrifices which used to accompany them in the original Greek, I could see so clearly that his way of thinking was the way of darkness, of hate, of wars, of crucifixion, of needless suffering. It was sad to hear him, but my sadness was momentary. It would be so easy to laugh at Bill Crang. But the next moment I was glad that he was talking at me, sitting on the bows of his boat with his back to the Parson, for then he did not see what I saw: and that was a small eye opening, and taking a look around. No other movement except the blinking of a small emerald eye.

The Parson's eye had a wary look in it. Then his mouth opened as though with astonishment that he was lying in a boat, and the same boat, too, in which he had nearly died before. For he had been caught three days previously in Bill Crang's net, and hauled out of the purse gasping and feebly kicking, to be held by the feet with his head under water until Bill Crang considered him drowned. While being rowed to the village he had stood up, coughed a sort of fish soup over Bill's head, and dived overboard.

"So you think, Mr. Crang," I said loudly, for the Parson was beginning to raise his head, "that I can avert the sulphur dioxide of this place, this diabolical place, you speak of, only by standing up to my middle in water, while your minister totally submerges my vile body?"

"Aiy, aiy," replied Bill stoutly, and the next moment a small hard shower came upon us. It rattled in the boat, and made a few spirts in the water. The Parson, who had been only stunned by the shot, was shaking the lead pellets out of his hard quills; after which, with a hoarse and doleful cry, he flew off down the estuary. The flight of his riddled black wings made a sighing whistle as he flew straight and low over the waters, after the manner of cormorants. Watching through my glass, I saw him brake with tail and wings and feet, saw the water torn as he slowed and settled, when he stood up, nearly as big as a goose, and flapped his wings to tighten the feathers for diving. He was hungry, having left his dinner at the edge of the sandbank for the gulls.

Next morning I saw him, one of a row of seven, perched on the sandbank. Four of them had the tails of mullet sticking out of open beaks. Their wings were held out to dry in the sun, and they worked their shoulder joints in order to shake down the fish which were distending their gullets. I recognized the Parson by his ragged appearance, and by the gaps in his flight quills. He was trying to smarten himself up by oiling them from the gland in his back above the tail.

Somebody else was watching the seven Isle of Wight Parsons, too, and that was Bill Crang. I must tell you that the Board of

Conservators paid a shilling for every Parson's head brought into the chief water-bailiff's office, and money, of course, was the real guiding force of Bill Crang; a fearful concern for one's whereabouts after death can hardly be called religion. Seven Parsons' heads meant seven shillings for Bill to put in the box under his bed, which was supposed to hold over five hundred pounds, all in small silver. One may wonder why all this money wasn't in the bank, or invested? Because Bill didn't want anyone to know how much he was worth. Like most of the people in the village, he was sensitive—no, that's the wrong word—he was cunning about his money. As a sort of camouflage, he would refer to his poverty. He was not a miser, but his pennies and sixpences had been gained laboriously. He had been wet in sea-labour nearly all his life, and never had any boots or shoes until he was thirteen years old. His wife was childless, so why, one may ask, was Bill so thrifty? Because he liked working, because the thought of increase—which, I remembered, was the earth's thought—inspired him to continue to store up treasure for the heaven, or haven, of old age. Hard work and hard preaching meant security in this world and the next for Bill Crang.

So Bill got out his line and hooks, and at high tide went what fishermen called rough fish-catching, that is, any fish for the taking of which no licence was required. (A May to September licence for salmon and sea-trout cost five pounds.) Bill caught several bass with his line, using bait of sand-eels, and the smaller ones he didn't bang on the head but threw them alive in the well of the boat. When the tide was ebbing he went down to the buoy and made fast the line to the stem. Then he foul-hooked the smaller live bass, and dropped them overboard. The tide went seawards in swirls and eddies, the ridge of the sandbank showed its newish ribs, the leaning buoy in its dreary spinning wound and unwound the line. Every minute the sandbank grew wider and longer, and an hour before slack-water the seven Parsons flew in from the sea and began to fish.

It may be of interest to know how *Phalacrocorax Carbo* (as he is known in museums) or the Isle of Wight Parson (as his kind had been called in the estuary before museums were made) caught his prey. When he was swimming under-water the short oily feathers of his head, neck, and back used to reflect streaks of light at all angles around and below him. These streaks gleamed like the sides of small fish shoaling, and seeing them above, cod, bass, pollack, and other fish would swim up for a meal. The Parson, cruising in a fathom of water, would espy the gleam of a big fish, and race in pursuit of it.

The wide webs of his black feet would drive his lean body swiftly through the water. A small fish of less than a pound in weight he would swallow underwater, but if it was big, usually he swam up with it. When on the surface again he would fling it up to catch it by the head, and swallow it. Sometimes when the sea was calm the Parson would watch while swimming with his head under water, but usually he prowled in a zigzag course just above the bed of the estuary.

On this afternoon I could imagine the cormorants swimming far down in the green crab-haunted waters, past stone-fastened weed which streamed with the tide, wings pressed close to sides, and moving at the pace of a trotting horse. The lean head on the long neck swung up. There was the gleam of a fish turning above. With decisive kicks of his feet he thrust upwards, blowing a string of bubbles in his excitement. The bass sped up the fairway, the Parson following, slim with his speed. Over the buoy's mooring chain, covered with mussels, went bass and cormorant, the bird following every twist and swerve of the fish. Suddenly the fish stopped, and hung still in two fathoms of water, the unseen line taut from it to the surface. The Parson braked with fourteen short tail feathers and two wide webs, and slid upon the fish, while the agitation of the sheared water arose and spun itself away in two buttons of foam on the surface. The bass was seized in the long beak with its preying curved upper mandible. It weighed two pounds, which was quite big enough for the Parson, but not too big to be gulped down when he swum into air and sunshine again. While he was shaking it into his gullet the fish was jerked away, but he caught it, and the hook fixed through the bass's side stuck in his throat.

For another cormorant was hooked, on a different part of Crang's multi-baited line . . .

Who can tell the agony of two birds both struggling for freedom, the frantic swimming rush upon each other, up the estuary against the ebb, down with the current, then in opposite directions again, until the agonising jerk checked them with a force which would have snapped the neckbones of less rapacious birds. The Parsons (who had been reared in the same home, i.e. on the same heap of rotting seaweed and fish) could not understand what was preventing them from flying. They dived, they cried, they bled, until they were weak, when they lay in the water with only their heads showing while they gasped for the air of life, hiding thus lest the dread enemy should observe them.

3

The buoy, after its hour upright, leaned wearily towards the main-land, and the flow whipped it into a sluggish spin. Night came with its stars, the moon looked down on the unresisting waters, and tarnished the troughs of waves. The five remaining Parsons were asleep on their roosting rock on the distant Isle. Salmon came over the bar, the bull seal after them, and the seal caught one of the hooked bass, and the barb of the hook fastened in the flesh of his throat. Mad with fear and pain he beat his flippers against the tide, dragging the two brothers on the line after him; soon, however, he champed through the line, and the birds were free, except for each other. When daylight came they were a mile from the land, and still trying to be themselves again. First one would dive to escape from the line, and pull the other under; and the other, terrified by an un-known enemy dragging it down to drown and devour it, would swim up and break the waters, a very sea-scarecrow to the gulls as it flapped and ran in the wave troughs before flying. It would fly until a tautened line flung it as though shot in mid-air, to tumble into the water, gasping.

After many days his brother died, and the corpse was dragged behind the Parson when by day he swam into the undersea world, soundless in its green gloom except for the throbbing beats which began when the currents set eastward. Southampton was miles away, yet the pulses of ships' screws travelled far under the Solent tides. The Parson was tortured by hunger, for he could catch only the smallest fishes. At night he slept among the waves, while from a cold and starless grave his dead brother swayed and beckoned as the currents filled its wings. Sometimes he was awakened by a tug on his head, and he had to struggle for air with web and wing, while the tug, tug, tug, on the line continued. Conger eels were pulling at the body far below.

These fish, so cold and powerful and slimy, tore the flesh of the corpse until the wings swayed on a frame of bones. Crabs picked out tongue and eyes, but even then the little fish were frightened by it, as it fled and bowed through the depths. Sharks and dogfish stared at it, sting-rays with blue bellies swam from the gape of its beak. Once the line drew it through an eddy about a skeleton resting on the bottom, a skeleton many times as big as itself, with the frames of its wings hung with barnacles. There were bones and skulls about this frame, and rusty engines shunned by crabs. Warped and split ply-wood of propellers looked like giant human hands held up for warn-ing from the netherworld. The line drew the Parson's skeleton across a machine-gun, in the handles of which its legbones became en-tangled; once, twice, thrice, the line jerked it on—but it was finished, like the airmen and their seaplane, and the ways of life beckon the dead in vain. It stayed; but the head, the shilling head, was pulled from the neck.

That was the end of the Parson's brother, and although the headless skeleton in the machine-gun has a further history, it has no place in a story which tells of life and hope.

4

Phalacrocorax Carbo, the Isle of Wight Parson, lived on among the waves, carrying wherever he went twenty yards of barked hempen line tied to a galvanised iron hook fixed in his throat. How thin he was! The herring gulls watched him. They rode the invisible wind waves in beautiful white flight, watching the sea with pitiless yellow eyes. Other diving birds they passed over in their slow sailing, but when they saw the Parson their level wings shifted, they banked for a turn, and lay above him. The Parson paddled faster as he cocked a green anxious eye. The gulls cried their vague flock-cries, of which no man knows the meaning. It was not the harsh, selfish jabber of excite-ment during a food scramble, as when a shoal of whitebait, or a dead porpoise, lies near the surface; it was not the screaming mutter of parental alarm. Men hear the flock-cries before a storm, when the birds are going inland; and old fishermen believe (but do not like to say in these radio days) that the bewailing spirits of drowned sailors are in the bodies of seagulls. The flock-cry is impersonal, like the loud wail of insanity's laughter, terrifying to man by its waste and mock of sunlight's spirit.

The imagination of Phalacrocorax was not so small that the gulls' cries did not affect him. He got away from them as quickly as he could. They waited for him to swim up; indeed, they watched him all the while he was submerged. They could see the line slanting behind him, and the head at its other end. More gulls drifted over, and cried the wild flock-cry. Two glided to within a yard of the Parson, their trailing feet an inch from the sea. They lifted their wings above their backs, settled on the water, and folded them. Others alighted with white hastelessness. The Parson dived from them.

A breeze sprang up in the afternoon, when they could not see him swimming below, so they circled in a screaming flock while they waited to tear from his beak any fish he caught and brought to the surface. I know this because I saw them from a sailing boat. The gulls screamed as I tacked after the Parson, who could fly about a score of yards before the weight of the line compelled him to flop into the water. Once we got to within boat-hook length of him, but he dived before I could snatch the line. We chased him for nearly two hours. It was hot in the boat, which smelt of new paint, so I got out of my clothes and went overboard when he appeared to be exhausted, while my wife took the tiller. I had been swimming for several minutes when she cried:

"You're absolutely filthy!"

At the same time I noticed the brown smears on my hands and arms. I was swimming with many curious dark bubbles level with my eyes. Whenever one touched my face it left a cluster of minute bubbles which broke and smeared my skin. I tried to rub off some of the smears, and found that I was only rubbing them in the more. Where the smirches were, the water ran off. And among these swarms of bubbles floated what looked like fragments of black decayed moss. I climbed back into the boat, and saw that we were moving in a patch of placid sea discoloured by the false rainbows of crude petroleum. The moss-like stuff was everywhere, in belts of dark scum which on touching the bows left a mark as of tar there. We saw the Parson rise some distance away, and watched him trying to fly. He flapped his wings vainly. His flight quills were clogged. He beat water over himself to clean them, the water of the false rainbows.

We tried to rescue him, pursuing him with the boat-hook until the low sun reddening in the sea vapours gave warning of the late hour. We left him gasping and bedraggled in the scum of oil-fuel cast overboard after the tank-cleaning of unknown ships. Perhaps some of it had come from the ships sunk by submarines during the Great War, or from the submarines sunk by other ships. The sun went down, and the small speck was lost to sight.

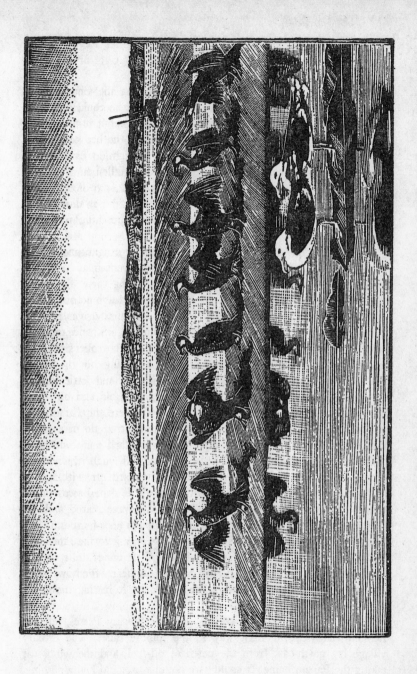

5

Sometimes a great liner from New York, tearing the Channel into whitest rage, bore down upon him so swiftly that he could not swim away in time. Then he would dive, to be thrown about in a darkness of roaring foam which shifted even the crabs on the bed of the sea. Week after week he endured the long agony of flightlessness. He saw other diving birds that were victims of oil-fuel, guillemots with long sharp dusky beaks and brown breasts that should have been white; terns who, in happier days, had graced the air like swallows; and miserable shags, who had left their communal perching rocks for ever.

The gulls robbed them of nearly every fish they caught, and waited for their dead bodies. One morning these gulls went inland, wailing the flock-cries. The wind went after them, hurling them along like feathers, so high were they. The storm wind could leave nothing alone —that blind and restless and uncared-for wind that drives as it is blindly driven. It harried the grey old wrinkled sea, and tore the hair of its billows. With furious gestures it set the rollers to their ancient tasks in slavery: of battering rocks, rolling buoys, tossing boats at their estuary moorings, breaking the slips and jetties of the quay. It knew not the living from the dead, being old and blind before life began. The sea heaved and hollowed where the Parson was swimming, the foam rolled upon his tail as he trod down a wave. He drifted into an area where waves were smoothed and controlled, their crests held under an oily skin. He paddled through it, while the wind wrinkled the sea's false skin, and a little bird ran with fragile feet upon the sullen swell, sipping with its beak. It skated away in the wind to play under a wave-top, and when the wave reared and fell lo! the little bird was under another. For hundreds of miles it had run with the storm, a darling sprite that knew only joy where men and birds found fear. Deep-water men said this little wingèd one carried its egg under a nimble pinion, and hatched it there: for how can it otherwise nest, they asked, when we have seen it in the middle of the Atlantic?

Mother Carey's Chicken, as they call the Stormy Petrel, left the Parson, and went its light way in the sombre mists. The estuary village lay north-east from the patch of oil-fuel, and the wind was taking the Parson home. It could care nothing, it could know nothing, of what would happen to a bird driven helpless to the very quays of its enemies who would be rewarded for its head. Throughout the night it drove him nearer land, past a buoy bearing in an iron cage a bell which clanged drearily in a grey-green waste of sea. When daylight came the Parson was in the estuary, striving in vain to swim out of the fairway where the force of the flood tide was throwing a plume of water over the stem of the rusty ridge buoy. Gush of wind and set of current carried the weak bird to the shore, and the surge flung him up.

He could crawl on the elbows of his wings. Dimly aware that the pounding surge would break him, he dragged himself to the rocks discovered by the last tide, rocks which for ages had been known as stumps and fangs and were now many feet high. In the shelter of one of the monoliths he lay for more than an hour, until he was found by a dog, who called a man by barking. The Parson was too feeble to peck with his hooked beak, too feeble to beat ragged wings. He lay on his side with closed eyes. The yapping of the dog grew louder as its master approached. Thus the Isle of Wight Parson, who had escaped death by water, lead, iron, and oil, fell into the hands of Bill Crang for the third time, to be picked up and carried to his home, by way of the quay, where stood an aged sailor with swollen legs, known as Old Mast-and-Yards, who nodded approvingly, and said in a slow voice cracked like his ancient sea-boots:

"If thee buries un for a week, and then thee bakes un wi' tetties and a bit o' bacon, 'er will taste proper, midear, like a turkey, 'er will, surenuff."

"Ay, aiy," replied Bill Crang, and passed on. He wouldn't eat no Pass'n, like they ould deep-sea chaps.

6

It was Old Mast-and-Yards who told me about the capture of the parson a few minutes after Bill Crang had passed him. I went down to the sands in order to see if any other divers had been washed ashore in the gale, and following the heavy footsteps of Bill Crang, I reached the rock where Phalacrocorax had taken refuge. Looking round the other sides, I found the fishing line which had been frayed against a sharp edge, and pulling it with difficulty out of the wet sand, I recovered the head on the hook. A shilling is a shilling these days—the price of an ounce of tobacco, of a pound of sausages,

of a quart of beer—so I put it in my pocket, and went round to see
Bill Crang.

I found him about to have his tea, to which he invited me. He
said, pointing with a knife at the dish, "I must have my fry for
tea, I must." The fry was pork chops, potatoes ('tetties'), kidneys,
mushrooms, eggs, and black pudding—this last a favourite country
dish, and made of the chopped chitterlings of the pig mixed with
groats and barley, the whole savoured by the blood caught when the
pig is stabbed. Bill loved it, the more since he had killed his pig
himself, and saved the butcher's fee. He liked food in quantity, did
old Bill. No wonder he bulged everywhere under his blue woollen
slop and serge trousers. A bulky man, with fixed ideas, a hearty
muncher of big mouthfuls, a hearty believer in a jealous Gawd ever
ready to 'ur-rl the sinner into the fiery furnace of 'ell heverlasting
furevurr'-an-evurr, brother! Hairs grew out of his ears and nostrils,
his chest was a hair-shirt unto itself.

Yet he was a good fellow, for he had asked me to tea out of his
heart's kindness; partly, I knew, in order to help persuade me to
join his Chapel, a thing for which he earnestly hoped.

"The Devil is everywhere!" he ejaculated, throwing down knife
and fork, and wiping egg fragments off his lips with the back of
his hand, and allowing the dog to lick it clean. The animal waited
for more, while Bill gazed at me for several minutes without speaking. Whenever his gaze met mine it shifted either to the floor or the
ceiling, and I imagined either that he was uncomfortable after
his meal, or that he was collecting his thoughts for a series of remarks
about the Devil.

He cleared his throat, tapped with his fingers on the arm of his
chair, and let out a throaty "Hur?"

I said, "What did you say, Mr Crang?"

He replied, winking several times at me, while his head seemed to
sink low into his shoulders, "You think I don't know nothing, don't
you?"

"What's the matter?" I asked.

He winked again, with a heavy air of timid aggressiveness, said
"Hur?" and after a pause, "So yer wants to know, hur?"

"Tell me, Mr Crang."

"With all yer studying and book-writing, yer don't know everything, so I'll ask yer now. Didden you once say as how you believed
a bird had a soul like a ooman being?"

"Yes."

"Including a Hisle-o'-Wight Pass'n?"

"Why not?"

Bill Crang chuckled, and picked up a match-stick from the floor. "What about Milton?"

I asked who Milton was.

"The celebrated poet as wrote 'Paradise Lost'."

"Well, what about him?"

Three slow winks, more confident winks.

"You think I ain't got no scholard's learning, huh? Milton wrote that poem when 'e were blind. Ye'll know it yerself, hur?"

I confessed that I was still young enough for the school-time distaste of Milton not to have left me; but ignoring my fragment of autobiography, he went on in a louder voice:

"I'm doin' this yurr Milton in my address next Sunday, so ye'd better come and listen, hur? Well, then. Now Milton says in the fourth book of 'Paradise Lost' that the Devil sat like a cor-mor-ant on the highest tree of life. Cor-mor-ant, that was the Devil. Well, then. This yer Hisle-o'-Wight Pass'n is the Hisle-o'-Wight Pass'n's proper name, hur?"

He was getting into stride now, the stride of Sunday afternoon.

"Answer me, brother. Look into yer own soul, and ask yerself this question: Do I still 'old wi' the notion of a Hisle-o'-Wight Pass'n 'aving a soul when I 'ave jes' 'eard Will Crang say as ow Milton said as ow the Devil sat like a cor-mor-ant on the 'ighest tree o' life?"

I replied something about evolution.

"Hevverlution idden no sense!" said Bill, with much contempt. "Now look at me, and ask yerself, do I look as though I were once a monkey? That's all hevverlution is! Why, darnee, midear, tidden about birds at all! Further, brother, suppose yer were to take a Hisle-o'-Wight Pass'n into Chapel, could a' sing a psalm? Could a' understand God's Word? Could a' know what I were a-saying'?"

"Why not?" I said. "God moves in a mysterious way, surely?"

"Get out, tidden no sense! Why, how would a Hisle-o'-Wight Pass'n conduct in a Holy Building?"

"Probably the bird, being natural and faithful to the forces which created it, as Man is seldom faithful, would do its best to get out of the building," I said.

"Exactly!" roared Mr Crang. "And for why? Because the Devil created it for to take the fish which The Almighty put in the sea for Man to feed upon."

In the distance, beyond the closed door, I thought I heard a cry.

"Milton," declared he, "is now a statoo in Westminster Abbey, which, I may tell you, is in Lunnon. Folks put a statoo up to 'im. You and me won't get no statoos, will us?"

Yes, it was a cry.

"You might get a statue," I suggested. His name was already gouged in a cement block on the Chapel wall. It had cost him five pounds.

He tried to look modest. He began, while contemplating the possibilities of a statue, to clean his few remaining teeth with the match. The small noises of his tongue at work were distinct with the brittle chirping of an elderly cricket above the kitchen range; one heard below them the subdued roar of the sea. Again I heard the cry, and the dog heard it too, for with ears cocked he shifted to where the stream of the draught under the door would draw across his nostrils. Yes, it came again, a groaning in the darkness, and I thought of the bird whose burial had been urged by Old Mast-and-Yards. An unbearable thought.

"I think I hear something outside," I said.

" 'Tis most probably they fool chaps up to pub," he replied.

Bill Crang never went into an inn, and he despised those who did.

"May I go in the garden?"

He waved permission with the burnt match. The subdued roar of the sea increased with the cold wind on my face as I opened the door, while holding the scruff of the dog lest it should slip past me. A word from its master made it sink on its paws and blink its eyes. I closed the door, and listened, waiting for the daze of the table lamp to leave my eyes. The sky was clear and starry after the storm. Outlines of things grew near me: I could see boxes, barrels, oars, and other gear take shape around my feet, and beyond them the stalks and leaves of cabbages and winter greens. I heard the sound of flapping, and moved with slow short steps down the garden, staring for guidance at the ground at my feet, which often kicked empty tins and cracked shards of china and glass. The flapping ceased.

I suppose I had been standing still about a minute when a groan broke out of the ground before me, a groan prolonged and feeble, immensely saddening in its remembered association, for had I not heard a friend groan like that, after a week's writhing at a base hospital, just before the spirit left the body pocked with the burns of a phosphorus bomb? The groan ceased in a long sigh, so

startlingly human that my heart thumped with the abrupt change in my mental picture of what was before me. No bird would sigh like that! I peered into the gloom, and saw a pale luminous movement, which in silence uprose before me, and spread sideways into the semblance of a headless cormorant.

It glimmered there. The ghost of the Parson! The apparition had wings and a body, all dimly luminous, and wavering as though behind smoke.

My back went cold, my hair moved.

I am observing a rising from the dead; this is an astral body; such a rising must have begun the legend of the phoenix: these thoughts ran in my head while I watched with a curious detachment of unreality in which I did not completely believe that such a thing could really happen. The ghost stood with outspread wings for perhaps five seconds, a phoenix risen in what strange fire—those wings flapped, and oh! they wafted upon me a most sickening stench of rotten fish.

The wretched Parson was not dead. Bill Crang had flung what he believed to be the corpse in his dressing-pit, with cabbage stalks, old fish and other such stuff put down to rot for next spring's top-dressing, for his garden. The Parson had lain there spread-winged and on his breast until he had recovered from the sea-buffeting. Perhaps the familiar phosphorescent glimmering—familiar because in spring every nesting rock is strewn with the waste catch of cormorants—had helped to revive him. Bruised and hurt by the waves and rocks, his flight quills clogged as with tar, his tongue pierced by a hook and nearly pulled from his throat, the flesh of his breast pitted by shot, scraggy from starvation and sleeplessness: thus was the Isle of Wight Parson whom I took home in a sack to my cottage, to be fed, and tended, until he was well again.

7

We turned over every large stone in two miles of the stream, for the eels which lived there; we gave him dead rats, and dog biscuits soaked in warm water; we stood for hours on the sands at low tide with rods in our hands for the taking of bass which fed on sand-eels in the breakers. All day we sought food for him. Still he flapped and croaked for more.

One day, when he had swallowed a bucketful of fish as fast as I tossed them to him, my wife said:

"He's quite well, except that he can't fly. Why not make him catch his own food?" And she added excitedly: "I say, why not food for us too? With a ring round his neck, so that he can't swallow the big fish!"

"Rather!" I cried. "We'll put the kitten's collar round his neck."

So the Parson was taken out in the boat, and he dived off a thwart carrying a thin line on a little collar round his neck, and swam under for nearly a minute. He came up with a lovely red mullet, which he tried to swallow, and swam about until we took it from him. That night we had a fine supper, while the Parson slept in a shed behind the cottage, tired after the labour of so much swimming and swallowing.

We kept him (or rather, he kept us) throughout the mild weather, and in the New Year he was so tame that he would follow us up the village street. When he flapped his wings, he looked just like a worn-out umbrella, torn and greenish with weather and blown inside-out. In February, however, he shed his old ruined feathers, and took on a new set, which gleamed with bronzy hues; and gay new white ones grew on his thighs, which had not been there when we got him. How could we keep him when we knew how much more those white feathers would be appreciated by eyes that were fishy? So the collar was taken off him, and put on its real owner, a cat. Phalacrocorax was taken to the beach in the side-car, and he flew off over his native sea. We know that he found a mate, and soon they were carrying bunches of seaweed to a rock where six other cormorants were nest-building. And for a while I fancy they will be safe, for the Fishery Board, which must needs economise because we have such big war debts to pay back, has abolished the reward for their destruction. The last shilling paid by the Board, it may be of interest to know, was paid to one who signed himself W. Crang, who tendered a head whose eyes and tongue had been picked out by crabs; the head, I believe, that he had readily accepted in exchange for the Isle of Wight Parson.

Redeye

Old Muggy Smith, the most honest man in the village, and one of the rare human beings in North Devon who refused to repeat or listen to scandal, told me the main incidents of the strange tale of Redeye one summer morning as he sat in the shade on the steps of the village club-room. The stream flowed below, and he used to rest on the third step from the top, in his shirt-sleeves, smoking cigarettes, calling cheery remarks to the passers-by, and meditating about life. Everyone knew him. He traded rabbits and their skins, took telegrams, sold watercress and mushrooms in season, fowls, did any odd jobs for people; he was the best whist player at the Nightcrow Inn. He knew all the details of Redeye's terrible adventure; of his cowardly assault upon the puppy-hound, Lightfoot; of Lightfoot's revenge; of Redeye's homecoming. Here they are.

When Tom Fitchey went to choose a lurcher pup from the litter six weeks old, four pups were playing near their mother, but one was asleep. Immediately Tom decided to have it. The pup was a dog, fawn coloured, with long legs and tail; it resembled its mother in appearance, although its father was a bulldog. Dogs of such divergent characteristics had been chosen as parents in order to obtain the speed of their mother and the courage, tenacity, silence, and scent of the bulldog. For lurchers are poaching dogs, working usually at night; gipsies have them; they must not bark when coursing hare or rabbit. Tom Fitchey chose the pup sleeping by day because his experience taught him that it would be a night-dog.

And he was right. When the pup grew up Tom trained him. The first thing was to break the bladder of a dead rabbit over his nose. Then he gave him skins to tear and play with. He was a lanky creature, very playful, often leaping round in excitement, seeming to swing round by the aid of his long ropey tail. He was gentle, but

Tom soon changed him to a snarling cur. Frequently he was kicked and beaten. Tom was a labourer in a hamlet of North Devon; he was fond of beer, and spent most of his money at the inn. This was a perpetual worry to his wife, who had seven small children. Tom was good to them by impulse; but his simple childlike nature was easily upset, and he behaved with rough cruelty for which, afterwards, he was profoundly but temporarily remorseful. He encouraged Redeye, as the dog was called on account of the tawny glow of its eyes in lamplight, to be shy of other men, and when he saw him inclined to be friendly he would kick him with his hobnailed boot.

Village children avoided Redeye. He was half a wild fox, some men declared. He slunk by them, tail curved between legs, eyes glancing sideways at them. By being brutal to the dog when it was young, Tom had made it brutal. At six months old its mouth was too hard, even for a lurcher. At night, after coming out of the inn, Tom would stroll up the lane, usually singing, or trying to sing in a fuddled voice, the only two bars of 'Roamin' in the Gloaming' that he knew. With a low sound he slipped Redeye from heel, who, creeping under a gate, ran silently up the leeward side of the field, keeping the wind in his nostrils. Tom took a bolt net from his pocket, and fixed it in the gap between the lowest bar of the gate and the ground, but it was hardly needed.

In the darkness to the waiting labourer (always a little fearful) would come a squealing, to which he replied by a squeaking sound made by drawing in wind through his lips and teeth. At the recall Redeye came with a rabbit limp in his mouth, its ribs crushed. Occasionally the yelps of a dog being beaten would follow the bringing of a mangled rabbit that after a longer absence he had partially eaten.

When Redeye was a year old, he met a foxhound puppy in a lane near his master's cottage. The puppy at that time was being walked by Farmer John Tucker, and it was friendly with every living thing it met. It was a whitey-yellow colour, with large pads and a thick neck, long-muzzled and its eyes showed the haw. Lightfoot—for that was its name—approached Redeye who was asleep in the sun, with tail swung so effusively in greeting that its progress seemed to be made by heavy wriggles. The puppy sidled up to Redeye with charming and inoffensive playfulness, but Redeye jumped up with bared teeth and a snarl that made it run away with tail tucked between its legs. Redeye chased Lightfoot, and bit the howling puppy about the neck and head, and for this he was kicked and thrashed by Tom

Fitchey, who worked for the owner of Owlacombe Farm. Light-foot's neck ever afterwards showed the scars of mauling.

But in spite of many other beatings, Redeye continued to serve his master. Often on Sunday, instead of going to chapel with his father and brothers, Tom used to go on the Down, a high expanse of stony ground, whence on fine days the grey Exmoor hills could be seen in one direction and the blue hills of Dartmoor to the south. He sang as he walked in the clear cold air of the sunlit hill. He sang with happiness, with the larks in the sky, the wheatears that flitted before him, and passing bees. His dog barked and danced around him, tail flung in a circle, jumping up at Tom who petted him affectionately. "Fetch 'un," whispered Tom, and Redeye was off roving; leaping on his hind legs many times and gazing for sight of bolting rabbits. One Sunday, when Redeye was two years old, he coursed a hare, quite a rare visitant to the down, a great tan hare with ears black-tipped, that bounded away out of its form. Redeye at its heels ran swiftly, silently, head stretched forward, straining sinew and muscle to reach and snap and crush. Suddenly the hare turned, doubling back; Redeye fell head over heels, and Tom, who was running and shouting encouragement, gave a cry of anguish, think-ing that he had dislocated a thigh, or worse, had broken it. But Redeye recovered and sped after the hare, who came within five yards of Tom, running with head tucked into shoulders, the large eyes looking back in terror at the dog. It did not see Tom, but winded him and altered its course. Tom flung his cap, hoping to bowl it over so that the lurcher might seize it. He missed. They passed him. He yelled and ran after them. The hare sped in curious zigzags about the Down while thinking whither it should run, and remembering a patch of gorse and bracken it made straight for it. Redeye followed, and the two were lost over the curve of the hill. A buzzard rose from its meal of a young rabbit and wailed as they rushed by, beating violently its great brown wings. The hare reached the cover and dashed through; and the dog fifty yards behind imagined, since his experience of rabbits taught him to seek a bury when his prey abruptly vanished, that it had gone into one of the holes under the gorse bushes. Tom came up panting, his heart throbbing, expecting to find the hare dead. He found only the lurcher scratching furiously at a hole, and cursed. Redeye dug the faster, since his mind—a very small mind, and one whose reason-ing was always at moments of excitement or stress dominated by his instincts—reacted to the curse. Tom choked down an impulse to weep; he was bitterly disappointed. The only hare for years in the district had been lost because the mazed loobey of a dog thought it was in a bury. The beating of his heart after the run made him giddy; he sat down and considered that he would not be able to throw the hare on the table, with a careless air, for the missus to exclaim at and the childer to say what a master dog was Redeye. No. And he would not be believed at the Nightcrow Inn, where at Election time many men had made the excuse to call him mazed, and a liar, and a bad workman. The lurcher had lost the hare; no one would listen to him, but laugh, shake their heads; he could have got five shillings from Muggy Smith for the hare.

Tom Fitchey was thin with narrow shoulders; his blue eyes were watery and held the suggestion of sleeplessness; he had a small head, he never brushed his hair, and the ragged ends of his brown moustache were a darker shade owing to regular dipping into ale. He got up and gave the digging lurcher a kick that made it howl for a moment. Redeye ran away, and would not return to him. It was hanging about the cottage when Tom got home, by this time remorseful for his cruelty. He called him, and he came slinking. Tom patted him, but Redeye gave him a quiet deliberate nip in the leg, and jumped away.

That night Tom went out in the lanes and made the recall noise with his lips, but no dog came to him. He grew depressed, and after a week decided either that someone had poisoned the dog and buried it secretly, or that it had been caught in a gin and knocked on the head. It was harvest-time, and he had no dog to chase the rabbits that dashed out of the corn as the machine cut the stalks. Autumn came, with the equinoctial gales, but no Redeye. Winter brought flocks of green plover to the ploughlands, but no Redeye.

2

One evening just before Christmas a young clean-shaven stranger arrived at the Nightcrow Inn. Muggy was playing whist, with Tom Fitchey as partner. The stranger seemed weary. His legs, booted and spurred, were splashed with mud. He wanted to stable his exhausted horse for the night, he said, and to sleep at the inn. He was Sub-Lieutenant Graham, R.N., on leave after six months' course at the Royal Naval College, Greenwich.

The landlord told his son to take the grey mare to the stall, and wisp its muddy legs with straw. While a bran-mash was being prepared, the stranger sat by the stove, drinking ale, and stretching his legs. He invited the dozen or so men sitting on the benches to drink with him. He was stiff and sore. He started to tell them a strange tale, and while he was telling it there was the bay of hounds in the night. His tale ceased. Something bumped into the door. They waited, and a howl, long and deathly-mournful, filled the passage. Someone opened the door. An animal stood there. It had the thin muzzle of a greyhound, wounded and bitten. Its fangs were bared in a snarl. It had a long ropey tail, woefully bedraggled. Stiff blood darkened one side of its head. An ear had been torn off. It stared into the room, its eyes glazed with the light of the paraffin lamp. The gennulmun, who had raised his pot to drink, spilled a lot of the ale on the stone floor. The animal did not move. Muggy was there, in his usual corner, and watched it. For this is what had happened.

At eleven o'clock that morning the hounds met on Exmoor at Brendon Two-Gates. The boundary wall between Devon and Somerset here breaks at the road; the Severn Sea is only a few miles northwards. It is wild moorland. The heather stalks were dark and wiry, bearing the rusted bells of dead summer that nevermore would shake to the wind in purple tune. The peaty ground was sodden, and covered with white tuffs of cotton grass. A few minutes before eleven o'clock the drab moor showed, a mile from the boundary gate, two specks of colour like holly berries. They came up from the low ground, over the curve of the heath, and were seen to be red-coated men on horseback. Between them a trickle seemed to be moving steadily uphill. The young man holding the reins of his tall mare as he lounged by the boundary gate stood upright, watching the huntsman and whip riding over the heather with nineteen and a half couple of lemon, white, and black foxhounds, led by a large yellow-white dog; and trotting at the rear, a wire-haired stumpy-legged terrier.

On the black and white horses the two hunt servants came at a steady trot over the heather. They wore velvet caps of dark blue, with stiff peaks, white stocks, white breeches, black riding boots with dark brown tops, and steel spurs. They carried hunting whips, each with a six-foot leather thong, and a six-inch blue cord lash. The elder man, the huntsman, had a clean-shaven face, brown and

weather-stained as the top of his boots. The whip was younger; his face was still red.

Along the Somerset side of the moorland road an old greybeard farmer was approaching, riding a small shaggy bay pony, once wild, but captured as a sucker and reclaimed. Half a mile behind him a man and a woman were trotting. Father away still, other people were coming to the meet. Across the heather a small schoolboy with a cap askew on head jig-jogged on a pony; there were young farmers; men in ratcatchers; and members of the hunt in West-of-England dark jackets and bowler hats.

The stranger watched lovingly the hounds as they walked around, or sat down; one or two rolling—the young hounds of that season's entry. Two were solemnly licking the neck and muzzle of an old hound named Pensioner; some were scratching flanks or ears with hind feet; one called Moonstone had curled up to sleep. The sun, low in the southern sky, glanced across the dry heather, shining in the black water where peat had been cut.

"Morning, Edward. How's your mother?" said the Master to the schoolboy, who flushed, grinned, murmured "shut up" to himself, raised his cap quickly, and, alarmed at the attention of various people, muttered: "G'morning, sir."

At a quarter past eleven a field of fourteen was at the meet. Mr. Graham, feeling himself a stranger and remaining aloof, had been spoken to by the courteous Secretary, who had advised him to follow the old farmer on the shaggy pony, as he knew every bog and every soft patch on the moor. The Secretary, having collected from him a cap, or day subscription, rode away to talk to the Master. This gentleman, mounted on a very fresh strawberry roan nearly sixteen hands high, was endeavouring to keep his beast still and at the same time to talk to a white-bearded old man with a long sheep-crook in his hand. This was a shepherd, who had come to tell the huntsman of a sheep-worrying fox that slept by day in the bracken of a narrow coombe.

"It be a master girt vox, zur. I didden like to trap or poison he, though he have worrited dree of my ewes to death. It be larger than a moor vox, zur, for it can crack the rib bones with its teeth, surenuff! I be proper plagued wi' voxes, and the yaws (ewes) in lamb, zur."

"Have you seen the fox yourself?" he heard the Master asking.

"Nobbut once, zur. I zeed un down to Bagery (Badgeworthy) Water. It were slinking after a pricket. It runned the pricket, too!"

"Good heavens! Do you hear that?" said the Master to a tall elderly lady standing near with grey melton riding-apron held up in right hand, her fair hair coiled under a bowler hat; the masculine appearance of her long brown face increased by an eyeglass. "Fox chasing a two-year deer."

"Then fox ought to give us a good run, Master!" replied the lady in a deep resonant voice, holding up her foot for the groom to throw her into the saddle.

The huntsman caught a nod from the Master and began to speak in a twangy tenor voice to hounds. Other men and women mounted. An infantry subaltern on leave, riding a hired horse from the stables at Minehead, adjusted his stirrup leathers for the third time; his companion touched his horse with a spur to make it prance—he may have wanted to be noticed by a small and beautiful girl, black-habited, with squirrel-brown hair, mounted on a milk-white Arab pony. This girl was called Diana by another girl riding astride, whom she called Mary. Mary was dark and brown-eyed.

The whip spoke sharply to those hounds that did not prepare to move immediately—Mayfly, Sorrel, Moonstone, Queenie, Trumpeter, Cornflower. The pack moved off, led by the big hound Lightfoot, and immediately behind him trotted his special pals—Magpie, Charmian, Pensioner, Emerald, and Sundew. The short-legged terrier trotted merrily with the pack, finding the heather hard going. He was called Dicky Doone, well known for his courage to tackle fox and badger in earth. He leapt over tufts of heather, following his friends' waving sterns.

For an hour they drew blank. The air of Exmoor, so high under the sky, was cold and keen and sun-frosty. From coombe to coombe the huntsman took his pack, making casts through the cover of bracken and heather on the steep sides. They passed horned sheep which stared at them. From the sea came a sparkling wind. Graham could see nothing but wild moorland and blue sky. During a wait he heard the lady with the eyeglass remark to a short man, dressed in black from pot hat to boots and riding a black gelding, that scent was lying badly. She addressed him as Judge: he had a lobster-red face, a lobster-claw nose, and merry blue eyes. The field was standing at the top of a valley, watching hounds working far away and below. Sometimes short notes on the huntsman's horn came to them, as though it were saying *blank-blank-blank*. A mile up wind a small herd of deer was watching anxiously. Some of the hinds had little prickets still beside them, as well as their calves. *Blank-blank-*

blank sang the faraway horn. Blank it was, and the field moved away to another covert.

This was a broad patch of bracken, and they spread out, cracking their whips in order to drive out any fox that might have his bed there. Sometimes a lark jumped up before them, and once five greyhen rose and flew away like big partridges. A wheeling buzzard watched them; when they were gone it would return to the rabbit it had been eating. They passed the skeleton of a sheep dead a year or more, with wool still on it, or scattered about; raven, crows and foxes had picked it clean. Some animal had been gnawing the skull. A herd of wild ponies cantered away, long tails flying. Often they drove out rabbits, to cries of 'Ware rabbit!', and the crack of a whip-lash.

"Well, it's the first blank day we've had this season," remarked the pink-coated Secretary to Graham; "it's very bad luck for you."

The young sailor noticed the tails of the Secretary's coat, rain-stained with purple, looked like a crushed poppy-petal. The drenching mists of Exmoor had often soaked him, the winds blown rain like ice splinters into his face, the gusts nearly unseating him. Fog often swept over the moor, resolving all things more than three yards away into white chaos. "Yes," repeated the Secretary, taking watch from a flapped pocket in his yellow waistcoat. "One o'clock. It's the first blank—"

He stopped. From the pack in front a hound spoke. It was the fastest hound, Lightfoot. Lightfoot spoke in a querulous high note. Another hound whimpered in excitement. Horses tossed their heads; bits jingled. One began to prance and neigh. Graham shortened the reins in his left hand, and began to tremble slightly at knees with excitement. He loosened the curb reins, not wishing to pull the soft mouth of the mare. He gripped the saddle flaps with his knees, excited and wondering if she would bolt with him and fling him into a bog. It was his first hunt on the moor. Graham was still shaken by recent sights of thousands of Greek bodies of women and children floating in Smyrna harbour, following massacre by Turks.

The leading hounds—Lightfoot, Magpie, Charmian, Pensioner, Emerald and Sundew—were whimpering, nosing the ground in a circle, their sterns a-feather. They waved furiously, just like feathers being tossed in a circle by the wind. Then Lightfoot threw a deep tongue, and ran swiftly with his nose to the ground. The huntsman blew notes on his horn, signalling *Gone away!* The whole pack gave tongue, and streamed after Lightfoot. All the horses cantered after them. The Judge was seen to be fighting his black horse, a boring, pulling gelding; he was swearing to himself, while in front the thirty-nine foxhounds filled the cold clear air with bell-like sounds. Graham's heart snag as the mare lifted him over a gorse bush; he yelled as he viewed a large fox two hundred yards in front.

Over a ditch they flew, the little ponies left behind. The hunted animal made a sudden left-handed turn, they saw him trying to leap a lichened stone wall; fall down; run back and leap again, hounds fifty yards away; saw him hang by his forefeet, draw himself up, scramble over. Hounds came up, baying, trying to follow. Lightfoot, the leader, leapt and fell backwards, leapt again. Five hundred yards behind, Edward the schoolboy on his fat pony Tansy was crying to it to go faster; he wanted to be in at the death. But pony went on at its own pace—an easy little canter. Two hundred yards behind them ran Dicky Doone, yapping for more speed, his stomach very near the ground.

After many falls, Lightfoot clung, pulled himself up, scrambled over. They heard him throwing his tongue in excitement as he ran the line. The wall was too tall to fly. The huntsman cursed. The Master, seeing a piece of glass near scrambling hounds, was heard to exclaim bitterly: "Damme, they're starting a soda-water factory up here!"

Some said there was a gap lower down, and they followed the huntsman. Crying hoarsely, the red-faced, red-coated whip urged the pack off the line, cracking thong-and-lash with noise of pistol shots. "Leu-leu-leu—on, Galloper! Hemlock! (*crack*) Magpie!" (*crack-crack*).

"Make way for hounds, damme!" bellowed the Master at Graham, who in alarm spurred the mare so that she leapt forward and nearly trod on Magpie.

"By heaven, sir!" glared the Master, "why not get inside your mare, sir, and let her use her brains?"

Graham mumbled an apology; the next moment the Master was cursing someone else. Downhill they galloped, finding the gap, holding back dancing horses while hounds poured over, giving tongue to the huntsman's horn. Lightfoot was half a mile away, at the bottom of the steep coombe, where rushed a trout stream over brown rocks. The pack streamed after him; whip and huntsman and groom followed on sliding horses. Above waited the field, looking for fox running up the other side. They saw nothing but a great stag leaping nimbly up to the sky-line. They waited. The minutes went by. The Judge, who resembled a starving Mr. Punch, remarked that the wind had changed. "There'll be a fog to-night, 'Lobster'," prophesied the Master. The Secretary came to Graham, who looked unhappy. "Don't worry," he whispered, "it happens to every one."

Just then a prolonged thin peal of the horn floated up the rocky coombe side.

"Gone to earth," grumbled every one, in tones of disappointment.

Horses started to crop the short grass. Dicky Doone panted up, passed them, went far down the steep slope to the hounds and red-coated men standing beside a granite rock. There was a hole under it. Dicky Doone, whimpering his excitement, plunged through the brown stream and ran to them. It was his show now. He growled as a young hound playfully touched his head with a paw. He panted at the hole's mouth. And just as he was about to enter, the huntsman, with a sudden movement, knelt to examine the marks of pads on the soft earth. They were larger than any he had seen. Hounds bayed, and crowded round; the whip cracked his lash, driving them back. Huntsman drew back, puzzled. Dicky Doone crept down the earth, his hackles raised.

Under the huntsman's orders, the whip kept back the pack, lash-cracking, and shouting in his tenor voice.

Hounds whined and whimpered. Lightfoot did a thing that never before had he done during a check in the chase—he snarled. At the entrance of the earth the huntsman still knelt, listening. There was the sound of worrying. It became deeper and more remote. Something thumped, softly. Flup. Flop.

The huntsman saw the white body of the terrier in the gloom. Then a long tawny animal, blood on its muzzle, white fangs bared, slipped out of the earth quicker than any fox, leapt the stream on boulders, and raced up the opposite coombe side towards the field. Shouts, cries, thunder of hound music in the goyal.

"It's a dog!" cried the Master. "The sheep-worrier! By Jove! it ought to give us a run!"

The huntsman pulled out Dicky Doone. The terrier's head hung lazily, as though he were a puppy, and very sleepy. Wind came wheezingly through a bloody tear in his windpipe. His left shoulder was lacerated. It was not necessary to urge hounds to the line. They ran up the hill like lemon and brown and black leaves before a wind. The hunted animal raced on, made an abrupt right-handed turn, and disappeared over the skyline. Lightfoot led the nineteen couple as they flung from deep throats a great burst of music. Field was mounting; huntsman and whip hastening over the stream; groom nursing Dicky Doone. Shouts and the thudding of hooves. The wild dog fled swiftly. It ran in terror for its life.

Lightfoot had set his pals upon Redeye.

3

Half an hour later Graham was cantering down a narrow lane miles away from where Redeye had broken covert. He was among the first-flighters. At the bottom of the lane there was a tarred road, and running beside it, a river. Just in front of him the Judge tried to pull up his horse; he heard him cursing; its iron shoes slipped, it staggered across the road, and blundering into a tree, tossed the rider into the Lyn with a big splash. A green petrol-tank lorry, drawn up by the roadside when the leading hound dashed down the lane, caused the horse to bolt up the road, one stirrup iron flying and banging the saddle flap. The other was still on the Judge's boot. Stopping to find out if he were hurt, and knowing by the oaths that he was only wet and angry, Graham tapped his mare's flank and plunged into the river. There was a ford at this point, and the water was only two feet deep. His breeches were instantly soaked by splashing. Hounds were giving tongue in a wood below the steep path up which the mare made long, plunging leaps. A hundred yards in front were the Master and the Secretary. It was very steep. He thought that if they slipped, horses and riders would roll down upon him.

He reached the top as the leading hounds came out from the edge of the wood. They ran about confusedly, whimpering, feathering sterns. From far down in the wood came the hoarse encouraging cry as the huntsman, cap in right hand furiously scooping the air, urged them on the line found again. Never had he seen girls so beautiful, thought Graham, seeing the bright eyes and the fresh faces of Diana and Mary, as they came up the hill.

Elsewhere, hoarse voices shouting, hats scooping air, mud on boots and breeches, sweat-lather on horses' necks where reins rubbed, blood-scratches on bellies, soaked girths, mud everywhere. Champing bits and wings of steam blown into the air from wide nostrils. No matter—on, on, on. Huntsman cheered hounds. Behind stringing-out pack the field followed at a canter, the men standing in stirrups. Through the wood, sending earth and leaves flying, while pheasants grated and rocketed away; rotten branches snapped and twigs of oak and hazel whipped hat and cheek. Graham was knocked off by a branch and caught his mount after many minutes. From the river below came the sound of rushing water, sometimes dissolving the mellow bay of hounds now far away. He climbed into the saddle, urging forward the mare with voice, whip and spur.

Half a mile away Redeye was running, tongue a-loll. Behind him, tirelessly following wherever he went, was Lightfoot. Sometimes Redeye knew terror, for the baying of many hounds told him their blood lust. He ran out of the wood, turned left-handed, got to the river and leapt into it. The cold water refreshed him, and he was carried down as he swam, so that he reached the opposite bank some distance downstream. Creeping out of the water he shook his coat, yawned, then leapt into the stream again, swimming with the current. Once again he crept out, shook himself, and loped across a field, coming to the road. Behind him he heard a new sound from the leading hound, a sharper, yelping sound. For Lightfoot had entered the stream where Redeye had entered, swum across, and was running the bank to discover where he had crept out. He ran nose to ground, mute, and coming to the place where Redeye had shaken himself, he spoke sharply, querulously. The leading hounds emerging from the wood with two red coats answered him. But the scent led nowhere. It was sprinkled about; the water held the scent of Redeye's breath.

In a circle Lightfoot cast, whimpering to himself. He could hear the huntsman's shouts to hounds as he told them to cross the stream; the whip was urging others to run the other side of the bank.

It looked to be a muddle.

4

Redeye ran on. He loped up a steep hill, where were bushes of furze and bramble. Several rabbits bolted, but he did not heed them. He felt a weariness in his legs, He scratched a small hollow in the earth, and lay down with his chest in it, to ease thumping heart. His hind legs were stretched out, his red tongue lolled as he panted, five breaths a second. He closed his eyes. Then came the baying of the pack from afar. They had found the line. Immediately he got up and loped on. It was a relief to run on level grass. He came to a five-barred gate, which usually he could leap without any effort, but now he struggled underneath. Grazing sheep in the next field stared at him, stamped forefeet, and bundled away; he ran after them, leaping on the backs of many, barking hoarsely. He was trying to destroy his scent. Twice round the field he drove them and suddenly springing sideways he was off, flying a gap in the bank and coming to a steep heathery slope leading to the skyline.

He was alone; the wild landscape was quiet. There was no sound of pursuit. Only a buzzard wailed high above him. He came to thick rush-clumps, and lay down. His pads were hot. He lay on his stomach, nose to the ground, pointing the way he had come, and panting nearly as quickly as a magpie chatters. It was quiet, and the wind made a sighing in the rushes. Then, once again, he heard the faint twang of the horn, and dreadfully near, the deep, excited tongueing of five hounds, the special friends of Lightfoot—Magpie, Charmian, Pensioner, Emerald and Sundew.

He rose silently, slinking up a steep track in the heather, trying to hold his breath. There was a slight dip in the moor, and when hidden by this he ran with tail flying behind him, and long tongue stretched out to be cooled of its slavering sweat. He came to heather and ran in a circle, trying to throw off hounds by tiring them, for the heather was hard to the feet. He ran for two miles, and came upon a flock of crows and daws feasting on a dead sheep. They rose flapping and cawing; distantly there was the shout of a man, the twanging of the horn, and a noise like confused murmurs of bells, swelling on the wind to many deep bayings.

Redeye remembered the sheep; he had worried and killed it three weeks previously. Cracks sounded, the yelp of a hound stung by lash; the pack was being whipped off the scent in order to be laid on again at the point where the huntsman had viewed him. The crows had betrayed him. *Leu leu leu*—and on again, where the heather gave way to tufts of yellow-white grass. Soft ground, ease for hot, cut feet. Ease for a little while only, then onwards, with the chorus ever behind.

On he ran, mile after mile. Hounds became mute, with a note now and then. One by one, far behind, horsemen dropped out with foundered horses. He splashed into black shallow water lying in the patches where peat had been cut; crossed a moorland road, ran over heather again, down a steep rocky coombe for half a mile, and then a moment's rest while ribs were cooled in amber water. Upwards

again, hounds ever following, till he reached the crest where the wind came cool. Onwards through wiry heather that hurt his feet. Snipe rose in zigzag flight before him, calling *skiap, skiap.*

He came to a place where the heather was scantier, where the cotton grass grew in clumps. The ground was very wet, and he loped over it, coming to another stream at the bottom of the slope. He lapped water, splashed through, and climbed again to a ridge, running on a desolate place of scree which added hurt to his feet. He ran down the slope into another coombe, through the stream that rushed over the boulders, and toiled wearily upwards with hanging head and dragging tail. He passed by green bog, wild duck getting up with a whistling clatter of wings before him.

There he flopped down. Two tiny figures on second horses were miles behind him. Hounds were running mute, but following. For several minutes Redeye lay and panted. Then coming up the slope, alone and very near, he saw Lightfoot. He staggered to his feet, and trotted on. Reached the crest of The Chains, where the sea breeze was blowing hard. Far away the sea was sombre, and the long headland of Hartland purple in the sunless light. He set his face for home, and trotted on.

Behind him Lightfoot pushed steadily on his scent. Less than half a mile behind the dingy white hound ran, mute and terrible in resolve, the loyal five. The hunted thought of rabbit smells, of the smell of the human who ages ago had fed him. He recalled the smell of the cat he had killed. The sea-wind opened his memory as he ran westwards to the wire boundary fence, crawling through it from Somerset into Devon. He passed the Longstone Barrow, loping onwards over Challacombe Common and past Blackmoor Gate. Often he lay down, whining at the memory of sleeps he had slept. Above him in the pale sky the buzzard wailed, *Finish, Finish.* He began to cough harshly, the exertion causing him to totter on puffy legs, but he staggered onwards, swaying and wheezing through failing light—and eyesight.

5

Sirius, the great star-hound of the winter heavens, woke and yawned silver in his kennel of evening-blue space. Dusk came, and the mighty Dogstar broke the chain of day, and gave tongue in green music, and glared fire i' th' eye, and bounded after Orion, and together they began the hunt of strange spirits over the horizon of time, where no mortal may follow.

But earthly chase lasts not for ever. Under the glimmering stars Tom Fitchey's runaway lurcher slunk into a farmyard not very far from his native village, and avoiding a particular spot between a wall and a haystack, collapsed.

A minute's run away the hound Lightfoot padded mute, nose to ground, on a weak scent. Scent was weak because Redeye was weak —it failed as his strength failed. On the high ground behind him a fog had come with the changing wind, creeping over Exmoor. In twos and threes the pack was wandering home to the kennels at Brendon, led by Moonstone and the lazy ones—Mayfly, Sorrel, Queenie, Trumpeter, Cornflower. Only Lightfoot kept on, with two and a half couple of hounds three minutes behind him—Magpie, Charmian, Pensioner, Emerald and Sundew.

Redeye lay still. A bat passed by the stack. A rat rustled in the straw. The puffy legs twitched. He shivered. It was thus that his old enemy found him, giving a great snarl and rushing at him, stern straight, hackles raised, teeth bared.

Redeye leapt up silently. He sprang a yard, over the spot he had avoided, and turned to meet the hound. Lightfoot dashed at him, seized his ear, but was abruptly checked by a metallic snapping noise that seemed to pitch him forward. He gave a scream of pain. A shudder passed over him; then he was snapping wildly the air, Redeye, the straw, his paw, the iron thing that held him. In the dark distance hounds gave tongue, but Redeye had him by the cheek and was tearing the skin. His hackles too were raised. His tail too was straight. The two dogs worried and snarled at each other's throats. Redeye fought with the fury and rage of a mad dog. He was chopped and bitten, but all he cared was to tear out the throat of the hound that had hunted him. He drew back; but Lightfoot did not leap at him. The hound in a whimpering fury of pain and fear snapped at the iron thing that clung to his broken leg, at the chain that held the fox-gin to the peg driven into the ground. He broke his teeth on the steel spring; and now Redeye's teeth sank into his throat, and he had him, worrying, shaking, twisting—*clump, clamp, clamp* went the fox-gin whose iron teeth had broken the leg-bone. The struggles of the trapped hound weakened, but Redeye still shook and worried, his teeth set like those of the gin. His ear was bitten off, but he did not know it, or feel anything. He had the hound

by the throat, and only when hair, skin and flesh, grasped in the bite, came away was Lightfoot released. Redeye gulped down the mouthful, and slunk away from the dying hound lying twisted across the gin set by the farmer to catch the animal (presumably a fox) that had been taking his fowls.

He slunk away, but half a minute later was loping over field and hedge, with five hounds following, running mute—Magpie, Charmian, Pensioner, Emerald and Sundew.

Muggy saw the beer spilling from the gennulmun's pot, and looked again at the open door, where stood an animal with the light of a smoky oil lamp glazing its eyes.

Hearing the baying of hounds again, and nearer, Tom Fitchey leapt up and closed the outer door, just in time. Hounds flung themselves against it, scratching, snarling, and whimpering.

Redeye stood motionless. One forefoot was advanced. His fangs were bared. Only his tail moved downwards, almost imperceptibly, as though with relief. Hounds bayed at the outer door. He stood still, on the threshold, facing the lamp. They watched for ten seconds, twenty seconds, half a minute. He never moved. His snarl was fixed. He stared straight. Slowly, very slowly, his tail went down till the tip touched the floor.

Hounds went on baying. Still Redeye stood in the doorway. Tom Fitchey touched him. He fell over dead—run stiff—heart burst and broken—muscles set. He lay as though frozen on the stone floor of the Nightcrow Inn.

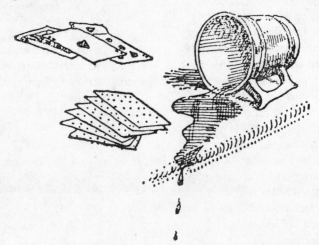

T'chackamma

Jafta Hallelujah, an old Kaffir shepherd with kick-scarred shinbones, who guarded the flocks of his master on the lower slopes of the mountain, saw the dark shapes of baboons moving high up across the ravine, and was frightened. He dared not run to Intaba Kraal and tell Baas, for Jafta Hallelujah feared the shapes more than the Boer farmer. Evil spirits dwelt in them, and the most dreaded is T'chackamma! *Maye Maye!** Jafta Hallelujah struck his wrinkled bald pate with his wrist, and wept.

Half an hour before sunset, the Cave of Bats held all the tribe. Dog-headed, with close-set eyes, they squatted round T'chackamma, whose low gibbering speech was made with many grimaces. Some scratched themselves as they listened to the plans of raiding Intaba Kraal. Often the Chief ceased speaking and held up his head, closing his eyes with the pleasure of being scratched by his wife. He grunted, fluttering his white eyelids, and the upper lips of his face curled back from his teeth. Such teeth! They had been magnificent, but T'chackamma was growing old, and the years of captivity spent behind iron bars, and the lack of scorpions had ruined them. Brown tartar nicked the necks of four incisors. T'chackamma wore a collar, which was the only article of civilization amongst the tribe. Many eyes watched him, but none so fixedly as the eyes of T'je. The little male, who had left his mother only a few months, sat at the feet of Chief, absorbed in every expression of the patriarch's face. He was awed by the collar Chief wore. So intense was his admiration, that whenever T'chackamma coughed, T'je usually needed to clear his own throat. Whenever T'chackamma hooked away something in a finger-nail, and crushed it in his teeth, this being the readiest revenge for torment, T'je usually happened to be bothered by a stinging itch

* O Grief, Grief!

at the same moment. As a fact, the youngster had few fleas; but he was at an age when he learned by imitating.

T'chackamma's voice ceased, and all began to talk. The air, already thickened with the warm breath of the assembled tribe, was stirred by gutteral cries and mutterings of excitement. Three males, detailed by the Chief as scouts, pushed their way through a group of females, some of whom had young at the breast, and climbed along and down the narrow ledges above the ravine. Sometimes they swung themselves, easily, down the tough, rope-like stems of creeping plants. The empurpled glow of sunset was fading off the peaks of the mountains, and stars were about to glitter in the sky.

T'chackamma sat and listened at the mouth of the cave, and they waited behind him. With a wafting of air many bats tumbled fluttering, one following another, out of the lifeless darkness of the remote cave into the rich gloom of African night. T'chackamma gave them one glance, and forgot them. He was thinking of the blood he would drink that night. He hated white men, and in both wakefulness and sleep he would sometimes groan as his memory made pictures of the thousands of white faces which had mocked him in captivity. That captivity had ended when one evening in the greatest rage he had broken his chain, and surprised the white man who had brought his supper, catching him by the arm that emptied a bucket of food into the trough, and pulling him through the door. The keeper had been a strong man, but in contest with T'chackamma his arms and spine were no more than mealie stems. At the subsequent inquiry, the written report of the doctor who had examined the body had not been made public, so awful had been the way of death. The escape of T'chackamma, which was cabled to every civilized country in the world, at the time thrilled and appalled the people of five continents; but the sequel was known only to the Kaffirs of Intaba Kraal and to the baboons of the Cave of Bats until Jafta, feeling death upon him, whispered to me out of his parching throat, years after it happened.

T'chackamma returned to his home on the mountain a year and a half after his escape. It is perfectly true that he was greeted with cries of joy, for Jafta Hallelujah heard them, and he saw T'chackamma's wife embrace him, and watched her efforts to tug off the steel collar which was fastened round his neck in an incomprehensible manner.

The moon's rim rose through the mists of the veldt. Like a ripe and heavy gourd it rolled up the sky, in a glow of its own yellow juice. It threw a shadow of T'chackamma on the rocky wall, framed with a tangle of creepers. He turned, and in the direct pale rays the face of the blood-drinker was ringed with two white patches of skin. As he dug the hair below the ribs with a hook of four black fingernails, he rolled his eyeballs and fluttered his eyelids. He muttered a curse against the fleas, and when a baboon bumped into his back, he turned with a deep-throated snarl, which made it cower back. Imprisonment and torture had lacerated his nervous temper.

The Cave of Bats was not a place of dwelling, but a place of congress, where the baboons went when a raid upon a veldt homestead was being planned, or in times of common danger; for every white man and his dog were their enemies, and the white man's law gave them no protection. The cave had one permanent occupant, a grey-headed ancient who had been old when T'chackamma was crawling round his mother's knees. She lived deep in the cave, beyond the shaft of daylight that came through a fissure in the roof. She was the guardian of that which was in the cave beyond the daylight crack, of that which no baboon had looked upon as it glimmered at the end of the cave under the mountain, and lived. They feared the guardian, for none who passed her had ever come back. Every day food was brought to her, and she never spoke.

They waited and listened. The precipices of the mountain across the ravine echoed multitudinous whisperings and devil-like chucklings which were water-noises from the river in its rocky bed below. A bird of the night, with great soft wings, flew with black flaps across the starlit mouth of the cave, returning as it came, in absolute feather-silence. As T'chackamma peered it let out a screech and tumbled in the air to clutch one of the bats which were hawking insects. The owl flew away, but like the ghosts of dead bats the screeches tumbled back, again and again, fainter and fainter, in an irregular sequence.

2

The swelled yellow gourd, freed of earth mists, shrunk hard and small and silver as it floated in the sky. A lion's roar came up from the river, and soon afterwards the cry of a scout. Immediately T'chackamma quitted the cave, and descended swiftly, followed by the tribe. He cared nothing for any lion which indeed, meeting the baboons, would have fled. The toes of their feet gripped the edges and juts of rocks as readily as their fingers.

By the side of the river, two hundred feet below the Cave of Bats, the warriors formed themselves into two columns, which protected the flanks of the main body of females and young. Some of the younger baboons, excited and frolicsome, bumped into the legs of their elders, and T'je, leaping away from a playmate, butted the naked hindquarters of the leader. He cowered, with hands on head. T'chackamma the Morose, T'chackamma the Terrible! Fingers caught playful T'je by the shoulder and dragged him off his legs, a hand thrust back his head, teeth gnashed by his shut eyes, hot breath made him whimper in a death-fear, another hand pressed nostrils and mouth so that T'je could neither cry nor breathe. Thus held, he was told that the least noise would mean his jaws being torn apart as a scorpion's tail is ripped out of its joint, and then he was flung on his back and left gasping in a yellow-bush. He picked himself up and followed quietly, at the very end of the main body, since T'chackamma was at the very beginning.

Hyenas slunk away when they winded what was coming, and slunk back to the carcase of the ox stricken at dusk by one of the lions which they had been following for many weeks; for hyena eats what lion leaves.

T'chackamma led them on. The stars flashed above, and the moon gave them shadows. The shufflings of pads on the dry veldt moved like a vast sigh of breathing. They advanced steadily and cautiously, although they were several miles from Intaba Kraal where lived Mijnheer van den Wenter, the farmer who had captured T'chackamma and sold him to a menagerie owner.

Jafta Hallelujah, who had lived with a wife in a stone hut in the midst of mountain pastures, had known for weeks T'chackamma had returned to the mountain, but he had not dared to tell Baas at Intaba Kraal. For Jafta knew whose spirit dwelt in the mortal frame of T'chackamma, a spirit who would be the more terrible if T'chackamma were killed, for then the spirit would be free. To Jafta the Kaffir, who had taken the Holy Bible name of Hallelujah as a protection against as many devils as possible, the baboon was sacred, that is, a revengeful power to be feared and conciliated. Inside the hut Jafta Hallelujah and his wife huddled on their bed strung with thongs of ox-hide, and waited for the first agitated *tottle tonk* of an iron sheep's bell that would mean that T'chackamma had come.

3

Miles away in the homestead of Intaba Kraal the Boer farmer sat before a smouldering fire of dried cow-dung and roots of yellow-bush. His hair was worn long and fell from his forehead down the sides of his long face in lustreless hanks like drying tobacco leaves. A scar, the shape of a stork's foot, drew together the flesh of one cheek; the scar of a clutch by T'chackamma. He munched his meagre supper of griddle cake, baked on the open hearth, and biltong, or sun-dried strips of meat, and sipped a mug of native beer made from the grain of dura. A barrel of the beer had been brought to the stone-built homestead that afternoon, and left in an outhouse.

The huts of Intaba Kraal, the native compound, were built of mud and thatched with reeds, under one roof of which psalms were sung on Sunday afternoons and the Bible read aloud to Kaffirs.

Many dogs padded about Intaba Kraal, big mangy animals which lived on what the Kaffir women did not want, and the vultures did not take, from the knacker-heap away from the farm buildings. They were cattle dogs, for Mijnheer van der Wenter had lately increased his stock. Sometimes when the moon was full these dogs went hunting on the veldt, their leader being Zwart Piet, a cross between boarhound and mastiff, and sire of more than half the dogs of Intaba Kraal.

On two nails driven into the ceiling beam in the homestead kitchen rested an old rifle and bayonet, which van den Wenter had taken during the South African War from one of the English prisoners. This weapon had killed subjects both of Queen Victoria and of T'chackamma. A bandolier, rubbed with mutton fat to preserve the leather, hung from another nail, beside the bags of dried herbs used in the cooking pots of the young Kaffir woman who lived in the house.

The moon was just rising when she removed Mijnheer van den Wenter's boots for him, before going to bed. The Boer farmer carried rifle and bandolier upstairs. It had been his custom to lay it along the wall under the head of his bed, loaded, for many years; ever since he had killed a Kaffir who had stolen a case of Schnapps. And on this night, when he heard cries of "Baas! Baas!" and the sound of blows striking the main doors of the building, the first thing he did after the sudden awakening was to lean over and under the edge of the bed until he felt the chill metal of the butt-plate.

With the rifle in one hand he pulled back the heavy dark curtains from the small window, and muttering to the native girl to stop her whining, unfastened the leather loop and opened the casement. The head boy, a Kaffir nearly sixty years of age, stood below, beating the door with a knobkerry. "Baas! Baas!" In the clickering jabber of his native tongue he shook out bits of his fearful tale. Baas shouted to him not to be a fool, but to say what was the matter. The head boy was beseeching the devils not to kill his little children—the little children being between the ages of six months and forty-seven years. While the terrified Kaffir jabbered on his scarred and bony knees, mixing prayers for his safety to his own particular god and wails to his master not to beat him, a white conical object fluttered past his head, and seeing it, the old man fell with a moaning wail upon his face. The farmer shouted *Suka bo!** many times, threatening that he would come down with the sjambok and beat him if he did not say what was the matter. When the head boy saw that it was only Baas' nightcap which had fallen upon him, and not the vengeance of the Alungunyani for coming to tell that the baboons were raiding the outhouses and the mealie fields, his terror went from him, and crying, "T'chackamma, Baas, T'chackamma!" he fled.

The young Kaffir girl had made a light, in which the gilt letterings of Scriptural texts in Dutch gleamed on the white-washed walls. He pulled on breeches and socks, thrust arms into coat, and with bandolier and rifle and candle, jumped down the stairs. Feet were stamped into boots on the warm hearthstone. He took a cowhorn from the wall, and running to the door, slid back the wooden bar. All things under the moon were unreal and dim, with blackest cut shapes which were shadows.

He placed the horn to his lips, and blew. He waited less than a second before blowing again and listening for the answering tongues of dogs. Silence, except for a far-away sound like the Deutscher cheer of *hoch!* once. He knew it for the alarm signal of one of the baboon scouts. He cursed the dogs, the scores of dogs that lived on him and were gone the moment they were needed. Again the alarm horn sounded in the starry night. He imagined the ruin of his crops, with nobody to help him as he began to run towards the large mealie field, blaspheming in his helplessness.

"Zwart Piet!" he yelled, "Zwart Piet! To me, Zwart Piet!" He raved against the mongrel mastiff with the great sullen head, whose teeth more than once had fastened in the heels of strangers' riding-

* Get up, blast you.

boots; and ripped the shoulders of a stranger's horse. "Come to me, Zwart Piet!"

No dog came. The pack was miles away on the veldt, hunting. He went on alone, with long strides of his big lean limbs. He knew his danger, but rage made him heedless. He thought only of shooting T'chackamma, who in the past had torn open scores of his lambs for the milk inside them, and with his tribe in one night had destroyed a season's crops.

He was panting when he stopped at a stone wall, on which the moon made shadows of his head and arms and rifle. The mealie field was still in its fixed and soundless extent. Even the mice did not squeak. He rested elbows on the top of the wall until a noise caused the end of the rifle shadow to slip below on the leaves of the mealies. His forefinger crooked round the trigger, for the noise had been that of an old Kaffir belching—exactly as the drunken Kaffir Ngoza had done when first he had slashed him with the whip of rhinoceros hide. While he stood with sweat dripping from under his raised shoulder (for that Kaffir had been flogged to death) the immobility of the field changed one fragment of its bewildering light and shade. A deep harsh cry broke out near him. The cry, so sharp and unexpected, seemed to give life to related patches of darkness. The patches moved with a running rustle of leaves. At once he saw that a bow of his enemies was drawn around him. Some crouched on the wall to the left and right of him, in soundless and threatening attitudes. They crouched so still that he could define them not at all after the first concerted movement. Every shadow was a baboon.

He became afraid. With a weakening feeling of horror he saw two white rings fixed directly in front of him, apparently in the air. They seemed to float in moonlight as they came forward slowly, without a sound, without a visible movement. He raised the rifle to fire, although he knew that his life would end a moment afterwards. While he stood there, physically unable to press the second joint of finger against the iron, the bow untautened into a ragged roar. He turned and ran. They did not follow. They departed from Intaba Kraal, for their homes in the mountain by way of the pasture land where Jafta Hallelujah on his wood-and-thong bed lay quaking as he waited for the cries of dying lambs to arise in the night.

4

Far above the ravine, over the peaks of the mountains, a bird soared as though unable to descend to heavier airs. Its shadow rushed through the ravine to the lower slopes of the mountain, and over the browning sward in which were embedded rocks. Already the life of the grass was being drawn upwards in a quivering ascent of torrid air, which, like glassy flames without colour, seemed about to melt and crumble the mountain. The sun blistered the sky. Wheeling in this airy place, the bird saw the baboons creeping on the earth as they fed. From nearly two miles above, its eyes could see T'chackamma pulling up stones. Those eyes could look at the sun: they had a third eyelid, a membrane which was like a darkened film. But they rarely looked sunwards. No food on the sun. Food below soon, for it saw the horsemen and dogs approaching the mountain. T'chackamma had not yet seen them. They were ten miles away.

T'chackamma was hungry again, and very thirsty. He left no stone, that was a stone, and not part of the mountain upjutting from the earth, unturned. Even big stones he pulled up, sometimes placing both feet against footholds and tugging with long hairy arms. He was looking for ants. He picked them, cocoons and all, out of the fibrous cavities which were their homes suddenly disrupted to the glare of the sky. He picked them off in thumbs and first fingers of both hands, and pounded them into paste in his grinder teeth. Every minute about a hundred, kicking and biting and stinging, went into the mouth. Ants were his favourite food.

He fed apart. He stepped as though with caution, sometimes glancing under his arms. An ignorant stranger spying through a telescope might have thought that T'chackamma was peering shyly at the little female following him. But no, T'chackamma was making sure that no one was getting any of the ants he might have missed. And the little baboon following was not a female, but T'je, who in spite of blows and tweaks, persisted in following T'chackamma. He followed him everywhere, filled with admiration, a desire to imitate.

T'je, rather stiff with unbloomed bruises and his pelt pitted with old and new holes where the teeth and nails of T'chackamma had dug for various punitive reasons, followed his Chief with many glances of his bright eyes.

T'je did not get many ants. Yet he got something that Chief had missed, for in wrenching up an insignificant lump of rock, T'je found a scorpion. With glee he flicked it out of its hole. Play first, and thought of how nice it would taste. He picked it up by a leg, and dropped it. He pretended to seize it by the sting in one hand, while he pinched a foreleg with the other. While amusing himself with the scorpion, he forgot about T'chackamma.

He soon tired of play, and was about to tear out the sting, when he happened to see, out of an eye's corner, that Chief was within two yards of him. T'chackamma walked upon him with exceeding slowness. T'je's mouth opened, and he jibbered *"Wo! Wi? Wo!"* He swallowed eat-water. He coughed a small cough. He pretended that it was necessary to scratch himself, but after three scrapes decided that the scorpion must be de-stinged immediately. He did so, with trembling fingers, and was jibbering to himself, possibly pretending that he had not seen Chief so near, when a very loud *Hoch!* made him aware that he was expected to look up.

Little T'je looked into the eyes of T'chackamma. Chief's white eyelids disappeared into his wrinkly head, as though with utter amazement at the audacity of T'je in daring to find a scorpion on ground that T'chackamma had passed over. Chief drew in a deep breath, and his eyes turned upon T'je, who was about to flee with the scorpion to his mother when it was snatched out of his hand and he was bitten through an ear and hurled downhill. With a grunt and a frown T'chackamma watched him going, shook his head slowly, swung round his hindquarters (which pointed upwards) and proceeded to divide the scorpion and to munch the portions. Then slowly, his pink callosities, naked from so much sitting on hot rocks, wrinkling at every step, he went down for the fourth time to drink water. He had a thirst. He had been very drunk the night before, on the barrel of dura beer found in the outhouse at Intaba Kraal.

T'je peered at him from behind a boulder, where he found a lizard, which he promptly ate. Afterwards he too went down to drink (when the Chief had gone), and, his thirst quenched, he walked uphill to be near T'chackamma.

5

It was T'je who, about an hour past noon, gave a barking cry of *hoch!* as a warning to Chief. T'je's cry preceded others by the time of an eye-blink. Baboons ran in their peculiar, cantering four-footed

shuffle to form a drawn bow, strung tense in common danger whose arrow of waitfulness was barbed by the scrutiny of T'chackamma acutely immobile on a rock a hundred yards in front of them. They saw horsemen, several native stirrup runners, and a pack of dogs.

They came nearer. T'chackamma crouched on his commanding rock, one foot crossed over the other. His head, which gave him the appearance of having had a boar and a dog for parents, never moved. High above them the vulture on widespread wings cut circles in the blue and open sky. The horsemen dismounted, and climbed the difficult ways in the kopjes of the mountain's base. Among the baboons, only T'je moved. He walked forward. He climbed Chief's rock, and sat on a crag behind him. In attitude he was a small statue of T'chackamma. He scratched himself, as though nothing was happening, even when T'chackamma got down from his rock and, step by step, walked towards the pack.

T'je watched Chief, wanting to follow him, but held to the rock by a sensation between a thrill and a fear which filled his mouth with eat-water. The more his glance lengthened and shortened between the enemy dogs and Chief, the more T'je was unable to move. He tried to cry out a warning as the dogs, viewing the solitary baboon, bayed together. He could not cry. He gurgled, and gripped the rock in terror when T'chackamma suddenly turned, and at a lumbering gallop came back, passing the rock and leaving him alone. T'je had never expected this! He cried out, but Chief never stopped. T'je wailed in the awfulness of his desolation, and shrieked when the dogs reached the rock and climbed upon the lower natural steps, trying to spring to where he crouched.

Three smaller birds were now watching from the sky. In a lower and hotter air they cut each other's circles of flight above the rock where sat T'je. One of them swooped at his head, and when he looked up he saw eyes with yellow rings and a curved beak and feet with black claws; and when he looked down he saw tongues and fangs and eyes. T'je cried to his mother, he cried to T'chackamma. Chattering through teeth he implored the hawks to fly away; and he told the dogs that he would tell T'chackamma if they did not stop snarling at him.

Upon other rocks three hundred yards up-mountain the baboons were perched, in their regular defensive formation of a bow so supple that at a command from the leader the ends would draw together in an immediate circular envelopment. The cries of the small baboon came to them with the snarls of the farm dogs.

T'chackamma barked.

Twenty-three grown baboons and a dozen youngsters climbed down and walked forward two hundred yards. T'chackamma walked before them, in the centre of the bow.

The patriarch, who had reckoned the numbers of his enemies when he had gone forward alone, continued to advance leisurely on all fours when the baboons of the defensive bow stopped and mounted rocks. T'chackamma carried his tail at first curved upwards, and then hanging down. As he neared the foremost dogs that tail swung left and right, moving with his gaze and the shifting of his feet.

He walked slowly, almost leisurely. Sometimes he stopped to beat the earth with his hands. Step by step the distance between baboon and pack was shortened. The bow behind drew into an arc of warning. Its ends began to outflank the pack. T'chackamma's eyes never blinked as his gaze swung over the faces of the dogs. *Pat-pat-pat* of hands on the brown and brittle grass, where in stony fragments glinted metallic ores. Slowly he walked nearer. As he approached Zwart Piet, the purple naked patches of his face deepened in hue. He was very angry. The dogs drew back, snarling and bristling. They were afraid. He was terrible and quiet. A shadow fled over the ground before him, flung down from where the vulture soared.

Slower and slower the big baboon walked towards the rock where the little baboon was crouched. He moved alone with his shadow, swinging left, swinging right, swinging left, swinging right, and in a sudden dust leapt over the head of Zwart Piet, and was beside T'je, and had knocked him on the head as a warning to cling to his rescuer in complete obedience.

Zwart Piet, the colour of dirt, ugly and strong and fearless, stirred the pack into a dusty upheaval of tails and teeth and hackles. With T'je clinging to his back, T'chackamma looked at them. The gaze of his close-set eyes fell upon Zwart Piet, and they opened wide, while his head went up and his mouth opened. He barked.

The bark appeared to break into fragments against the rocks whereon the warriors sat. Flying chips seemed to detonate in the sunshine. After the cracks one baboon sprang into the air and caught its tail as though it would climb up its own spine. Another baboon screamed as it rolled off a rock, to twitch and lie still across an ant's highway below. Another, who had been yawning, ceased to yawn, and with a drowsy mutter lay down as though to sleep.

Baboons quitted their seats in a panic. Another volley was fired. The defensive bow formation was broken, as the females and young retired before the males. T'chackamma looked down at the dogs and at the fleeing tribe. He sat still with T'je and gazed at the lengthening distance. A shot struck the rock at his feet and whined over his head in ricochet. With T'je clinging with all fours to his back, suddenly he sprang among them, bounding through the way which opened in their midst, and with the pack at his tail, galloped towards the fugitives.

Zwart Piet headed him off, and he turned to the left, towards the ravine, making for Lamm'gei's Rock, where he could climb to safety. The dogs gained on him so swiftly that they pulled him down by the tail as he reached the pinnacle, the base of which was strewn with the fragments of old bones.

6

High above, from the terraces and ledges before the cave of Bats, the females and young of the tribe looked down upon him. The vulture soared level with them, watching fourteen dogs attacking the baboon, and waiting for the flesh of the slain.

The tails of the mongrels, of many hues and shapes, some short and bushy, others long and mangy, waved as though from the hindquarters of headless dogs. Their bristling backs heaved. A bass vibrating sound, neither growl nor snarl nor howl, came from the pack. It was as though much water was boiling under the rock. It was the sound of worrying, for a boar-hound, brother of Zwart Piet, had got its teeth in the skin of T'chackamma's throat, and other teeth were biting upon the body. Dog-teeth bit dog in the excitement of the easy victory. Baboon-teeth gnashed on bone, and the nerves of the brown-nicked incisors, inflamed by the drunken night before, released a spasm of strength that empowered him to turn in a somersault, and kick, with his hind legs, the boar-hound into the abyss. Upright again, he let out a bellow.

Without pausing, the mastiff sprang at T'chackamma, who tightened his legs for a leap sideways from his sitting position, in order to have his back guarded by Lamm'gei's Rock. T'je, who all the time had clung to Chief's back, snapped at the mastiff in its mid-air spring, and bit its tail. Zwart turned his lined and sullen face upon the little baboon, and would have had T'je off and under his forelegs while he tore his throat, *if* T'chackamma had remained where he was; but T'chackamma had leapt, and taken T'je with him.

Back to the wall, he faced thirteen dogs, twelve of them quailing when they saw his black head set, almost without neck, upon his terrific shoulders. He patted the ground with one hand, as though with irritable impatience. He turned his inflamed eyes, in their white circles of creased skin, from one to another. They feared to attack him, and infuriated by their barking, he put T'je behind him, ran forward, snatched a dog, and threw it over the precipice. Jafta Hallelujah saw it falling. They rushed upon him, trying to fix their teeth in his legs and thighs, and springing for his head. He clasped one in each arm, biting left and right, and so powerful the muscles of his jaws that both their spinal columns were broken. He flung them after the other corpses. Zwart Piet tore a mouthful of skin from his belly, and, avoiding the death-hug of the long arms, ran back, to await a better chance. T'chackamma embraced another dog, who before dying fastened its teeth in his left hand, cracking three of the finger bones. As he dropped it a frothing muzzle thrust over the lolling head of the slain, and bit T'je in the leg. T'chackamma leaned over and paralysed the dog by biting through the nerve at the base of the skull; and even as they hesitated, he picked up the body and flung it at Zwart Piet.

T'je, crouched behind his Chief, was gibbering in pain and fear. T'chackamma stood on a raised platform of rock, his eyes smeared with the gore of his enemies, and his own blood welling from many bites. A swarm of flies buzzed about his ragged coat. Seven of his enemies were slain.

The others ran at him together. He met them with open jaws and arms, and bit thrice. Three dogs fell back and spun crookedly as they tried to lick away the agony in three splintered thigh bones. The baboon took one in a grasp upon the scruff of the neck that tore hair from skin, pulled it to him, bit through the neck, and fell over, panting.

He pushed himself back on to three limbs, while T'je cowered under him, and he was almost balanced for a sitting position when Zwart Piet ran in upon him with lowered head and set his teeth in T'chackamma's thigh. The baboon roared, and bent over to bite the mastiff. His teeth snapped on the steel studs of the thick leather collar, and with all the power of his jaws he tried to bite through it. He broke some teeth, and unable to make the mastiff loosen its hold, he seized the head and wrenched it away, and sank back afterwards, with the sinews of his thigh stripped from the muscles by the clenching teeth. Another dog mouthed at his right flank, but fell back in its own fear, to lie with the other dogs ten yards off, and pant and watch T'chackamma.

7

Dwarfed shadows began to creep out of the bases of rocks, and to spread over the hot ground. Below on the slopes, where the advance line of the baboons had squatted, three bodies lay and stank in the sunshine. Each body was marked for the great soaring bird by two dark lines extending away from it. The ants were busy, one dark column approaching empty-jawed, the other staggering along the return track with chunks and masses of rich food for the store-houses. They hurried twenty abreast up and down the tracks. The vulture dared not alight near one of the bodies and feed while the ants were there. It would carry up the bones and drop them for their marrow when the ants had finished in a few hours' time. It ceased to watch the ants, and soared above its own rock, watching for movement below.

It had no sense of time. The shadows grew wider and softer. Dogs slunk off down the mountain, hiding when they saw their master coming up. The bird circled unwearied in the cool air. T'chackamma's head was hanging on his breast, as he squatted still, holding T'je in one arm. Flies settled and swarmed in heavy clusters as they blew their eggs on his wounds. The mastiff was lying down five yards from him, in a plash of its own drying blood. It lay as though dozing, but it was watching the baboon through one eye.

And then the bird came down. It had a span of more than three yards, a dark grey back and tawny breast. In ponderous slowness it alighted on the whitened pinnacle of rock above them. It was dreadful and old. Its narrow head, so small in proportion to its body, was bare of feathers, and the bright scarlet rings round its scabby eyes gave it a mean and wicked look. It stared at T'chackamma, and blinked, and opened its beak and screamed a miserable and whining cry—the cry of Lamm'gei the vulture, who knocked sheep over precipices, who tore sods from the earth for its nest, who carried up tortoises and dropped them to break their shells. The bones it had cracked would have girdled the base of the mountain. On the rock Lamm'gei sat and blinked and waited.

Zwart Piet laid his head on his paws again, and groaned through a mask of flies. T'je slept. T'chackamma's head swivelled slowly round until it was fallen on his chest.

8

The action of Lamm'gei unfolding great wings and jumping off the pinnacle some time later made T'chackamma look up again. At the same moment Zwart Piet tottered upon his legs, and howled. His tail began to wag in the flopping irregular motion of a compound fracture. One of his ears hung below his jowl. T'chackamma's clutch. T'chackamma the Terrible! With a ragged tongue he tried to lick his master's hand. He fell over.

"Ah-ha!" cried van den Wenter, his grip tightening on the rifle. He had climbed the higher slopes, sniping as he climbed. He knew the risks, but his crops had been ruined. Rage drove out fear. With loaded rifle he moved upon T'chackamma, and raising it, took aim and fired. As the bullet, its blunt head nicked with a cross, spun through the baboon, it split and opened, and passed out of the back by a hole as big as a man's fist. The Boer ejected the brass case, and fumbled in the bandolier for another cartridge. When he had reloaded, he stared at T'chackamma, who had made no movement, except for a shudder when the dumdum bullet had struck him. T'je clung to him, and whimpered.

The Boer moved upon what he thought to be a baboon mortally stricken. Holding the bayonet before him, he advanced upon T'chackamma, whom he recognized by the collar. The baboon sat with fallen head, one arm limp beside him. The mastiff moved forward with his master. The man walked nearer, cautiously, step by step. When his enemy was near, T'chackamma's eyes filled with life, and he sprang, and the point of the bayonet pierced his throat.

Tearing it out, he seized the muzzle of the rifle as the trigger was pulled, and lurched upon the man, his ears ringing with the detonation. Wheezing through the pierced windpipe, he wrenched the rifle from his enemy's hand, meaning to rip him as he had ripped Zwart Piet, with the thumbnails of his hands. Those nails had once slashed open a lion. They were sharp and jagged as broken glass. And his feet were like his hands; he could pull four ways at once. The Boer screamed as a hand fell on his shoulder and the cloth of his coat broke; but T'chackamma was coughing and wheezing, and his hand slipped off the shoulder as he sank to the ground, still holding T'je. At his master's feet the mastiff was shivering and groaning as he tried in vain to climb over the fallen body and fix his teeth in T'chackamma's throat. T'je gibbered at him, and presently jumped on his back and bit him, and Zwart Piet died.

Van den Wenter's leg was held by the baboon's hand, and to free it, he picked up the rifle and brought down the butt-plate on its wrist. He was unplucking the fingers from their grasp when a shadow of spread wings glided upon him, and Lamm'gei with its talons knocked him over the precipice.

Jafta Hallelujah saw him hurtling down, and he knew that it was the vengeance of the *alungunyani*, the dreaded baboon gods, who had sent Lamm'gei the Bearded to the help of T'chackamma. The old Kaffir declared that T'chackamma climbed with T'je to the Cave of Bats, leaving the young baboon to be tended by the females there, and passing beyond the grey-haired guardian of the inner cave, who was blind, he lay down and slept into death among the bones of his ancestors. Jafta told me that the baboons never raided Intaba Kraal again, for the homestead fell into ruin, prickly pears and weeds grew in the mealie fields, and no one came to claim it. It was well that it should return to wildness, the old man muttered, for the spirit of T'chackamma, which was the spirit of Ngoza, the Kaffir sjamboked to death by Baas years before, would never leave at peace any white man who dwelt under the mountain.

The Rape of the Pale Pink Pyjamas

One sunny morning in the month of May, as I was lying across the tank of my Norton 499 c.c motor-bicycle—a machine with belt drive, no gear-box, yet flexible with a Phillipson pulley—one pushed off and when the engine fired, leapt over the saddle and roared away —I noticed in the sky a tiny cloud of peculiar shape and colour. Closing the throttle, I stopped beside a wind-gnarled ash and focussed my glass. What appeared to be a pair of trousers was sailing by themselves at a great height, the legs were filled with air, and trailing behind a dark and narrow object like a fragment of eyelash, was a sort of buzzard hawk, but with narrower wings and a forked tail. I watched this odd sight until bird and what it was towing dropped into a distant wood.

Then on to my destination, a house in the valley beyond, where I was going to meet a friend who had recently returned from Norway where he had been making photographic studies of bird-life.

I was eager to meet C--- again, and had been delighted when, by the eight o'clock post that morning, I received a letter telling me that he had observed a very rare 'hush hush' bird flying over Dartmoor, one of a species which he had believed to be extinct in Great Britain. 'Come over any time you like.'

The journey south from my cottage had been a pleasant run through hilly country grooved by deep wooded coombes, or valleys.

I was moving along a very rough drive to the low soft beats of my engine when I saw the low grey house, built of granite. My friend was standing under an oak-tree and whistling, while looking up into the leafy branches overhead. A leather gauntlet was worn on his left hand and wrist, with an object that looked like a badly stuffed bird.

C---, I should explain, was an amateur falconer. He had, in his

mews, a tame kite and a pair of Swedish goshawks. I suppose there
was hardly a boy in any preparatory or public school where C---
had lectured and shown his unique films and slides of wild life who
didn't remember him with enthusiasm. He must have worn out
several gold nibs in signing his name in autograph books. One of
the few survivors of the original Royal Flying Corps, he had ended
the war with the 'scrambled eggs' of a Group-Captain on the peak
of his service cap. More I cannot say; neither of us wants any 'col-
lectors' of rare birds, after their skins and/or eggs, to spot who
and where he is—

I waited beside him. One of the goshawks was settled in the tree.
It was a brown bird about two feet long from beak to tail. Its eyes
had a morose, almost sullen expression. C--- explained that the affair
of wings on his left arm was a lure by which a hawk was attracted
back to the fist after a flight. I noticed that small bells were tied to
its legs, which were almost hidden as it huddled there with its breast
feathers puffed out.

"She's sulking," said C---, and told me why. He said that the finest
exhibition of flying he had ever seen had taken place an hour
before my arrival, and when I considered this statement from a
man who, at the age of twenty-three, had brought down nine German
scout 'planes—'Albatri, Fokkers, and Tripes'—it may be realized how
I wished I had seen it. He told me all the details in his calm, off-
hand manner; and I wish I could convey them as objectively as he
told me.

2

At ten o'clock that morning C--- had gone to his desk to begin an
essay which he had meditated several days. He wrote slowly,
distracted by many sights from his paper, *The Lost Red Kite of
Great Britain*. He found it more pleasant to watch the finches in
the garden, the butterflies which danced their sun-dance over the
flowers, and his wife hanging out washed garments on the line which
stretched from a laburnum tree to a hook in the wall above the
window where he was sitting.

These garments were being stroked in a valley wind not strong
enough to ruffle a wren's breast feather or sway a floret of sweet-

william. White blouses, two pale blue camisoles, a sextet of tiny handkerchiefs, the trousers and jacket of a pair of pink pyjamas—all of silk. His wife went away, and he glanced at what he had written.

For centuries the wild Red Kite lived in London under the protection of the Lord Mayor, as it was a scavenger of the city, seeking its food among the garbage and offal of the streets. It nested amicably with the pigeons on the ledges of St. Paul's Cathedral and other high buildings.

The shrilling cry of a blackbird made him think of a cat in the garden (he had a fear of cats) as he cleaned his nib and prepared to write another paragraph, when the voice of his wife from the garden said:

"How silly of me! I thought I had hung the two there, and I hadn't!"

He enquired what was silly, and she said she was certain that she had hung two camisoles on the line, whereas one only was there.

She suggested that he had hidden it for a joke. She looked under the lavender bushes which grew behind the wallflowers and sweet-williams. Frowning and smiling and puzzled Mrs. C---, after a further search, returned to the house.

At eleven o'clock her husband got up from his desk, and went through the kitchen into the yard, where in a loose-box used as a falconers' mews three hawks were perching, leashed to blocks. He slipped the leashes of one bird, and putting on a leather gauntlet carried a kite on his wrist to a bow perch in the lawn. The bird, he told me, was grieving for its mate, which had died soon after arrival in Devon. Then he fetched the goshawks for their daily airing, and returned to his desk.

He tried to write while the shrilling of a blackbird above an almost continuous chatter of finches and titmice from the bushes and shrubs around the lawn was like glass bottles being broken against a sack of steel chains. The garden birds were scolding the glaring raptors.

While the kite squatted still, the goshawks flapped their wings and spread their tail feathers, turning their heads repeatedly to gaze about them. Their perches were made of willow sticks whose ends, sharpened to points, were thrust into the turf.

Barcud the kite (C--- had given it the old Welsh name of the Red Kite) sat miserable and still. It was thin, and ate less every day, for it was pining. Often C--- had regretted that he had not released the pair before the death of the male bird, for his reason in bringing them to England was to free them when tame in the hope that they would nest in the oak-wood on the valley side, where he might photograph them.

He wrote on.

The peculiar sailing or gliding flight of this bird led to the name of Glead, or The Glider, by which it was formerly known. Grace of flight, its rich chestnut colouring, and its useful service for centuries to Englishmen as a refuse remover in his towns, have not saved it from annihilation. Persecution by landowners, for the sake of pheasant shooting, and by poultry owners, who had only to poison a sheep's carcase and leave it in the fields to destroy the Glider, reduced its numbers so that it became a rare bird.

In the garden the miserable kite began to utter a whistling cry, which he had never heard before. The goshawks were moving their feet on the curved willow perches, and cocking eyes at the sky, but as they stared at every passing bird, he had no thought of what bird was sailing out of his sight.

Its rarity saved it from further persecution by gamekeeper and roost owner, for the Red Kite soared no more above England's fields and woods. A few pairs still lived in the wilder forests, but their eyries were sought out by men who robbed the nests and shot the parent birds, for by reason of the kite's rarity, its eggshells and skin were worth man's gold. Before the Great War five pairs were known in the British Isles, four of them being in Wales. This year, wishing to photograph a nest before it became too late, I sought the owners of the properties where these birds lived, only to learn, to my regret, that the kites were no longer there.

It is to be feared that this beautiful bird, of whom Shakespeare wrote, 'When the kite builds, look to lesser linen', has vanished from the land.

He put down his pen, determined to abandon the essay. What was the use of repeating what naturalists knew already, when he had no original facts to record about it, and little chance of ever filming its flight, so famous in olden times? He pushed back his chair, swaying it on its back legs. He had made a rule to write only in the morning, between the hours of ten and one; but usually at twelve o'clock his natural indolence (he told me) overcame completely his self-disciplinary desire. While he was pressing tobacco into a pipe, he heard again the wailing whistle from Barcud and saw her flap her wings in an attempt to rise from her perch. The goshawks showed, by their dipping as though for a take-off, that they were disturbed by the presence of something in the sky beyond his own sight. He sprang up, and was stretching over the desk to lean out of the window, when he heard a sudden soughing of wings and saw a shadow sweep over the lawn, and as it vanished two clothes pegs dropped on the grass.

He jumped out of the window, and when his wife ran out in response to his shouts she saw the extraordinary sight of the lower portion of a pair of pale pink pyjamas filled with air and borne from the earth by a bird holding the fastening cord in its talons.

3

Now I had, forty miles north of C---'s place, known of that kite's existence for over a year. I saw it first during the previous spring, at the time of change of colour on the forest's floor from brown to blue. Bees came to the bluebells hiding the dead leaves, and one morning, wandering under the pines which crested the oak-wood on the hill, I saw in the beams of the sun rising above the line of the distant moor a big bird hawking them with the ease of a swallow. I had never seen a bird like it before, but when it turned, and showed a long forked tail, I knew it for a Red Kite! Morning after morning I had watched this rare and solitary bird, as I lay in a hide of heather and bracken on the southern slope of a hill. He roosted always in the same tree, perched on a particular branch. At the joint of this branch with the trunk was a flat nest of sticks, to which he added honeysuckle bines and leaves every day, but I never saw a mate with him. I named him Glead.

Sometimes, the weather being fine, I slept in the wood. I awoke at songlight. The badgers lumbered home to their holt near the roots of Glead's tree; the tawny owl hunched itself against a pine trunk and blinked like a cat into slumber; the carrion crow croaked near its treetop nest; the kite flapped its long narrow wings and yawned. From the valley below came the sound of water running in a stony bed, but the sky-gleams had not yet come on the brook when the first lark sprang from the tussock beside its mate and aspired with its song of life.

During the days of watching, I grew to believe that the hopes and desires of wild birds were equal with man's. I was convinced that Glead had an imagination, that he imagined he had a mate (a dangerous thing for man to do), and that the objects he brought to the empty nest were pleasing to her.

Every dawn he awakened as the soft white orb of the morning star was shrinking into a gold bead, as though melted in the pale light flowing to the zenith from the unrisen sun. He flapped his long red narrow wings, and looked at the dim and spectral trees of the forest, and whistled, and jumped off the branch to begin the day's search. He was searching always, at every season, but between the times of sap-rising and leaf-unfolding his lack was more acute. Before the sun came up over Dunkery Beacon he soared to meet it, whistling a wild call as he threw his pinions, and as light deepened with the beams of the sun bending over the world, his eyes scanned the spaces above and below him. When the air was clear he could see many birds in many miles of airy desert, but never a fork-tailed bird with wings spread like his own. He espied a drift of peacock butterflies below him, and dived down to snatch one in the claws of his short toes. He liked, also, grasshoppers which were numerous on the slopes yellow with birdsfoot trefoil.

Only once did I see him attacking another bird, and then I think he chased it because it was insolent to him. The bird was an oodmall,* or green woodpecker, whose cry, as of derision, rang in the forest while it flew from tree to tree. From his branch Glead watched it hammering a rotten oak-tree, tearing away pieces as long as a man's finger and dropping them below while clinging to the trunk by claw and tailquill. Maggots bored the wood, and the wood-pecker's long tongue, thin as wire, darted into their tunnels and drew them out. When it had fed it flew to Glead's tree and perching a yard away opened its beak, threw back its scarlet head, and cackled at the kite for quite half a minute, until Glead launched himself at the oodmall and drove it away. He twisted in flight among the branches, swerving and avoiding twigs with the ease of a swallow. The tip of a wing missed a tree by an inch, but the brain which ordered the full stroke of the pinion knew that not one filament barb would be unhooked. Sometime he tilted out of the way of a branch in twirling throw of wings like the ruddy spokes of a swift carriage wheel. Then he came with suddenness upon Oodmall, who had perched against a vertical trunk. Glead turned beak over

* Possibly a corruption of wood-awl, from the bird's beak, with which it bores in rotten wood, to abstract grubs, etc.

tail in the space of his span, to clutch at the green back, but Oodmall had pushed himself with his stiff tail round the tree. His cry, so startlingly mocking to human ears, rang out like a jibe. The kite, seeming to pivot round the trunk on one wing-tip, viewed him again, and the woodpecker flew away. Glead pursued him in and out and around trees, while Oodmall, closing the short wings of his sturdy body went straight through foliage and twigs as though a bolt, rust-red and moss-green, were pursued by the cross-bar that had shot it.

The chase was ended by the woodpecker disappearing inside a tree which it struck in flight, seeming to pierce the hole with its beak and head. At the base of the tree scores of chips and fragments of sappy wood were scattered, gouged out of the living timber by Oodmall and his wife during many weeks. The entrance to his home was a straight hole for several inches, when it opened downwards into a bottle-shape, on the floor of which, resting on wood dust, were five white shining shells. Five little oodmalls were tucked inside these eggs, heads between legs, and not so much as a feather among them; but they were very warm, for their mother was sitting on them. Beside her the woodpecker rested for a few minutes, and then it climbed out to fly with a ringing cry to Glead's tree, to pick woodlice out of the sticks of the rotten nest.

He sought the food for his mate in safety, for Glead was a mile high in the sky, sweeping in wide circles and searching for another bird like himself. He soared with hardly a thrust or throw of pinion. Sometimes he rushed into vapour, when the sun was hidden from him, and whenever again he saw its shining disc and the wood below him, a wild whistling cry fell from his beak. Never was there answer.

Once he broke his fast on a rat, filched from a magpie. The rat had been caught in a gin set by a farmer, and flung dead among the blades of young barley. From the lofty sky Glead watched a black and white bird with a long tail flicker off a thorn by a gate and alight on the field. Although more than a mile of air was between kite and magpie, his eyes saw the magpie's beak battering that on which it was perched. He saw the long tail of the magpie open as it balanced itself for quick blows. Glead dropped to a thousand feet, level with the trees on the hillside, and fell still lower, so that he was hidden from the magpie. With flaps of long hollow wings he beat over the grass and up the slope to the hedge, throwing himself up and buoyantly over the thorns, and was upon the magpie before that hardworking and hungry bird could rattle its note of hate.

Glead did not attack it, for he had come only for the rat, which he lifted in his left foot before swinging away. The magpie's harsh chatter brought other magpies and a carrion crow out of the wood, who followed the kite and tried to peck him from below and dash upon him from above, while the crow sought to wound him with its open beak. Glead easily avoided the crow, and flew leisurely to his tree to eat the rat on the old nest.

That 'nest' must have been several seasons old, for many of the sticks of the flat structure were brittle and grown with lichens and moss. They were of elm, holly, and oak, and bore a load of decorations. Bines of honeysuckle, with the leaves still green, trailed across the four feet of its width. There were flowers—foxgloves, dandelions, and orchids. Glead's taste was catholic, for he saw an adorning beauty in a crumpled square of white cloth marked in red letters: PROPERTY OF THE GREAT WESTERN RAILWAY. The sun only knows where he got it from!

After his meal Glead cleaned toes and talons with his beak, and rearranged the flowers and the hand-towel. While he was doing this, Oodmall, seeing an earwig crawling along a stick near the edge of the nest, flew from a tree from where he had been watching, picked it up, and sped away with a loud cry. Glead was too busy tearing up *The Times Literary Supplement,* which he had taken from my shelter, to chase the oodmall, but I saw him turn and swear at it.

The meal of the rat was a poor one, but when he had eaten nine bees, three beetles, a worm, a lizard, and a small rabbit (leaving only its ears beside the snare of brass wire pegged into the turf by a run) he was gorged and satisfied. He flew home and perched on the bough above the nest until he felt less sleepy, when he mounted a little wind and soared southwards above the earth, solitary under the sun as he uncoiled his mortal destiny in flight.

Then, for days, I had not seen him. I wondered if he had been shot—the usual ending of a rare bird.

As I have said, C---'s place was about forty miles south, as the falcon glides, of that wood I had come to know so well. And now, it seemed that Glead, in his wanderings, had spied a bird like himself, perched on a wooden block on grass near a house; and to lure her to him, had started to build a nest near C---'s home!

Let me try to reconstruct what may have happened. Soaring over one valley he had seen smoke rising from a chimney-stack in the orange-coloured lichened roof of a grey house, and had espied some linen on a line over a lawn. He glided lower, regarding the linen so intently that the desire to bear some away overcame his fear of buildings from which smoke arose. He swooped, snatched at one of the garments, ripping it from the pegs which held it, and carried it back to some new nesting tree—perhaps to the ruins of an old nest originally built by a buzzard.

Glead returned to the house, meaning to get some more from the line, and as he circled above the roof and treetops, preparing to make his swoop, he heard something which made the featherlets of his neck stand out in excitement. As he glided down a wailing whistle came up to meet him, for the tame kite had seen him; and his reply was so joyful that it was hoarse. Recklessly he swooped upon the line, hidden from view of C--- by the top of the window, who, seeing the extraordinary sight of his pyjama trousers sailing off, apparently by themselves, gave a shout and ran out into the garden.

The goshawks on their perches were jumping in agitation, and flapping their wings, while the tame kite cocked a wild silver eye skywards and whistled to Glead. C--- ran indoors for his tripod and camera, which was loaded with a spool of film, and when he returned Glead was still circling above the house, calling repeatedly for the leashed kite to fly up to him. C--- tried to conceal himself and his camera in the hope that the bird would descend; and the hands, which during flying combat at ten thousand feet had been without a tremor, now holding tripod and handle were shaking with suspense. For he was thinking that if the wild kite wouldn't descend, why not fly the goshawks, in the hope that they would force the kite to come within camera range? What pictures the flight would make!

His wife came out, in answer to his call, and looked up, her hand shielding from her eyes the glare of the sky. Glead, trailing the air-bellied trousers by the cord which was entangled in his talons, saw the glint of the camera lens, and feared to fly lower.

C--- acted almost immediately the thought had come into his mind. In general outline and appearance when resting, the goshawks resembled Glead, having hooked beaks, yellow legs and toes, and strong curved black talons for binding on to their prey. But in hue of plumage and shape of wing they differed. The eyes of the goshawks were fiercer, and ringed with lemon rings and their dull white breasts

were barred with thin black lines like the charred cracks of ashen logs in a fire. They were sturdier than the kite, although not so long. C--- focussed his camera on the male bird while his wife pulled the leashes of soft leather through the brass swivels of the jesses attached to its feet, and threw up the bird. As soon as it recovered flying balance the short wings flickered and it climbed upwind, to turn when level with Glead and dash at him. Meanwhile Mrs. C--- had unleashed the larger female goshawk, which sprang off the perch as the male struck at Glead and the kite took evasive action.

Now the hand turning the handle was steady. The birds were above the house, perfectly grouped and in focus as a foot-stroke of a goshawk slashed one leg of the pyjamas from knee to ankle.

Barcud on the low perch on the lawn was flapping her wings and wailing as she watched Glead trying to evade the goshawks, whose shorter and wider wings enabled them to fly up under the slower bird with toes spread and talons sharp as needles ready to bind on to him. At each grab Glead shifted and tumbled, for he was hampered by the stolen garment, of which he could not rid himself. Sometimes he stooped upon one of his enemies as it missed him; at other times he threw his head between his legs (as the camera afterwards revealed) in an effort to tear away the entanglement on his feet. The satisfaction of the photographer gave way to a feeling of dismay and apprehension for the safety of the wild kite, whose wailing had changed to screaming as it realized that its attackers were too strong for it. The female goshawk was the first to strike the quarry, knocking away many small feathers which the swallows and martins, wheeling in a flock above the hawks, descended to take in their beaks; and C--- declared that they dropped these feathers and caught them again, twittering as though jubilantly at the disaster to one of their dreaded enemies.

Barcud was straining at her leashes as she tried to fly from the perch, and on impulse C--- took out his knife and cut through the thongs of porpoise hide above the swivels, and the strings of gut holding the small bells to her legs, thus giving her a token freedom. Heavily on frayed pinions she flapped away, and as she rose the female goshawk dashed up at her. She slipped sideways, and flew to join Glead. For many minutes C--- watched the play of the four birds, which ascended higher and higher, until above the line of the valley Glead and Barcud found the breeze which has been the friend of all kites since the beginning of wings.

Both goshawks gave up, and flew to a tree. And when I arrived, there was old C--- trying to lure one down to the ground with a contraption of feathers, swung in circles around his head, and called the lure. Nothing doing!

By now the two kites had found a stream of warm air ascending; and on pinions widespread and motionless, forked tails open, tilting wings to get the pressure of air at the turns, Glead and Barcud mounted higher at each gyration. The curves of their superb soaring were broken many times by a few beats of pinions—each stroke of which began when the wings nearly met overhead and ended with the tips pointing to the earth beneath, to regain entry into their invisible airy wheels; and they soared thus while C--- and I and his lady wife gazed into the blue, eyes shielded by hands as we lay on the grass and watched in comfort. Smaller and smaller became the birds, until the sight of one pair of human eyes, aided by lenses and prisms of glass, saw them as motes of dust which merged into the blue. These motes vanished from aided human sight, but something dropped into visibility, something pink and tattered, and after it came the kites, sometimes dropping with wings closed, at other times swooping down. The female returned to the lure, and was fed; but Glead, who had swooped again upon the silk rags drifting earthwards, had disappeared into the wood. It seemed that he had deposited it, like luggage on a honeymoon, at some new nesting site, for soon he returned for his mate, who followed him up a thermal of warm air, while C--- exclaimed, "They're the most graceful birds of heaven!"

And there, as summer came to its full flush, four British kitelets were reared in safety, mocked in the forest by the cries of oodmalls, and cursed by rapscallion crows and jays.

My Day with the Beagles

His shadow came round the corner first, for the sun was not high in the southern February sky. When he saw the hounds on the green before the Feathers Inn, a grin cracked his dirty face, his eyes shone, and he gave a whoop of joy. Turning round he swung a sleeve of an officer's discarded khaki service tunic which his skinny arm animated, and shrieked:

"Crikey, whata lota dawgs! Corlumme! 'Ere, quick, boys!"

A man in a brown tweed golfing suit, wearing Service tie and black naval shoes without toe-caps, watched the urchin as he padded across the muddy road, and said almost to himself:

"How charming."

The girl in the broken-rainbow-coloured jersey beside him said slowly, without moving her head:

"What's charming?"

"That boy."

She laughed in her throat, softly, so that I just heard the derision, and her murmured drawl of:

"That dirty little urchin charming. Why?"

"The impulse to share a delight. So human," replied the man in a low voice.

He clenched the three fingers of his left hand hanging by his side. A pink weal was where the second knuckle should have been. He did not look at her. She was about nineteen, and he was perhaps thirty years of age. There were grey hairs in the dark hair of his head. She wore a brown felt hat, and her gold hair was plaited in coils hiding the ears. Standing behind her was a tall lounging man, in grey flannel trousers and threadbare coat of tweed. A stranger. He was watching the girl stealthily. He saw the curves of cheek and chin, and hoped she would turn her head and show her face. A brooch was fastened to the left side of her hat, made of a hare's pad mounted on a silver pin. It was a meet of the jelly-dogs, as beagles are sometimes called, to hunt a hare known to be couched in a near cornfield.

The man who had spoken about the urchin did not speak again. The friends of the urchin came round the corner at the double, three of them, and stood on the grass near the tiny hounds. There were twelve couple. Some hounds were standing on hind legs with paws on the skirts of girls fondling long thin ears, stroking short and tapering muzzles or patting shoulders that sloped and ribs round and deep. Some sat shivering in the grass, gazing with soft, full eyes at the kennel-huntsman. Warily the urchin advanced, and put out a grimy paw to pat one of them. Columbine looked at him, and he snatched back his hand.

"I saie, mister," he piped in his Cockney voice to a youth who stood near.

"What do you want?" asked the honorary whip, on his just-left-school dignity before the assembling field, and knowing that small boys in the country near London were usually cocky and impertinent. Many people were looking amusedly at the child in the enveloping tunic, torn knickers, and bare bony shanks thrust into dirty-white cricketing boots, too large for him.

"Willy bate?"

"What?" said the youth, frowning.

"I said, willy bate?" replied the urchin, with mock politeness. "Will your dorg bate if aye stroke him? Will your d'horg mind if aye give him a pat?" And as this made his tongue tired he ceased to mimic, and said: "No, straight, guv'nor, willy snap me arm off if I tries to get pally like wiv 'im?"

"Here, you be off!" ordered the huntsman, to the relief of the young whip, who was so neatly uniformed in green cap and coat, white stock and breeches, and pipe-clayed canvas boots with rubber soles. His whale-bone whip was held in yellow-gloved hand.

2

Huntsman put horn to lips and blew a blast. Immediately the tiny hounds clustered round him, yapping their delight, jumping up at him as they lashed eagerly their gay sterns. He moved off at a quick

pace, with the excited jelly-dogs at his rubber'd heels. Then came the
two honorary whips, one on each side of the black, tan, and white
pack. The natty youth was flushed no more. His colleague was a
young man with a red and jolly countenance. who worked in a stock-
jobber's office five days a week and whipped in every Saturday to
the pack. He was a younger son of a Surrey squire whose estate
had been sold to a syndicate of builders of small semi-detached villas
and bungalows.

The third whip kept the rear of the pack. He was the second
hunt servant, a lad of fifteen with an incipient moustache and beard,
big feet and raw hands. He walked stiltedly because his feet were
swelled with chilblains; he had told nobody lest he might lose his
job, which he loved. He had a shy smile, a soft voice and childish
brown eyes; ladies often gave him sandwiches, which he ate in
crammed mouthfuls.

Then came the Master, an elderly man who lived in a south-
eastern suburb of London and was a chartered accountant by pro-
fession. He was popular because he managed to find time to speak
to most of the field, and he remembered all their names. He was talking to an architect out with his smallest son, a boy who at that
moment was stuffing a woollen muffler into his greatcoat pocket, for
the morning had been cold and his mother had insisted on his taking
it with him. Behind the Master walked an underwriter's clerk at
Lloyd's who had been a temporary major during the war; the three-
guinea annual subscription (he thought) was a good investment
(although the rules permitted but six Saturday mornings 'off' a
year) since it entitled him to membership of the Hunt, and therefore
he felt himself to be a Somebody, especially after his photograph
had appeared in *The Tatler*.

Then came three girls, in the early twenties, one of them fair
and fat, another dark and serious, and the face of the third was
carelessly powdered. They wore coloured jumpers, tweed skirts and
soft felt hats, and the fat girl 'rather liked the look of the man that
Calmady girl had in tow'. I gathered that the Calmady girl was the
girl with the ear-plaits and that her 'tow' was an officer retired
from the Royal Navy who had been in the same ship as Miss
Calmady's brother, who had been killed at Zeebrugge. Older ladies
and gentlemen followed; the field numbered about fifty people. The
daughters of the local doctor and lawyer were there, with walking-
sticks and brogue shoes worn at heel. Jolly girls, one holding a panting black cocker spaniel straining at leash. By them, but always

changing pace, progressed the urchins. All walked on the asphalt of the main road. Red motor omnibuses from London crept past, and cars and motor-bicycles. People peered at the jelly-dogs packed into the kerb by anxious whips, smiled, and passed on.

"Oh, *look* at those dear little dogs!"

"Aren't they too sweet."

"Mummie, Mummie, what's those dogs for?"

"Hunting, sonny."

"What's that?"

"They fight foxes, and bite them up."

The bus passed on with the peering faces.

Near the tail of the field, as though they wanted to be apart from others, walked the girl with the ear-plaits and the sailor. She walked from her hips levelly on rubber shoes bound to her feet by anklets of some brown cloth. The tall stranger followed. He imagined she could dance on her toes; she had the form and carriage of a dancer. Her tweed skirt was unfastened from the four leather buttons on her left flank, and as she swung along in her cool maiden grace he could see that she wore dark breeches and fawn-coloured stockings. The many-coloured jumper was cut low, showing where base of neck joined her back, and the flesh was white. He followed purposely to see her. There was a celandine open on the bank of the lane up which they had turned, the first he had seen that year, and the sight of the yellow star put joy into his heart. Planetary life might be chaotic and purposeless he thought, as some philosophers made it their life-work to prove, but the things of the earth were beautiful to themselves. The celandine turned to the sun, ardent to itself; the hare day-dreamed in the cornfield; the stranger's imagination was quickened by female loveliness. Always near her he walked, unnoticed and solitary, neither attractive nor unattractive, of the Celtic type so despised by the German thinkers. He was a 'writer of little stories about swallows and weeds, old men, children, dogs, and other humble things'.

Through a gate—"last through fasten that gate, please!"—into a field of loam, scattered with broken flints and thin blades of corn. A lark sang sunwards. Eagerly hounds rushed over the corn, and almost at once the pack gave tongue as a hare sprang up from its form and ran away. Its long hind legs were thrust between its fore-pads and its ears were upright. The excited yapping increased as hounds lost view behind a hedge, and they tore through the gap, scrambling on one another and helping in an agony of frustration and excitement.

"Crikey, boys, come on!" yelled the urchin, running over the field with all the speed his too large cricketing boots would allow him. His friends followed. Several members of the field began to run towards a gate, not wishing to break a larger gap in the farmer's fence. It was not a good day for scent, as a cold wind blew from the north-west, and the beams of the sun had not yet melted the rime in the fields. On the other side of the hedge was a boggy meadow, and through this the hare ran, under a gate, and into another cornfield. There she waited, crouched on the ground, listening in terror to the beagles and the horn of the huntsman. Columbine was apparently a babbler, because many times the whips rated her. She spoke when there was no scent; immediately half the pack rushed after her, giving tongue, wagging their sterns and unable to contain the eager excitement. When the line was found again they rushed away, each straining muscle and sinew to be leader, and with a spasmodic but sonorous burst of music that made the stranger's blood glow and his feet desire to run.

The hare crouched by the headland of the field until the pack, babbling and rushing everywhere, was fifty yards from her. Then she laid her long ears on her neck and sped away, looking back at them with large hazel eyes. Over the plough she went, the beagles driving her and yelling their loudest. Soon they had crossed a ditch into another meadow, leaving the runners far behind. Only the huntsman kept close to them, calling them by name, while the first whip rated the more blatant liars. The other whips went wide to the flanks, in order to watch which way the hare would run. The followers could hear the pack in full cry returning, for the hare had doubled back across the field and passed about a hundred yards in front of the laggard runners, or rather, walkers.

About half-an-hour later the line took them to a quarry, where a crane was swinging a bucket of earth into a truck standing on rails. The crane was a tall web of steel, painted scarlet. About a dozen men were digging crude Fuller's earth on ledges, or steps, thirty feet below the field edge, which was guarded by a fence made of rotting railway sleepers and two sagging, rusty steel-wire cables, the higher about a yard from the ground. The writer of stories saw the gold-haired girl leap the fence and stand still about three inches from the edge, calmly looking down. The position apparently caused her companion some alarm, for he begged her to come back She did not heed him. He saw the stranger approaching, and waited with anxious face until he had gone on, when again he asked her to be careful. He called her Betty.

"My dear Gerry, you are absurd," and again the derision in the laugh.

The horn sounded on the top of the slope, the chase was on again. The hare had been hiding in a hedge, watching with terror the approach of the pack, unable to forbear the suspense, perhaps, of not knowing definitely if they were owning her scent. She had been leaping sideways as she ran, in order to break the line. She ran over the lane and by an oak-tree into another field. Hounds followed, but the scent was difficult owing to the heaps of midden dumped every few yards in straight lines, awaiting the four-pronged forks of the labourers who would scatter the top-dressing before ploughing in. However, she was seen by the stockbroking whip, who yelled: "*Yoi-yoi-yoi, Whirligig, Reveller, Snowdrop, Yoi-yoi*," and they rushed at full speed to him.

3

The hare ran for two more hours, roughly in a figure of eight, covering many miles. Other hares were put up, but huntsman and whips lifted the pack from the 'cutting-in pussies' and laid them on the line of the original animal. She ran noticeably slower, and scrambled through thick quick-set hedges that would baulk a fresh hare. The stranger was wet to his knees, having slipped at a take-off on the bank of a brook and fallen into the water. He was more fortunate, however, than a fat butcher in flannel trousers and sports jacket who, in attempting to leap a ditch, fell sprawling, to crawl out covered with black leaves. Over this ditch the girl leapt with easy grace; she ran tirelessly, and often her companion was left half a mile behind. But the stranger followed. Barb-wire, the curse of the foxhunter, was his friend that day, for it caught in her Fair Isle jersey, and he was able to unhook her. Her shoulders were broad, and she had rolled her sleeves to the elbow, revealing lovely arms which he dared to see only from the corners of his eyes. She thanked her helper again; he dared a glance at her eyes.

The intense blue of the spring gentian that grows where the snow has melted on the Pyrenees, the gleam of our English kingfisher over

the brook, the night heaven watched from among midsummer meadow grasses, the sunlit sea calm over drowned chalk, were not bluer than the eyes which looked into his for a moment of time that civilized man alone reckons. She turned away and ran on. He followed, his heels blistered and his calves aching. He watched the muscles of her calves working under the fawn stockings at' each pressing lift of her toes. More wire, a single strand this time, at the end of the field, a gap in the thorns. She bent and put her head under the strand, turning sideways to pass through. The skirt slipped away and under the stretched materials of the breeches he saw the shape of the huntress' thigh. Again he dared only to regard indirectly the line of leg, ankle, knee, as the maiden body bent under the rusty wire. She gave a little cry, for a thorn had drawn a line on her neck. There was a drop of blood on the white skin. He grasped in his hand the spray of prickle-guarded buds and tore them away. The thorns went deep into his hand. "I think you can pass now," he said, with a slight, impersonal smile.

"Thank you," she said, and ran on, effortlessly as before, always leaning forward slightly, arms loose by her side. He followed, a stitch in left lung and shoes filled with gravel rasping the blisters on toes and heels. Pain was nothing to him. Two more miles he followed, sometimes (dreading lest he give offence) at a distance of a hundred yards.

4

He cared nothing for the hunting. Beagles were amusing little creatures to watch, but his sympathies were with the hare, one of the purest and most timid of animals. He had hunted the wild boar of the Black Forest, on foot with spear upheld to ward the slashing tusks; sought the spoor of the lion whose paw-stroke is instant death. He had hunted the English fox, which is murderous to many birds and animals, and would be extinct, except in the wildest parts of England, were it not for the partial protection of fox-hunters and its cunning when chased. To follow hounds was to be filled with the joy of living dangerously, even if bury-rotten banks and boggy Devon 'bottoms' were not exactly dangerous. He hoped the hare would escape, but he feared she was doomed. Already she was stiffening with exhaustion and stopping every hundred yards. The beagles were in a fury of desire and excitement as they ran here, there, and everywhere to find the line of failing scent.

The chase took them near a railway embankment, when huntsman became fearful for his pack, the noise of a train coming from the distance. Hare doubled, however, and led them away. The field was by this time scattered. The line led them past another quarry, but deserted and partly flooded. A dead dog floated at the verge, near a sunken wicker basket and an old boat. There were allotments here, with dry stems of weeds among yellow cabbage stalks. To shorten the distance between hounds and herself, the girl ran down into the quarry and climbed the loose rock-like lumps that were piled against a cutting. The stranger watched her leaping from stone to stone, until she reached the crest and disappeared. He scrambled up, grazing his ankle, and at the top he paused to get his breath. She ran on, seeming to rise from the hard clods with the lightness of thistle-seed bounding in the wind on its silver filaments. Yet she was no frail, gazelle-like maid; she was thewed and shouldered like a Viking's daughter. He loped on again, pleasing to force sinew and muscle. It was a pleasure to endure. He was not running for his life.

The hare had crawled under a wooden fence into a shrubbery of rhododendron and holly surrounding the gardens and paddock of a house. Half a mile away and below smoke rose from the chimney-pots of Redhill. The fence was five feet high, and placing her right hand on the wood, she sprang. Her legs were level with the top of the fence as she hurled herself over, but she must have landed with a crash on the other side, for when next he saw her (having climbed the fence) several sere holly leaves were hooked to skirt and jumper. She gave him a cool and casual look. He was breathing heavily through his mouth; she was entirely at ease, breathing through nostrils slightly expanded.

Hounds were speaking in the cover, and the huntsman called out: "Stand up by the railings, sir, please. She may be close to the house. She won't leave here. Stop shouting, boy!"

His last words were addressed to the urchin who was yelling at three of the questing hounds. He grinned, and came to stand by the stranger. The girl stood ten yards away, with her back to the house, one foot on the lowest rail of the fence. She glanced indifferently but repeatedly at the gate through which they had entered into the paddock. A man and a girl came through, and several others, to stand about in the grass while the pack drew cover and a colt cantered about the paddock, sometimes stopping to whinny its dismay. The urchin talked to the stranger, who regarded him with friendly eyes.

" 'Ave yer sin the rabbit, guv'nor? I 'ave. Cor, it wasn't 'alf a big 'un!

"It coudden 'arf run, couddenit? Lumme, I wisht the boys dahn our street had seen it!

" 'Ark at the dorgs.

"They can't find it. What'll the dorgs do when they ketch the rabbit?"

Halbert, or Bert, was his name, he confided to the stranger, who could not help smiling with him. Bert smiled back most pleasantly. He said he was ten, and had come from Waterloo that morning, by motor. By hundreds of motor-buses and lorries. But he hadn't paid. Not bloomin' likely. He and his companions had hung on to lorry tailboard and motorbus footboard until detected and ordered off, when they waited for another. Cor, it was lovely in the country, mister. 'E was coming 'unting again next Saturday, not 'arf 'e warn't. Strike him pink, it was better than the pictures. 'E 'ad a grinnat at 'ome, 'e 'ad. What was a grinnat? Sorry, he meant a gr-heen hat. Grinnat, to wear onnisead. 'Is 'ead, where 'is 'air grew. Onnisead. Like a proper bloke 'unting. Would the rabbit bite the dorgs? 'E'd sin a rat bite a dorg dahn by the river. Could yer eat it when the dorgs caught it? What, the dorgs ate it? "Go on, whatsyernaime, yer ain't kidding?"

At last came the sailor called Gerry. He limped. When he saw Betty he came towards her, trying hard, it appeared to the observant stranger, to walk without the limp. She did not move. He glanced at the stranger as he came near. A reserved, impersonal glance, but the other thought there was an anxiety behind it. He wondered how the sailor had lost a finger; there was a scar on his hollow cheek; his limp. Perhaps splinters of a German shell, or a flight of nickel machine-gun bullets, at Zeebrugge. His eyes were thoughtful and steady. Yet when he looked at her his gaze faltered. He was in love with her. The stranger thought that she scorned him.

"How's the leg, Gerry?"

"Bit stiff, Betty. Sorry I couldn't keep up with you."

"Have some chocolate?"

"Not now, thanks."

He gave some to the urchin.

"Thank you, guv'nor," said Halbert. "Sorry yer leg ain't all right."

"Thanks," smiled his patron, and the girl gave an amused sidelong glance, slightly disdainful, at his rags. They moved away a few minutes later. The sun was failing, and it was chilly after the hot rays. Then the stranger saw the hare. It appeared on a grassy border near the house. It dragged itself slowly, a few steps at a time, this little child of the clover fields. It was wet and exhausted, its ears laid back, its innocent eyes dulled with approaching death. Its splendid heart, which enabled it to spring out of its form swiftly, was failing now, for the long chase had clogged blood and muscle. It seemed to be pulling itself along, trying to reach the cover of a holly bush, where it might hide itself and die. Stranger remained silent, thinking, among other things, of that famous nineteenth century sportsman of the West Country, Parson Jack Russell, who once had leapt a five-barred gate before harriers in order to pick up in his arms an exhausted hare. The stranger remained still, despising himself, unable either to holloa or to pick it up. But Halbert the urchin was no craven.

"There's the rabbit, whatsyernaime!"

"Hush."

"What's up with it, mister?"

"It's broken its heart with running."

"Lorlumme. Will it bite yer?"

"No, it's the gentlest animal alive."

Halbert stared a moment, and a frown came on his grubby face.

"It's a —— shame, mister!" he whined. He used an inappropriate word before 'shame', or rather 'shime'. The hare dragged itself another three inches. Hounds were babbling fifty yards away, unseen, behind the house.

"Shall I rescue it, mister?"

"Yes! Go and take it," he whispered. No one was near.

"Yer won't split if I do, guv'nor?"

"No."

"Take yer oath on it?"

"Yes."

"Spit through yer 'and?"

Thus adjured, the other spat through his hand. Bert looked round furtively before climbing the fence. He ran to the hare and picked it up. It did not struggle, being stiff. He held it under an arm and ran with it out of sight into the rhododendron bushes. The stranger listened with beating heart, but his unsporting behaviour had apparently passed undetected.

The huntsman called off hounds and drew the allotments, through which they had run, as he thought that the hare might be lying out there. The sterns of the little jelly-dogs wagged eagerly as ever, and the more excitable babbled occasionally. Through the fields they went. The north-west wind was cooler, the sunbeams more yellow, the moon was pale in the afternoon sky. Several hounds bit corn-blades in a field; there would be no more scent that day. Through the fields they walked, those who had not gone home, towards the village where they had met in the morning, to take up coats and change shoes left at the Feathers Inn.

5

While standing in the dim passage within, smoking his pipe and holding a tankard of ale, the stranger heard voices in a room. The door was opposite him and half open. He could see in a mirror the head of Betty. Her hat was thrown on the floor. Perhaps they were awaiting poached eggs on muffins for tea, as they sat by the fire. He made no movement. In a few minutes he would be leaving Surrey in the London train, and probably never see her again. He looked in the mirror. She could not see him, as he stood in darkness, a long shadow of a man, for she was surrounded by light. The sailor said:

"Who was that tall dark fellow following you, Betty?"

"I don't know. I've never seen him out before."

"I rather liked the look of him."

She shrugged her shoulders. The stranger was forgotten.

"Sorry I couldn't keep up, Bets." The sailor spoke in a restrained voice. She looked at him, and smiled her peculiar smile.

"Poor old Gerry," she said a few seconds later.

"Bet," he said unevenly, "are you really angry because I didn't interfere when the boy took the hare? I couldn't, Bet. I've dragged myself like that, and I know. Bet, they say animals don't feel, but I—"

"Hush!" she interrupted, touching lightly his hand. "You mustn't talk like that; I've told you so before."

She mocked him still. He stared into the fire and was dumb. The stranger remained still: if he left, they might think he was eaves-dropping; so he did not move. He had felt as the other was feeling then. She despised pity, thinking it weakness. Hopeless to try and explain. He fell into a reverie, in which his thoughts seemed to burn away in the brightness of his vision, until all was a celestial radiance. At the end of the world, he stood . . . Beyond the end of the world, when pity was shining and free and one with beauty in the white radiance of eternity, the lonely ones would be understood ... So he thought, in agitation, a lonely man of twenty-five who felt himself at times to be seventy years old. The old world was still in ruins from the War, the new world yet unformed ... then he saw actual objects again. Betty. He had been wrong about Betty, for the mirror revealed a strange look on her face. Her companion, with the downcast head, did not see it. Her lips were parted and she was smiling in the way that a virgin smiles to herself when suddenly she feels she can resist no more, but must surrender to love. Never again could she torment him. O, she was young and beautiful and her eyes were misty with love. As the sailor would not look up she leaned forward and took his broken hand. She said something to him. The shadow in the passage dared not gaze any more, but gulped his beer and, pushing the entrance door, went outside and along the road to the station.

He had to hobble back, with the tankard he had absent-mindedly taken away with him. Returning to the road which the motor-buses from London used he saw at a corner of a lane Halbert and his three companions sitting on the bank under the hedge. They were sharing a cigarette, and Halbert was ending what appeared to be his account of the hunt.

"Yuss," his voice was saying dramatically, "it didden 'arf bite the dorgs! 'Lumme, I won't 'ave one left', cried the bloke wiv the grinnat onnisead. ' 'Ere, mate', I says to im, 'give us yer whip', and I dashed in and dots it one on the boko. Crikey, boys, it didden 'arf come for me. I 'it it 'arder and 'arder, and when it was dead the bloke says to me, 'e says, 'you kin 'ave it, me boy, and thank you fer saving me dorgs, and tell yer ma to cook it fer Sundis dinner,' he says."

"Blime," murmured his pals, stroking the dead hare hidden in one of the large pockets of Halbert's tunic.

The writer of little stories heard the train coming into the station and broke into a run. He was just in time, and in a carriage by himself tried to pick with his tie-pin four black thorns out of his hand.

Tales of Moorland and Estuary

Preface

These stories had to wait some considerable time—nearly three decades, indeed!—before they were published in book form by Macdonald & Co. The earliest was written in 1923—two years before my marriage. This was *The Yellow Boots*. I wrote it after reading in a local paper that an entire pack of hounds had, after being lost in fog during a chase on Dartmoor, been poisoned by the Master as soon as they returned to kennels. He had not waited even to inform the Hunt Committee which owned the pack.

The Crake had a filleted appearance in one number of the U.S.A. magazine, the bogus *Esquire*. In fact, not only was my story extensively cut, but entirely rewritten until it became a parody of what I had written. It was done without permission, too; and when I wrote and protested to the Chicago editor, an explanation was made that the 'reader', or re-write man, was a confirmed alcoholic who no longer worked for that florid periodical.

In 1926 I set myself to assemble the final version of *Tarka*, writing all night while nursing a sick baby and wife. It took about six weeks of exhausting labour. *Tarka* appeared in 1927: it brought fame in 1928, while I was composing the ultimate novel (*The Pathway*) of my youthful tetralogy called 'The Flax of Dream'.

That novel, published in October, 1928, brought many visitors on a pilgrimage to see the author. I was then herding various village sketches and stories into two books: *Tales of a Devon Village*, and *Life in a Devon Village*. Thus ended my first seven years in Ham, the original name of that village; and not so long afterwards a new-broom incumbent from a London suburb glorified it to Ham St. George. This didn't last even so long as the small years of his rectorship.

Shaking the dust of rectorial criticism of *The Pathway* from my shoes, I took the family of two small sons to live beside a trout stream descending from Exmoor through the Bray valley and to pass by a thatched house called Shallowford. There I composed a rather silly volume, a sort of bogus guide and walking-tour affair, with characters more appropriate to 'Beachcomber's' column in the *Daily Express* than a serious book. It was an 'I-I-I' book; that is, narrated by my then satirical self. This concoction was called *Devon Holiday*. It contained some short stories, which now reappear between these covers.

Life at Shallowford was, at first, all bits and pieces. Frustration was my lot: I had been paid a fairly large sum of money by Dick de la Mare, of Messrs. Faber & Faber to write a companion book to *Tarka*. About a trout? A salmon? I hadn't the slightest idea what to write. I became irritable and moody. Months passed, and became years. I spent much of my time with a 2-ounce fly rod, wading up a 2-mile beat of the rocky river Bray. I bought several hundred Loch Leven trout from the fish-farm below Dulverton, and put them in the river; not to be caught, but to bring back grace to an over-fished stream. I watched for salmon, during freshets, from several places on the river banks, including a big alder tree. Downstream were several near-impassable weirs, each built to contain a flow of reservoir water: to be led-off by leats, or narrow ducts, to grist mills still being worked, for the grinding, between millstones, of barley—the chief food of bacon-pigs.

And so the summers went on; to be lost in the mists of autumn, the cold river flowing fast, outside our cottage standing below hill plantations of larch and spruce. All the rooms were sunless during six or seven weeks at the dead-end of the year, in our frosty valley.

One winter night the first paragraph of *Salar the Salmon* was written. It was now the New Year of 1935, six years after we had moved to Shallowford. Since 1929 a daughter and another boy had joined the two small brothers; and a fifth child was on the way. I continued the writing of the book day after day. It seemed dull to me; 'every word chipped from the breast-bone', as V. M. Yeates wrote of himself while writing, at Eltham in Kent, his classic *Winged Victory*. Almost uncaringly I saw the sun's rim appear over the tree-tops; the white rime of winter's dark melted on the two lawns, each set with its yew tree; fuller light came in the sky with the swallows home again; then, in early May, an annoyance of cuckoos was calling and gabbling from tree to tree in the Deer Park through which ran clear cold moorland water in which salmon leapt at dawn, and again at twilight. My rod remained in its stand: I left for my field above Ham village, to write in the hut, or outside in the blazing sun of June ... July ...

Chapters went off, uncorrected, to the publishers in London; thence to Plymouth to be set-up in page-proof by the printers. Page-proofs meant that no excisions could be made, or paragraphs added. I felt cold in the August sun sitting day after day beside a small pine tree, feeding myself occasionally on biscuits and cheese—and feeling that if Salar did not die soon, the author would: a deserved death, for surely it was the dullest prose ever written.

The book was published two months later, and sold well at once, with splendid reviews. I did not care; there had been too much anxiety; I must change my life—

So the family migrated to Norfolk, to start a new life; I to became a jolly red-faced chuckling extrovert farmer on 240 derelict acres. But in Norfolk, with little capital, the wages had to be paid from money earned at night by B.B.C. scripts on farming, and articles in the *Daily Express*, while by day one learned to use the body in tasks of remaking roads, rebuilding 'condemned' cottages; ploughing, making seed-beds, and selling barley at a loss—for it was, in 1937–39, the greatest slump in British farming for 150 years.

So we dug and loaded into an old lorry over 1700 tons of gravel and chalk; then, besides working in the fields, our team of four hauled hundreds of tons of mud from choked meadow-dykes dividing five grazing meadows, and spread a splendid compost on the arable. For years the meadows had been white with thistle-floss in summer and water-logged in winter; now they were drained, and bullocks grazed revitalized pasture between April and October, before going into the yards to be fattened.

Thus I worked the body hard during eight years; five of them during the Second World War which confirmed my ideas of the white races going wrong.

Almost ended was my little trade with British magazines. All of the war ended in general chaos.

But in the U.S.A. an outstanding magazine of quality managed to survive: and I must record my gratitude to *The Atlantic Monthly* which published half-a-dozen or so of the short stories during those war years; and for sending to the family parcels of food, which, during those dark days, were shared with town friends who were less fortunate than ourselves.

The Crake

It is a wonderful feeling a man has when he is exploring a country for the first time, especially when he is young, with a war behind him, put away, he thinks, for ever. He is in a new country; he is a writer with the highest ambition; he lives in a thatched cottage said to have been built in the reign of King John, for a rent of eighteen pence a week.

Everything he sees and hears (when it is not about himself) is tremendously interesting, and forming into stories. The wild, beautiful, unexplored Atlantic seaboard! The falcons, the badgers, the otters, the character of the people! When he sits down to the table, the stories write themselves, out of his excitements.

That is the feeling I had when, one morning in the time of primroses and celandines in the hedge banks, and gloss on the coats of grass-feeding red Devon cattle, I left my cottage, spurning to lock the door, and with stick in hand set out to explore the fishing village across the estuary. The way led down the valley for a mile or so until there was a sharp bend in the lane where a little stream ran across the road—Forda, the little ford—and at the turn I went up another lane and past a farmhouse lying under the hill which I looked forward to climbing.

That farm and the outbuildings was a place to linger by. White owls nested under the thatched roof of the cart-shed; there was a pound-house where in autumn a horse turned a great cogged wheel which ground apples in a circular stone trough for the making of cider; and the men about the farm were so friendly. They seemed willing for a talk. I was not merely wasting their time, for in those days a motor-car in the lanes was a rare sight, and if the village had half a dozen visitors in the summer months it was said that "the place was opening-up-of quite a lot."

But no one was about this fine morning, and my destination was the estuary. The way led up a steep and narrow lane, or rather gulley, for its stony bed was a-trickle with water, as one entered a dark tunnel under blackthorn bushes. The lane, sunken below the fields on either side, was used only by dogs, drovers and cattle. It was too steep for a horse and butt, so there was little need to cut back the thorns and brambles which nearly choked the way. Higher up, hazel and ash clumps met overhead and made it a place of shade and sun in dapple and glister. I had been told that it was a disused sled-track: that years ago sacks of flailed corn were brought up and spread on the hilltop, for the winds to winnow off the doust, or shucks.

It was a steady pull up the lane, but at the top there was bright reward. I stood in the clear air of morning gazing over hundreds of square miles of land and sea. Far below, spread out like a model contour map, were the sandhills of the Burrows, blown by the sea-winds into a desert extending behind a shallow shore. A long head-land enclosed the southern ocean, ending at Harty Point. There, across the steely-blue sea, on the horizon of sky and ocean, was Lundy, standing high; its cliffs, like those of the promontory, seen in clear detail in the low rays of the eastern sun. My watch said seven o'clock, but the world had been fresh and bright for over two hours. Across the Burrows I saw the white stalk of the lighthouse, among sandhills this side of the estuary of the Two Rivers: and across the water, the village which was my destination, built around the base of a green hill.

Usually I walked between twelve and fifteen miles every day. The thought of being indoors was unbearable. With happy anticipation I gazed at the route before me, of the miles along broad sands in which the ribs of wooden ships were embedded.

Descending the hill, I crossed the sandhills, and soon was walking in the spindrift at the edge of the sea. For a change, I traversed the sands, with their shells of razor-fish and cockle, and walked along the upper-tide-lines among the corks and feathers and notched skeletons of birds struck down and plucked by the peregrine falcons. There were pink crab shells and sand-blasted bottles, dry seaweed thongs and barnacle-riddled driftwood, among which ran the ring-plovers upon stone and shell, piping their frail cries as they arose in flight before one; and after a swift wing-jerking circular flight they would glide to their feet again, to stand as still as the stones and watch the stranger whose bare feet were purring in the dry sand above the tide-line, where they were dreaming of laying their eggs.

Beyond the wrack-strewn hollows in the breaches of the sandhills lay the estuary, with waves breaking white on the submerged shoal called the South Tail. As I strode along the shore, still carrying my shoes, I saw oyster-catchers on a shingle bank; and rounding Aery Point, was soon trudging on wet loose gravel to the lighthouse, and thence upon the lower rocks, among pools where crabs hurried from my shadow, and strange small fish, locked in by the lapsed tide, reamed into the dark, seaweed-haunted depths. I was making for the middle ridge from where a waved handkerchief would bring a boat from the far shore, to row the traveller across the estuary for a shilling.

Such is a walk on a spring morning, when a man is free and facing life with zest: a timeless walk, every moment lived in peace; a walk that seems to go on for ever, and then it is all behind one, but living in the mind, timelessly.

2

I had made two previous visits to the village, the first by way of the mossy pans behind the sandhills, the second along the shore. Now, on my third visit, I felt that it was already a particular place of my own. The village was said to be natural and wild. That suited me! There were seventeen inns and taverns in its narrow wandering streets and along its quays. Each was filled, after the day's work, with a life rich enough to stimulate any writer. There was never any drunkenness in the inns, but plenty of good fun and talk. The low-ceilinged rooms, with their bars, benches, settles, and tables were lit by oil-lamps. They were the social meeting-places of men who worked in the shipyards, the boat-houses, and the fishermen whose lives were almost entirely lived in thoughts of salmon.

There were sailors, too, some of them from the Baltic, the Indian Ocean, the China Sea. Steam had brought most of them; but an occasional three-masted timber-ship from Finland or Scandinavia sailed over the bar on the spring-tides, the extra depth of water floating them up the river to Bideford.

The scene that met my eyes on that early spring day was one that by now was becoming part of my new and wonderful life. The steep, wave-wet slip, grown with seaweed below, led up from a rocky foreshore littered with old pots and pans, fish-heads, rusty bicycle frames, and other jettisoned rubbish; dark salmon nets hanging on walls during repairs; fishermen working at them, clad in dark-blue jerseys, salt-encrusted trousers, bare-footed like the children. The Seamen's Mission, with its biblical text painted over the door, and a lonely looking Lascar, face more green than brown, disconsolately standing against the wall outside. The chemist's shop with the big blue and red globes of coloured water in the window and the little corked phials of odd objects blanched in alcohol—a viper, a frog with two heads, a sea-horse, a lamprey. The ship-chandler's with the copper and brass fittings displayed in the window, with splendid new port and starboard lamps in polished phosphor-bronze which did not corrode in salt water; the anchors, boathooks, and yacht's fenders, the neat coils of Manila rope.

Having had my fill of staring, I padded back the way I had come, up and down narrow sett-stone streets filled with the shouts and happy cries of scores of bare-footed children. I was making for the Royal George. On the way thither I had to pass the War Memorial, the design of which, I felt with relief, was no oppression of the spirit. There were upon it no winged seraphs holding aloft torches or swords; no draped female figures with ecstatic or self-righteous faces gazed into the sky. Such memorials were common elsewhere in Britain at that time: the commissioned, directed work of third-rate pretentious sculptors obeying the wishes of committees dictating the disposal of the subscribed money. They reflected not the truth of men who had died, but only commonplace civilian feeling unaware of its own sentimental obscurity.

While my twenty-four-year-old self was musing thus, standing by the plain cross and thinking of my friends of long ago, I noticed an old man walking slowly towards the memorial from another direction. He looked to be much worn by the sea. The elements had long since taken the dye out of shapeless peaked cap and jersey alike; the eyes which looked at me out of the round face were vacant, a faded blue, the lower lids fallen and red. To the tops of his legs he wore sea-boots of cracked leather, seemingly nearly as old as himself. They had been botched many times.

Seeing his eyes fixed on me, I bade him good morning, and with respect for his obvious great age and maritime experience I saluted him with my right hand.

He made no reply, but slowly raised a finger to the peak of his cap. Otherwise he continued to stand still. As he also continued to gaze at me, I bent down, as though intent upon reading the names on the memorial.

Nearly all the names were of sailors, lost in the Royal Navy and the Merchant Service. When I looked up again, the old man was still regarding me with his anxious eyes. At last he spoke.

"A man must splice a rope," he said.

"Yes, of course," I replied, while wondering what he meant.

About a quarter of an hour later, as I strolled barefoot upon the narrow sett-stoned way, I came upon a small cul-de-sac called Irsha Court. There I saw the old fellow again. He was pouring water out of a battered copper kettle into a tub. I noticed how it left the spout in a shaky splashing. Some of it had gone over his boots. Was that perhaps why he wore them?

The water in the tub was brown with dissolved essence of oak bark, in which the nets and sails of fishermen were preserved. The tub stood just outside the open door; but what took my fancy at once was a carved wooden woman, painted in blue and pink and black, fixed on the wall above the door. Figurehead of a sailing ship! It was startlingly beautiful, with all the mystery of remote deep water, of coral isle and the peaks of the Andes. Inside the cottage, in the single downstairs room, someone was at work on a net.

Now a stranger to what, for him, is an entirely new world often shows a curiosity which reveals his own gaping inexperience; and a young writer, of course, is always questing for material for his work. I took a quick glance into the room, which I felt to be a treasure-house of bygone age. Would there be stuffed and varnished flying fish, small brilliant birds of the tropics under glass domes? Strange sea-shells, perhaps the skin of a monkey, or a necklace of human teeth? A painted shield taken from the cannibal chief of a war-canoe among the islands of Polynesia? And, of course, models of full-rigged ships in bottles on the kitchen shelf.

Glancing in, I got a shock. Upon a chair sat a man with no ears. Part of his nose was missing. His jaw and cheeks and neck and hairless skull looked as though he had been made of wax and melted in fire.

"Oh, do forgive me," I said. "I have lost my way to the Royal George."

The apparition came to the door and pointed down the street, with an accompaniment of mumbled words and a kind of nasal whistling. I pretended gratitude for the information and hastened away.

3

As I drank my beer, and ate my lunch of bread and cheese and pickled onions in the Royal George, I learned from the landlord that the injured man was the only surviving son of the old fellow, who himself was one of the last of the deep-water sailors of the village. He was what the landlord called a masts-and-yards man. Four of his five sons had been lost at sea, three of them in the war. The fifth, and youngest, who lived with his father in Irsha Court, was known locally as Whistling Paddy. He had served in an oil-tanker, which had been torpedoed. When the crew had abandoned ship and taken to the boats a roar of flame and billowing smoke had suddenly arisen like forest fire in the dark Atlantic night. The boat crews had rowed desperately to escape the widening fringes of fire sliding down the slopes of the swell, and they were gaining on the roaring furnace when the tanker exploded, and flaming spirit had dropped out of the sky upon one of the boats in which Paddy had been rowing.

I gathered that, with his wound-gratuity paid recently, Whistling Paddy and his father had bought an old salmon boat from a certain fish agent, together with a net and, most important of all, a licence. They had had to pay a lot of money, for licences were coveted things, and limited in number by the Two Rivers' Conservancy Board.

Apparently the fish agent, who in some of his spare time was a preacher, had driven a hard bargain. But it is only fair to say that everything was scarce, and therefore dear, in those days immediately after the ending of the war. Salmon were dear, too; and if the season, which no man could foretell, turned out to be a good one, there would be a fair return for the money, as the agent had declared, quoting "Render unto Caesar the things which are Caesar's", before his final "Take it or leave it, midear, there be plenty others after my boat and gear, tidden no odds to me who buys what an honest man has to sell." After that business-like remark the fish agent had been known as Julius Caesar.

With two others, out-of-work ex-service men (there were many such at that time), a crew of four had been assembled. One share for the boat, another for the net; and a share for each of the four men. That was usual, and considered fair. It meant that old Masts-and-Yards and Paddy took two-thirds of the money paid for salmon by the agent who bought the fish from the boats, paying the best market price, wholesale, less a small commission for the work of collecting the fish. Live and let live—the principle that satisfied all in the village.

There was much speculation in the Royal George about the wisdom of this particular venture. The licence cost five pounds a season; the old man was beyond such heavy work, while the son was a cripple, suffering at times, particularly at the full of the moon, from headaches, which made him feeble. He would be unable to haul properly on a rope. It was during the spring tides, the biggest tides coming with the new moon and again with the full moon, that fish ran up better than on the neaps; and the spring tides, it was thought, would prove too much for such a crew of cripples and men ignorant of the currents.

The draughts from the lower estuary, shot from off the sandbanks of the bar, were dangerous to those who did not know how uncertain the swell could be there. Many a boat had been swamped on the North and South Tails, upon which a swell might roll in unawares, in calmest weather. Apart from the danger, the work was hard, much harder than they had bargained for. The old man was fit only to chew tobacco with the stumps of his teeth and stand about on the quay in fine weather; he was too masterful, "he never took no advice, whether from doctor, parson, or them as knew the tides". What did he know about fishing? He had been a deep-water man all his born days, an old masts-and-yards man, who didn't understand shoaling water. But " 'twadden no good tellin'm. He wouldn't listen to no man"!

I gathered that there was considerable animosity in the village between the fishermen and the water-bailiffs employed by the Conservancy Board. The Board was the legal authority which ruled when salmon-fishing should begin and when the season should end. It controlled the netting in salt water, and the rod-fishing in the fresh water of the rivers which flowed into the estuary. It decided the number of the boat licences, and the cost of licences for both nets and rods. Apparently netsmen had a deep grudge against the Board.

Angrily they told me of the differences between the season of netting in the sea, and that of fishing in the rivers. The rod-and-line men on the river-banks were allowed to fish for salmon and sea-trout a month before the nets were permitted to start; and at the back-end, or autumn, the nets were off a month before the rod-and-line men were stopped by law from fishing. In the eyes of the nets-men, to whom salmon were their living, this was unfair. You could take fish for sport eight weeks more in a season than for your living! Many a water-bailiff was, in imagination, thrown into the sea for that fancied injustice. Indeed, on one occasion, during netting, or poach-ing, in the close season, the bailiffs' boat was rammed in the Pool, in an attempt to upset and drown them, apparently.

There was more than the eight weeks, too. For whereas a poor man, they declared, had his living to get by hard work, he was restricted during the season to five days a week only; a rich man, a rod-and-line man, could fish six days a week, and six nights, too, if he'd a mind to! Ah, there was one law for the rich, another for the poor! Money talked! The water-baillies were there only to serve the interests of the rich man, not those of the poor fisherman.

What was the reason for the five days a week fishing for the nets, I enquired; and my innocent question was answered by a roar, and such angry looks, that I did not repeat it in the Royal George. I had the answer, however, a little later in the season.

4

There was a young doctor in the district who was also a fly-fisherman. He did a lot of work, for a hobby, in compiling a natural history of the Two Rivers. He analysed the waters of the various streams which fed the parent rivers coming from the southern watershed of Exmoor and the north-western slopes of Dartmoor. He collected in little close-mesh nets, the summer fish-food in the rivers, comprising plankton, daphnia, nymphs, creepers, shrimps, snails, and other small forms of life. The doctor believed that truth would always prevail with men, were the facts presented to them in a way they could comprehend. The rivers were the nurseries of the young stock, and salmon were not unlimited in number.

Trying to do good, to replace ignorance and selfishness with know-ledge and co-operation, the doctor volunteered to give a lecture in the village one night. He would like to talk to the fishermen, to tell them about his adventures up the rivers, which were the nurseries of the baby salmon. Unless a proper number of mature fish were allowed to get up the rivers to spawn, he said, the stock would decline and die out—and the netsmen's livelihood with them.

The talk was sponsored by the Clerk to the Board. Bills announcing the lecture on the Life Cycle of the Salmonidae were posted about the village. Admission free. I made it my business to attend.

Knowing the habits of fishermen, the lecturer timed his talk to take place one evening when the tide was high, when all the netsmen would be ashore. Net fishing could be done only on the last of the ebb and the beginning of the flow, when the channels were narrow and the currents not too strong for the hauling of the nets.

The doctor was liked in the village. He played skittles in some of the inns with the men; he had brought many of their children into the world; he did not press for his bills to be paid. Because he was popular, many fishermen went to the Mission Hall to hear him, while determined not to accept a lot of book-stuff and words which had nothing to do with their necessity to earn money to buy food and clothes for the missus and kids. He might be a good doctor, and no man would say otherwise and not be contradicted, but did he know about salmon and peal? Had he ever worked in a crew, had he ever hauled a net, beyond giving a hand now and again when he was out messing about down the estuary? What could a mere water-whipper know about real fish-catching? Did he deny that salmon spawned in the gravel pits left on the Shrarshook by the gravel boats? Salmon, as all men knew, were saltwater fish, and so it was nature that they spawned in salt water! 'Twas a dirty lie, about laying their eggs in river water, a lie just to cheat the poor man of his living, so that rich gentry could have their sport whipping water, wi' hartifissal flies, up the valleys! Ah, they were not going to be sucked in by any old flimflam talk!

The doctor knew all this; but he remained cheerful, even confident. He had borrowed a magic lantern, and had some slides to throw on the screen made of a borrowed bed-sheet tacked up on the wall of the Mission House.

Before the assembled rugged faces, from which arose much rank tobacco smoke, the doctor began his lecture. He started by saying that he would tell them only of what he had seen himself, and they ought to know him well enough to know that he would not tell them any falsehood. He had seen fish laying their eggs in the gravel beds, called redds, of little brooks and runners far up under the moors. These salmon, in spawning dress, were all colours. The keepers, or cock fish, were usually red and yellow; while the sows or hen-fish were usually dark brown, a bronze colour.

He described the fighting among the male salmon; the eels which attacked them when, weak after spawning, and often covered with the same sort of yellow fungus which attacked riverside trees, they were too feeble to make the return journey to the sea. But if a salmon after spawning, he said, could get down to salt water, perhaps as thin as a sprat, yet with its silver coat come upon it again, it might be restored to healthy life and growth.

"It cleans itself!" shouted a voice. "Us calls'n kelts, midear!"

"Exactly!" agreed the doctor. After a while he went on. "Now the eggs which hatch, usually in the early months of the new year, turn into what we call alevins. They are little fish with their egg-sacs, just like the yolk of a hen's egg, shrinking into their bellies. Soon the alevin becomes a fry, a tiny little spotted fish, looking just like a trout. It has red and black spots, when only an inch long. It takes two years of living in freshwater to grow to about six inches in length, feeding on flies which have hatched, snails and shrimps, in fact anything it can get. In this stage it is called a parr. Alevin first, then fry, then parr. It feeds hungrily, in competition with the native non-migratory brown trout of the stream—and with the parr of the migratory sea-trout, what you call peal, as well.

"Then, usually in the month of May, the parr in its third year of river-growth begins to change into a smolt. Its scales become silvery, and in some excitement it drops down the river, to find the estuary and the sea. You must have seen many smolts jumping in the Pool here, in May."

"Us have midear, us have! Go on, doctor, go on, us be waiting for 'ee!"

"Right! Grand little fellows, the smolt. Away to sea they go —if they survive their enemies in the estuary, that is. There are many bass waiting for them in the String, where the two rivers meet—you all know the String much better than I do, where the two ebb-tides meet and jabber against one another—well, if the smolt escape the bass and the cormorants they reach deeper water and grow rapidly as they eat the rich and strange food of the ocean. Some return after a few months, weighing four or five pounds. They are called grilse. Others stay longer in the Atlantic, and grow to great weights, eating prawns, herrings, and all sorts of smaller fish; but always, if they survive those greedy herring hogs and seals, they try to return to the rivers again, to spawn, and so to continue the race or species. If too many are lost in the sea, or when lying in the rivers—"

"Aah, they rod-and-line boogers!" roared a voice.

"Quite right!" said the doctor. "Some must be left to spawn, for stock fish! I agree with what you said, Billy. Now, with your permission, I propose to show you some magic-lantern slides of salmon scales. Here is the first one. You will see that it is like the cross-section of a tree. Or like a thumb-print; but the likeness to a tree is better. These scales grow with the fish; they reveal its growth. This is one off a four-year-old fish. Observe those inner rings, evenly spread; they tell the growing period of the parr, of its first summer in the river, when food was plentiful. Beyond them, you see the rings are jammed up, clotted together, dark and thinly spaced: that is the winter period, when the fish made little or no growth, from little or no food. Now observe what happens to a scale when the fish reached the good food in the sea! Look at the expansion! If it wore one of those excellent jerseys knitted by your good wives, it would nearly burst it open! That was when the smolt began to gulp down shrimps, sprats, and anything it could get. That little bit of growth in the middle, the small rings in the inner scale, show the two years' river-feeding: these wide and wavy rings on the edge show the next two years' growth, for it remained two years in the sea—and grew to twenty-nine pounds' weight in that time! The first two years of the fish's life produced about three ounces of growth, in bone and flesh; the next two years, nearly thirty pounds! Wonderful, isn't it? Now then, I'll be pleased to answer any questions. Only remember—when I want to have a bathe I'll dive in by myself—I don't want any help this evening!"

There was a roar of laughter. The lights were turned up. The doctor began to pack a pipe, while sitting easily on the side of the lecturer's table, swinging a leg.

"Come on, don't be shy! Ask anything you like."

No response.

"Why, what's happened? Have you all been hearing the Crake?"

It was perhaps not a tactful question; but the doctor was well pleased with himself, a little over-confident at the good humour of his audience. He felt he knew them, and that they would take what he said, from knowing him to be a 'proper chap'. They needed education; they were prejudiced, from ignorance; some even believed in that relic of superstition, the Crake, as a portent of death approaching one of themselves. Obviously it was some bird calling at night; but should the call or cry happen to coincide with a death by drowning, perhaps half the world away, when the news arrived, weeks afterwards perhaps, someone remembered that the Crake was heard about that time. Nonsense! Relic of the age of witch-hunting and mental darkness!

"Come on, chaps, let's hear from you. I don't know everything, but I'll do my best to answer any question."

Yes, they were a rough lot, but good boys when treated properly. Had they not been dead against the Tory candidate, all Liberal to a man until the Tory member of Parliament got them the right to have their votes, when they were at sea during an election, by proxy? In generosity for that, to a man they had turned Tory; and next time the Liberal candidate had come to address them, it was his turn to have flat tyres to his motorcar! And hadn't two policemen, not so long ago, been caught, in nets flung upon them as they walked side by side for safety at night, and soused in the sea, suspended in the net from the top of the quay? They thought the police were in league with the water-bailiffs to stop the poor man's right to take salmon in the closed season.

"Surely you must want to ask me something?"

At this point a burly individual got on his feet and spat carefully between his boots. This was Bob Kift, one of the strongest of the fishermen, who was usually most violent in his words about the water-baillies. Was he not the man who had actually, single-handed, dipped the two policemen in the net? He was a big-headed man, as powerful as a bull seal. Where his stretched and faded woollen jersey ended at his hairy wrists and massive neck his skin was almost as brown as a sail or net. He could eat a dozen herrings for his tea and then could manage a pound of steak, if he could get it. Eighteen stone of bone and meat, otherwise muscle, stood on feet encased in black rubber thigh-boots which were patched in places with red rubber motor-tyre patches. The human seal cleared his throat, but no words came.

"Well, Bob Kift, I didn't think you were a shy man!"

"Ooh, I ban't shy, doctor," replied Robert Kift. "I ban't shy, noomye! But 'ee zaid us could ask ee questions, didn't ee, surenuff?" He spoke softly.

"Certainly, Bob. Ask anything you like," replied the doctor, deceived by the softness of the big man's voice.

"Wull then," Bob Kift suddenly roared out, "what about they bliddy water-whippin' rod-and-line men killing parr and stock fish with their bissley li'l bits o' fluffy feather and 'ooks up the rivers for a pastime?"

Shouts and bellows of laughter greeted the comedian. Thus encouraged, the bull seal plunged to the attack. His mouth wide open, so that his bristly grey moustache hid most of his nose, he hollered, "Why should they dolled-up niminypiminy loobeys be allowed to take the bread out o' the' mouths o' our chillen? They gentry fishes for pleasure only, while us does so for a living! Aye, 'tes true! They can fish in March, when the big run o' fish be comin' in, but us chaps has to wait till April! Tidden right! They stops the nets in March, when the fish be runnin' plentiful, so that salmon can get up the rivers, for to provide sport for the rich man! If salmon spawn in autumn, there's plenty o' sojers rinnin' up then, red as mullets, to keep the stock goin'!"

"Red hake, you mean, don't you, Bob Kift?"

"Aye, red 'ake us has to call'm, like yippocrits, in the close season, else us'd be fined or sent to gaol, if they water-baillies had their way! And I'll tell 'ee this, midear, for to put through your magic lantern when you'm showing it off to the gentry what sits on the Bench! Ask they magistrates, what fines poor men for poachin', as they calls it, ask they niminypiminy water-whippers if their cooks 'ave ever bought red 'ake at the backdoor, for the gentry to sit at their tables and eat at night! Why, if they had their desserts, they'd all be in gaol, that's my question to your answer, Doctor!" And the bull seal sat down.

The Mission Hall was in an uproar of laughter and shouts, of stamped feet and rolling heads.

The doctor was a man of courage, which may be the same thing as obstinacy at times. When the laughter had subsided a little, and they were waiting for more fun, he said, "Ah, Bob Kift, you ought to be on the Board, with your eloquence! But now let's be serious a moment. If all the fish are caught before they can spawn, your living, as well as the river fishing, will simply die out. You are agreed about that, surely? Come now!"

"Tidden true, you know," intoned a solemn voice.

They looked round, at the figure of Julius Caesar, the fish agent, who had risen on his feet. The audience at once settled quieter. They preferred Bob Kift to speak for them; but let a man have his say. And from what they knew of Julius Caesar, his say would be something.

"I have somep'n to say," said the solemn voice. Aye, it was coming, trust Julius Caesar. "The Lord put the fish into the sea, no man can deny that, durin' the creation of the earth in six days. Fish were created for the food o' men. Can anyone deny that?"

"What about seals and 'errin' 'ogs?" cried a voice from the back of the room.

"I ham concerned with the truth o' the Book, and let no man deny it except at the peril of his immortal soul, and the chanst o' hivverlastin' damnation." Julius Caesar looked around. All eyes avoided his eyes. "Wull then, since no man can deny the truth, I can illustrate what we have heard tonight by bringin' to you the miracle o' the loaves and fishes, which the Book—"

But the man who had mentioned seals and herring hogs, otherwise porpoises, did not appear to have any respect for Julius Caesar. He interrupted the threatened sermon by calling out, "Let they as be saved, or think they are, save their voices for Sundays! Meanwhile, why don't the Board shift they rocks below Middle Ridge? If they profess to be servin' the interests of the working man, why don't they clear away the rocks? Shall I tell you why? Because they care nothing for the workers, though they pretend to, like all capitalist yippocrits. It be a bourjois swindle, to keep down the Workers' Revolution. Lenin said—"

"Us don't want no red flag yurr, midear," cried Bob Kift, getting on his feet, "All the same, Doctor, there be some sense in gettin' the Board, if they'm a mind to it, to dredge up they rocks which tears the seines of our nets time and time agen. Now, Doctor, us knows 'ee, but with all respect, you ban't very old, midear, and some on us chaps have bin yurr saison after saison three score years and more. You'll do more good if you ask the Board to shift they rocks, but they won't tackle it, and shall I tell 'ee for why? Because they want netsmen to have broken nets, for to let the fish through, for their pals on the riverside upalong to get the fish!"

The noise of agreement was terrific. The meeting seemed to be out of control. Vainly the doctor's voice cried out that the Board had no money to undertake the work; that if the men wanted to do it, why didn't they do it themselves? The Board wasn't all-powerful; it merely tried to preserve the stock of fish for year after year... They went out noisily to the pubs. Nothing apparently had been achieved by the good intentions of the doctor.

When we were alone in the room, he said to me, "You won't get any objective thinking from men who still believe in such palpable superstition as the Crake."

I agreed with the doctor. Obviously they were as prejudiced as the limpets on the rocks.

In the Royal George I heard old Masts-and-Yards declaring that salmon did not spawn in the rivers; in his father's time, and grandfather's before him, he said, fish spawned on the gravel of the Middle Ridge, which some called Shrarshook, since Cap'n Charles Hook had bin drowned there in his young days by the Crake, but Middle Ridge was allus the proper name.

The old man's son, Whistling Paddy, sat beside him. I avoided speaking to him. I felt that he was shy of speaking, for he could not articulate his words properly, his jaws having been set askew after being broken by the torpedo explosion which had preceded the burning in petrol flames. Also, the ear of anyone he was confiding in was liable to be sprayed by a whistle of beer.

The trend of the talk was that someone had got at the doctor, someone on the Board, and sucked him in, ah, that was the only explanation, for he was a nice little fellow, who paid his way, and harmed no man by either word nor deed. The lecture was the subject of much talk that night; but by the following week, when the season was opened, something was reported which put nearly everything else from their minds.

The Crake had been heard by three boat crews fishing from the Shrarshook, in the darkness. It was no exaggeration, it was a fact; a dozen men told me that they had heard it quite clearly in the darkness. The doctor laughed at the story. I did not know what to think.

Meanwhile, I was learning more about the art of salmon fishing.

5

The tides ruled when the netsmen could fish. Once every day and once every night the lunar Atlantic pulse moved up the estuary, filling the arms of the Two Rivers. The sea went up far beyond the old bridges of Barnstaple and Bideford, pressing back the fresh waters of the moorland rivers; and at the tide-heads, at the very end of ocean's impulse, the flow hesitated and became the ebb. Unless there was enough water in the rivers for the fish to run up farther, they returned with the tide, to come back again in the following flow. Each journey up and down the estuarine reaches was perilous for salmon; for when the tide was making, and again when it was nearly ebbed away, the boats went from their moorings below the sea-wall, each with its crew of four, to take salmon and peal in nets two hundred yards in length, each with a mesh of two inches, the size determined by law to permit the escape of immature fish.

6

It so happened that on the day of my next visit it was the turn of the boat owned by Whistling Paddy and skippered by his father (out of courtesy to the old man) to start the morning's fishing upon the sandbank of the dangerous shoal called the South Tail. The licensed boats of the estuary took turns at the various fishing places, so that all should have an equal chance. So the boat skippered by old Masts-and-Yards, its number painted on its bows according to the law, left its mooring below the Royal George in advance of the other boats and went down upon the massive green and wimpling glide of the ebb.

It was a spring tide; the moon was new; the weight of incoming press of water had made the currents the fastest of the month; the ebb was equally rapid. It swilled along down to the North and South Tails, marked by their successive lines of the dreaded white water.

With placid dips of sweeps the boat drifted down on the tide, passing a leaning buoy on which was perched a herring-gull with one leg. The bird was waiting for the water to lapse, for the wide expanse of the middle ridge to show itself. Then it would fly by custom thither, prise off mussels with its beak, carry them into the air, drop them on the stones below, and follow them down to eat out of the smashed shells. The pitiless yellow eye of the bird stared at the old sailor sitting on the piled net in the stern, who saw it without a thought.

Sometimes a wave, driven by the west wind, slapped against the bows of the boat, and skits of water were flung into it. Soon the buoy, marking the edge of the fairway, was left behind.

A mile and more seawards, waves were breaking on the tails of the bar with a dull and ceaseless roar. Beyond in the bay a tramp steamer was lying at anchor, awaiting the iron ball on the post by the lighthouse in the sandhills to arise, a sign that the bar was navigable. The ship would have to wait several hours for high water.

To left of the salmon boat was a ridge of grey pebbles, above which were low cliffs of sand worn by wind, the ragged dunes held by marram grasses. This was the Westward Ho! Pebble Ridge, made famous by Kipling in *Stalky & Co*. The old man looked without interest at the long bleak stretch of sand; his mind was far away, perhaps looking upon scenes of the South Pacific, the green slopes of Peru, the immense towering Andes flushing pink in the sunrise which had not yet looked upon the top-s'ls of the three-masted schooner, whose holystoned decks he trod with his wooden shoon. He had worn these as a lad, on returning to port the first time after rounding the Horn, and known the exhilaration of the trade winds.

The sixteen-foot salmon boat passed by the Hurleyburlies uncovering in the lapsing water, their black edges ripping white; it passed the checkered Pulling buoy floundering in the hollow swirl of waters; but still the old man was away in thought and fancy. Only when a salmon leapt out of a wave not fifty yards from the boat, followed by a big, black object, and at the shout of " 'Errin' 'og!" from one of the rowers, did his eyes focus upon the moment, to see the porpoise rolling up and down again, like a great blubbered bottle. There were others, farther off.

"Tidden right to allow them, I say," said one of the rowers. "There be several on'm! They'm taking of the fish, you know, all the time. If the water-baillies would do some work with a rifle out yurr sometimes there'd be some sense to it."

There was a school of porpoises. They had followed a run of salmon from the Lundy Race, a dozen miles and more westward from the bar. Several salmon leapt to escape the predacious mammals, each of which would tear away its bite from a fish, then pursue another. They were hunting not from hunger but for sport. The sight of many dark shapes rolling up and under again filled each man with hatred. The sweeps ceased to ply, as they watched. It seemed that there were at least a dozen porpoises in the school. Another rolled up just behind the stern of the boat. In its mouth was pink flesh, and a glint of silvery scales, together with the fin torn from near the salmon's vent. In his anger Old Masts-and-Yards spat at it, squirting brown tobacco juice at it, his only weapon of offence. When his anger had gone, he said:

"There be fish about, so pull hard, lads. They'm running! I never seed so many leaping like this all my born days."

Whistling Paddy hissed with excitement.

7

The boat went down towards a spit of sand on which gulls, white in the sunshine rushing before and after the shadows of clouds, were perched head to wind. The starboard sweep was eased, the sandbank grew nearer. When with a slight bump the keel-shoe grazed the sand, Whistling Paddy jumped out and a coil of rope was flung to him. Winding the end round his waist, he shoved out the boat again, and at once it was rowed with long strong pulls into the current. The old man paid out the rope over the stern, and then the net followed, the dark two hundred yards of it, eight feet deep, corked along its head rope and leaded at the heel. The heel rope sank away immediately, leaving the corks on the choppy surface to hold the net vertical.

The cast was made on the shape of a horseshoe, and by the time all of the net had dropped over the stern the ankle boots of Whistling Paddy leaning back on the rope were sunken in wet sand beyond their tops. He tugged them free, and with all his strength began to plod along the water line towards the boat which, having come round its loop against the tide, had touched into the bank again. The three men clambered out; one ran to join Whistling Paddy, whose head was bowed, for the pull of the tide on the net was almost beyond his strength.

The second man bent the dark and dripping net over his shoulder, and together they slowly plodded towards the other pair, likewise hauling. When about thirty paces apart they stopped, and began to pull hand under hand, slowly; short slow pulls against the weight of water which had crushed the horseshoe shape and borne the seine past the idle boat.

Minute after minute the four men hauled unspeaking, two at the head rope, two at the heel rope. The dull morning grew lighter; the waves were washed with tinny sunlight. The porpoises were now around the distant bar buoy. As the distorted arc of the corks was drawn imperceptibly small, hauling was easier. When only the purse remained in the sea the bodies of the men were bent forward and they hauled rapidly, the net falling at their feet, while their eyes stared for sight of fish.

The purse, drawn in fast, was empty except for green crabs and stones with bladder weed growing on them.

No word was spoken. The youngest man ran away to the boat

and started to pull it to the piled net. His mate ran to help him. "They 'errin' 'ogs've drove the fish out agen, I reckon." They walked the boat up in the shallow water. In the meantime the old man and his son, one at heel and t'other at head rope, were shaking the net free of stone and crab—crushing crabs underfoot—and piling the net on the sand, preparatory to repiling it upon the boat's stern. Afterwards a rest of a couple of minutes while they gazed seawards for sign of jumping fish. Nothing: but the press of the tide was lessening, and at a word from the skipper a second draught was shot.

Once again the shedding of the net; the full-strength pulling on the heavy sweeps; the slow plodding haul from the sandbank; the emerging after twenty minutes of the purse; again only crabs and seaweed and insignificent flat fish shaken free. No cursing of luck after the vain fatigue of labour which made the backs of the recently unemployed men, unused to such work, painful to straighten again. Again the youngest went for the boat; again the piling and repiling of the net; and when the third draught was shot and hauled in, as before, the tide was slack and almost at once began to flow.

Wind was freshening, flinging afar sprays from the tops of combers before they curled and plunged in bounding white turmoil upon the hidden shoals of the bar. The tide began to move in faster, creeping up the sandbank. A large bird flew with powerful thrusts of wings up the estuary, settling with a splash beside the Pulling buoy.

"He knows where th' vish be, I reckon," said one of the amateur netsmen. The skipper did not reply.

He was afraid of shoaling water. White water was death to all deep-water sailors. So the salmon boat left the bank for the light-house shore, where the fourth draught of the day was shot. The porpoises were seen nearer in the fairway, heading for the place the boat had left. One of the new men grumbled. He glanced, as he hauled, now and again at the black bird near the pulling buoy. Tipping up and disappearing underwater, and swimming with rapid thrusts of its webbed feet, the shag caught two codling and a sea-trout, returning to the surface with each fish to tip it head first into its hooked beak before gulping it down. After each swallowing, and before the succeeding tip-up and dive, its small emerald eye stared at the men, its enemies, across the widening gulf of water.

"There be fish over yonder," said the youngest man to his mate.

"Don't waste your breath, lad; save it for hauling," said the skipper.

"I could've made more on th' dole this last month, had I known it," replied the other.

A fish leapt inside the arc of the corks. A big 'un! In silent intentness the purse of the net was drawn in, and there was the salmon, threshing upon the watery shingle. Steady, lad! Whistling Paddy got his hand round the wrist of the fish by the tail and, securing his grip, lifted it sinuating up the shingle, where he dropped it to thump it on the base of the skull with a sodden length of drift-wood.

"Fifteen pun, I reckon, Father!"

Fifteen pounds at two shillings a pound from Julius Caesar, who collected fish for the lorry which came from Bristol to meet every tide. Thirty shillings. That was something, but they would have to take many more fish before the licence and wear of boat and net was paid for, let alone their living.

After another draught there was danger of the tide taking the net among the rocks lying off the shingle shore; so they rowed up-tide to the Shrarshook ridge. They rowed hard to get into the fair-way. The tide was tumbling over the low rocks, but they reached the Pulling buoy in safety, and from there approached rapidly the lower end of the bank. Behind them, between ridge and lighthouse, the tide was leaping and pouring. On a rock raised above the others squatted the black bird, with wings half spread and a fish-tail sticking out of its gullet. It moved its wings at the elbows, in order to shake down into its crop the live eel which was trying to writhe a way out of the scalding juices of the crop, past a flatfish and a small bass, both inert but still breathing. The shag's crop was gorged; the out-held wings eased the weight.

"That bliddy bird picks up a livin' easy," complained the youngest man. "The bliddy thing ought to be shot."

8

There was no need to do more than paddle in the fairway, to keep control of the boat, with the tide flowing fast. There was time for one more draught only. Amid the chop of wavelets that broke irregularly with foamy tops, with bubbles rushing under, the open boat glided past the decreasing extent of the Shrarshook at five knots. The wooden props which shored the barges, while gravel had been dug and shovelled on board at low tide, had been taken aboard the squat tarred vessels. Frothy flumes of water were pouring into the pits beside the barges, rocking the matchsticks flung away by the men at work, as they had lit their fags. Now the gravel-diggers were resting. Smoke wandered from galley chimneys.

A heron flew across the Pool with heavy hollow flight, making for the duckponds in the marshes behind the sea-wall.

"One more draught, lads; the tide be makin' fast."

They shot the draught, while other boats coming in from the bar passed over their floating corks. The salmon boats swept by, making for the backwash or eddy which lay off the curve of the sea-wall. It was hard work hauling in the net against the pull of the tide; and underwater the heel rope was carried against the big rocks on the bed of the Pool. The net was hung up; it had to be pulled free, for now time was against the crew. As they hauled, it was seen that at least half a dozen salmon were on the right side of the corks. The fish drove about to find a way out of the net; their back fins reamed along the top of the water and caused some excitement among the two amateur fishermen. Visions of much money at the week-end made their eyes keen; but the skipper and his son, whom the seas had taught patience, hauled stoically as before. One fish rushed unseen towards the edge of the gravel, turning in a great boil of sand and water and sped back, the sounds of its acceleration being just audible as drumming or thruddling through the noises of pouring water. It was a big sea-trout.

They hauled in; but when the seine came into near water, and finally upon the gravel, it was empty, a hole torn in the purse. Then the skipper dropped his rope and, raising his fist to the sky, began to curse the water-baillies for not dredgin' up they flamin' hellerin' rocks instead of tryin' to stop honest men arter a lifetime o' work on the high seas from keepin' out o' the' Grubber (workhouse or poor-house) by turnin' an honest penny! They dalled blasphemin' Board Boogers mocked Holy Writ, and they water-baillies were disciples o' Satan Hisself!

His words were heard by Julius Caesar, skipper of another boat, as it moved past the ridge.

"Takin the Holy Book's name in vain won't never pay you, midear!" came the warning from the bulky solemn-faced man. "You watch what you'm about, you a Masts-and-Yards man and all; you ought to knaw better than take the Book's words in vain!"

"Go and caulk yourself, you psalm-singing hellfire trader of a bliddy boy, you longshore beachcombin' son o' a ship's cat!"

Julius Caesar was a mere fifty years of age; thirty years younger than Masts-and-Yards.

"You should knaw better at your age than to talk like that, midear,' called back the other, from his boat rapidly receding. The current took it past the Pool buoy leaning at a steep angle upstream, a plume of water flung over its top. "Aiy, you should knaw better, old man, God is not mocked!" came over the water.

The stentorian tones had been heard by several of the crews of the gravel barges, waiting on the Shrarshook for the tide to float them off and take them up to the ports of Bideford and Barnstaple. Some men, looking on, laughed with derision. Because of his known hardness for money, Julius Caesar was not popular; but he thought they derided, not himself or his manner, but the Word. So he felt he was fighting the Good Fight.

Old Masts-and-Yards growled and spat as he repiled the torn net, muttering to himself about a local praicher who had nivver been beyond shoaling water. The younger men, the ex-soldiers, were amused and superior, winking to one another at the nonsense of old men, both so daft as each other. But even they, sceptical of so much since their return home from the war, were quietened when, only a little more than twelve hours later, they recalled the preacher's words.

The Crake came again in the darkness; this time with Death.

9

Towards midnight old Masts-and-Yards got out of bed, where he had been sleeping partly clothed, awoke his son, and went downstairs in his socks. After a cup of strong hot tea and some bread and beef-dripping, the two put on several extra garments, all frayed and worn—jersey, waistcoat, trousers, jacket—which had been hanging to dry on a line across the ceiling. Clad thus against the cold night air, they left Irsha Court, each carrying a sweep, which had been brought up from the boat during the afternoon tide lest they be stolen.

Tiny bluish-yellow jets of gas-light marked the sett-stoned streets and broad quay, beside which black masts and rigging of coastal craft arose among the stars. The night was almost silent, with faint slappings and murmurs of the ebb on boat and mooring and wet step of slip. On the farther shore lights shone in unseen houses, their thin reflections wriggling like golden eels beyond shapes of darkest shadow which were the moored salmon boats.

Father and son, unspeaking, waited by a bollard, to which the rope of a quayside ketch was made fast. At last voices were heard. A red spark came nearer, with the sounds of shuffling soft footfalls of boots worn to the uppers.

Without a word the four men went down the wet stone slip to the rocks and sand; hauled in their boat by the dripping painter; then away down on the ebb, by the spinning sea-top of the Pool buoy; and so to the dark rising ridge of the Shrarshook, now musical with the cries of wading birds. At steady intervals the roving beam of the lighthouse caressed the boat, and lit in a frail flash the outlines of gravel barges anchored there for the tidal shift.

There was money to be made in gravel during the immediate post-war years. Government subsidies to builders for new houses were £260 a house, and many an ugly little square building was going up, built by men who were one-man builders, masons seizing their chance to get on and make money. Gravel, sharp Two Rivers gravel, after washing in fresh water to remove the salt, made the best mortar.

Hoarse human tones came from the water-lapped dark of the Shrarshook, followed by the thud of wood baulks and the crush of boots on wet shell fragments and stone, as sleepy men jumped after the props to shore upright their barges. A blot of intense light swept over the ridge, stared blindingly a moment on the dark scene, blinked into darkness, and leapt again into seaward shine of vigilance clear and unfaltering for some seconds. Distantly came the roar of waves on the bar.

The two men dipped the sweeps, to keep steering way on the boat. Flashes of phosphorescence glimmered green and died in every placid swirl left by the blades. Old Masts-and-Yards and his son sat aft, the piled seine between them. In silence the boat glided away, leaving behind the ridge and the lonely lighthouse among the sand-hills. Past the Pulling buoy, writhing heavily ahead of the racing troughs and crests of the tide on the rocks, the dreaded Hurleyburlies, and down the fairway to the loose sandbank near the South Tail. The water flickered with pale-green lights of phosphoric plankton, minute life of the summer sea.

There was little wind, the air was heavy with moisture, and rain began to fall as they were shooting the first draught. At first a soft drizzle, then a steady suent wetness which laid the thin clothes of the ex-service men against their bodies. They did not mind being wet; their minds held memories of hopeless cold nights and days in the flooded winter crater-zones of Somme and Ypres which kept them fortified, in that they thought of the roof over their heads when they should return, where they were safe, secure, where they could be warm, and to which they might go and come at will. So they toiled without loss of spirit in darkness that might have been water, except that it could be breathed.

After slow heaving, they heard something in the purse, and, pulling in the net, were disappointed to find within, threshing and flacking, squat fish with thin rasping tails and heavy angular bodies nearly flat.

"Thorn-backs!" one man cried in disgust.

Whistling Paddy sought a Swedish knife from his pocket, flicked open the single blade, and stabbed the two great fish many times, to sever the spinal cords. They were skate. On their backs were bony talons. They shone palely as they were lifted up, to be slithered into the well of the boat. Of little value, parts of the fish were used in the fish-and-chip shop, poor men's food.

The crew waited for the ebb to slacken. When the tide was low, the skipper shot another draught, but instead of rowing round and hauling in directly, he told the two men at the sweeps to linger in the fairway, with the net gently bellied by the tide just on the make. This was illegal; it prevented fish from ascending, the net became a 'fixed engine for the taking of salmon', thus, in both theory and practice, stopping fish from reaching the nets higher up.

The salmon either were not running or were remaining over the bar, afraid of the porpoises which had been seen several times during the day. Some of them had gone up with the previous tide almost to the towns' bridges. At any rate, the net was empty.

The skipper shot one more draught; then he left, afraid of shoaling water, ever mindful of the dreadful menace of white water.

The boat went up to the next place. Here they took two salmon, and were jubilant: two grilse, of only about nine pounds, but they were *fish*, and made three that day!

"There be a school comin' in, I reckon," said one of the men. They hastened to shake out the net, for the skipper said that they would bestways cast from the lower end of the ridge. There were no loose rocks in the fairway at that place. It had taken him and his son three hours to repair the torn purse.

10

It was from the lower end of the Shrarshook that the last draught of the little company of four was shot, before the boat was burned. The tragic circumstances of that final draught were discussed for many weeks, even months, afterwards. While Whistling Paddy held the rope on the ridge, his figure silhouetted now and again by the sweeping beams of the lighthouse, the boat pulled across the tide, while being carried aslant the drift of water. It was turning round in a wide arc amidst its own wake of phosphorescence, the rowers straining at the sweeps to bring the boat back quickly to the ridge, when a big salmon, thought to be all of forty pounds, leapt from the water and fell with a splash only a few feet away from the skipper in the stern. As he called to the rowing men to bend their backs a hissing noise accomanied by a tremendous downpour made him peer into the gloom.

"Keep you a-going lads, keep you a-going!" he called out.

Almost immediately afterwards a scream, strange and plaintive, seemed to be coming from the agitated water beside the boat. The upheaval was so severe that the boat was violently rocked. Water poured over the starboard gunwale. One of the rowers lost his sweep, and fell over backwards; the other swore in his fear.

"Keep you a-going, lads!" said the skipper.

A dim white patch arose out of the murk. The sea became lashed with foam, filled with green flecks of fire, and the moaning scream came again, arising out of the turmoil, and filling all with terror.

Others heard the noise. There was a shout from way up the ridge —"The Crake!"

Whistling Paddy on shore was yelling. His words were indistinct, but it was thought he cried that he was not able to hold the rope. At the same time the net was being hauled off the stern-sheets of the boat by something big in the water. Seeing what was happening, one of the rowers clambered aft and grabbed the rope coiled under the remaining bulk of the net, now leaping off the boat into the water.

The old man began to curse him. "Get you back to the thole-pins, you loobey, or I'll have 'ee in irons afore us be finished!"

The younger man took no notice, as he took a couple of turns of rope round his sweep.

"Don't get the wind up, Dad," he said. "Us wull lose the net else.

'Tes a school of mullet; I seen 'em in Cork Harbour in bliddy thousands."

"Leave me to mind th' net! Git you back to the sweep, you g'rt fool, you!" cried the skipper.

The man had hardly got back to his thwart when the cries on shore changed into yelps of distress.

"I can't hold'n no longer, I can't hold'n, Feyther," came Paddy's voice faintly.

"All right, boy, us be comin'; keep you a-goin'!" cried the old man.

The rope-end in the boat was still turned round the handle of the sweep. The boat was drifting fast with the tide, though seemingly still. The man who held the sweep placed it between the oaken pins and braced himself to hold it there, for the rope was now snaking over the gunwale, giving little leaps and slashing the surface of the water. He braced himself for the tug to come. The skipper was by now without speech; he had no power left to compel the mutinous man to do his bidding, to row ashore to help his boy, whom he already saw, in a moment of insight, as lost. A deep-water man, a masts-and-yards sailor for fifty years, he knew what the spouting of water portended; he had seen monsters of the deep ocean main; but in his very experience, by his knowledge of the ways of God upon the face of the waters, he was helpless; for only the old knew the truth, and nobody listened to an old'n.

When the rope had run out of the boat the jerk on its beam was so heavy that it almost capsized. Then the boat was being turned about as it was pulled sideways, its gunwale almost under water.

"Loose the rope end, loose it, you sod!" cried the other man.

His mate responded by tipping up the sweep so that it slid over-board. The boat was now free.

Other shouts were coming from the darkness. The cries of Whistling Paddy had ceased.

When the old man found his voice he called out, "Be ee all right, Paddy boy?" and when there was no reply he stood up, took the other sweep, and, putting it over the stern, began to scull towards the ridge, working it to and fro with a rolling motion.

The two men sat still on the thwarts, and the bump into the shore of the Shrarshook, near the barges now waiting to go home on the tide after the night's work, flung them on their backs among the cold and slippery skates.

Old Masts-and-Yards walked down the ridge, calling to his

son. There was no answer. A hailing voice from beyond the barges cried out that there was something beating about in the Pool. Another voice was heard, " 'Tes the vengeance of the Lord come among sinners; 'tes the Lord's wrath come among us!" It was the voice of Julius Caesar.

The old man went down the length of the Shrarshook, calling the name of his son. The two men stood dejectedly by the boat. The net was gone; there would be no seeing that again. They would have to find other work. Rain was falling lightly; the rotating beam of the lighthouse was an opaque blur.

I I

From the quay across the water one or two women, who had heard the shouting, and thought it might be trouble with the water-bailiffs, watched in the darkness. The mournful hail of old Masts-and-Yards came over the water. As the onlookers waited, they saw an insignificant light burning upon the ridge; they watched it wavering about like a will-o'-the-wisp, before it fell and died out.

"Oh, my Gor, what be that, midear? Did 'ee zee'n, surenuff?"

" 'Tes trouble I shouldn't wonder, maybe 'tes they water-baillies."

The flare had been burned by Julius Caesar, whose practice it was to enwrap himself with newspapers at night under his jersey, as a protection against cold. Now, like a picture prophet of old, except for his bulk and girth, which certainly did not accord with any fasting in the wilderness, he was advancing down the southern shore of the Shrarshook, bearing aloft a torch of rolled newspapers in one hand, while with the other he pulled more paper from around his middle.

"Brothers!" he chanted to the night, out of a feeling of self-justified joy. "Brothers, fellow sinners all, the wages of sin is death, and 'e what taketh the Lord's name in vain shall be in danger of hivverlastin' 'ell fire." He waved the burning newspapers.

Other boats were appearing on the water-line of the ridge. One was rowing hard against the tide, a man in the bows standing up and looking for sign of floating corks. Men gathered round Julius Caesar. The feeble flare, with an occasional spark fleeting down towards the coppery crescent moon low in the vapours of the west, revealed their quiet faces. Stealthily the water crept up the sloping bank. From the direction of the lighthouse came a rushing roar as the sea poured into the rocky pools and lagoons below the shingle shore. The men discussed what had happened.

The net had been torn away from the boat, that was certain. As for Paddy on shore, the rope enwound about his middle and over his shoulder, and held by a half hitch—as was his habit—had pulled him into the water. The boat crew at the top of the ridge had heard his feeble cries in the water, following a great shower of spray, and the slashing plunge of some fish or animal.

" 'Tes no use for to strive with a man's reason," intoned Julius Caesar. "What be the Lord's hidden purpose, no man can dispoot. 'Tes the Crake come agen, for to warn sinful men, hanimated by their own pride, which goeth before a fall, for to teach us, sinners all, to live humbly in the ways o' th' Lord."

"Put a sock in it," muttered one of the ex-service men; but the words were unheard in the general response of "Amen".

12

Boats searched, in the chill light of the descendant moon, up the courses of the Two Rivers until dawn, looking for floating corks which would reveal the net. They had little hope of finding the missing man alive; they searched as an act of reverence to themselves, and to their neighbours, to bring the body home, for the churchyard. That was the natural place of a man when he was cut off, to be laid to rest in the place where he was born, where there was love for him, surely, lingering in the stones he had known, in the faces of friends and comrades, and most of all in the heart of his father.

That is how it seemed to me, when I learned the story of Masts-and-Yards, and found out why, so often, in sunny weather and rainy times too he was to be seen by the War Memorial. Had not all his sons been lost at sea? His neighbours knew it, and so they searched for the boy Paddy, to bring him home to his father.

The boats which searched until dawn found nothing. One volunteer crew kept a look-out during the ebb, but saw nothing of the net. The mystery remained for another day; and as has been said, provided the only real topic of talk in the village, and its seventeen taverns and inns, until the matter became clear the following morning.

The pilot of the Lundy boat *Lerina*, going out top of the tide, saw something floating near the bar buoy. Standing in nearer, he saw what were apparently the corks of the missing net. The ropes were twisted round the chain to which the buoy was anchored. The *Lerina* heaved to, and a boat hook caught the head rope. Hauling part of the net aboard, they recovered the body of Whistling Paddy, distended with water. It was even as had been said: the rope was made fast to his chest by two turns secured by a half hitch. It was drawn tight, confirming the belief that he had been pulled at a considerable pace through the water.

The *Lerina* turned back, to where on the quay a stretcher on wheels was waiting: for the boat had been watched from the lighthouse, the keeper of which had telephoned to the police in the village and to the doctor.

The body, covered by a canvas, was taken off in the rowing boat, after which the Lundy packet, prepared to encounter the formidable tide sweeping down the Irish Sea into the open Atlantic, set her sails to aid the efforts of the oil engine which drove the screw.

On her way across Bideford Bay the captain of the *Lerina* saw ahead a school of porpoises. They were not rolling and leaping through the sea in the usual manner of herring-hogs; indeed, when the captain of the *Lerina* looked through his glass he saw that one was jumping in the manner of a salmon trying to escape the pursuit of seal or porpoise. The porpoises, about a score of them, were appearing in all directions, quite unlike a school following a leader in a drive after food. The porpoises were being pursued.

Suddenly he saw what was after them. An immense shape arose out of the water, a little whale, which opened its wide mouth, set with teeth like tent-pegs, to snap at, but to miss, its prey, before diving down again and showing a fluked tail as it disappeared.

The *Lerina* kept on her course, which would cross that of the line of porpoises. The next time the monster appeared, it was with a porpoise being champed in its jaws, which were red with blood. The killer's head was blunt, shining smooth and black, with two patches of white above and behind its two small eyes. From a spiracle in the top of the head a jet of vaporous water rose hissing. It was a killer whale, a carnivorous animal which fed on flesh and fish alike. In companies the killers sometimes attacked the largest sperm whales, springing at the vast flippers to tear away flesh with chop of jaws able to crush seal or man with equal ease. *Orca Gladiator*, the grampus . . .

So that was the origin of the Crake! Well, not exactly the origin, for the screaming cries in the night had probably been made by a seal in its death agonies. The grampus had followed the porpoises and seals up the estuary, themselves following the runs of salmon, and, coming up against the net, had simply carried it away. Such was its weight that, had it chanced to arise under a sixteen-foot salmon boat, it could have overturned it and scarcely been checked in its movement through air and water.

Whistling Paddy was buried by the Vicar, himself an old naval chaplain, with traditional ritual and discipline. The net was re-covered, torn in the middle, and burned; so was the boat. Old Masts-and-Yards continued to live in Irsha Court. And the last time I saw him was as the first: he was standing in the sunshine by the War Memorial.

I knew then that he was there to be near his sons. In his thoughts he saw them, and talked to them; they were all ages to him, from small children to grown youths. He told their ghosts about the youngest, little Paddy; he saw their mother with them, too, she who had died when they were children, so that they were brought up, while he was away for months at a time, sailing the deep waters of the seven seas, by a sister of his, who now lay in the churchyard. One day they would all be together again; the good Book said so. He had always believed it to be true, although he had never wanted any man, certainly not one like Julius Caesar, to tell him so.

Until they should all meet again, there was work to be done.

"A man must splice a rope," he said, and now I understood the meaning, the experience, behind the simple phrase. This man had lived by courage all his life in the perils of the sea; and until his own final dissolution he would continue that way.

A Hero of the Sands

A dog fight is always stimulating, usually interesting, occasionally amusing, rarely dangerous. Once on the summer sands, in the glorious days of wearing a beard, no shirt, trousers tied up with string, and shoes without socks, I came upon a very funny scene. There before me was a Pekinese dog, hanging to the lower part of one section of a visitor's trousers! I was prepared to enjoy myself to the full for the sight the gods had provided, when my mood of detached amusement changed. The action looked to be complicated; for while the embarrassed fellow was trying to knock away the little beast with a newspaper, a big Alsatian wolfhound loped over to see what was doing and, picking up the Pekinese, proceeded to shake it.

The visitor, a mild-looking man, realized that, being British, he would have to be a hero, as only women and children were near—myself remaining conveniently aloof, as all objective artists should be. Accordingly he grabbed the hindlegs of the wolfhound, which, thus suspended, continued to shake the Pekinese until the little dog dropped off.

And then, suddenly, a situation of the gravest peril! There the fellow was, holding the great snarling brute by the hindlegs, fortunately with its back towards his front, while his arms sagged gradually and the jaws of the angry animal clashed nearer and nearer his knees. And while he was thus engaged, the Pekinese, fluff-snuffling up behind him, retook its hold on his trousers. What could the hero do?

What could *I*, no hero, do? I hitched up my trousers, and tying the string tighter round my middle, prepared for action. Swallowing the saliva in my mouth, I advanced upon the struggle. I felt courage coming into my stomach, empty but for a rind of stale cheese and an old piece of bread—food, in those days, was generally scorned as an unspiritual thing.

Meanwhile the real hero had walked into the sea. The Alsatian, no hydrophile, quit at the first breaker, but the Pekinese was nearly drowned before it let go. Bravo! I thought: he is another Solomon. I was wrong. Hardly had the hero waded on shore again, than he was attacked by an hysterical woman who was nursing the Pekinese in her arms. Solomon then proceeded to get it back from both plaintiffs at once; for while the Pekinese owner was describing him to himself in terms of herself, the owner of the wolfhound was shouting at him: (a) it was a valuable animal he had been injuring, (b) it was not British to be cruel to animals, and (c) he deserved flogging.

That night in the pub in the village up the valley, kept by Charley, himself a very tough customer on occasion, I heard the hero, over his fourth glass of whisky, explaining the ironies of his predicament that morning; for the Pekinese, apparently, belonged to his mother-in-law.

"Ah, there's all sorts about nowadays," remarked Charley noncommittally, as he leaned over the bar beside his pint of beer and rum, and spat past a customer's ear into a cuspidor placed on the lime-ash floor.

After a while the visitor asked about the heads of animals on the wall behind the bar. There were four of them, close together, greasy-looking objects stained by years of fug and tobacco smoke. Fixed to a piece of wood by the neck, the dead and stuffed existed among various knives. Two of the heads had once belonged to badgers. A year or two back Charley used to go badger-digging with his famous terrier, the Mad Mullah. The other two were un-British.

"That's him, that's the Mullah," remarked Charley, pointing at the dingy old dog sniffing at the visitor's trousers. "Get away, Mullah!"

The old dog took no notice, but continued to sniff without emotion and almost without movement.

"He's old now, the Mullah," went on Charley musingly. "He don't take the slightest notice of what I tells him. He's slow, and don't care no more, see? But when 'e 'ad 'is teeth, Mullah'd tackle the biggest boar badger, and when once he'd got a holt o' any brock Mullah'd hang on. Aye, he'd hang on for a pastime! Not like other terriers, all barking and fuss, but well away from a badger, noomye! Mullah'd be right up, facing the badger, yesmye!"

"Would he ever fight other dogs in the village?" enquired that morning's hero of the sands.

"Not unless another dog tackled'n first," replied Charley. "But no dog would interfere with the Mullah in they days, they knew'n too well, see."

As so often happens, dog and master seemed to share the same temperament. Both were undemonstrative, loyal, easy-going, but awkward customers if roused. And yet (such is the paradox of life on occasion) I was to observe, on the following morning, certain behaviour of Charley and his dog in the street outside my cottage which was contrary to what I had observed about him heretofore.

2

There was a gaunt, somewhat argumentative and awkward old farmer who lived opposite my cottage, nicknamed 'Stroyle' George. He was going downhill. He had only his grown-up daughter to help him; his rented arable fields were foul with weed, particularly of couch grass, locally called stroyle.

As Charley was walking down the street, with the old terrier Mad Mullah, 'Stroyle' George came out of his yard followed by Roy, his cattle-dog. Roy was a timid dog, afraid of lightning and thunder. I had observed this recently, during a sudden storm. "The rain come down like aught out of a sieve," 'Stroyle' George had said to me, "and the bliddy dog cleared at the first clap." 'Stroyle' George usually spoke as he ploughed; he drove the straightest of furrows, he was a master worker; but his argumentative tongue, working so hard against the irregularities of others, had been his ruin. He thought too much. His speech was simple, direct, and with the least use of words. Thus, cantankerous and poor, he spent most of his time arguing, protesting, declaiming against the obvious faults and deficiencies of others. And, since men impose on their dog or dogs, Roy was a bit of a nervous wreck.

When I saw the farmer and the publican approaching one another, and the farmer's dog dodging behind his master when it saw the Mad Mullah, I got up from my desk and watched from the window, for it looked to be interesting.

Roy, the timid but handsome cattle-dog, had been afraid of the Mullah for several years. Shouted at by his master since puppyhood, Roy was usually hysterically responsive to a friendly word. He was uncertain, afraid of his neighbours. Roy's mother had been the same; she was the successor to an old dog which 'Stroyle' George had shot, and the bitch had witnessed the shooting. She appeared to me to have a semi-human intelligence; she used to send waves of semi-human appeal to me with her eyes as she showed her teeth in nervous grins and wriggled her belly on the ground, often rolling over before me in subjection. Many of her puppies, of mixed breed, had been drowned. Eventually 'Stroyle' George gave her away, keeping one of her dog pups, who grew up to be the handsome Roy, afraid of lightning, thunder, the report of a gun, and many other things, including the Mad Mullah.

Nowadays, the Mullah, slow and aged, was as inoffensive as he was independent. He lay about in the road, scratching and biting his coat, sleeping on his side in the sun. Wheels of passing motorcars whizzed a few inches from his head; he did not trouble. Sometimes a car, hooting and with squealing brakes, stopped just short of him, when the Mullah would raise his grey scarred head, give a glance, sigh, and settle down to sleep again. "He'll be runned over one day," Charley used to explain. "I've told 'n again and again not to lie in the road, but he goes his own way. I can't help it. It makes no odds what I tells him, he don't trouble." Both man and terrier went their own ways, both were fearless and independent; they shared the same spirit, accepted the same world, the same kind of living. Charley may have thought that he took the Mullah for a walk on fine mornings; but it might have been that the Mullah was taking Charley for a walk, for the sake of old times. That is how it appeared to me, as the two shuffled down the street, looking slowly about them, each sufficient to himself. On this morning Charley carried his old muzzle-loader, for he was going to try for a rabbit on a little splat of land he had recently bought.

As they came down the street the yard-door of Hole Farm opened and 'Stroyle' George came out, Roy prancing around the near-ragged figure of his master. Then Roy, aware of the Mullah, slipped with wolf-like lope behind Charley and let out a sharp querulous bark.

The Mullah turned and looked at Roy over his shoulder. Roy, still loping, ran round again behind his master. The Mullah trotted after him slowly, but straight at him. Roy started to lope away, glancing back fearfully at the older dog following him slowly. Round and round the two men the almost leisurely procession went, until Roy, with another sudden sharp bark, turned and gripped the Mullah across the neck and shook him slightly.

"A-ah!" cried 'Stroyle' George. "Roy! A-ah you!"

With a nervous glance at his master, Roy began to lope around his wide orbit again. The Mullah followed, quietly, almost leisurely.

"He's got no teeth, you know," said Charley, surprisingly gentle, to the other man. "He can't do naught, but he's game—yesmye, he's game!"

"A-ah, you heller!" growled 'Stroyle' George, for Roy had turned and gripped the Mullah across the neck again, and worried him a moment before turning away.

As before, the Mullah followed the big cattle-dog.

"He won't leave him now," remarked Charley, in his reedy, conversational voice. "The Mullah fights for a pastime, you see. One day he'll be killed—he's got no teeth, you see. I tells him so often, but he don't trouble, noomye!" Charley spat, to disclaim further responsibility.

Round and round the two men went the slow lope-and-trot, Roy glancing first at his master then at the old terrier.

"Roy don't want to fight, you know," said 'Stroyle' George. "He could kill 'n sure enough, and knoweth it; but he's a-feared, all the same."

"Mullah bant afraid of nought," said Charley shortly. "Mullah! *Mullah!!* Come yurr, you bad old jack, you!" for the Mullah had rushed at Roy and nipped him in the loose skin below the eye. He lost his grip immediately, against toothless gums.

"Only brown stumps, you see," repeated Charley in his quiet little reedy voice. "No teeth, you know. One day he'll be killed. I knows it. I told'n, too. Mullah!"

The Mullah ignored his master. He was going to get Roy.

"Darn the dog!" shouted 'Stroyle' George. "ROY! A-ah, you boogerin' booger, you!"

There was Roy, after another light worry, followed by the Mullah, who, without expression on his grey scarred face, trotted after him as though he were going to look at an indifferent bone hidden some distance away.

Suddenly 'Stroyle' George roared out, "Git 'oom!"; and Roy, after a glance at the Mullah, got home—he slipped through the stream-hole in the wall above the culvert which took the stream beside Hole Farm.

"Mullah! MULLAH!!" yelled Charley, in his old Cardiff-docks

fishporter voice; but uselessly, for the terrier, heedless of his master, likewise vanished down the hole.

A minute later, having run on his long legs down the bed of the stream beside the farmhouse, through the orchard and so into the yard, Roy appeared on the stone wall higher up the lane, beside the dwarf furze bush which had been trying to grow there for a score of years. Easily he leapt down and trotted to stand by his master.

A minute or so later the door of Hole Farm opened and the voice of the farmer's daughter yelled, "Git 'oom! Out of it, you mangy old flea bag!" and a broom was used to impel the Mullah over the threshold.

"Gordarn the girl!" cried 'Stroyle' George. "You've set one on t'other again!"

"I didn't know!" protested the daughter. "Mullah came sniffin' about the place, cockin' his leg in my dairy, and I ban't standing for that!" The door slammed.

The dogs were revolving once more. Roy's tail was between his legs, and his backward glance more frequent. He showed his teeth. His was the weak spirit goaded: like the spirit of a former timid, peace-loving villager who once lived in the cottage I was occupying now. Goaded, they said in the village, bullied by the policeman for months, suddenly the cobbler seized a bill-hook and killed his tormentor—to die of grief the night before he was to have been hanged. But who, in the orbit of pads and tails and hanging tongues, was goading who this fine morning? The Mullah, that old toothless badger-dog, was enjoying himself, by the light in his eyes; until abruptly he found himself on his back while the powerful jaws of the hysterical Roy were mumbling about his throat.

Did the Mullah's owner, well known for his rages at times, raise his gun and shoot Roy? Did he curse Roy, and Roy's owner? Charley had been a bold fighter with fists in his day. In his bar, too, he could use a rough tongue at times; liable to order you outside if he didn't like your face or if you put your foot on one of the benches within the dark little room. How would Charley react to the murder of his old pet? I was amazed to see that he remained in his detached, almost nonchalant posture, deliberately giving every freedom of action to the farmer, all side-whiskers and gaunt peering nose. 'Stroyle' George raised his stick, shouting at his dog; and Roy sprang back, still yelping hysterically, and ran once again down the stream-hole. Mullah slowly picked himself up, shook himself, then followed leisurely after the cattle-dog.

"I said it," remarked Charley, in his twittering-finch voice, addressing the sky, as he leaned an elbow on the wall. "Mullah won't give in."

"My dog won't always be so nervous of him, you know!"

Charley spat. "Well, I told'n. I can't do no more."

I waited, watching the furze bush. No shaggy dog appeared on the skyline.

The farmhouse door opened, a voice cried out, "Roy and Mullah have gone down the stream to Cryde sands, I reckon," and the door was slammed again.

"Well," said Charley, "Mullah'll be back when he comes," and after a few more amiable words with the farmer, he slung his gun on his shoulder and went back up the road, his morning walk over.

3

About an hour later Roy was seen trotting through Cryde village, and, a long way after him, came the Mullah. It is possible that Roy had forgotten the Mullah, or rather that the Mullah's image was now obscured behind Roy's mental pictures of sea-weed pools and cake-owning summer visitors. The moon was almost at the full, and the spring-tides left the rocky pools of Down End exposed for a long way at midday.

Now Roy, who was usually so faithful and vigilant to attend the farmer and his daughter, who waited to be of use for cows in the street outside the farm every day, occasionally deserted his watch and went down to the bay when the moon was full in summer. It was his habit then to attach himself to any party with bare legs and prawning nets and sandwiches, to keep with them faithfully for a couple of days or so, then to return after his holiday to the village. During such excursions I had sometimes watched Roy standing on the rocks, looking down with great interest at one or another of his temporary friends prodding with gaffs into clefts and holes and pushing nets under the sea-weed fringe of pools.

This must have been in his mind that day, for Roy was observed trotting through the barley field and across the sandy burrows beside the stream which eventually cut through a gap in the sandhills and splayed out upon the shore. Arriving there, Roy sniffed at the strong and varied scents in the jetsam of the tide-line, before starting to cross the shore in the direction of the black ridges of rocks below Down End. On his way there he crossed an interesting scent. Following this up and down the sands, at length he came to a diminutive dog being led by a stout woman.

"Grr-r! Get away, you brute!" cried the woman, and picked up the Pekinese. "Don't be upset by the nasty dog, Consuelo darling; Mummie won't let it hurt you. Grr-r! Go away at once, you horrid brute! The impertinence!"

The brute, however, was obviously attractive to Consuelo; and panting with excitement, she managed to scramble out of her barreline owner's arms. Galloping away, Consuelo reached the handsome Roy and then, turning her back to him, she stared at the sea in a provoking attitude.

Roy, however, had seen some prawners on the rocks. As though ridding his pads of the scents of the old world, he kicked up a certain amount of sand with his hind feet, and then loped away, followed by the galloping Pekinese dragging her lead, heedless of her owner's entreaties, through the wet delta of the stream in the sands. Roy's mind was set on lobsters and crabs, which terrified and therefore absorbed him; he made straight for the rocks.

As he was nearing the first ridge, having outrun the unattractive little dog, he heard a familiar sound, and turning round he saw the Pekinese being attacked by a big dog. Naturally Roy had to return to see what was happening; but the grey apparition of the Alsatian made him afraid, so that he ran backwards and forwards, shifting always to be behind the big dog, while yelping and making other hysterical noises.

Then the Mad Mullah, who had been following Roy's scent, appeared on the sands. He trotted towards the grey-hackled Alsatian as casually as though he were going into the kitchen of the Lower House for his dinner. Trotting directly up to the Alsatian, the Mullah bit the wolfhound in the loose skin of the jaws. At once the Alsatian flung the Pekinese away and, springing upon the Mullah, bit him in the shoulder and began to shake him. Neither dog made any sound, either of growling or yelping; both dogs were killers. The Alsatian worried the smaller terrier in the furious silence of killing.

Roy had been throwing up his head and uttering shrill howls, but the silence of the deadly struggle seemed to change hysteria into strength. With hackles raised he ran at the Alsatian and bit him across the neck. Several visitors were warily approaching, including the son-in-law of the owner of the Pekinese, yesterday's hero of the sands, who was being urged by his wife to do something. Mothers were exhorting their children to keep back. Two men dared to approach and to thwack the Alsatian with their children's spades, while one boy had already thrown in vain his friend's model yacht, while the friend was scooping up pailfuls of sand to throw at the dogs from afar.

"Go on, *do* something!" cried the owner of the Pekinese.

Roy seemed to be fighting silently, locked to the wolfhound's jaw. A power seemed to be upon him, for he swung the grey dog about as though it were no heavier than the Mullah.

One of the men who had vainly tried to stop the fight with a child's spade was the owner of the Alsatian. The fellow now appeared with his wife's sunshade, open, which he prodded and spun in the faces of the writhing dogs. All that happened was the sunshade got slightly buckled; but bravely he persisted, possibly seeing himself in the role of bullfighter, in a position of great danger; but to the on-lookers he was merely funny, as he cavorted about, just this side of danger.

Like a wrestler Roy swung the wolfhound, trying to put his enemy on its back. The Mullah had no interest in the fight: he stood some distance away, with drooping head, shivering, as though dazed by the realization of what had happened to him. Grey and tired, he limped away homewards.

Meanwhile the hero who the day before had held up the Alsatian by its hindlegs now had got hold of those legs again, after shouting to the parasol-flutterer to get hold of the other dog by its hindlegs. The two dogs held grimly to their bites upon one another's neck-skin, as their legs were drawn out.

"Now," said the hero of the sands, "Will someone light a newspaper and just bring it near their noses, please."

This was done. Flames of *The Daily Wail* separated the heads; whereupon the Alsatian turned and ran away in great long determined strides towards the north side of the bay.

As for Roy, he was making friends with everyone, looking up into many human eyes and panting happily, a new four-legged hero of the sands.

4

"You wouldn't do what I told you, would you?" jeered Charley to his dog blinking on the mat by the kitchen fire that afternoon. "You thought you knew better, didn't you, eh? And let me tell you again, you obstinate old toad you, you'll get runned over if you continue to lie in the road. And you leave Roy alone in the future, see?"

The Mullah swelled; and slowly he sighed. His wounds were yellow with iodine.

The very next day he was lying in the road again, on his side, and Charley was lounging against his doorpost, when 'Stroyle' George came up with his cows, followed by Roy. Charley noticed that Roy was making as if to dodge behind the farmer when he saw the Mullah; he watched him hesitate; then swiftly and silently, as the old dog's head was raised, Roy bounded forward with feathery tail and lightly touched nose-to-nose with the Mullah.

The Mullah's head sank again; he swelled for a sigh of contentment: and with a joyous bark Roy leapt around his master. From first to last the behaviour of both men and dogs had seemed to me to be wonderful.

Incidents of an Afternoon's Walk

This author's aim in writing has always been to re-create, or bring to life again on paper with print, the life around him as he has seen and heard it. Never merely to write a beautiful style, or to make a perfect form for its own sake. Here is the world—always with awareness that it is but one man's limited world—and here is that which is to be seen, heard, and occasionally to be smelled and tasted. Take it or leave it, that is up to the reader; the writer cannot do better than try to bring some of the life he has known to paper. As for the dialogue, or the way people speak—well, he tries to reproduce the manner of speaking, and the words. Sometimes fortune smiles on him: thus the following dialogue occurred in a Devon court of Summary Jurisdiction, and was reported in a local paper. Someone had summoned a neighbour, suspected of getting rid of that someone's noisy dog.

Cross-examination of defendant by the plaintiff's solicitor:

"What did the dog die of?"

" 'A died of a Vriday, zur."

"Yes, but how did he die?"

"On 'a's back, zur."

"Yes, but what made him die?"

" 'A's heart gived out, zur." ·

"Yes, yes, but how did he come by his death?"

" 'A didden come to it, zur, it came to be."

"Yes, yes, yes, my good man, but what was the complaint?"

"There wadden nivver no complaint, zur; the neighbours was all satisfied."

That, of course, is a gift. But such repartee and wit is not rare, if one listens at the right places. Local speaking is usually good because it arises directly off work or action. I have only to listen to a neighbour of mine, on this hilltop, to hear graphic English which derives from the living scenery of that energetic smallholder's world.

One afternoon, upon setting out for a walk, I saw in the sunken lane outside my gate a bramble-torn cap, covering the shaggy hair of my neighbour. He was speaking to another farmer on the subject of what the Ministry of Agriculture, reverting to language of Latin rootage, was beginning to call *Rodent Control*.

"Aiy, there be a lot of bliddy rats about the viels now. In a month or two, the boogers will be down in the barns and stacks. Hundred and thousands o' the bliddy things; why, t'other night I stood by the gate upalong and if one bliddy rat rinned over me boots, why, I tell 'ee midear, there was bliddy thousands! I kep still; I had me gun, too; I could have shut a score with each barrel, but I knew if I so much as kecked one of the boogers with me boot, t'others would have mobilized me.

"I'll tell 'ee, the government should do zomething 'bout rats. They'm all for taking your money, but what about ridding us of rats? Last winter I took ninety-three of the boogers one morning out of my gins tilled in one viel. Ninety-three! Then there was thousands of the bliddy critturs left in the rabbuts' buries. Aiy, thousands and thousands! Booger, I caught one and tarred it, a bliddy girt stag-rat, and I let'n go agen, hoping he'd drave the others. But still I couldn't keep no eggs or chickens or chicken food, they ate the bliddy lot. Fast as I'd trap a couple of hundred, the'd spring up agen. One night, I'll tell 'ee, midear, listen to this, I hear'd a bliddy great galloping about on the ceiling over me aid (head) and my missus zaid to me, It be like a cart and hoss passing overaid, whatever can it be, Jack. I zaid, 'Tis they bliddy rats up auver. I coudden get a wink of slape all night, back and 'vore the boggers was proper bliddy galloping, like a bliddy aerial durby it was up there. Aiy. But I'll tell 'ee what I did! I tilled a gin for the boogers, but coudden catch nought. One day, tho', I cornered one behind the cupboard, and a bliddy girt stag-rat 'twas, jimmering and chammering at me, clinging to the bliddy wall, just out of reach of my bliddy stick it was, and wan bliddy cat on the top of the cupboard, anither on the shelf, and a couple of bliddy dogs waiting below! I kept the booger pressed there agen the bliddy wall with me stick, I warn't going vor leave'n now I'd got'n, not if I stayed there all bliddy night, and the cat and the bliddy dogs biding there too. Missus fetched a long stick but the bliddy thing was bent, and wouldn't titch the stag-rat, which opened its mouth and showed its bliddy teeth to me, and jimmering and chammering it was, with the bliddy cats howling up above and the dogs a-roaring and a-bawling down below and me yelling at the missus to yett (heat) the bliddy poker in the vire, I'd burn the booger out if it wouldn't come out, cruelty or no cruelty. Of course I knowed if one of they inspectors for the abolition of cruelty to hanimals was to have comed along, I should have been in Town, but what about cruelty of the bliddy rats to me, unable to get a wink of slape with them tritting 'bout overhead like a bliddy hossrace? So missus yett up th' poker, and I pressed 'n into the rat, saying burn you booger, burn, and gor'darn! the withering thing burst into vlames and rinned down the wall and not a bliddy dog would titch it. Lucky the door was shut, else 'twould have rinned out and maybe set vire to me neighbour's ricks, for 'twas the selfsame bliddy rat I had tarred. I 'spose the ither rats had drove'n, because of the smell, and the booger had comed into my place. I tell 'ee, there's hundreds and thousands of rats in the viels today."

The ragged cap was lifted, and the shaggy scalp scraped by broken nails. Then the conversation or monologue continued in the same language, the trapper telling the identical story again, word for word, laugh for laugh, in the traditional Devon manner.

2

Having taken this in, I set out on my walk. I crossed several fields, climbing over stone-and-earth banks, always on the look-out for a bull, for it was cattle country. I followed a small runner, grown with watercress and brook-lime, which led eventually to a pond. This little bit of water was a favourite place to visit, for I was always hoping to see a trout there. Not to kill; but to feel it being alive.

The stream which fed the pond was hardly more than a trickle, scarcely more than a yard in width and six or seven inches deep; but it was pure water, eventually joining the stream passing through Cryde village which was reputed to hold the biggest fish in Devon, owing to its teeming insect life. (I ought to say that this was before the motorcar generally "opened up the place", with consequent increase of summer visitors and the stream's inevitable pollution.)

The little pond was triangular and silted. It lay in the corner of the field, holding a few thousand gallons dammed by the stone wall. The water worked a grist-mill in the farm behind the manor house three hundred paces below. It was a haunt of moorfowl and other water-birds.

As I came down the slope of the field I saw a heron standing at its muddy edge. The tall grey bird flapped away when I was four or five gunshots distant.

Not that I carried a gun; but herons know the habits of men, and, taking no chances, are up and away, usually, when well out of range.

Seeing me, the heron jumped, its broad grey wings scooping the air; but it was caught by the wind as it tried to rise, and could make no headway; so it turned down the wind and was carried in a long glide over the next field, where it swung round again, and alighted among the rough grass clumps and thistles. I could see the head on the long neck held up anxiously to watch me away, when it would return to its feeding.

I jumped over the earth-and-stone hedge, to find out what it had been eating. The mud under the broken turf had been made arrowy by its feet, as the bird had stalked from the pond's apex to the deeper water by the stone dam. After every dozen steps it had turned to peer into the pond, and at these stances the mud was much trodden; the heron had taken many steps forward to snick its prey out of the water. What had attracted it? I could see nothing.

I sat down and waited. Wind ruffled the pond's surface; wavelets lapped the margin, erasing and silting the arrowy footmarks. Very soon from the direction of the wooden fender came a noise like a duck quietly calling her ducklings; but it was a dryer, more brittle noise. A similar cry came from the bank, and then another: a chorus broke out over the pond.

I saw a rat running along with a frog in its mouth. It went into a hole in the bank continuing the stone dam. There was a well-trodden track leading into this hole, two inches wide—the path of the rats. One of the colony must have come out as the heron flew up, and seeing a frog on the bank, picked it up.

Many frogs were now apparent in the pond. Most of them were bull-frogs, smaller than the females. The glitter of the sun and the lessening cold had excited them to begin the search and struggle for mates. All things in nature have their seasons, and the males usually await the females; it is so with the bull-frog, which finding a female, makes sure of her by climbing upon her broad back, and clinging there in the attitude of a jockey at the gallop. I was, all unsuspecting, to be on this afternoon a spectator of a mad, whirling, ranine romance and tragedy.

A female walked out of the water as I watched, and the movement drew four unattached bull-frogs. She was mounted by the quickest, but carried him six inches only before the other frogs began to muscle in on his racket. I am sorry if this American slang phrase hurts the reader's susceptibilities, but I am no stylistic writer: I repeat, my aim is always to convey to the reader what my eyesight puts into my brain. The frogs were muscular creatures; they made a racket, or noise; they were competitive, pitiless, entirely selfish. The phrase therefore is used, although it belongs to the gangsters of the U.S.A. who have probably never heard of the little pond behind the hamlet of Putsborough in North Devon.

The jockey was prepared for musclers-in. With a slow but well-judged shove with his off-hind foot he laid one on its back. Then he croaked, as though trying to get his mount to start again. She carried him forward another three inches and stopped. He dug his hands deeper under her armpits, urging her on with calf and spur. She remained motionless. A rival greener than the jockey climbed leisurely up, avoiding the thrust of elastic hind-legs; and digging his arms in, the green rival bent his head forward and slowly arched his back, in an attempt to unseat the jockey. Their stifled croaking stirred to movement the three other frogs who had been squatting behind them. These would-be jockeys hopped forward, to receive immediate thrusts of feet in their faces. Two of them overturned. They got upright again, and squatted still, as though in oblivion.

The greener frog who had scrambled up was now trying to throttle the jockey. The three fingers and thumb of each hand were clenched with his striving. In other words, *he was muscling-in.*

For nearly a minute the muscling-in continued. Then the female decided to move; she took two heavy hops forward. The squeaky cries of the jockeys began again. The three also-rans moved after them. Two of them collided, and as though in despair one hopped astride the other. He was carried forward a few inches, but dismounted, and turned back. The movement of my foot had drawn him; he leapt at the toe of my shoe, fell off, and went back disconsolately towards the water, passing another aspirant who was hurrying forward, gay with a bit of weed round his neck.

Meanwhile the race was continuing. The steed was walking and hopping forward with her double load. During one of her pauses the fourth frog sprang, receiving from the green rival a quiet, sure kick in the throat which laid him out; but picking himself up, he tried again. The original jockey sat still, croaking weakly, vainly, for motion; but the green super-jockey, the line of whose back was now almost oval with the strain of throttling, kicked out again at a fresh aspirant, and missed. Immediately the aspirant gripped his leg and hung on, while the steed moved forward a few more paces. During the next interval the aspirant managed to grip the other leg of the green super-jockey, and stepping up on the wide haunches of the female, secured what may have given a satisfying illusion of superiority.

It was no longer a race; it was an omnibus. The omnibus progressed unevenly, with noises like the tooting of horns blown asthmatically. It had four pairs of protuberant headlights, the reflection of which glinted in the sun. It appeared to have been broken down completely, so I left it, having other business with a raven's nest on the headland. I climbed over the stone dam, jumping down to a place out of the wind, pleasantly warmed by the sun.

I was now hidden from the waiting heron by a screen of ash boughs cut and laid along the top of the bank. Shoots and twigs growing upright gave cover for my head as I peered under a horizontal grey bough. The heron was still standing in the farther field, among last year's thistle stalks and grass-clumps, its head held high and anxious. It was doubtful if it had the sense of continuity: that it would remember I had not reappeared.

I had been standing there for about a minute when rustlings and small thumpings became audible on the bank, with the squeaks of rats. I had forgotten the rats. Were they fighting over the frog brought into the tunnels when first I had sat by the pond?

I listened, keeping still; and peering over the dam, I saw a rat running along the side of the pond, followed by two other rats. They made straight for the omnibus—still in the attitude of breakdown—and through my glass I watched two rats pulling the frogs apart. The jockey, the green super-jockey, and the aspirant hung on to each other, kicking and croaking; but the rats, the zestful and murderous rats, braced their hind legs and bit and tugged. The aspirant was the first to go; he was dragged immediately along the path to the hole. Vainly the green super-jockey croaked for speed; he was nipped by a leg, but the strength of two tugging rats could not shift him. After a while, for a minute I should think, the rats ceased to pull each for himself; they appeared to organize themselves, and set about removing the omnibus as it stood. Each with a leg in its mouth, and with heads held high, they trotted along the bank, sharing the weight of muscled frogflesh.

Another rat ran to meet them, and yet another. There was a squeak and scuffle, and the newcomers ran on, plainly told to mind their own affairs. They ran to the water, where, putting their heads down, they swam under like small unskilful otters.

Squeaks inside the bank told me that the rats had entered with their booty, and I remained there, hoping to get a glimpse of them, for there were many rabbit holes in the bank. Noises of tugging and thumping came with more squeaks out of a low tunnel, and tiring of my position, I stood upright again to watch the swimming rats. Long thin legs and wide grey wings upheld and dropping blurred in the retina of my eye: the heron had flown back to the pond.

It folded its wings, while raising its head and looking round for movement that might mean danger. Knowing how keen was the sight of this shy bird, I tried not to blink an eyelid, for the section of my face under the laid ash-bough was silhouetted (from the heron's point of view) against the sky.

Suddenly the heron lowered its beak. I saw a rat swimming across the pond, its whiskered head exposed with something unwieldy before it. It was carrying a frog. The heron's body, seeming so loose and thin within the shell of soft grey wings, their big flight quills tipped with black, seemed to stiffen and sharpen. It moved head and neck low and forward, an unobtrusive action against the background of its body. The rat could not have seen it, for it swam on steadily until it was within twenty inches of the heron's sharp beak, when the beak struck and the rat was lifted out of the water. It squealed and twisted; its feet ran on air; its tail whipped its body. The heron turned round to strike it on the bank, but its beak was wedged in the rat's skull. It lifted a long leg and tried to claw it with its toes, and the weight of the rat and the wind caused it to stagger.

Then the heron saw my eyes under the bough of the ash tree, and jumped into the air with fright. It flapped and tumbled; but before I had time to clamber over the bank, it had recovered, and was steady on the wing. In the air it clawed its beak again, and the rat fell with a splash into the water. When I reached the bank opposite the splash I saw a dead rat floating in the wavelets, with a jockey already riding on its shoulders, croaking defiance to another whose head, set with glazed and bulging eyes, was poked up alongside.

Swagdagger Crosses a Field

There is something in the nature of most men, arising on certain uneasy occasions, which has a basis so universal that everywhere it commands the sympathetic understanding of reasonable folk—an attitude of which the commonest vocal expression is 'Why do you want to interfere with me? I don't want to interfere with you! But if you're looking for trouble you'll damn'd well find it!' And as with men, so with animals who live the life, wild and free and pitiless, that men, more or less—chiefly less—have quit.

This attitude in the wild is liable to instant reverse; the trouble seeker of one moment may be the troubled of the next. The rights and wrongs—many of them as old as life itself—of Swagdagger happily crossing a field on a certain morning in early June cannot be discussed in this story, which is able only to hold an account of all the trouble which began when I looked over the western bank of my hilltop property in North Devon—a field I had recently bought.

Who had been leaving litter in my field? There the evidence was —a long strip of paper, blowing across the grass! I had seen no-one there a moment before, when I had been in the field.

The sooner a proper palisade gate replaced the ramshackle tangle of rotten bars and posts, the better! Also, I must see that the gap in the bank—made by bullocks, so the farmer had said—was filled with level thorn branches pegged down.

I vaulted over this formless ruin, meaning to pick up the paper; but when I got to where it had lain, it was gone. Had a magpie picked it up for a nest lining? But magpies always built with dark twigs, and put a top of thorns to cover the nest.

Three red lanes, metal'd with ironstone—one of them already bearing much motor traffic in summer—met at the south-western corner of the field, near the deciduous gate. Just above this gate was a small spinney of beech trees which I call Windwhistle

Cross. The road divides the spinney, and leads on over the down to Ilfracombe. It was toward these trees that I had looked when I passed the gap in the bank. Now, I considered myself to be both shrewd and observant; yet it only occurred to me a few moments later that the long white strip, rippling as paper in wind, had been moving in a direction *contrary* to that in which the wind was blowing.

As I was soon to learn, the white object in the middle of the field was moving on a track it had run along many times before, a track belonging to itself. Indeed, it owned the entire field, with every other field it ran in. Its sense of ownership was similar to that of my own, but more elemental; its angry defiance of any intrusion was coupled with a raging desire to break with teeth the jugular vein of its enemy. Nearly everything was its enemy, and nearly everything ran from it; for it was Swagdagger the stoat. Swagdagger lived a life harder and more eventful than any other stoat in the West Country, for he had been born without colour, except for his eyes, which were pink, and the tip of his tail, which was black. Swagdagger's hairy coat, covering a long and sinuous body, was white as the snow which so seldom fell in the fields. Nearly everything saw Swagdagger as he ran prowling, low and swift and sniffing the air, over green pasture and brown ploughland, and through the thorns and brambles growing on the banks dividing the fields.

During the days that followed, I, keeping up wind, and focusing my Zeiss monocular, saw much of Swagdagger, as I called him. He was usually hurrying, but not always hunting. Many times a day he ran with eagerness across his fields into Windwhistle Cross, to play with the five stoats who lived under a wood stack at the foot of a beech tree. Such rough-and-tumble games they played together— Swagdagger, his mate, and their cubs.

One morning as he moved in the field a dark brown bird, with a wing span of more than four feet, wheeled in the sky a quarter of a mile away, and slanted down over the wind-sheared tree tops of the spinney. Swagdagger saw it coming, and ran faster. It was a buzzard hawk, whose wailing cry often came down from the sky. It fed on rabbits, moles, and snakes, which it dropped on from above and clutched in its yellow feet, piercing with black talons, and tearing with its hooked beak. The hawk was stronger and much heavier than the stoat, who saw its eyes and beak and hanging legs, under the line of outspread wings, grow larger and larger as it glided upon him. Swagdagger stopped, forepaws on ground, head and neck raised and pointing at the buzzard. He crouched until it lifted great wings to drop on him, and then he stood on his hind legs. The buzzard, who had meant to grip him across the back, saw a small white flattened circle, set with whiskers, that broke across with sharp clicking teeth.

The stoat stood like a lean mushroom stalk; the hawk seemed to bounce off its angry pointed nose. It flapped broad wings, to keep safely above the furious pale eyes. It flapped heavily over the stoat toward the spinney, but rippling white movement lured it back again. It turned and swept down on the stoat, spreading yellow toes for the attack. The white ripple stopped, becoming fixed and upright under the snatch of talons. Again the buzzard quailed before the snapping teeth, and, beating into the air, sent a wailing cry down the wind. *Whee-ee-i-oo!*

Another bird, black from bristled beak to toe, that was perching on the highest bough of an elderberry tree, stunted and lichen-crusted at the south-western point of the spinney, heard the cry, and started out of its reverie—for it was contemplating the old nest from which it had driven the last of its grown winglings that morning. Immediately it stretched its head higher. Every black feather tightened when it saw the buzzard. Its craw swelled, its tail dipped, its beak opened, and *Scarl! Scarl!* it called, harshly and rapidly.

Another carrion crow heard the call, and left the broken carcass it had been eating—rabbit in snare set by labourer—and flew toward the elderberry. The crows built their nest in one or other of the trees of Windwhistle Cross every year; they owned the spinney and the fields around it, and whenever they saw a winged or a four-legged intruder they drove it away from their property.

Krok! Krok!—Hawk! Hawk! said the first crow, flying up to meet her mate. Together they flew, silently, just above the green slope of the wind-sheared tree tops. They appeared suddenly over the spinney, seeing the field below. *Krok! Krok! Krok!* said the crow again, and flew faster toward the buzzard, meaning to peck out its feathers—a thing which the crows tried to do whenever they flew near a buzzard, not liking its face.

Before its beak had closed again, the male crow saw the stoat. Scarl had seen Swagdagger many times before. *Krarr! Krarr! Krarr!* cried Scarl and his mate together, turning across the wind, and slanting over the red lane and the bramble-grown bank.

Every day, antagonism increased between stoat and crow. Usually, Swagdagger was not far from Windwhistle Cross when the crows dived at him. He recognized the voice of Scarl, and ground his teeth. With open beak Scarl dived, but a yard from the ground the crow flattened his wings and with a jeering *Krarr!* passed over him. Scarl alighted two yards behind Swagdagger, while his mate flapped above and in front of him. The stoat stood up to meet the peck of the crow, and Scarl, hopping quickly over the grass from behind, nipped the black tip of his tail.

In this way they teased Swagdagger, while he grew more and more angry. Every time he attempted to run forward he was poked and jabbed from behind by one or another of the crows, and still he was not far from the bank whence he had started.

Meanwhile the buzzard was soaring higher, watching the shifting white streak. It was being stared at by a bird perched on a thorn growing out of the eastern bank of the field. This bird was the size of a crow, but more huddled-looking; and it had a whitey-grey face of bare skin. The buzzard saw it looking up, and wailed for its mate again. The grey-faced bird launched itself off the thorn, and with leisured beat of wings climbed into the air to look around. It was a sentinel rook, and the buzzard was wary of rooks, for often they mobbed him.

It flew under the hawk, and cried *Caa! Caa-r!* Hearing the summons, several rooks looked up from the earth where they were digging new potatoes. Buzzard never harmed, and potatoes were good. They went on digging again, knowing the old self-appointed sentinel rook to be at times over-officious.

Now Scarl the carrion crow saw the rook flying under the buzzard, and, I feel sure, began to *think*. First one eye was cocked at them, then the other—for a crow does not reason until he has taken a double squint. His beak lifted higher, his craw swelled, he dipped, and *Krok-krok-krok-krok!* he cried. The stoat bounded upon him, but the crow, still looking at the sky, hopped over his head, alighted behind him, and gave four more croaks. *Ca-ar!* answered the sentinel rook, leaving the buzzard, and flying over the field to find out why crow had called him. He saw, turned, and flew back quickly, in silence.

Usually rooks flew wide of crows, whom they distrusted, for crows had been known to chase the little red mousehawks, or kestrels, over their rookery in spring, and, in the general uproar that greeted the hawk, to sneak into the trees and suck rooks' eggs. But against Swagdagger every bird's beak and wing was raised. *Krok-krok-krok-krok!* cried the rook, wheeling over the edge of the potato patch, and calling them in a voice like a crow's. This time every rook flew up. The potato diggers (my potatoes) glided and swooped down to the grass as soon as they saw the white ripple. They filled the air with cawing and the sound of wings. They alighted to make around the stoat a rough excited circle, which broke wherever Swagdagger ran in his grinding rage.

Each rook appeared to be urging its neighbour to hop forward and dab him one on the head. Each rook was determined not to be the one to dab first. Their wide and simple eyes, filled with scared thoughts, looked from stoat to crow, from crow to one another. Scarl and his mate hopped about in the ring, feeling safe with so many beaks near them, and enjoying the game of peck and jump. And all the while they were playing the crows were watching their chance to peck out Swagdagger's eyes.

Sometimes nervous rooks would fly up with squawks of alarm, but the croaks of the bolder crows were reassuring, and they alighted in the circle again. Jackdaws passing over the spinney dropped among them, like flakes of burnt paper out of the blue sky, and croaked with deep voices, for they too belonged to the powerful family of *Corvidae*, sharing ownership of all the fields and woods. They poked their grey polls and hard azure eyes between the dishevelled shoulders of the rooks, and cursed Swagdagger, who in hot rage was giving off a most penetrating stench, which in itself was almost enough to keep them at a distance. Then came four magpies, sloping over the field, their wings flickering black and white as they made slow way against the wind. They scolded loudly when they saw Swagdagger. After them came a pair of missel thrushes, who flew down boldly, the smallest birds present, and screamed in the face of Swagdagger as he stood, with swishing tail, with bared teeth, with blazing eyes, in a green space enclosed by the black and shifting mass. Suddenly every bird looked up into the air, and remained motionless, as though frozen.

Three miles westward, on his pitch two thousand feet above the sea, Chakchek the Backbreaker, the peregrine falcon, had seen the commotion of wings in the field, and a white speck in the centre.

His family owned the air of the world; even the eagle shifted under his stoop. Across the sky on level pinions he had glided, cutting round into the wind above Windwhistle Cross. He saw upheld beaks and eyes watching him anxiously. Crows and a stoat! He turned, and swept away.

2

The sentinel rook, sire of many birds of the rookery in the village below, an old bird whose life was set in duty to others, watched the Backbreaker an eye-blink longer than the other rooks watched. He forgot Swagdagger as he stared at the pointed wings, which often he had heard hissing in the dreaded stoop. Then a whiteness flashed, and the old rook was on his back, his feathers were flying, his legs were kicking. He tried to screech a warning, but as his beak opened he shuddered; and Swagdagger, red on teeth and whiskers, ran at the next rook. The grass was flattened by the draught of beating wings.

Cra! cried Scarl, who had jumped a yard, but alighted again. *Cra!* as he hopped to the stricken rook, and pecked out his eyes.

As soon as the rooks and daws had flown up, Swagdagger started to run towards the spinney, carrying his head high. He had gone one third of the way along his track when the rooks, flying at him with open beaks, but swerving a safe distance off, checked him again. Other birds came to the field—tomtits and wagtails, sparrows, finches, and stonechats. They perched on the brambles of the banks, each one adding his tick or squall or stitter to the general outcry. Some of them had lost mates or fledglings when last they had seen the white horror.

Kron-n-n-n-n-n-k!

The sound, prolonged and deep, was audible through the screeching and cawing. It came from above the spinney. Swagdagger stopped, sniffing the air. Only one thing had such an acrid smell, and whenever he encountered it Swagdagger got out of daylight into the nearest rabbit hole.

The owner of the deep and penetrating voice had flown inland when he had seen Chakchek the Backbreaker slip off his pitch; for sometimes he robbed the falcon of what he had struck down. The raven alighted on a branch at the top of a tree, which bowed to his weight. Scarl the crow saw him—he was perching on Scarl's own lookout branch, which commanded nearly all the ground around the spinney—but Scarl said nothing. For the newcomer was Kronk, King of the Crows, the powerful and aged owner of seven miles of coast—from Pencil Rock to the Morte Stone, where the realm of his great-grandson, the Gaping Raven, began—and of thousands of acres of forest, heath, field, spinney, and down.

Kron-n-n-k!

The raven, looking blacker than any crow, he was so big, jumped off the lookout branch, and climbed almost vertically into the air. When about twenty feet above the tree tops he rolled on one wing, dropped a yard, and rolled level again. Then, his playful movement over, he pointed his great black beak at the stoat, and glided down to kill him.

But Swagdagger did not wait while Kronk was growing bigger in his downward glide. He turned, and galloped back along the track he had started to follow more than ten minutes before. *Whee-oo!* cried the buzzard from the sky, soaring on still, cleaver-shaped wings, as he watched Swagdagger fleeing before more than fifty clamorous birds, almost to be overtaken by the fast raven.

Swagdagger rippled up the bank, and got among the top cover. The withered sword grasses, and tough strings of bindweed tying brambles and briars, and dry thorn branches laid lengthways across old bullock-broken gaps, moved and rustled as he drew his lean body under them. Crows and rooks followed him, flapping to where patches of white showed in the long net of grasses, below stalks of tansy, dock, and hogweed. Three times he was pecked as he travelled along the southern bank, but he reached the corner safely, and turned up the western bank towards Windwhistle Spinney.

He pushed his sharp way among the brambles and grasses to the break made by the feet of bullocks scrambling over into the sunken lane below—where first I had seen the white paper, as I had thought of it. The gap of earth and stone was bare for two yards. On a stone bedded in the dry earth stood the great raven.

Now stoats—and their smaller relations, the weasels—possess strength and determination which last in fullness unto the moment of death; and the mind of Swagdagger was set upon getting to Windwhistle Cross. His small flat head pushed out of the grasses, moved up and down, swung sideways, while the nostrils worked nervously at all the hostile scents. The quick movements wove a hole in the grasses, which set around the thin neck like a collar. The gaze of the eyes wandered, then it rested on Kronk, standing a yard away.

Raven and stoat remained still, brown and pink eyes fixed in the same stare. All the lithe furious power of Swagdagger blazed in his eyes, for he dared not run forward. His tail swished the grasses behind him; fumes of anger drove the rooks into the upper air. And then, suddenly, at a new short *Kra!* from Scarl the crow, the clamour ceased, and the air above Swagdagger's head emptied of wings.

Raven, crows, rooks, daws, pies, thrushes, finches, tits, all flew away silently, big birds over the field, little birds along the hedge, leaving Swagdagger alone.

The stoat stepped through his grassy collar, smelled only furze bloom and foxglove in the air, saw the birds flying away, and forgot them. Without hesitation he ran down the bank and across the grass to his track; for he had never entered Windwhistle Spinney any other way.

He was near the northern bank when the noise of wings made him stop and throw up his head. The buzzard which had been sitting on the bank by the far corner, watching in curiosity the behaviour of the birds, had been alarmed when they had suddenly flown away; but not having heard what they had seen in the sunken lane beyond, and being fearful of taking the air when raven and crow were about, it had continued to sit there. The white moving lure of Swagdagger was too strong for its caution; it forgot the general alarm, and flew over to the stoat.

On broad brown wings it sank upon Swagdagger, flapping to check its glide and stiffening its legs for the clutch. Swagdagger stood up to meet it with his teeth, but, as the buzzard was about to strike, it looked away, apparently startled by my face, set with the grey Zeiss glass.

The buzzard's wings beat violently in alarm; and instantly they beat wildly, for Swagdagger's teeth had pierced one of its legs above the knee. It rose up above the level of the bank, and tumbled sideways, the weight of the stoat struggling and twisting under it.

The buzzard unclenched its feet to be free, but they were clutched on nothing. It dived and tumbled, but could not shake off the jerking weight on its leg. It dropped towards the field again, meaning to stand on the stoat and rip it up with its hooked beak, as it had ripped up many rats and rabbits, but the shout of a man made it fly up into the air.

Many feathers floated away in the wind over the spinney, as the hawk swooped and tumbled and recovered. The rooks, back at their potato digging (my potatoes), looked up at the struggle. Some flew around the buzzard as it zigzagged overhead, and added their cawing to the wailing whistle of the hawk. Swagdagger held to the leg with his teeth and the long claws of his forepaws, and whenever the buzzard's beak came forward to cut open his head he loosened his bite and snapped at the throat. Sometimes his tail was over his head, as he swung to the turns and somersaults of his enemy.

The flight took them away over the adjacent grazing field. I hastened to the gate, and saw that the wings of the buzzard appeared to be flapping more heavily, and its tumblings were slower. Two claws of its right uninjured foot had pierced the loose skin of Swagdagger's neck, and were clenched tightly. It flew as before, in and out of the cawing rooks, until its bitten leg began to give it pain, it twirled and wailed towards the ground.

A final frenzied tumble in the air flung Swagdagger's head near its own, and the buzzard's beak opened to break his skull; but Swagdagger was quicker, and his teeth, like two rows of bone thorns, sank into the feathers of the buzzard's throat. The feathers sailed away, and he snapped again, but his teeth did not click. Hanging there, he steadily changed colour, his head and back and dripping tail, from white to dark red, while both predators sank down to the earth. There the hawk began to strike with its feet and buffet with its wings while snapping its beak; but Swagdagger held on, his eyes closed as he drew warm strength from his enemy.

The dying hawk flapped upon the ground, Swagdagger rippled away, leaving a trail of small feathers sticking to the grasses. The idea of getting to his mate was still, apparently, firmly fixed in his mind. He galloped gleefully, licking his jaws as he thought of the game he would play with his cubs.

He reached my field, and ran along his track. Halfway across he stopped, his nose working at the air that came in swirls from the bank. There was the smell of fresh-turned earth, blown with a strange and puzzling taint. He left his track, making a loop to avoid the unseen danger; for everything strange was dangerous to Swagdagger. Ten yards off the north bank he seemed to freeze, for his nostrils had dipped into a stream of strong, familiar scent—my own.

I had heard of stoats having a strange power to scare men, and decided to find out what this one would do, after his recent exertions. So I started after him, shouting "Hi!" when Swagdagger ran up the bank. When I got to the place where Swagdagger had climbed, I saw nothing there.

Picking up a stick (just in case) I hurried round the outside corner of the lane. I was in time to see a tail, tipped with black, disappear over the low bank at the edge of the spinney. I scrambled through the brambles, holding out an arm to ward off low branches from knocking my face. Grasping the stick firmly, and with head held tense, I walked warily through the beech trees, peering left and right.

I came to a woodpile, and had a glimpse of a smaller animal, with white patches on its light brown body, before it disappeared. Exhilarated by excitement, I crept forward, and waited for it to run out again. I could almost touch it with my stick. Of course I didn't want to kill it, merely to see what it would do. I saw another peep out, and then another.

I began to pull at a branch on the top of the pile. I felt strong as I levered it up, and with a vigorous turning movement threw it down. Lovely white skins: they must be ermines! I saw myself in the midst of wondering villagers, but swiftly thought, *No, keep it quiet!* as I levered another heavy bough off the top of the pile. I was enjoying myself immensely.

I had thrown down four boughs when Swagdagger ran out of the pile. Swagdagger was in a rage. He had been pestered and thwarted nearly all the morning, his play was interrupted (four cubs rolling him over and biting him with their milk teeth) and now his mate and cubs were threatened. He stood still, uttering whiny, champing noises—for a translation of which into colloquial English see the first paragraph of this story. When I moved forward with uplifted stick, Swagdagger also moved forward. His harsh chakkering cry rattled in the spinney. He continued to approach me—fourteen inches of warning and aggression—and I heard myself saying, "*Grrr!* Get out of it, you beast!" as I held up the stick.

Hak! Hak! Hak! Hak! Hak! Hak!

I have been accused by 'scientific' chaps of anthropomorphism in my writing about animals; but I have always believed that birds and animals are near in instincts and feelings to men and women, being of the original flesh and spirit; what I hadn't realized was that Swagdagger's forefathers had run in Windwhistle Cross since the beech spinney had been planted nearly a century ago by a Devon landowner with an eye to adding beauty to the skyline. I was a little surprised, therefore, when Swagdagger ran forward and started to climb up my trousers. I yelled when the sharp claws pricked my knee, and struck at the animal with my hand; but so quick was Swagdagger, and so sure his eye, that he bit through the tip of a finger before a blow knocked him off.

I turned to leave the spinney. I heard myself shouting for help when I saw other little animals running out of the woodpile. I blundered through the low branches to the bank, brambles clawing my clothes, and filling me with fear. I stopped in the lane, and to my horror saw that I was being followed. *Hak! Hak! Hak! Hak! Hak! Hak!*

Wheeling high over Windwhistle Cross, above the rooks and crows, Kronk the raven must have seen me legging it down the lane, now oddly stimulated by *fear*.

I was pulling my Zeiss glass out of its case when the skewbald pack of Swagdagger ran round the corner.

Hak! Chakker! Hak!

I ran to the middle of my field, then turned, and stared at the pack. I felt a dreadful desire to remain standing still.

High in the air the raven, who also must have felt the fascination of being approached by a pack of hunting stoats, watched me standing still until the white threads were almost to me. Only then did I make for the lower bank. I scrambled up, and stood among the brambles, until the damned white threads reached the bank. I jumped down, with head turned to see if they were following.

Hak! Hak! Chakker-hak!

Wheeling on firm wings, the raven watched me haring across the next field, and the plunging canter of bullocks down wind when they got the musky scent of stoat. He watched me across another field, and so to the road.

I ran on, slower and slower, groaning that if I only got out of this, I would give up smoking. I was chased almost to the cottage at the bottom of the hill, where a cattle dog, which had been lying in the roadway, got up and loped forward to see what the trouble was; and made off at full speed when it smelled and saw.

Swagdagger appeared to forget all about me; he went under a gate into another field, where was one of his playgrounds, a quarry, from which ironstone had been blasted for the widening of the motor road, and which the brambles were always trying to reclaim. Here I fancy they played awhile, and hunted rabbits, and washed themselves after their meal, imitating Swagdagger, who was busy with his tongue on ribs and back and tail. When they had played again, the white leader led the way back to Windwhistle and crossed my field for what was probably the first time with that season's jolly cubs.

We grew to respect each other; to live and let live. I saw the old predator sometimes; but kept my distance!

The Yellow Boots

Unlike many Hunts, the Inclefell Harriers—who also hunted fox—held a meet on the day before their annual Hunt Ball, and not the day after. The meet on the morning of the last Hunt Ball will be remembered long. The mounted followers and those on foot waited till midday, but no pack was led to the crossroads. The meet had been advertised in the local papers to be held at eleven o'clock. At a quarter to twelve about one-third of the field, including every farmer, had gone homewards. A few minutes after noon Jim Huggins rode up. He was the huntsman, an old and fog-seasoned man. In his high voice he said that he had been sent to say, with the Master's compliments, that the meet was cancelled. That was all. In answer to questions, he made but one reply—"I don't know, s'm". It was his habit to address both ladies and gentlemen as "s'm". He never said "sir" or "ma'am".

"But what's happened, Jim? Anything the matter with hounds?"

He sat upright and still on his stocky bay cob.

"I don't know, s'm."

"But how extraordinary! Are they sick?"

A week ago they had been fed on donkey flesh, and had fought in the kennels, all the way to the meet, and even when drawing covert. The unusual diet had been the cause of many jokes.

"I don't know, s'm."

"Is General Inclefell all right?"

They walked their hunters nearer to him. They were made curious by his rigid reticence.

"I don't know, s'm."

He shifted slightly on his right thigh the angle of his whip.

"You don't know! Haven't you seen the Master this morning, Jim?"

The kennels, and the huntsman's cottage, were in a wood two hundred yards behind the Manor.

"Not this morning, s'm. Second footman came with the General's message, s'm."

"Have you seen Miss Mollie?"

She was the honorary whipper-in to her father's hounds.

"Not this morning, s'm."

Jim in his green cap and green coat sat on his bay cob, looking straight ahead, avoiding every eye. He was like a gnarled and mossy limb of one of the dwarf oaks of Wistman's Wood—trees rooted on Dartmoor, thick as they are tall, and said to be ancient before Domesday.

The voice of a boy said timidly:

"Plaize, zur, us didden hear no dogs zinging this morning."

"Hold your rattle, young tacker!" commanded Jim Huggins in the sharp, hound-rating voice he had not used since whiphood days. Only his jaw moved; the mist of breath vanished in the cold air. He looked at his horse's ears. People exchanged glances. The tacker was abashed.

He lived near the kennels, whence had come no singing of hounds that morning.

"Good day, s'm," said Jim, raising his cap, laying the near rein on the horse's neck and pressing its off flank with his boot. The cob turned with smart obedience and trotted home. The word "extraordinary" was ejaculated by nearly everyone present in the saddle.

That night, while people were arriving at the Bedford Hotel in Tavistock for the Hunt Ball, the secretary—'Pops' Russell, who often said that life would be a bore without hunting, billiards, and Bass's beer—was surrounded by many black- and pink- and green-coated friends, to whom he told the astounding news that neither Bimbo nor Moll was coming that evening.

"But, Pops, old man, what's up with Bimbo? What's all this mystery about?"

Bimbo was the name by which the Master was known to his friends.

"Asked me to tell you he was awfully sorry, but he isn't feeling very fit."

"And Moll?"

"Same, 'parently."

Everyone was discussing the peculiar happening. Somehow by supper-time it was known that the entire pack had been destroyed. It was incomprehensible, for the Master was known everywhere for his fatherly tenderness to the hounds. However, the dance went merrily on. The band was voted a good one.

At two o'clock in the morning 'Pops' Russell and three of his pals were drinking in the bar. The middle-aged secretary was drinking his thirteenth bottle of Bass.

"What's the mystery, Pops?" asked 'Naps' Spreycombe, M.F.H. in another country.

"Rioted," replied Captain Russell, staring at the lethargic bubbles rising to the flattened froth half-way down his glass. He was an honest man who disliked subterfuge, but he had to lie. "I suppose it's bound to get known, anyhow. Won't do hunting any good."

With a sudden movement he emptied his glass. "Don't tell anyone I told you. Rioted after sheep. Bimbo's poisoned 'em, every dog and every little bitch. Cyanide of potassium."

"Strewth!" drawled Spreycombe. "What about your committee? And subscribers?"

"That's the very devil of it," muttered the secretary. "I shall have the dirty work of explaining to subscribers. Bimbo's got enemies and they're not his own hounds—or weren't, I should say. There'll be the very devil if anyone gets nasty."

"Was it that run on Monday, when they got lost in the mist?" inquired a young man wearing the uniform of the Lamerton Hunt.

Captain Russell nodded.

"Put up hare, changed to a screaming scent up by Links Tor— must have been fox, I think—disappeared into the mist. Jim couldn't find'm. Stragglers began to come into kennels about eight hours later. Moll heard'm in Tavy Cleave, and saw'm eating sheep. Everyone of'm eating. Once get the flavour of hot mutton, and it's all up with your chance of catching fox or hare. Myself I believe it was that dem donkey flesh."

Next day the *West Country Morning News* published a statement, displayed prominently, that Major-General T. F. M. Inclefell, C.M.G., D.S.O., the Master of the Inclefell Harriers, had destroyed the entire pack for sheep-worrying. It was followed, in the issues of succeeding days, by an extended correspondence. General Inclefell was accused of acting hastily; he was held blameworthy for the faulty and irregular feeding of hounds in kennels. The incident was amplified into a general attack upon fox- and hare- and stag-hunting. A letter signed W. H. Starcross, Lt.-Col., R.E., complained of the expense the writer 'had undergone in bringing hunters to the district and the enforced dismissal of his two temporary grooms in the worst part of the winter consequent upon the folly of General Inclefell shown by the needless and callous annihilation of the innocent hounds with the guilty'. The secretary replied, stating that he had searched the Army List, and his Subscribers' List, and had been unable to find the name of W. H. Starcross in either.

This surprised everyone, except the writer of the letter, an eighteen-year-old youth named Cocks, a mechanic to an unqualified dentist, whose hunting experiences were confined to (1) stalking lovers in the summer evening fields, and (2) stamping mice to death during the threshing of a corn-rick in his uncle's farmyard.

There were letters from *Not a Nut-Eater*, who wrote about the "Appalling danger of rabies *via* the butcher's shop"; from *Dog-Lover*, who wrote "on behalf of poor little dogs who cannot defend themselves"; from *Only a Schoolgirl*—"We of the Upper Fifth have had a debate, and we have decided to let it be known that it was a jolly rotten thing to kill hounds. *Two blacks never yet made a white*, was our unanimous conclusion"; and from indignant butchers in Plymouth, answering the allegations of *Not a Nut-Eater*. And various others. Some funny, some silly; but all based upon ignorance.

Every letter was read in the West Country Club with great interest and often amusement, except by the uneasy Captain Russell, the secretary of the packless Hunt. His ruddy face appeared every day for its morning Basses, which were drunken, as usual, under the stuffed badger in the case above the fireplace. Often he declared that he wasn't interested in what was said, and as often he spent the morning morosely interested in what was said. He knew the main facts about the run in moorland fog, as told by a pale Molly Inclefell to her father in the evening of the disastrous Monday; and they were quite different from the explanation given at the Extraordinary General Meeting a few days later.

It was remarked that the Master had looked "positively uneasy, when Valentine Potstacker got up on his hind legs" and demanded the name of the farmer to whom compensation would be paid for the loss of sheep by worrying. The Master said that he would personally investigate and settle all claims. Major Potstacker, a lawyer speaking for a clique of subscribers, repeated that he would very much like the meeting to know the name of the farmer who had lost sheep by worrying. The Master replied in a voice weary but courteous that the Scotch sheep on the moors roamed at large; that some time must elapse before any loss could be discovered. Major Potstacker, following his line, suggested that all claims that were to be made had been notified already.

The Secretary then got up and said that surely everybody except the only non-subscriber present had been able to grasp what the Master had just told the meeting: that the committee would be called upon to examine no claims whatsoever, in respect of sheep worried by the pack. And further, he himself, as secretary, would announce that the Master, whom he understood was about to offer his resignation to the committee (which, in passing, he would say, he hoped would not be accepted). To that he would add that the Master had guaranteed the cost of a new pack. He sat down, feeling hot.

Major Potstacker thereupon said, gently, that he was representing some of the subscribers, and that on their behalf he would like to suggest that the price of new hounds would be the only expense to be borne by the Master and that he would further suggest that the Master might possibly have had another reason than the one given for the slaughtering of the hounds ... Voices said, "Oh, shut up"; "Put a curb in his mouth someone"; and "Sit down, sit down".

Captain Russell jumped on his feet and said, "Mean to say I'm a liar?" Major Potstacker said, "Certainly not, Mr Secretary. I am seeking information. Now, I see many farmers present, men who call a spade a spade ...' (A quiet voice: "Us calls'n shovels, maister," and laughter.) ... "Well, shovels. Now farmers are exact in what they say; they insist on a shovel being called a shovel." And when loud laughter of only the farmers had ceased, Major Potstacker said distinctly, "Who among you lost sheep by worrying last Monday?" He looked round. "No one claims a loss! Well then. Who among you has counted your sheep?" Many gave an immediate "Aiy, aiy!" At this point he was called to order, and told curtly to address his questions to the chair. "Dem swine," Captain Russell was heard to mutter.

Major Potstacker knew that no sheep had been killed. He had been making inquiries; but he had learned only negative information. And after the meeting, although he tried to pump Jim Huggins, he got nothing from him. "Warn't ee to the meeting, s'm?" Jim murmured plainly. "Aw, ee missed a rare lot o' rattling; but I be dalled if I knaws what 'twas all about." Yet even Jim, close and firm as a Wistman oak, didn't know everything.

2

The cracked tenor bell of the church had ceased its franging hum when a man crawled furtively through the garderobe hole at the base of the wall of Lydford Castle. The four walls of this Norman ruin were open to the stars; the ivy pushing its roots into the yellow mortar between the hewn granite blocks and inner rubble shook with the exploring winds. The crumbling hollow square stood upon a motte, or raised mound of earth. For centuries it had been used as a stannary prison, but now its dungeon was fallen in; brambles grew where men had lain in chains. Owls and jackdaws cried around the walls by night and by day.

In the north-eastern wall of the keep was a mural chamber, built for hiding in an age of violence; it was dilapidated, the home of grasses and nettles. Stalks and blades were broken and bent; some blades were raising themselves, for the man who had been hiding in the wall all that Sunday, shivering and sometimes groaning, had just climbed along the ledge and jumped down. He was peering through the garderobe hole.

Once he had had a name; he still bore the name, but it was never spoken on any lips except his own. To have heard other men speaking the names bestowed upon him with pride and tenderness at his christening would have been to him warning of a calamity more terrible to anticipate than death. For he was one of the most wretched of breathing things, a convict escaped from Princetown.

The number of his cell had been 76. He was known to the warders as Seventy-Six—the warders to whom it was forbidden to speak, unless he were asked a question. He was Seventy-Six, a corrupted animal that for years had quarried stone for other men's buildings, dug turf for other men's fires, sewn bags for other men's letters; had his hair cropped, his chin shaved, worn khaki clothes marked with the possessive broad-arrow of His Majesty's Government. An animal, not wild and pure, but with rot in its mind, that had done with life, but with which life had not yet done. He was godless.

The castle ruin was remembered from a happy visit from Plymouth, just before the Great War, when he had been on his honeymoon. From August 1914—when he had jacked up his job and stood for hours before a recruiting office, hoping with his pals to be sent off to fight before the fun was ended—until his escape the day before, he had had practically no sense of time. He had exchanged one number of military servitude for another of penal servitude with only one period of tentative freedom—when he had murdered a man and a woman. Now he had another interval of freedom. The day before, Seventy-Six, who was serving a commuted death sentence, had dropped, from the scaffolding where he had been working, a block of stone on a warder's head, and escaped by running through the fog. He had scooped in his hands the icy waters of the moor, drinking on his knees. He had eaten grass. Repeatedly he had touched the hem of his jacket, fearful lest he might have lost his only companion.

Seventy-Six crept through the hole and listened. A row of larches grew between the castle and the church. The fog was gone, and moisture dripped from the branches. Organ music came with a dim light through the windows of the holy building. People were singing the evening psalms. Seventy-Six sneered mentally.

After listening he slunk down the slope of the motte to the larches, jumped softly down a bank, and walked to a gate. Once again he listened, but hearing no footfalls climbed the gate and crossed the road. He entered the rectory garden, startling from a laurel bush a bird that flew away with shrill squealing cries of alarm. Seventy-Six cursed and touched his jacket again. Reassured by the contact of his index fingertip with the head of what he sought, he crept towards the house, stooping, with silent steps on the grass border of the main path.

A cautious inspection of the lightless building told him that all the lower windows were secured. He felt along one pane, wondering if he dare risk the noise of putting his elbow through it. While he was hesitating, he heard above the thudding of his heart the voices of men in the village street. He hurried away, going down a steep slope among spruce and larch trees where it was very dark, but safe. The river roared below in the gorge. He turned to the left, and walked on, often blundering into ants'-nests as tall as himself, and mossy-wet trunks of trees. He bruised his head, and a sudden mood of happiness came upon him.

The wood was thinner by a viaduct with arches that spanned the gorge. A thought came to him that it would be easy to climb the embankment and lay his head on the rail and end it all. But while he waited a train thundered above him. Sparks rained into the dark gorge. He was still free; but so hungry. Seventy-Six choked back a desire to cry, and walked on. The path was rough with shillets, and led down to a cottage before which were scattered bits of paper and empty tins. Washed underwear, some of it ragged, was thrown on a hedge in front. He scrounged two shirts and a pair of trousers hanging with the lining inside-out. He chucked one shirt back on the hedge, thinking that the bloke as owned it was a poor man.

An abandoned water-mill stood near a footbridge, with broken roof and walls, and he was about to explore when he heard a man's voice above the rushing sounds of the river. Thinking that the owner of the clothes had discovered the loss, Seventy-Six crossed by the footbridge. He had stepped down to the path on the other side when he saw the glow of a cigarette in the darkness above him. Someone was coming down the path through the wood. He crouched on the earth, hiding his face, and felt about for a stone or stick. The voice spoke again, high and eager, and of the quality that Seventy-Six had often laughed at when coming from the lips of music-hall comedians before the war. The red point came near, and now a girl was speaking. Seventy-Six listened to the first feminine voice he had heard since his trial at the Old Bailey.

"What fun, I say! But you know, we mustn't ever let daddy know we did it."

"Rather not! I feel rather a rotter to have done it, really, without his knowing. Of course, he doesn't hunt, but after all I'm his guest. He's on the committee, too."

They stopped by the bridge.

"Shall we do it, Bid? Or shall we go up to the village and make a present of it to old Atters? It's damned heavy to carry."

"Oh, let's do it! Daddy will laugh when he hears," persuaded the girl. "He doesn't like Captain Russell for killing all the badgers, but he didn't like to say anything, as the farmer wanted them killed."

"The farmer was probably thinking of the free drinks next month at the Badger Club supper," said the young man scornfully. "And he probably believes they do harm, as Russell says they do, the fat liar! The other day I heard him telling someone in the West Country Club that he had 'dug out a hundred and thirty pounds of badger flesh from one holt!' His very words. Whereas two labourers did the digging, three terriers got bitten, one a broken jaw, and all the work he did was sometimes to kneel at the hole, thrusting down an ear to hear what was happening, and then to tootle-too on a copper horn with what little beery breath he possessed after his athletic feat of kneeling. Pah! And, of course, he stabbed the poor brocks when someone had banged them on the nose with a shovel."

"Pah!" said the young girl delightedly. "He calls that *sport!*" The man's eager voice spoke as they were moving away. "You know,

Bid, it will be a great scene when hounds leave the hare's line and crash off down to the marsh! And when Russell and the rest of them arrive at the holt—and find hounds at dinner!"

The conversation was meaningless for Seventy-Six, except the word dinner. He allowed them to get a safe distance ahead of him before following along a footpath under trees beside the river. He climbed a wooden fence, dropped down to a single plank over a ditch, and walked away from the river and up a path which lay on the rock, past a waterfall that thundered white in the darkness, and on to grass again.

Half an hour later, he was trying to find what they had been hiding on the side of a hillock above the marshy ground by the river. The word dinner had so filled his mind while he had been staring in the direction of the voices, that he was convinced they had been hiding food. Reasons for the concealment of food did not occur to him. He stopped among the furze and bracken, to get the dinner that was waiting for him if only he could find the right place. His forehead knocked a thorny branch, and he was rubbing the pain away when he fell into a hole, where immediately he smelled a strong smell. Wondering if it led to a cave where he might hide by day, he felt with his hands. Chopped roots stuck out of its sides and roof. It led about six feet into the gravelly earth. At its end the tunnel narrowed, and was blocked by something soft. He pulled out a heavy bundle and unwrapped the cloth around it, to feel a cold smooth object, with a rough covering. It was a pie.

Seventy-Six pushed his thumb through the crust, and tasted. He tore off the pastry, and pulled out a handful of meat. He crammed it into his mouth, swallowing without chewing, gulping with dry wheezings in his throat. He muttered and thought phrases like "Gorblime, mate, you're in luck," and "Stuff to give'm!" The food gave him sharp pains, and he went to the river to drink. When he returned, he ate less quickly. It was a steak and kidney pie, flavoured with onions and hard-boiled eggs. The gravy was rich, tasty with salt and pepper. The dish was big, holding enough for a dozen men.

When he had eaten his fill he again felt about the place. It ended in a tunnel too small for him to crawl into. He found a pair of light walking boots, with rubber pads fixed on the soles. With them were the skin of an animal, stuffed with straw, a coat, and a bowler hat. The smell he had noticed when he found the hole was thick on the skin. It dimly recalled the pain of caned hands in boyhood.

Some hours later, wandering on the lower heather slope of the moor, he found a hiding place under an oblong slab of granite. It was sealed on all sides save one, by which he entered. Low-growing furze and heather and whortleberry formed a springy door. He crawled out again, and tore, with difficulty, handfuls of heather from the sodden ground, while a herd of small wild grazing cattle stared and sniffed near him. A wan white moon gleamed above low clouds moving over from the south-west. Seventy-Six made his bed, and placed in a far corner the dish with its life-making food. He wore the khaki, arrow-marked clothes no longer. At first he had hidden them in the pillaged badger-holt, but cunning had made him pull out the bundle, and, going back the way he had come, drop it, boots and all, in a waterfall of the gorge under the viaduct. But before discarding his prison clothes, he had withdrawn something from his jacket and placed it in the hem of the new coat.

To Seventy-Six, warm and happy, came the old thoughts he had had just before his marriage, when one Sunday night he had listened idly, his girl on his arm, to a street preacher, and believed what he had heard. He recalled another preacher before whom the battalion had been marched, and formed into a hollow square, and ordered to lie down, while the chaplain stood up and preached. The old sweats 'ad said afterwards that they were for it again, because the padre 'ad talked about Gawd being on their side, which 'e always did just before a push.

The words were realized now by Seventy-Six for the first time since that September church parade before Loos in 1915. Gawd saved sinners! Gawd had arranged for the pie to be hid there! He sat on the granite slab, and said "Gorblime!" which was the vocal accompaniment of his poor darkened spirit's aspiration. He did not really pray to be blinded.

A rising wind stirred the heather, and curlew cries were blown across the sky. Seventy-Six thought, Gawd, please go hon 'elping me. Then he drew out from the hem of his coat the thing he cared for more than anything on the earth, and played with it. It had been with him through his trial. He tossed it a few inches into the air, and caught it lightly between finger and thumb. He had played like this in his cell for hours, often watched by warders. It had shared his hopes for a better life—for Seventy-Six was still young enough to hope for a happier future. So acquainted was he with the ways of his companion that Seventy-Six could jerk it up and catch it again in the dark. He caught it by his front teeth and, biting on to its head, nicked it with a finger-nail. It made the least musical note, which was as a loved voice, comforting him. It fell, and he trembled; his throat was dry until he found it. How glad he was when it prickled his finger, and he picked it up and put it in its place. It was an ordinary pin, made of brass, the bright plating of which had long since worn off.

Seventy-Six crawled into the refuge and fell into a deep sleep before he had tucked in his legs. All night the rain was driven slantingly upon his boots. An old dog-fox trotted down to where he lay, made curious by the strange scent carried upwind to Links Tor where it had been seeking beetles. Three stoats visited the boots during the night; and when the rain ceased at daylight a pair of ravens, flying to the moor from their rocky fastness in the gorge, dipped from a height of two hundred yards to inspect the yellow things in the heather. After much flapping of wings and dipping of beaks over the granite slab, one dared to alight. With sidling walk and glances of little eyes, and uneasy hops into the air, it made a swift lunge with its beak, ripping a toe-cap. A grunt came from under the stone, and the ravens departed, fearing a trap. They were puzzled as the fox and stoats had been at the unfamiliar taint in the air.

3

A few hours later the Inclefell Harriers met at the Dartmoor Inn. A small field was present, about two dozen in the saddle, including farmers. Miss Mollie Inclefell stood talking to Jim Huggins the huntsman. She was a slight fair girl, wearing black coat and breeches. Six motorcars had brought people. The Squire was there, on foot with his sons and daughters. With them was a young man who hid a nervous restlessness under an assumed lack of interest in the meet.

When the huntsman took hounds to a certain slope of bracken where a hare was usually to be found, the youngest daughter of the Squire set off with her companion, at a tangent from the curve made by the mounted and foot followers. When over the brow of the slope they started to run. Unseen, they crossed the river Lyd by leaping on boulders. Quickly they climbed up the other slope. The two friends were making for high ground whence the old badger holt might be seen. For a quarter of a mile they climbed in sunlight, and then they sat down on an oblong block of granite embedded in heather.

They had been sitting down less than a minute when hounds far away and below gave tongue. A hare had been started from its form. The high voice of Jim Huggins sang faintly in the wind. They watched the hare making a right-handed turn towards the field of flat-poll cabbages behind the Dartmoor Inn. The hare sped away from the leading hounds. They watched it crossing the place where, the previous afternoon, the young man had taken off his brogues and pulled from a haversack a pair of yellow boots . . . suddenly hounds checked, they clamoured, they pushed their muzzles together so that they looked like a great fungus suddenly grown on the moor, only to break up into fragments that streamed along a new line. They over-ran the place where the hare had branched, and raced along the crest of the hill above the stream. The extended field cantered behind.

When the young man turned to speak to the girl standing a few yards away, he was startled by her white cheeks. She was staring at something near. Following her gaze, he saw the pair of boots which he had imagined to be with other things in the badger holt. The boots were covering the sockless feet of a hidden man.

· The girl whispered, "Oh, it may be the escaped convict!"

The young man stared at the boots again, and said, "Oh, my God!" Then he leapt through the heather and clutched one of the heels. His hand was kicked away.

"Come out, I say," he said quickly. "There isn't a moment to be lost."

"Oo are yer?" snarled a voice.

"On my honour I won't hurt you," cried the other, certain that the man was the escaped convict. "You are wearing the boots I hid in the badger holt. It was meant for a joke. I really should advise you to clear off as soon as possible."

He was deeply alarmed, and had tried to talk in an ordinary voice to reassure his companion. She was a nervous and imaginative girl, but recently recovered from scarlet fever.

"Why can't a bloke 'ave a bit of a kip if 'e wants to?" threatened the voice. And then, "If yer tries any monkey tricks, I'll bash yer, straight I will!"

"Please come away, please," implored the trembling girl, looking at her companion.

· The baying of the pack grew fainter as hounds sank the hill to the holt two miles away. After more persuasion, the man came out, clutching a piece of granite in his left hand. He wore a pair of labourer's trousers with the lining on the outside, a grey shirt, a Lovat tweed jacket, and a grey bowler hat. The wan blue eyes of his ruined face looked about him with such an ailing wildness in them that the young man felt he had to deal with a madman.

"Don't be alarmed, I say," he said, aghast and smiling. "Look here, you ought really to clear off as quickly as possible. In about ten minutes or less hounds may be running your line. I laid a drag yesterday with those boots you've got on now. Wherever you've been walking they may follow. Now if you'll only run to Links Tor over there on the skyline, you'll find a narrow crack in the granite, up which you can climb to the top. It's hard to get up the Chimney, but once there you'll be safe until they can whip hounds off. Look here, I'll follow you and give you a pound for the trouble you've had through my damned foolishness. And I'll give you my word I won't breathe a word to anyone that I've seen you. After all, I haven't the least idea who you are, and it's none of my business— I mean, not my affair who you are. Now go, as quick as you can."

Seventy-Six, having been born and bred in a Bermondsey slum, had never seen a live hound in his life. He looked at the summit of Links Tor.

"Climb up on the skyline to be sniped at, eh? Not a hope! See any green in my eye?"

The young man said earnestly. "Well, look here, change boots. I've got you in this mess, and I can run. But ... all right, Bid, don't worry. But it wouldn't be any good, unless you hide that jacket! Clear off, there's a good fellow. Oh, my God, do hurry. Look, they're running to the badger holt."

The girl never forgot the look in the convict's eyes. She was unable to cry, she was fixed as though in a nightmare. The face became set in her mind, as a symbol, not of human spoliation and despair, but of cruelty and evil. She knew nothing of war. She heard him mutter something as he flung the granite lump at the face of her companion, who groaned and dropped into the heather. She could not breathe. She heard hounds in the distance, and thought, Come soon, come soon. She watched the blood beginning to run from the purple mark on his forehead. She was dizzy and sick, and vaguely realized that the man was ramming her father's old otter-hunting hat on his head as he ran. The hillside seemed to slide up the sky.

4

Long before he reached the tor, Seventy-Six had to use his hands to aid him. After splashing and slipping through soggy ground he came to a clitter of rocks overgrown with turf and mosses. A holly had its roots in a granite crevice, a tree twisted and hoary with lichen and without a red berry among its spineless leaves. The holly grew near a mountain ash. Both had been planted by birds.

Looking down, while holding a branch of holly, Seventy-Six could see the toff kneeling by the girl and below them, the river at the base of the hill. He neither saw nor heard hounds, for they were running down the unseen slope which led from the marshy ground. Beyond the marsh, on the opposite hillock, was the badger holt.

He climbed the clitter, and went at a steady pace onwards. Here was drier ground that dipped gradually to a saucer-like depression rising to Links Tor about a mile away against the sky. Being under the everlasting wind the heather was knee-deep and springy. There were no rocks to hinder. The flagpole on Hare Tor to the south— erected to give the signal when gunners were firing on the artillery ranges—lost its dark outline in a drift of cloud as he started to ascend again.

Seventy-Six began to hear the wind as he climbed towards Links Tor. From a sighing in the stalks of heather it swelled to a chilly whistling, and his clothes were blown against his form. About fifty yards from the summit, where was lodged a squat roundish mass of black granite grooved and scalloped and smoothed by wind and rain of a thousand centuries, he sat down and rested. Turning in a northerly direction he saw a great brown and grey ball of a hill, at whose base ran the leaden vein of the Lyd. He looked across the Great Nodden to fields in sunlight and shadow, and away to a blue infinity of land and sky. The south was dim and grey. Rain. Seventy-Six was glad, for it would hide him. He thought that he would strike inland to the moor behind him and hide till dusk, when he would return and make for the sea. As he became hopeful again he felt sorry that he had slung the brick at that young toff. It had been done in fear.

A sudden deep croaking over his shoulder made him turn his head. He was in time to see black cartwheeling wings as a bird swerved and dropped out of sight behind the tor again. The raven had meant to alight there, but something had disturbed it. As Seventy-Six stared he saw a thin object, like a stick, thrust up from the centre of the granite. It thickened towards its end, and then it disappeared. In its place was an arm, followed by a head and shoulders. A man then levered himself upon the platform, picked up a rifle, and staggered to his feet, his legs crooked as he braced himself against the blast of the wind.

Seventy-Six tried to force his head back to its normal position, but it was held there as though by a spring fixed to his spine. He continued to stare at the crooked figure on Links Tor. He had to stiffen the muscles of throat and neck before he could force his head away. He sat rigidly, wondering when he would be shot in the back. He waited, until the feeling in his spine compelled him to twist his head again. The warder had dropped on one knee, and was covering the convict with his rifle.

Seventy-Six pretended not to have seen him. The curiosity of dread made him turn round once more, just as a shout enfeebled by wind came from the warder. He was beckoning Seventy-Six, standing as upright as the wind would permit, and holding the rifle in his right hand at the position of trail. Seventy-Six got on his feet, and while he was walking towards the tor, the warden pulled a whistle from his breast pocket and blew a long blast. As though in answer a ragged edge of mist trailed in cold silence past the convict, and washed around the monolith of granite. Links Tor faded out, but the whistle continued its double note—*fran-n-n-n* in the fog.

5

Seventy-Six stood irresolute. He felt for the head of the pin. The touch of its head was like a double dose of rum before going over the bags. He laughed, and was turning it in finger and thumb when a hound spoke below. It was the leader, a dog named Lamplight. The pack was less than a mile away, running the line of the yellow boots, whose scent was pungent in the mist. Again Seventy-Six thought of being caned on his hands, before the boys and girls of the fifth standard of the Council School. He remembered the bag of aniseed balls, which he had been made to throw in the master's waste-paper basket—his mother's birthday gift, bought with one of her scanty spare pennies. And afterwards the master had made him face the class, and had used the little boy's tearful gulping for a crudely sarcastic lecture on the subject of Heroism. He had not known that a son felt that his mother's heart was thrown in the basket.

Seventy-Six thought, This fog is a bit of all right! Stuff to give the troops! He set off at a run, on his toes. He had been the champion runner of his battalion. The moor was a chaos of whitey-grey, cold and dim. Soon his eyelashes were damp. The ground was firm, and he leapt over the ling. The rubber pads gave a good grip. After a quarter of an hour his breath came quickly, and he felt a relief when the ground began to slope down. The noise of water was before him. Lower and lower he descended until he came to the Rattlebrook fretting its stony bed. He crossed without wetting his feet, and listened. In front of him the ground rose again, and a remote baying seemed to float down through the mist. He pushed on up the hill, but was forced to rest at the top. He imagined that as he was invisible, he was safe, because he did not know that hounds followed by nose alone. As he lay on a couch of ling he heard them giving tongue, not an echo this time. They had reached the unseen crest of the coombe. He jumped up and hastened onwards, cursing them because he thought they would betray him to the warders. The clamour suddenly increased—where Seventy-Six had rested—and he ran on again.

His next rest was half an hour later, when he flung himself by a thread of a stream which had cut for itself a channel in the peaty soil. He dipped his hat in the brown water, flinging it over his face and washing out his mouth. In the old running days, when the Guards Division had been out of the line, he had been trained never to drink before or during a long-distance run. He lay on his back, wishing he had a pal with him; one minute, two minutes, three minutes, and then the baying of hounds.

Patches of ling and grass tufts became scantier. Everywhere was water. The rubber soles of his boots often slid. He ran flat-footed over a maze of water-threads. An idea came to him that he must jump them all, that he would have bad luck if he slipped into one. To ease himself he carried the hat in his left hand. It began to impede him, but he dared not throw it away, as he would need it until his hair grew. It hindered more when carried under an arm, so he rammed it on his head again. During the next half hour, toiling up a long hill, he changed its position more than a dozen times.

Eventually the hat was thrown away beside a layer of turves that had been cut and laid in wide arrow-shaped lines to drain and dry, where it was found long afterwards. Disturbed in their feeding, three golden plover rose in the mist before the runner with swift anchor-winged flight and with gentle cries of alarm. Snipe, thrusting long bills into the soft ground, were driven up from their feeding. Sometimes a raven croaked over his head.

He was so fatigued when he reached the Great Knesset that he had to walk. His feet, with blistered toes and heels, felt as hot and heavy as they had felt when he had trench-feet swelled and red as tomatoes. He flung away the stolen shirt, soggy with sweat, on the morass where the river Tavy rises. His trousers to the knees were wet and black with peat. He had blundered into many shallow bogs. The deep sucking quakers, which shook and rippled at his passing, were bright green and easily seen.

He staggered across the plash in the peaty hollow of an old tarn, hid by swirls of fog. A broken spade was stuck into a heap of turves in the hollow, and in the turves was an iron box holding a metal stamp, a bottle of violet ink, and a book wherein many names were signed. Its fly-leaf was ringed and smudged by intersecting violet circles holding the letters CRANMERE. Seventy-Six remembered. Past and present were mingled as reality in his confused brain. In the early summer of 1914 a London-born youth and his wife, on their honeymoon, had scrawled their names across a page, with the remark, *It's all rite*. And now, nearly ten years later, the mortal remains of the woman mouldered in a South London graveyard and neither age nor name mattered further for the husband. Seventy-Six, grey-haired, was resting the weight of his head and shoulders on forehead and knees; but a younger man, in khaki, was writing a letter to a wife still living: *Dear Dol, i write hoping you are quite all rite, as it leaves me at present, in the pink. Are you getting the seperation allowence all rite. I hopes so. We are not alowed to say where we are but it isn't so bad, although a bit of mud about. I hope to get Blighty leaf soon it is my turn soon and i hops the Sarjint Major don't forgit. No more now from your lovin husband Bob.*
P.S. This war is a Bastard.

He blacked out the last word, remembering that his officer would read the letter.

And SWAK on the envelope flap—Sealed With A Kiss. The pencil-stump, paper, and sand-bagged traverse, sun shining, plank he sat on, all dropped into darkness. He heard the whining of ricochets, saw the greenish flares quivering in the water-filled shell-holes as the relieved right-wing company filed down the wooden track to the Menin Road. Jerry's machine guns were clacking from many points. Going out at last! Rest billets reached, and rum-in-tea dished out. The S.M. was calling out names for Blighty leaf. Christ, 'ow 'is 'eart thumped! 'Is own number, 'is name! He saw again the lorry in which he had hopped to railhead, after fourteen months in the mud of Artois and the shallow water trenches of the Salient. During the slow journey in the train, clanking and stopping and jerking on again past sandhills and pines to Boulogne, the young Coalie was singing and shouting, happy at the thought of seeing again the wife he had constantly thought of, but infrequently written to, during so many evenings in smoky estaminets, candle-dim billets, and lousy cubbie-holes. A stay of two days in the rest camp owing to submarines in the Channel, and again he was singing with his chums as they marched down the quay. Horse-nosed officer bloke with A.M.L.O. on his brassard, at the gangway with red-cap sergeant and two policemen scrutinizing the yellow pass. Then the pitch and roll of the boat, the nausea and prostration, the grey cliffs of England, the pulling-himself-together and the tottering off at Folkestone, the train with the black-painted lamps and drawn blinds, the faces in smoke and the crush of equipment, the glide into Victoria Station so vast and dark and subdued, yet noisy with feet and engine steam. Outside the women he didn't want to talk to saying, "Hullo, dearie," and then—the first drink of good old English beer, a pint of mild-and-bitter . . . How strange civvy suits looked!

One reality faded; nausea remained. Seventy-Six lifted his head and harkened to hounds following him in the mist. Two hours before they had streamed over the ragged grass below Links Tor. They were unfatigued, but had veered off the line, following the aniseed straying in the mist. Seventy-Six thought that the warders would see his name in the book, and know that he had been past Cranmere. He carried the book away with him, and trod it into a bog, where it was never found . . . afterwards it was indignantly stated that someone had taken it because it contained the autograph of the Prince of Wales.

6

Seventy-Six loped on for another half-hour, descending to a coombe where the mist was thinner. He fell over a rock beside a stream, and choked as he tried to suck up water which turned his teeth to icicles. When he tried to rise again he had to draw his feet from off the rock; he felt as though he were dragging the rock with them. He prayed with broken shouts, as he had prayed under the barrage at Festubert. His ribs were hugging him to death, the prison shirt was smothering him. He tore it off and left it on the rock, and pulled himself onwards, as a child in a nightmare. Now he was clad only in trousers and boots, and the Union Jack tattooed on his back. The flag was one of the patriotic relics of 1914, done in a Caterham shop after cheers and beers with pals, following flaring mental hatred of the sergeant-instructor drilling the squad to breaking point on the parade ground.

Over rocks and rushy tufts, while thirty-four hounds followed less than three hundred yards behind. His line of running had been in a loop, and he was approaching the Rattlebrook again, where it merged into the yellow winter water of the Tavy. He plunged into the river foaming and swirling among black and pink-blotched boulders and rocky tables, which for centuries the floods had slowly carved. It sucked him under and spun him in its twist. A spur of rock held him by the trousers, until they ripped, and wrapped round his legs. Hauling himself out, Seventy-Six waded back into the river again when the leading hounds viewed him and gave tongue.

He was carried a hundred yards down the water in less than a minute, to where a tree-grown islet divided the current. All the air was knocked from his chest. On hands and knees he crawled to the right bank. The strings of his thigh and calf muscles were drawn tight, and each lung was bayoneted. A spike of rock had torn his back, and the Union Jack was fouled by the blood of the ruined patriot.

A mist strayed through Tavy Cleave, and the broken screes towering hundreds of feet above were revealed and hidden by clouds. An old hill-fox deep in a clitter sniffed as he passed below and listened contentedly to the hounds which had crossed the river. The raven that had observed Seventy-Six for nearly three hours croaked a treble croak to its mate from a scaur of rock four hundred feet above the toiling figure.

It was now between half-past two and three o'clock in the afternoon. Feeling for the pin, Seventy-Six realized that he had thrown it away with the clothes.

Ever since he had been blown by a high-explosive shell out of a communication trench in the Hohenzollern Redoubt, with burst sandbags and pieces of a shattered Coalie, his chum, a spectre had fretted his life. Always—and especially in drink—since his fourteen days in the hospital of Hazebrouck 'recovering' from the shock of the bright shell-blast, he had been liable to moods both morose and violent. At Hazebrouck an inspecting Surgeon-General, a regular officer with two rows of ribbons and honours, suspected him of malingering, and ordered him immediately to be sent back to duty in the line.

The thought of his wife had kept the spectre away; as afterwards, the companionship of the pin in his cell had been a barrier against the dark fears which came into his poor disrupted mind. When he knew that the pin was lost, Seventy-Six threw up his arms and wailed. He saw what other men would not have seen, had they been with him. The new consciousness was accompanied by a sense of ease and lightness. All pain and fatigue left him. He seemed to be floating along, with the least touch of his toes on rocks and water.

The body of Seventy-Six was hobbling in the smooth and shallow bed of the leat which, serpentining through the moor, eventually brought water for use in the arsenic mines of Mary Tavy; but a Coldstream Guardsman also was walking on the platform of the Tube Railway at the Elephant and Castle Station. The platform was thick with the smell of many women and children sitting and lying against the wall. He was relieved that the journey was finished, and hitching up rifle on right shoulder he shoved a way into the lift. Outside the dear old boozer, where he had first met his wife. Now there was a war on, and a bloke couldn't get a pint after nine o'clock. The street was dark. A tramcar passed him, bumping and clattering, all its lights blacked over, except for the least glimmers. He lit a cigarette, and the voice of a special constable riding past on a lamp-less bicycle cried out in agitated sternness: *Put that light out! Second warning's been given!* He answered with a laugh, *Don't get the wind up, mate!* As he strode along the Old Kent Road, gunfire broke out, and a hundred white beams swept the sky. The yelling civvies might cut and run, but not a Coalie! He whistled as he walked. *Z-z-z-z-zim-z-zz-zop* fell the splinters of anti-aircraft shells. *Wh-oo-sh! Crack!* that was a nosecap that had split the paving stone just behind him. He walked on to his street, erect and with cap-peak pulled low over his eyes. Near his house he stopped and looked upwards. A groaning had opened in the sky above him. It filled the street, it snored gigantically through the darkness. *Whooursh, whooursh*, an immense slow corkscrewing of sound, that grew as though the earth was falling out of its orbit. The soldier crouched under a window ledge, while a starving cat miaowed to him, and rubbed itself against his cheek. Poor moggy, he 'adn't no milk to give. He stroked the cat, whose purring was drowned in the tremendous rushing noise descending. It was like a thousand minnies coming down. (The minenwerfen in the Salient had made a lesser noise.) He waited and sweated, for it was coming straight at him. He pressed himself against the wall, against the bricks made greasy by children's hands, holding the cat protected in his arms, his eyes closed, his breath stopped. A red glare showed through his lids, and immediately a stunning detonation flung him with the cat into the gutter. Houses swayed and tumbled and roared down in clouds of bricks and dust. He ran up the street, for the Zeppelin torpedo had fallen just about where he lived. The bomb had flattened a row of houses, but his house was safe, except for a splintered door. Won't Old Dol be surprised to see me, he thought, jubilant that he was still alive. He pushed the door down, crashing in upon the landlady, an old widow woman who was wearing a crimson flannel nightgown. Her bluish-white face was beyond speech. She moaned something, and pointed at a broken methylated spirit bottle on the floor. *Where's Doll?* he asked, *Upstairs?* She stood and moaned in the crude fumes of her own breath. *You're boozed, Ma!* he said. She let out a shriek when he pointed upstairs. *I to'd her not to do it! I to'd 'er not to!* she moaned. Her candle wobbled and fell. He ran up the stairs, pulling himself up with his hands and stones out of the wall fell away with his clutch. (Seventy-Six had reached the ruin of Redford Farm.) He turned the handle of the bed-sitting-room. The door was locked. A man's voice said, *What the bleedin' 'ell.* With the butt of his rifle he broke in the panels, and burst the lock. A gas jet burned with a small blue flame. The soldier turned the tap, and it flittered like a yellow bat. He snarled and drew his bayonet out of the scabbard, and fixed it. The man whined, *'Ere, I say, maite, what's the bleedin' gaime?* Then he shrieked and hid his face under the bedclothes, with the soldier's wife. The soldier stabbed them under the patched counterpane. He saw the spirit of his wife fly up on white wings. (The owl flew out of the chimney of Redford Farm.) But the bloke she had picked up wouldn't die. After each lunge of the bayonet he came alive again with more and more faces, which tried to bite him with their fangs. The soldier thrust and pointed and parried, *groin—belly —right nipple—left nipple—throat—in—out—on guard!* Just as the sergeant-instructor had yelled at him during bayonet practice on the stuffed sacks at Caterham. He smashed with the butt-stroke on their jaws and eyes, but the faces pulled him down. He did not care, they did not hurt him, and with a laugh he felt himself withdrawn from them, into darkness.

7

Redford Farm, near the leat which leads to the arsenic mines, had been a ruin many years before the last run of the Inclefell Harriers. One chimney-stack was still standing at the eastern end of the farm-house the Saturday before, for on that day, wandering over the moor, the young man who was the guest of the squire of Lydford had disturbed a white owl that was dozing away the daylight up the flue, among the fire-marked stones. But on the Monday, when Miss Mollie Inclefell, lost in the mist for some hours, and leading her mare lame in the near fore, arrived at Redford Farm about three o'clock, it had collapsed, as though someone had tried to climb up it. A raven flew over the heap of stones and damp mortar-dust lying on the ground. Several red-muzzled hounds came to her and leapt up affectionately. They remained by her, two of them licking her face, while she lay pale and still in a fainting fit caused by the sight of two shinbones sticking out a pair of yellow boots.

Crime and Punishment

This is the story of a dog called Snapper—a good name for him—
and an American gentleman who lived for a month or two in Devon,
on the funds provided by a travelling research scholarship. The
Assistant Professor went to Devon with the idea of writing a history
of the French Revolution.

Our story opens one fine May morning, when the Assistant Professor of Comparative Literature—to give him his proper style and
title—looked out of his study window and cursed. In the middle
of the lawn below was a small circular flower-bed, out of which
grew a cypress tree. It was not the sight of the tree that caused
annoyance, but the fact, as it appeared to him, that it was rapidly
being dug up.

In fact the tree had stood there for a couple of hundred years or
more, the age of the digger was scarcely half a couple of hundred
days, and the hole was not more than a foot deep and about five
inches wide. Nevertheless, a shower of earth was descending upon
the lawn.

The Assistant Professor pushed open the casement and bawled,
"Hey, Snapper! Grr, you! Go some place else, go kill real rats!
Where did that darned woman put the soda? I guess the farmer's
pork is all nobs and gas inside me." He patted his waistcoat with
mournful self-sympathy. "Jeese, I wish I had the dog's outlook on
life," he said to himself. "He doesn't trouble about the French
Revolution."

The soil which had been increasing for the past few minutes
between the hind legs of the terrier ceased to heave; a head and
ears dishevelled with earth were withdrawn, and the thing called
Snapper wagged its tail once, uncertainly. It turned its earthy face to
the window, laid back its long ears, and showed its teeth in a grin.

"Naughty boy!" said the Assistant Professor, in a tone of voice that caused the back of the puppy to straighten, its ears and tail-stump to become vertical. "Mustn't dig up other folks' trees! The British author I rent the house from will sock me for dilapidations, although strictly speaking it should be deracinations, except that the word deracination doesn't occur in my lease. Mind you don't wag that tail right off, Snapper. Go play with that bull again. I'll try and take you for a walk this afternoon. Goo' boy, Snapper! Jeese, you're a cheerful little guy. What a lot of kicks you get out of life!"

The puppy was now running round the lawn at its fastest pace, round and round the cypress tree. At speed its hair was pressed against its body, and it seemed to have enormous black eyebrows.

"Wish I could feel like you do," said the Assistant Professor. "I guess it's an illusion to grade you a lower species just because your ears are long and hairy, and you run on four legs and catch your fleas without mental poise and philosophical detachment. Wal, there you are enjoying yourself in the sunshine, never needing soda after your meals, without giving a darn why you are or who you are, and here am I, sitting day after day writing a lot of bunk about something that probably never happened among a lot of cockaded cock-eyed morons nearly a hundred and fifty years ago. Wait till I've broken the back of this chapter on Talleyrand, Snapper, then I'll take you for a walk this afternoon, a real walk."

The Assistant Professor went back to his chair and stared gloomily at the mass of books and papers cluttering the desk.

2

Left alone, the puppy lifted his nose and sniffed the air for an interesting smell. He was at that stage of his self-education when the allurements of reality and imagination were almost equal. No interesting smells being on the air, he began to imagine a colony of rats at the end of the hole under the cypress. He was about to dig for them when the scent of his favourite cat set across his nostrils. Up went his tail and ears.

A few moments later he saw the cat walking with slow unconcern up the rose path on its way to the kitchen door and the dustbin. He rushed forward jubilantly. The cat fluffed herself, flattened her ears, opened her claws, and spat. Snapper barked with joy. Very soon he had manoeuvred her to his favourite pitch at the edge of the lawn. He pranced before her, darting left and right, making feints forward and then springing back. She lay under the edge of the lawn on the path, showing only her moving tail-tip and her flattened ears. *Waugh waugh waugh!* Then occurred what Snapper had been deliriously awaiting: the cat sprang and struck at him. Snapper, feeling very clever, nimbly avoided her clip. She clawed the grass, and after a baffled hiss, chased him round the tree.

Snapper was so happy that he ran round the tree three times after the cat had retired to her base on the path at the edge of the lawn. To the left and to right he pranced again, defying her, baring his teeth at her, feinting forward, always alert to dodge the sudden lunge and hook of claws.

Glad of the excuse to quit the pangs of writing a masterpiece, the Assistant Professor looked down at them from his window. Then he saw the farmer, whose horrid pork was resisting every assault of the Assistant Professor's gastric juices, walking up the garden path.

The terrier raised its long bat-like ears, uttered a bark, and trotted to meet the farmer.

In one hand the farmer held a dead pullet by its yellow legs. Snapper nosed the bird and leapt up, uttering a gurgling growl of delight. The farmer grunted, knocked it against the terrier's head, and growled "Get off, you limmer! Next time I catch you nosing round my shed, you'll get something you aren't expecting. That's the second bird you've had in one day, you bissley li'l beggar!"

"Good morning!" the Professor called from the window, in an English accent. Then reverting to his native Connecticut, "Hello, has my darned dog been at your chickens again? Just a minute, I'll be right down!"

Five minutes afterwards the farmer was returning down the garden path, and the Assistant Professor, a methodical, industrious and ambitious young man, was entering in his *Diary of Work in Progress, Europe,* under the heading *Incidental Expenses,* the item:

One chicken, bought from Whiskers   *4s.*

Six weeks before, there had been this entry:

*One pedigree Jack Russell terrier, bought from
Henry Williamson*   *£5 5s. 0d.*

3

That afternoon the Assistant Professor sat in his study, groaning, forcing the pen slowly across the paper. Six weeks of his vacation were gone, and he had not yet got half-way through his schedule, which was to bring him to Chapter Eighty of Volume Four of *An Historical Outline of the French Revolution*. He had been working on his masterpiece for more than ten years. For more than ten years the Assistant Professor had been reading every available book already published on the subject; for more than ten years he had been reading, and reviewing for various highbrow literary weeklies, every new book on the subject published in the U.S. When one highbrow literary weekly folded, the Professor continued to review for its successor, until that died, and then he went after the next one. During the ten years he had fairly established within himself the idea that he was *the* American authority on how not to write about the French Revolution. Every book on the French Revolution reviewed by the Assistant Professor was discovered to be deficient in this or that aspect of behaviourism, faulty in this or that interpretation of psychological or character motivation. This book, or that book, declared the reviewer, was not the comprehensive masterpiece that was awaited by the world, the masterpiece that would reveal the decline and fall of idealism in the light of modern knowledge, that would transcend even Thomas Carlyle. A few highballs helped to clarify, now and again, the essential urgency of his own mission in the matter of writing *the* definite *opus* on the French Revolution.

Nevertheless, in spite of deficiencies in aspects of behaviourism and faults in interpretation of psychological or character motivation, every new book on the French Revolution added a weight to the appalling mass of material, to be worked into the comprehensive masterpiece awaited by the world, which accompanied the Assistant Professor everywhere; a mass, which at the moment when the Professor bought a pullet for twice its market value, filled three immense trunks and weighed over a quarter of a ton.

If this awful fact, and what it signifies, has not already flattened the reader of this little story, please be reassured immediately: pray remain seated: in a moment or two you will be watching the little dog, who waited in vain for its promised walk, playing with its friend the bull. You'll hear only once more of the manuscript of *An Historical Outline of the French Revolution*, which with its five hundred pounds of parasites was only dragged in to show how, in spite of his modern way of talking, the Assistant Professor was really a very cultured person. So while with weary determination he is digging into one of his several trunks, among the moths and mildew, in order to verify and embody—away with culture, the word is pinch—in order to pinch a few facts from one of the old review copies therein, come on tip-toe beside me, and watch the technique of Snapper with the bull.

4

The bull does not want to play with any silly little dog. He is a young bull, but recently separated from his mother the Aberdeen-Angus pedigree cow, all of whose milk he has sucked during the first eight months of his life. He is square, almost, when seen from behind; and the line of his back is straight. Shoulders all beef. He is what is called polled; he has no horns. Which is perhaps as well for Snapper; who anyway, would not care. Was he not descended from a line of fierce and eager little earth-dogs, bred to tackle badger and fox underground? The bull is standing in the shade of a beech tree as Snapper trots to within two yards of him. Snapper crouches in the grass.

The bull turns his head, with its curly black poll, and stares at the white crouching object with the bright eyes. Snapper makes his ears-cock—or rather, he makes them stand up straight, for they are too ludicrously tall for the action to be called cocking—and lies still in the grass, taunting the bull to play.

"*Humph!*" says the bull, and swishes his tail.

"*Worro-worro-wough!*" replies Snapper, making a sort of amiable growling in his throat. The bull slowly turns away his head, and gives an extra flick to his tail. Snapper leaps up, and runs round to face him, collapsing in the grass again. The bull bends his neck and gently lifts his nose, with the copper ring, in the direction of the dog.

"*Worro-worro,*" growls Snapper, with delight. He runs to and fro before the bull several times, before collapsing in the grass, pointing himself at the bull with shining eyes, inviting him to lower his head so that he, Snapper, may have the pleasure of springing away from the thrilling snort of his nostril.

The bull turns away.

Snapper barks. Raucousness is now in his voice. The bull does not want to play, so Snapper runs twistedly at the bull, showing his eye-teeth in a grin, and snapping a couple of inches away from the bull's muzzle. *Wough wough!*

The bull glares and snorts.

"*Ha ha!*" pants Snapper, prancing. "*Wough wough!*" He runs at the bull again, leaping aside, falling over, wriggling quickly upright, and making a circle away from his glaring friend the enemy.

So happy is Snapper that he dashes round the bull half a dozen times, before crouching again at the challenge. The bull paws the ground, and pretends to graze.

Snapper, after several feints in the grass, then threatens the bull by pushing himself on his belly towards him. To lure the bull he gets up again, shakes himself, and pretends to stare at a pigeon flying over. He yawns, making a plaintive sound. Nothing happens.

The bull crops, or pretends to crop, at a tuft of rank marsh-grass, which cattle never eat. Snapper walks behind him, collapses to scratch himself, then suddenly runs in and nips the idly swinging tail at its tuft.

The bull swings round, snorting, and paws the ground. Snapper barks, crouches on his forepaws. The bull trots forward with lowered head. His eyes gleam as he runs at the dog.

Snapper flees swiftly. Only when he has scrambled under the gate does he face the bull. Very bravely he thrusts his head between the lower bars and snarls a challenge. The bull has scared him.

"*Poof!*" snorts the bull, jarring the gate with his curly brow. Snapper nips his nose, not hard, but enough to make the bull swish his tail violently. The bull holds up his head, preparing to shut his eyes and to toss gate and dog over his back. *Crash! Crack!* Snapper turns tail and flees silently.

"Aa-ah-you," roars the farmer, coming down the hedge, and hearing the splintering of the lower bar of the gate. "You young limmer, you! Wait till I get near enough to put my stick about 'ee! Go after something your own size, why don't 'ee?" he yells after the dog. "Go and kill some of the ould rats round the stables!"

The small white dog, its long black ears raised in alarm, rapidly vanishes.

Amusing little cove, isn't he?

5

As soon as he was out of sight of the farmer Snapper stopped and rolled luxuriously in the grass. Something very nice and sweet-smelling lay in the grass. He had rolled on it many times before. During several weeks he had played with it, shaking and tearing with rage; but now the feeling he had for it was quite different. Of course there are, in the U.S.A., canine psychologists, whose work precedes that of the genii who inhabit the Halls of Memory, of Doggy Delight, wherein pets are embalmed, stuffed, and otherwise preserved in the Happy Hunting Grounds of Eternity, Inc. Without doubt, a doctor of that school of canine psychology would gravely have pronounced, Snapper has a manic-depressive complex. Was it caused by some fixation in early life? the Professor might have inquired, some dread shock in whelphood? Certainly the dog had bad dreams, wherein his legs and nose worked agitatedly and his ears rose and fell like English railway signals at the end of a prolonged fog.

Snapper is the first morbid dog in fiction: definitely he had the Cadaver Complex, or maybe the Dingo Complex: for he delighted to roll on the flattened corpse of a rat.

After rolling for several minutes, he arose, shook himself, inspected the corpse, performed a thoughtful ceremony upon it, and trotted off. He had recalled one of the sounds issuing from the farmer—*rats*.

6

The farmer at this period was much troubled by rats. His farm was near a hunting stables. Recently some of the stable buildings had been improved. Rickety wooden bins for oats and bran and other food had been replaced by modern bins of galvanised iron. The rats which had grown numerous and fat on plundered corn were now shut out. Their runs and highways had been stopped with wads of wire netting rammed into the holes, and the floor covered with concrete. A determined rat might eventually gnaw through concrete, unless it were made of granite chip, but the sharp points of wire defeated them. So they migrated to the farm.

Snapper had spent much time in digging and blowing and snuffling and whining in the farmer's wood shed, his long ears stiff with excitement, but only in dreams had he got his teeth across one.

As he went towards the farmyard he forgot the rats, for he saw his friends the fifteen pigs. At least, Snapper must have considered them his friends, for he always ran gleefully towards them when he saw them; but it is doubtful if the pigs thought of him as their friend. One of them, however, the sow, who weighed about a quarter of a ton, definitely regarded Snapper as her friend.

They were all pink. Their family name was Long White Lop-eared Pig. Snapper made two discriminations among them: one was much bigger than the others, and unplayable; the other was much smaller than the rest, and could be rolled over in the mud squealing. This wretched individual was the smallest of the farrow, his head was too big and his body too small, and only laziness on the farmer's part had prevented him from being killed at birth. A 'nestledraff', as farmers called this oddment, would make neither pork nor bacon. In the farmer's words, he 'ate more than the head o'n was worth'. Even so, the poor nestledraff ate little enough, always being squeezed out in the scramble. He was Snapper's favourite, for Snapper could do what he liked with him. He could pull the little creature's tail, nip his ears and jowl and nose, chase him all through the midden, and roll him on his back in the muck.

Play with it, however, did not usually last very long, because what Snapper really liked was a fight, or what to him was a fight. The larger pigs would run and dodge him for a while, and then stand still looking at him from between their ears. This gave Snapper a thrill, for when they stood like that they were ready to snap at him. Then he could dance around on his toes. As for the lumbering sow, she grunted and snuffled about the farmyard, and took no heed of him. She had long given up hope of any excitement from his presence. Once Snapper had rolled by accident off an empty barrel lying on its side outside the farmhouse door, and fallen sprawling on her back, in the precise place where she needed to be scratched. He had not known that the sow's grunts were of pleasure; he had been wary of her long snout every since.

Snapper had been playing with the piglets, causing squeaks and grunts and sudden patterings in the mud, for about ten minutes, and was in the act of pulling the curl out of a pink tail, when he was startled by a gruff voice shouting terribly near:

"Ah, you'm here again, be 'ee? Well, I like your bliddy cheek! Go on, out of it!" the farmer bellowed, his red face working. "Us'll be seeing master, soon, to get 'ee a good trimming. You'll come here once too often, my little boy, and find yourself looking at the wrong end of my gun!"

The farmer held another dead chicken in his hand. Nearly all its breast feathers had been torn off, and it was bitten in many places. Snapper fled.

The howls of a dog being trimmed came from the Assistant Professor's hired house. Afterwards the dead fowl was solemnly fastened by string to the dog's neck. The Professor hurled a stick into the hedge. "Remember—'ware feather, Snapper!" he intoned solemnly, in an Englishman's sporting voice: adding, "Gee, I'm sorry, but I've got to do it."

Shortly afterwards an entry was made under the heading *Incidental Expenses* in the *Diary of Work in Progress, Europe:*
One chicken, bought from Whiskers   *5s.*

7

The Assistant Professor stood by the window of the study. Papers, books, pens, pipes, and cigarette ends were everywhere. He addressed the woebegone figure of the dog sitting under the cypress tree below.

"Morally speaking, I ought to be wearing the darned thing next my gullet," he soliloquised. "Let me get the back of this chapter broken, then I'll take you walks."

Hearing the voice Snapper looked up, and wagged his tail. Whereupon the voice said sternly, " 'Ware feather, Snapper! 'Ware feather! Isn't that the correct Britisher's admonition? 'Ware feather, Snapper! Poor little devil, you're all fire and fun, and no one to play with. Wait till I've gotten rid of this moron Mirabeau, then we'll have some swell walks right across Exmoor. Meanwhile—'ware feather, Snapper!"

Snapper watched the window for a few minutes after master had disappeared, and then stared about him, wondering what to do. He sighed, and tried half-heartedly to play with the chicken slung around his neck; but it did not respond, and he thought he would sleep.

At that moment his favourite cat, one of half a dozen that lived in the barns and sheds of the farm, walked across the lawn, on its way to the dustbin. Immediately his ears stood up. He ran at her, but the weight attached to his collar made him stumble and fall over.

Instantly the cat pounced, bit him through the ear, got in several pleasing rips with her hind legs on his back, spat at him, smacked him on the nose as he struggled up yelping, then fled, leaving him to walk slowly back to his hole under the cypress, wondering why he had been hurt. He tried to lick his nose, and in doing so got tangled up with the chicken.

Hearing the yelp, the Assistant Professor flung down the pen he had been gnawing, got up, and walked to the window. He was in time to see Snapper, as he thought, trying to eat the chicken. That would never do! It was intended that the dog should drag about his victim for two days, becoming so humiliated, so sick of chicken that he would never look at another one in his life; but if Snapper were treating it as a joke . . .

" 'Ware feather, Snapper!" bellowed the Professor.

"Aiy aiy!" cried the voice of the farmer, who was hastening up the garden path. "You'm just in time with your advice sir!" Indignantly he held up the corpse of a third chicken.

"Well, I'm darned," said the Professor. He thought a moment. "But surely the dog has not had time to go around to your place and come back here again. Why, I've scarcely had time to write a sentence between the time of licking him and tying that chicken round his neck, and this your third visit."

"I'm very sorry, sir," said the farmer, "but here's my poult, bootiful little bird it be, too, and there, if you'll please to look, be the marks of worrying, identical with the marks on the other poults. If you'll please to step down a minute, sir, I'll show 'ee. Ah, you may well cringe!" he growled to Snapper, who was creeping off in a sidling walk, ears down, body curved, his tail-stump nervously fluttering.

"Come here, sir!" shouted the Professor. Snapper turned on his back, held his pointed nose up as though he were trying to smell a cloud in the sky, and waited for inevitable pain.

Together the Assistant Professor and the farmer compared the marks on the fresh chicken with those of the bedraggled thing attached to the dog. Snapper, lying on his back, looked first at one face, then at the other, anxiously awaiting their verdict. His eyes, under the black eyebrows, rolled, showing the whites, as he watched master going towards that part of the hedge where the stick had been flung. Master returned with the stick. Snapper sprang up, meaning to run away and hide in the new hole he had been excavating in the coal-shed, but he was handicapped by the weight round his neck.

Master caught him and whacked him, and as Snapper crept away into the hedge with both ears pressed flat on his skull, the farmer said, putting five shillings and sixpence into his pocket:

"Well, thank you, sir, I don't want to raise trouble, but I'm a poor man and I've got my living to make. The price be market price for growing birds, which put on a lot of flesh at this season o' the year, sir."

"The law of supply and demand has always puzzled me," said the Professor. "But at least I see quite clearly that as the supply diminishes so the value increases. Say, I've an idea. Why not let me buy the remaining pullets from you now at five shillings each. Then those that Snapper doesn't want, I'll sell back to you at the end of the month for what I pay for them now."

"Thank you, sir, I'm sure, but who'll be paying for their food meanwhile?"

"Jeese, I guess you've got me licked," said the Professor. "I understand why all revolutions are bound to fail. I'll have to keep Snapper tied up, that's all. Good afternoon."

The Professor returned to his study, and made a further entry into his diary of expenses.

Further contribution to the chicken racket　　　　　　　*5s. 6d.*

"The horney old buzzard," he muttered. "And he took the durned thing away with him, too!"

After walking round the room several times and trying to light a pipe that was too tightly packed, the Assistant Professor sat down at his desk once more. To his surprise and delight his pen began to move over the paper rapidly, in pursuit of a scathing criticism of French peasantry, small farmers, and all bourgeoisie. Page after page he filled with what he felt to be a brilliantly argued plea for the necessity of authoritarianism. At last he ceased, and looking at his watch was astonished to see that nearly two hours had elapsed. He had forgotten all about Snapper! Anyhow, now he could take the dog for a walk with a clear conscience.

He went downstairs into the garden and was about to whistle for the puppy-dog when from the farmyard across the lane he heard the roar of the farmer's voice, followed by two shots and the high yelping of a dog.

Clenching his fists, the Assistant Professor ran in the direction of the farmyard.

8

Now after the second thrashing, the trembling Snapper had remained in the hedge. But soon one of his ears had raised itself, and he yawned. Gazing around, he smelled nothing to do. He arose and shook himself. Then he walked away, dragging the cold thing beside him, and sat for a while under the holly bush by the kitchen door. He watched the cat eating the remains of his dinner, without even uttering one growl of querulous protest. Having licked the plate clean, the cat then sat beside it and thoroughly washed his face and paws, watched by the shivering Snapper, who had curled himself on an uneasy bed of dead holly leaves, his head pillowed on the thing which was fastened to him. Having completed her leisurely toilet, the cat got up and walked back towards the farmhouse. Snapper then walked over and woefully inspected the empty plate. He yawned, stretched himself, and trotted back to the cypress tree, animated by the thought of digging out imaginary rats.

Encumbered by the dead weight round his neck, he soon grew tired, and collapsing into the hole, went to sleep. Sometimes he whined in his sleep, dreaming of master chasing him with a stick as big as master, the end of which was a cat's paw with great curved claws, master and cat's-paw always just behind his tail however hard he tried to race away, and although he was running his fastest, he was not moving, and although he was not moving, the terrible cat's-paw never actually struck him.

With relief Snapper awoke from this nightmare, and looked about him, shivering. Master's window was blank. He heard sounds of distant pigs grunting, cows lowing, hens clucking, but they excited no desire in him. He curled into a tighter circle, settled his head across his paws, swallowed the water in his mouth, sighed with contentment that he was not really being beaten but was safely tucked into his retreat, and went to sleep again.

As the Assistant Professor was writing the last of his indictment (which was scrapped that same evening, for reasons that soon will be apparent) Snapper awoke, remembered his plate by the kitchen door, and went back to see if he had dreamed about the cat, or if the rest of his dinner was still there. Finding the plate empty, and the scent of the cat still lying strong, he decided to follow it. The line took him down the garden path, through the cabbages and potatoes, through the radish bed, among the marrow plants, through the

beans, down another lesser gardener's path made of cinders, and so
to the garden gate. The cat had jumped the gate, but Snapper
crawled underneath, dragging the dead chicken with him. He sniffed
for a while at a place where the cat had sat and completed its toilet,
and then followed beside a hedge until he came to the woodstacks
beyond which was the woodshed adjoining the chicken house in
which the farmer had discovered the succession of marketable
corpses.

This shed was a place of much interest for Snapper. His tail went
up, his ears went up, his nose went down to the earth, and forgetting
his humiliation, he started to work along one of the many lines of
scent which were laid on the earth. The line led him to a new hole
in the corner of the shed, into which he began to dig with great
excitement. While he was working his forepaws as fast as he could,
with pauses for deep sniffs into the earth, he heard the loud clucking
of a poult beyond the opposite wooden wall of the shed. He heard
it as he heard the lowing of cows in the meadow waiting to be
milked, as he heard the rooks in the lime-trees, and took no heed of
the clucking until additional rustlings and squeakings very near made
him withdraw his head from the hole and look in their direction.

To Snapper's wildest delight he saw what hitherto he had only
seen in dreams—rats, many rats, struggling together as they dragged
a chicken towards the corner where he was standing.

In the commotion of flapping wings and squawking the rats had
not observed him until he was among them. He nipped one lightly
with his teeth and drew back quivering from ear-tip to tail-tip as it
turned at him and jibbered. Before he could do anything one had
bitten him on the nose. Snapper leapt back in astonishment for about
half a second, then with a growl of rage he ran forward and bit the
rat across the back. The rat squealed, and the noise made him shake
it furiously. Meanwhile the other rats had abandoned the chicken,
which was squatting on the earth spread-winged and gaping. Without
pause Snapper darted after another rat, which turned on him and
bared its teeth as it sat up against the wall of the shed and squealed.
Snapper chopped it in his teeth, shook it as he had the other, and
flung it away in order to get one more. Then from the hole in the
corner, from other holes around the base of the shed, and from the
faggot-stacks outside, other rats began to appear. They sat up on
their hind legs and sniffed together, baring their curved yellow
teeth. Snapper had disturbed the colony which only two days before
had finally abandoned, owing to hunger, their assault on the new

concrete floors of the granary of the hunting stables. These rats swarmed out of the holes and formed a ring around the dog, jibbering and whispering among themselves, sitting on their hindlegs and dropping again to run little distances on their fore-feet, then sitting up again. Snapper barked at them, but they did not run away. Then a big old buck rat squeaked, and Snapper ran at it. The buck rat let out a squeal, and all the rats ran to Snapper and began to swarm over him as they bit him.

It was at this moment that the farmer, having heard the cries of the pullet, and coming up in a rage from his farmyard, carrying his loaded gun in his hand, ready to shoot the dog, saw the dog in the corner beset by more than two score of rats biting his legs and his ears, hanging on to the dead chicken round his neck, while he was snarling and turning all ways to snap and bite. So astonished was the farmer that he let out a shout, and raising his gun, fired both barrels together into the rats.

When the Assistant Professor arrived at the farmyard a minute later the first thing he saw was Snapper being nursed in the arms of the farmer's wife, while the farmer was standing among a group of neighbours, quite breathless as he repeated again and again what he had seen. There were the nine rats which had been killed, three by the dog, and six by the shot. And not one pellet, declared the farmer, had harmed a hair of the dear little dog's head, bless the little b'uty. But one of the lead pellets had cut the string which attached the chicken to his neck.

The live chicken, which the rats had been dragging into the shed, had escaped, and was sitting on the tailboard of a cart, looking bedraggled and very subdued, but otherwise uninjured.

9

"Yes, sir," the Professor tells successive classes of stoodents, "that's Snapper, the dorg you've seen with me, that's the dorg that ate his punishment. That's the original Shaggy Dorg."

It happened way back in Devon, England. Snapper is now a respectable old toothless gentleman dog, fed on slops, inclined to be a little stiff and portly, who has his own cushions and sets of rubber bones and invariable ceremonies and ways of procedure inside and outside the house. Sometimes, however, as when the moon is full, he may go out on the campus, and dig for imaginary rats under imaginary cypress trees, shaking them in imaginary teeth. The Professor, after a shot or two of imaginary Scotch, talks of his imaginary masterpiece on the French Revolution, which one day he intends to finish. The sophomores, or freshmen, are not particularly interested in the projected masterpiece, however, but all of them want to know the reason why the Professor refers in the course of his story to "the dorg who ate his punishment". Oh, he and Snapper went for a long walk, the Professor tells them, and when they returned the farmer's wife came up with a big plateful of carefully boned chicken which she had prepared for the little dog from the poults which the rats had killed.

Trout

Motorists from London know the winding road which leads from Taunton to the sunsets of the west; up hills and round bends with valleys below, twisting and turning above wooded coombes and plunging down to cross over little bridges, through villages with ancient names, and at last to the high ridge between beechen hedges where the sombre line of the moor can be seen to the north.

As this road upon the ridge begins to descend, the observant motorist may discern, in the mists and wooded prospects below him, a distant church tower, in the shape of an owl; and here is the town of South Dulton.

The main road to London—one hundred and eighty miles eastward —runs through South Dulton. The motorist rolls through its square, and away to the western sea-board, with visions of sand and green combers, of Devonshire cream and pleasant nights in the local inns. He is gone, followed by others; the wheels roll westward, away from the town. Few stop there. It is said by the superficial that nothing ever happens in South Dulton: that its golden age departed with the stage coach and the jingle of harness. Maybe this is so; but before we, too, pass on, let us for a moment think about Mrs. Houghton-Hawton (of Hawton) before she is forgotten.

The new generation remembers its own events. Who will forget, while they live, the great event of the roasting of the ox, in the market-place, and in summer, too, during the Forces Welcome Home reception? Six hundred people attended, most of them taking but the briefest glance at what was considered to be a gruesome sight—the great coal-fire in a brick open-sided box, and the monstrous horned and staring-eyed carcass frizzling on a horizontal bar of iron. The free beer cheered things up a bit, when they sat down to trestle-tables set out in rows and ate slices of the ox with potatoes and boiled cabbage.

Lest the above be interpreted as a criticism of the Town Council's lack of imagination, let it be said at once that South Dulton, in one respect, is in the van of modernity and progress. It possesses that which exists elsewhere only in the dreams of fly-fishermen of modest means—for South Dulton, having acquired the land adjoining half a mile of the main river into which the Hawton brook flowed, then decided that the fishing rights should belong to everybody. Free salmon, sea-trout, and brown trout fishing for all comers. God made the fishes for man and here men, uninhibited by selfish landlord or vested interests, take their rights.

The River Dull runs below the town. At the bottom of the hill the London road is carried by a bridge with a grey stone parapet. The bridge marks the upper limit of the free fishing. Immediately below the bridge is a high weir with a stone apron sloping too steeply for the ascent of any fish except in an almost phenomenal flood. Salmon and trout running up to spawn are forced to remain below the weir—in the water of the free fishing. And just below the weir stands the inadequate town sewage plant. After that was built, the Town Council had been able to buy the fishing rights of their half-mile at their own price.

2

Motorists passing down the London road at night slow up at the bridge, for the road bends beyond it. Occasionally one stops, attracted and puzzled by the strange flashing and dancing of lights in the valley below. Scrutiny reveals that the lights are moving apparently in the river itself. Are these the fabled lights of Will-o'-the-wisp? Surely not, for in addition to the lights are to be heard shouts, accompanied by noises of splashing and beating of the water. There may be a dull explosion, and a momentary fountain arising below. The sounds of quarrelling and the snarling of dogs are not unknown in that stretch of the town's free fishing. Here no keeper, hired by selfish capitalist, can prevent men from taking their rights; no water-bailiff, hated agent of the Board of Conservancy, dare show his face on the bank.

Dazed by the little searchlights, the salmon which has run up to spawn, its skin dark brown, its flesh infirm, its body full of milt or eggs, lies close to the bottom of the pool, while gaff or wire-noose on long ash-pole is moved nearer the tail, nearer and nearer, gaff just below the ventral fin, or noose over the dark square tail. Then jerk—out he comes! Hide'n under a vuzz-bush, midear, and keep an eye on'm, for rogues abound; there are always folk ready to steal the work of honest men.

Sometimes when many fish are lying there, gangs at night blow the pits with gelignite cartridges, killing by concussion everything living in the pool. Sometimes a couple of sportsmen will throw in a large screw-top beer-bottle filled with quicklime and a little water, and weighted so that it sinks to the bottom. The carbonic-acid gas increases until its pressure shatters the bottle; and in its rush to the surface enough gas is absorbed by the water to poison nearly every fish for scores of yards. Another method is to put an old stocking filled with chloride of lime into the stream; the first mouthful of dissolved chlorine gas passing through delicate gills—the lungs of a fish—causes twisting, leaping torture, until the fish turns on its side and floats down to where on the shallows hands await to grasp and pitch their spoil on the bank.

During days of summer, when the river is dead low and bright, small boys can be observed stalking the few tiny trout, mere finger-lings, that have come up from below. Bare-legged and intent, each with a stick to which is attached a fine brass-wire noose, the boys creep after the darting fish until they are fatigued and cowed. Noose is worked over the tail. Jerk! Put it in the pocket and go after that other one. Only four inches long, and ungrown? Yes, but if I don't have'n someone else will, so I'll have'n first. That's right, my boy. You look after yourself, no one else will.

3

A mile away, on the side of a hill, stands a house, gaunt and unpainted behind the Palladian pillars of its main entrance. Once life flowed from the Big House, as Hawton Hall was called, to all the farms around it, for many miles. Now, at night, sometimes a solitary light is to be seen in one of its windows, until nine o'clock precisely: when the light goes out, and the night is to the ghosts, which are memories.

For Hawton Hall is one of those English, or it might well be said, European houses which have had their day. Hawton awaits demolition for its valuable teak and oak and mahogany doors, its beams and rafters, the lead on its roof, the oak and pitch-pine planking of its floors and the panelling of its walls. Even its stones have a value in the post-war shortage of every kind of material in Britain. There are several eager builders waiting for the death of Mrs. Houghton-Hawton (of Hawton) and the sale by auction of that valuable repository of building materials. But the châtelaine of Hawton Hall, who has known four wars and five generations of her family, is still alive.

During the second World War Hawton Hall was occupied by many families, evacuated from the towns. The parkland—which had been sold after the first war—was a camp. Concrete roads and paths and scores of squat black huts of tarred corrugated-iron and brick, shaped like headless elephants in repose, had taken the place of the beautiful timber trees and the herd of fallow-deer. But Mrs. Houghton-Hawton (of Hawton) remained, occupying four rooms of the mansion, including the old music-room, which faced west, and the sloping land to the river.

4

Nearly every morning the old lady made her way to that room, walking by the aid of an ebony stick with an ivory handle, and looked through the wide west window. The scene had long ceased actively to distress her, for she lived almost entirely in her memories. These were by no means sad—for she had a great-grandson who was, to her, all that had been, and was to be.

Upon the piano, which had not been tuned or played for many years, stood a large silver photograph-frame. Within the frame were several photographs of young men: each was clad in tweeds; each was holding a fishing-rod in one hand, and a trout in the other.

One morning when she entered the music room Mrs. Houghton-Hawton noticed that the frame was not standing as it should have been, exactly facing the west window. The sight disturbed her, and she said aloud to the air: "Oh Matilda, pray see that the frame be replaced after polishing, exactly as before." Her voice was low; a little tired; and as she spoke she was seeing the face of her lady's maid before her; and she heard the reply, dignified and quiet: "Yes, ma'am, of course the gentlemen must always see the river." But Matilda Parker had died at the age of seventy-three, a dozen years before.

Mrs. Houghton-Hawton peered at the frame and noticed with agitation that there were fingermarks on its rim. She did not see that they were small fingermarks, as of a boy's hands; and she was moving to the wire bell-pull beside the door when she remembered in time that there would be nobody in the servants' hall to answer it. How foolish of her! Of course, the house was now divided into five parts, four of them occupied by the young wives and families of Royal Air Force officers stationed at the airfield beyond the river and the valley, on level ground on which once had stood three of the Hawton farms. Nevertheless, she was disturbed. Could Mr. Ridd the ironmonger have called again, and taken the frame in his hands to remark on it? How had he come into the room?

As a fact, Mr. Ridd, the ironmonger of South Dulton, had last come to see Mrs. Houghton-Hawton more than thirty years before. Mr. Ridd had called at Hawton Hall shortly after the opening of the fishing season one March to express his deep sorrow at "the Captain's death, as proper a young gentleman as ever whipped water with rod and line", and then in his nervousness he had taken the photograph-frame, with its embossed coat-armour, off the piano and, after staring at it with an expression of dolour, had respectfully suggested that if at any time madam would like a few trout for her breakfast, he would be only too willing to catch them for her, just for the sport of it, if she understood his meaning. Mrs. Houghton-Hawton had entirely understood Mr. Ridd's meaning, and graciously she had thanked Mr. Ridd, saying that it was most kind of Mr. Ridd to have offered his services, but at the moment . .

Mr. Ridd had left almost hurriedly, and gone out to his Ford van standing in the courtyard of the empty stables behind the mansion, wondering if the old girl had made arrangements to let the fishing.

Mrs. Houghton-Hawton had no intention of letting the fishing. Certainly not to Mr. Ridd! The way the fellow had handled the frame, turning it about, peering at it from various angles; and then the cunning look in his eyes as he had revealed the true purpose of his visit!

In truth, Mr. Ridd, a keen fly-fisherman, had not called for the purpose of getting some fishing for himself. When he had come into the presence of the old lady, and had seen the photographs in the frame an awful doubt had entered into him that she might think he had only pretended to sympathy that her son in the Royal Flying Corps had been killed, in order to get some trouting. Mr. Ridd's sympathy had been genuine; he had admired the tall, handsome figure of the Captain, and the fine way he could throw a dry-fly (as though he were able to know how a fish felt) with the delicacy and lightness of one of the hatching water-flies rising from the surface of the stream. And Mr. Ridd, talking it over with his wife at breakfast of bacon, egg, and sausage that morning, had almost convinced himself that by offering to supply Mrs. Houghton-Hawton's table with trout he was doing so solely as a tribute to her bereavement and loneliness.

5

On the occasion of Mr. Ridd's visit, the silver frame had contained three photographs, and the space for a fourth. The two lower photographs were of the kind known as snapshots, while the uppermost was a faded daguerreotype. Each was identical in subject and composition: a young man, a rod, and a fish.

The uppermost portrait was entirely of a past age—that is to say, it had been taken when Alethea Houghton (an heiress in her own right) had been a child. The details were nearly, but not entirely, obscure by the fadings of time. There was the figure of her father-in-law, Major Hawton, wearing a small close-fitting, small-peaked cap, with high lapels to his jacket, and tight knickerbockers and high fawn gaiters. With a magnifying glass, the beholder might just discern a face with the incipient moustaches and beard and whiskers of a youth in mid-Victorian times. He held a fourteen-foot green-heart rod in one hand, a two-pound trout in the other, a couple of fingers through one of its gills. He had been killed soon afterwards, with the Light Brigade in the Crimean War.

Below the daguerreotype was an early photograph, faded and yellow, of his son, who married Alethea Houghton, thus joining two landed estates and conjoining his coat-armour with that of his heiress-bride. Following the family tradition, the youth in the Norfolk jacket holding an eleven-foot rod with a ten-ounce fish had in due course become a soldier, who, leaving wife and small son at Hawton Hall, had died of enteric fever in the South African War.

The third photograph was that of the son, taken while still a schoolboy. He wore a straw boater and a jacket of Donegal tweed, while his rod was a nine-foot length of split-cane, with which he had taken his first fish, a somewhat lean half-pounder. The first World War had taken him, and with most of his generation he had found his grave in that immense desolation of linked shell-holes stretching from North Flanders to the downland country of Artois and Picardy. But before his death as an observer in the balloon section of the Royal Flying Corps he had married a girl serving with the Red Cross, and she had had a son who had grown up never having seen, or been seen by, his father. The boy had gone to the same school which many generations of Hawtons had attended; and, like them, he had learned to fish for trout with an artificial fly. In due course a fourth photograph had been added to the three others in the frame. The fish had been a six-ounce trout, taken on a three-ounce rod of split-cane eight feet long; and likewise in due course he had found a soldier's grave far from his native land, in action with his regiment of the Royal Armoured Corps, the 17th Lancers, the Death or Glory Boys, in the desert warfare with the Afrika Korps.

After her grandson's death Mrs. Houghton-Hawton had kept his rod and tackle for his son. This was the boy who had returned on holiday from school the day before our story began with Mrs. Houghton-Hawton peering at the fingermarks on her silver frame. The boy's hands had been greasy, for the first thing he had done after returning home was to rub his enamelled and tapered silk line with a piece of wash-leather on which was some paraffin-wax, in order to make the line float when he went fishing on the morrow.

Somewhat nervously the boy had surveyed the blank space in the family picture record, and wondered if he would be there with his first trout, and if it would be the biggest of them all, before the Easter holidays were over.

6

The declining weights and conditions of those fish in the photographs might have suggested to a philosophical ichthyologist a parallel in decline of the human scene and substance at Hawton Hall. For the same changes in human values had affected both land and river equally. These changes had been accepted by nearly everyone as the changes due to modern progress.

Soon after the death of the husband of Alethea Hawton the road running through the valley above the stream had been metalled and tarred for the new motor traffic which was gradually replacing the horse and the iron-shod wooden wheel. From off the sealed surfaces, laid to keep down dust, rainwater drained quickly into the river, causing it to rise and fall swiftly, and so to scour the gravel-beds which were the homes of the creepers and nymphs on which the trout fed. In addition to this disturbance, deadly tar-acids poisoned the microscopic life—the daphnia and plankton, on which the new-hatched trout fry fed.

After some years, and much endeavour to remedy injustice, deadly tar was replaced by harmless bitumen as a stone-binding surface; but by then increased drainage had caused other pollution. The fish found little on which to feed, for the gravelly bottom was silted, and most of the nymphs and other delicate water-life that can exist only in pure water had vanished. Lacking natural food, the bigger fish became cannibals, before slow starvation came upon them. A few were to be seen day after day in the same places, growing leaner and blacker, until they disappeared; only the occasional ring of a small rising fish broke the smooth flow of the water in the clear light of morning and the mellow dusk of a mid-summer evening. No mayflies arose and danced over the pools, no dark sedgeflies sped and whirled over the runs at night. The silt absorbed oxygen faster than the stream could replace it from the air in bubbles broken by every fall and run and jabble and stony shallow.

In vain the unhappy owner took legal action, pleading that the chronic pollution contravened the Rivers Pollution Act and the Public Health Acts. In vain samples of river-water were taken, in the presence of witnesses, and put into bottles which were then sealed, before being analysed and chemists' reports offered as evidence in courts of law. Technically pollution in some cases was proved, but no damages were awarded. The pollution continued as before; it was cheaper for the offending factories to face further summonses for pollution than to spend money to install filter beds and tanks.

With the building of more houses the pollution increased; but the owner did not lose heart. Little dams of tree-trunks were made, in the hope that high-water winter spates would cause turbulence to sweep away the deadly silt. In spring new water-plants were introduced, in the hope that while growing in sunlight they might absorb the noxious carbon dioxide gas, and release the oxygen which was the life of the stream, by which all things breathed. More trout were turned into the water.

The Hawton estate, once of flourishing farms held by a sturdy tenantry maintaining the fertility of the soil and looking to the squire for leadership in all things, had likewise declined. Agricultural depression, caused by importation of cheap foreign food, had been interrupted by wars which at base were trade wars. Every death in the family succession meant that a large sum had to be found to pay the death-duties to a government which was composed almost exclusively of those serving and served by the trading interests. Death-duties could be met only by the sale of farm-lands.

When all the land had of necessity been sold off, only the park and mansion remained. Further taxation caused the park and its splendid timber to be sold. A syndicate of speculators interested only in making money bought the park and sold the trees to a timber-merchant, who forthwith felled them and dragged the trunks away. A milk-canning factory was built where the old grist-mill had stood by the stream; its effluents finally killed the last of the weary trout. A gas-works did the rest. Birds forsook the banks; the last king-fisher flashed across the bends in the meadow, the last heron flapped away from water which even eels had left.

Rows of box-like houses, built of concrete, with asbestos roofs, grew where once fallow-deer had grazed. Modernity had come right up to the walls of the Hall.

A fence of galvanized wire set with concrete posts, and a macrocarpa hedge growing rapidly, as though with wild desire to hide with its greenery the change without, enclosed the unpainted mansion and its four acres of gardens, which were too costly to keep up. Slowly a wilderness of weeds arose there, until the Council rented the gardens for a nominal sum as allotments for whomsoever in South Dulton wanted an allotment. That was in the 'thirties, when the money value of English land was lower than it had been for nearly two centuries.

7

The better to inspect the photographs every morning, Mrs. Houghton-Hawton polished the lenses of her spectacles on a piece of silk which had lived in its special ivory box on the chimney-piece of the music-room for nearly thirty years. The constant friction against glass, gentle though it had been, had so worn the silk, that it looked as if it were begetting its life anew from the silkworm. In her care of that piece of silk, in her fidelity to it, might be seen the source of the old woman's fortitude to conserve what was left, after the ruin of another war, for her great-grandson.

The fragment of silk had been part of a white shining strength that swung a man slowly to earth, below the observation balloon from which he had jumped at a telephone-message of "Hun Over!" from the group frenziedly winding in the hauling-gear below; and having jumped and tugged at the release-cord, he had been pulled up with a jerk and flung about, knowing while he swung upon the wild beats of his heart that he was safe. The wind was taking him away from the slanting cable of the balloon. His fellow-observer had jumped after him, and was two hundred feet above, between himself and the balloon. Then the skirl and crack of shrapnel was joined by the hiss and clack of machine-gun bullets from above and below. He watched the vague smoky line of tracers passing diagonally by the balloon, surely through it: and yes, there was a slow curl of flame from its top. Then he saw the Hun, an Albatross, make an Immelmann turn, only to dive away to hedge-hop back to Hunland; and looking up, he saw two Sopwith Camels following the Hun down, and shooting at him. The bullets passed near; the *claquement* made his ears ring and sing, until a sudden terrific shock made him feel himself to be very far away, as he swung gently under the parachute, so gently that the sensation of swinging changed to one of gliding, then to a rippling as of the surface of a river.

As he listened, he could hear under the gentle noises of the stream on the gravelly shallows, the singing of the water-ouzel. He saw the little sturdy black and white bird perching on a mossy stone at the tail of the pool where the water ran clear and fast. He saw his father beside him, and felt the excitement of tying a dry-fly for the first time. He saw the spinners of the live duns rising and falling over the stream in the June evening. He saw the females descending to drop the eggs from their long whisks into the water. He heard the sip-sucking noises of trout invisible in the fast runs, as imperceptibly they thrust up their nebs while sucking in the spent flies. He saw himself crouching beside his father on the edge of the gravel under the bank, and heard his reassuring "You'll get him, take your time, be easy." He felt clumsy. The fly would catch in the alders in front, or in the thistles on the meadow behind. He was nervous because Father was there, and as in a dream he drew out line while working the rod to and fro until the tiny hackled fly was passing overhead, and as he measured the distance to the rising trout with his eye, he felt himself suddenly to be his father, and then he was casting exactly as Father did. He shot his line and tapered cast and brown hackled fly out straight and light; the fly dropped almost dreamily on the quiet bubble-riding water beside the mossy stone where the trout lay. The fly fell lightly, and rode down beside a bubble; the neb of a fish arose and quietly sucked in the fly; a light jerk of his wrist, and the tiny hook was driven into the corner of the trout's mouth. The fish dashed downstream, the rod bent, the fish leapt shaking its head, and he saw the red spots on its golden-brown length. Careful lest it break away, for the last two links of the cast were single horsehair!

He played the trout for at least five minutes, before it turned on its side, dead-beat. His first fish! Quick, the spring-balance, before it lost weight by drying! Father had never got a trout of more than eight ounces that season! It looked so beautiful, he wanted to put it back into the river; but when it flapped nearer the edge of the grassy bank he grabbed it in alarm. As he was working the hook from the bony mouth, the hook suddenly grew very big and fixed itself in his own mouth, attached to a monstrous line which tore at his jaw. He cried out for Father, but Father was gone. He could not find Father. He cried out: "Mother!" for the river was roaring. It was swelling and turning red. The line dragged violently at his head—so terribly violently that he was dragged farther and farther from himself, until at last something snapped, and after that everything was dim and unsubstantial, and fading into vacancy.

From below they watched the cable whipping and coiling on the ground, dragging down in a smoking tangle of rope and wicker basket the body of the observer and his torn parachute. Later they sent to his mother, together with his personal belongings, a piece of the silk, and a photograph of his grave at Ervillers.

That had been in 1917. Since then there had been another grave, in the desert of North Africa. But there was also another Nigel, just home from school for the Easter holidays, and eager to catch his first fish. All the eldest Hawton sons, back to the Tudors and beyond, had borne the name of Nigel.

But where could Nigel fish? Grannie had been worrying about it; and in the end had remembered Mr. Jones, who once had mentioned something about the free fishing below the London road.

8

Mr. Jones was known as a taxi-driver. This was a misnomer in some respect, for Mr. Jones's motorcar was not fitted with a taximeter, and it was, moreover, a Rolls-Royce, licensed to carry six passengers, certainly, but—well, no more need be said, except that the Silver Ghost chassis dated from 1914, and that its first owner had been the châtelaine of Hawton Hall.

The present owner-driver of the elderly motorcar was by name Jones; but he was prepared to resent anyone calling him by that name, especially any old die-hard Tory. Most of his fares called him either nothing, or Mr. Jones, or Charley; but Jones, he wouldn't have any of that, especially from any old geezer who never spent more than a couple of quid a year with him!

To the South Dulton free-fishing went Mrs. Hawton and her great-grandson Nigel on the second day of the Easter holidays. They arrived in Mr. Jones's motor. After the rather long business of the old lady removing herself, with the aid of her ebony walking-stick, from the back of the landau, the two began to move towards the bank. Mr. Jones walked behind them, carrying, at Mrs. Hawton's request, the tea-basket, Mr. Nigel's rod, and a landing net.

Mr. Jones (who was not, it need hardly be said, a native of South Dulton, but a comparatively recent immigrant) thought, as he puffed at his fag, that he didn't mind carrying the rod to oblige the dame, but, as far as he was concerned, he wasn't going to Mister no blooming boy, or man either for that matter.

The party of three stopped by the river-bank. The water ran clear over stones with sandy scours at the eddies, for the outfall of the sewage plant was below, hidden by trees. Unspeaking, with a faint smile, the driver handed the hollow bamboo rod-case to the boy.

"I say, Gran, this *is* the Palakoma split-cane that Daddy killed his first fish with, isn't it? It's wizard! Look, it's a hexagon pattern,

Mr. Jones! They're awfully hard to get now. Bayley-Martin at school says it's the best rod for small streams in the world!"

Pleased with the way he had been addressed, Mr. Jones watched the eager fingers attaching the reel, and drawing out line to pass it through the rings. Despite the rubbing with paraffin-wax and wash-leather, the line was tacky with age, and seemed reluctant to leave the spool.

"Now I believe I ought to have kept it on the line-drier!" the old lady remarked, watching the boy's actions intently through her lorgnette. "I recollect your grandfather always kept his lines between the pages of a copy of *The Times* every year, until the season opened again. I do hope you will find the flies of use, my dear. I don't suppose the change of fashion in flies is so marked as in other things." Her voice quavered a little; she was lost awhile; but recovered herself, and saw the boy before her once again.

The boy and the man were examining the several variegated objects in their little compartments, each with its minute hinged mica lid that flipped open at a touch.

"Now I wonder which flies you should use?" the frail voice enquired, with careful distinctiveness of tone. "Your grandfather was always saying something about wet-flies and dry-flies. Now what is the difference, I wonder?"

"Bayley-Martin always swears by the dry-fly, Gran. He says he's a dry-fly purist, and would never think of fishing wet."

As a fact, the fourteen-year-old boy referred to as a dry-fly purist had never caught any fish bigger than a salmon-parr, that voracious six-inch snap-all-that-floats-and-swims fish looking like a trout but with dark fingerprints on its side; and his fishing had been confined to the moorland stream of his Cumberland home; but Bayley-Martin was a great reader, and lived mainly in the imagination.

"A pity Bayley-Martin isn't here," observed Mr. Jones. "Myself, I'm a worm poorist. None of this whipping water for me. When the river's in flood, and muddy, that's the time to yank 'em out."

"Don't you think that as at the moment the water has the appearance of what used to be described as gin-clear," remarked the old lady, "it might be as well to try a dry-fly?"

"Well, others may be a better judge o' gin than what I be," retorted the driver, looking up at the sky, and wishing that his pals in the Ring of Bells could hear him.

"Now will you please be so good as to tell Mr. Nigel which are the dry-flies, and which are the wet, Mr. Jones?"

Mr. Jones was so relieved at the obvious respect shown to himself that he replied earnestly: "I'm sorry I don't know, ma'am. But mebbe one's so good as another. To tell you the honest truth, ma'am, I've watched them as knows putting on a fly and taking it off again, and trying others, and when they weren't no good, whipping 'em off again and picking out another, quizzing it, and putting it back, sticking it into their hat until they look like a fly-paper. Never satisfied, is a fly-fisherman. I don't wonder, either, when you come to think of it. All these colours ain't natural. Look at this one—" He dropped a minute and delicate affair of red and green peacock-feather, silk, varnish, and steel into his palm and held it out. "What fish is going to recognize that as anything he's seen before? And this —what natural fly, in a manner o' speaking, has two white wings and a lot of ginger whiskers growing out of its body?" He turned to the boy. "See? I ask you! But a worm's a worm all the world over, and the natural food of a fish, if you see my meaning."

Nigel, conscious of his school motto *Manners makyth man*, smiled pleasantly. But he thought: A wormer! "I wonder if this fly is meant to represent a worm?" he asked, picking up an object of fluffy cinnamon with a double hook.

Mr. Jones gave it a glance, and said emphatically: "Na-ow! That's an eel fly, for the eel has a double lock to its jaws, and can wriggle out o' one hook, but never two."

Nigel thought this an odd explanation, for according to the coloured plates in his book it was a Scottish loch-fly for big trout.

"I should try this one, if I were you," advised Mr. Jones, picking up a mayfly. "It's a juicy mouthful." As he spoke the stub of a cigarette was wagging about on his lower lip.

"Yes, Nigel," said Mrs. Houghton-Hawton, "I am sure that Mr. Jones is right about the choice of fly being not of the greatest importance. Your grandfather used to say, I remember, that to fish with a fly you believe in, is nine-tenths of the way to persuading a fish to believe in it also."

"How about this red and green joker?" asked Mr. Jones. "Here, give us the gut."

"I say, thank you so much, but I can tie it on," assured the boy, struggling to conceal his anxiety. "I know the turle knot—Bayley-Martin swears that's the best."

"I've nearly done it now," said the driver.

"Thank you," replied Nigel, politely, while his lip trembled.

"There you are, my lad," exclaimed Mr. Jones, flipping the fly away on the gut leader with his finger and thumb. At the same time he loosened the cigarette from his lower lip and neatly using an expulsion of air compressed within his cheeks flipped the stub into the river. At that moment a salmon rolled up to the top of the pool, showed a yellow-grey blue as it turned, and went under again. "There, did you see that, Nigel?" he cried, pointing to the water. "A bloomin' great fish come up and nosed it! Quick, chuck your fly in the same place!"

"I saw it, Gran, a salmon!" cried the boy. He dropped the fly-box in his excitement, and went on his hands and knees to seek the flies which had shot out of some of the compartments. "Oh, curse, just my luck."

"Here, try this white-winged thing," suggested Mr. Jones. "After all, my fag-end was white."

"Yes, why not take Mr. Jones's advice, Nigel? The rise may be over at any moment. I remember your grandfather used to say a rise might begin suddenly, and end as suddenly."

"Some water-whippers use several flies at once," said the driver, when he had tied the red-and-green Alexandra to the end of the cast. "That's your tail-fly. I'll tie white-wings above it." He snapped a length of gut from the cast. "That's all right, don't worry. It'll tie again. Have it hanging like this, see, on a bit by itself. That's called a dropper. One more on top, any one'll do, that's your tickler. Here, you tie it, and I'll find a worm to shove on fur luck." He began kicking up the turf, ceasing as another man came through the gate at the top of the slope, carrying a rod-case in one hand and a net in the other.

"Ah, here's Mr. Ridd," cried Mrs. Houghton-Hawton. "He'll be able to tell us what is the best fly to use, I have no doubt."

Jones abruptly ceased his prospecting for worms, and standing up, stretched his arm, pushed back his driver's cap, yawned, and sought a cigarette. Another old-fashioned codger!

9

Mr. Ridd's respectful pleasure in meeting Mrs. Houghton-Hawton and Master Nigel at the river was genuine. Any eager mental pictures he had had of getting a salmon with his new American stainless steel three-foot rod, using a small bronze Devon spinner on a thread-line of gut-substitute with a Pffleuger spinning-reel, were put aside. This new outfit, given him by an American officer after a day's fishing together, was capable of throwing a minnow weighing an ounce for great distances, and of dropping it within a foot of where he wanted to drop it. With such a rod and reel the American expert had cast well up-river, and worked the minnow downstream in a deadly manner, which had taken several sea-trout and a salmon in one afternoon, while Mr. Ridd had caught nothing. He had received the outfit by post that morning as a parting gift from the American officer, who was going back to the States. All the morning Mr. Ridd had been awaiting one o'clock, for it was the day of South Dulton's early-closing; but now, seeing Mrs. Houghton-Hawton by the river-side, and apprehending her gracious request for advice, Mr. Ridd forgot his ambition in a desire to be of service.

Immediately he declared that the red-and-green silver-bodied Alexandra was no good. It might be all right in Blagdon reservoir near Bristol, but it was useless in the present water. The Coachman was no good, either. All right for the late evening, with its white wings, but not a bit of use during the day. As for the bob-fly goodness gracious, wherever did it come from? A proper Irish sea-trout lough lure—a Parson Hughes it looked like, or it might be a Fiery Forbes, or even a local variation of Grouse and Claret. Off it came. What he would recommend was one or another of the Pale Wateries.

Finally Mr. Ridd selected a Blue Upright, a Cow Dung, and a Coch-y-Bondhu, which he pronounced Cocky Bundy, for the bob-fly. A Cocky Bundy, he explained, was a Welsh beetle found near bracken, and was a killing fly all the year. You couldn't beat a Cocky Bundy.

"I bet it don't beat a worm," remarked Mr. Jones.

"Mr. Jones has a single-minded faith in worms," said the old lady, and Mr. Ridd nodded politely in agreement. He, too, fished the worm in coloured water; it was catch-as-catch-can on the Free Fishing.

The flies having been tied, Mr. Ridd suggested that Master Nigel should kneel on the bank, lest the fish see him or the flash of his rod. Would madam kindly step back with him and Mr. Jones?

They retired, and the boy, praying that his nervousness would not be noticed, began to cast. He waved his arm from the shoulder, forgetting the instructions of Bayley-Martin.

"Keep that elbow well into your side, sir!" cried Mr. Ridd.

"You'll excuse me telling of him, ma'am? Imagine you're holding a whisky bottle under your arm, and use the wrist only, with the spring of the rod." Then, an awful thought of what he had said occurring to him, he turned to Mrs. Houghton-Hawton, stammering: "No particular reference intended, ma'am, about the whisky bottle. Really, ma'am, it's just the usual advice to the tyro, if you understand my meaning, ma'am."

"I think Mr. Nigel will understand, Mr. Ridd. He comes of a family of fly-fishermen."

"Of course, ma'am. And if you'll pardon the remark, ma'am, but I sincerely hope that the photograph of his first trout will be took this very day."

Just as he had spoken, the boy leapt up: he struck violently in his excitement; there was a glint in the air with the backward flinging of the line: a small fish leaping on the grass.

"A proper trout," was Mr. Ridd's verdict. "Three ounces, a sizeable fish. Well over the seven-inch limit."

The boy's hand trembled as he worked the hook from the prickly tongue, afterwards breaking the fish's neck. "Oh, Gran, aren't the red spots lovely? I say, I'm a fool to have struck so hard, but it was so unexpected. I'll leave it here with you. I mustn't lose any time, now the rise is on, must I? I say, if only Bayley-Martin were here!"

During the rest of the afternoon Mr. Jones resigned himself to the incurable obstinacy of some people who wouldn't learn that a worm was the natural food of a trout. A fluke, that solitary sprat of Nigel's. Old Ridd got nothing, neither, for all his talk of invisible line and minnows coming downstream so fast that no trout could resist having a bash at it. Call that fishing? Whipping water, that's what it was, he thought, as he drove them home in the high-bodied 1914 Rolls-Royce landau which once had belonged to Hawton Hall.

10

Having helped Gran from the car, Nigel rushed away on a most important mission. In the kitchen he explained to Mrs Bowden that the fish must be cooked for Gran's dinner. Cook said that she would fry it in olive-oil before the plaice, and she would serve it with a slip of lemon—that was the way the Captain best liked a trout done. "Leave it to me, dearie, I'll make it—hullo, there's her royal highness calling me." Mrs. Bowden shuffled away, to return a short while afterwards, saying that she wasn't sure if there was such a thing as a bottle of beer in the pantry.

In the hall stood Mr. Jones, cap in hand, fag-end pinched out and stuck behind his ear, and an expression of anxious friendliness on his face, as he listened to Mrs. Houghton-Hawton saying to the boy: "You'd like to ask Mr. Jones to have some beer, wouldn't you, darling? He was a most helpful ghillie, wasn't he? I'm sure his selection of flies would have been as suitable as any other selection. Thank you, Bowden, may we have it on the table? Please help yourself, Mr. Jones."

While Mr. Jones was absorbing the gassy bottled beer as swiftly as he could in order to get away, Grannie called Nigel into the library, and behind the door entirely concealed by rows of dummy books bound in calf she put half-a-crown into his hand. "One should tip one's ghillie, don't you think, darling? When he goes. I won't look, then he will think it's your own idea. Just say, 'Jones, thank you for your help'. Perhaps if you called him Mr. Jones he might be offended. Ghillies are most particular about such things, dear."

"Yes, Gran," said Nigel.

The old lady had the satisfaction of observing her grandson performing this rite, and of hearing the words: "Thank you, I'm sure, Master Nigel, sir."

Grannie produced the line-drier, and the boy carefully wound the sticky, ruined line upon it. Afterwards he went to his bedroom to examine a shelf of books that had been saved specially for him when the library had been sold to help pay death-duties when his father had been killed in 1941. He was reading a little book called *The Art of Trout Fishing on Rapid Streams; comprising a Complete System of Fishing in North Devon Streams, and their Like: with detailed instructions in the Art of Fishing with the Artificial Fly, the Natural Fly, the Fern Web, Beetle, Maggot, Worm, and Minnow, both Natural and Artificial*, when the dressing gong sounded. As he went upstairs to put on his dark-blue suit he remembered something suddenly; and the thought struck through him with almost a physical blow. He ran down the stairs shouting: "Oh, Grannie, Grannie, we forgot to take the photograph! Grannie, the photograph! Quick, quick!"

He leapt down the last flight of stairs two and three at a time, lost count in his agitation, fell over the last four steps, picked himself up in desperate haste on the tessellated white-and-black floor of the hall, and dashed down a corridor into the kitchen. Even his haste did not prevent him pausing a moment to knock on the door before opening it. "Oh, Mrs. Bowden! Quick! The photograph! Where's my trout, quick! Oh, it's cooked, it's cooked," he cried, and ran out of the kitchen again. Biting his lip against the tears that would not be stopped, he hid himself in a dark corner for a moment. Then, hearing Grannie's voice calling him, he went to find her, trying hard to smile and to suppress his sobs.

"But, darling, it isn't too late to take a photograph—there's still a little sunshine left," said Grannie in her tremulous tones, as she stroked his head. "And think how original a photograph it will be, with you holding your first trout, all ready cooked on a plate! I don't suppose Bayley-Martin has thought of that. Now put your rod together, and Bowden, who has a very steady hand, shall take the photograph, just where the others were taken. Perhaps two photographs, in case one goes wrong."

So it was done, and everything was happy again.

II

Visitors to Hawton Hall now see the photographs of five generations of fly-fishermen in the big silver frame on the piano in the music-room; and when they ask about Nigel Hawton, they are told that he is in New Zealand, where he is working on a farm, and where the trout, he writes, are simply monsters, the finest in the world. Mrs. Houghton-Hawton (of Hawton), who will be a hundred years old next year, is living for the moment when she will see again the son of her dear boy's son, and perhaps *his* little boy; and then she is lost in memories centred on the photographs in the silver frame which faces the river, and the sunset which she awaits with trust and serenity.

The Heller

In March the high spring-tides lap with their ragged and undulating riband of flotsam the grasses near the top of the sea-wall; and once in a score of years the south-west gale piles the sea in the estuary so high that it lops over the bank and rushes down to the reclaimed grazing marsh within. The land-locked water returns on the ebb by way of the reedy dykes, through the culverts under the wall with their one-way hinged wooden doors, and by muddy channels to the sea again.

I was unfortunate enough to miss seeing such a flood following the Great Gale, when many big trees, most of them elms but not a few beech and oak, went down; but hearing of it, I went down to the marsh the next afternoon before the time of high tide, hoping to see the water brimming over again. I wandered along the sea-wall, where the hoof-holed path of clay still held sea-water, as far as the black hospital ship *Nyphen*, and then I returned. The gale had blown itself out, a blue sky lay beyond Hartland Point, far out over the calm Atlantic.

There is a slanting path leading to the road below by the marsh-man's cottage, and by this I left the wide prospect seen from the sea-wall. While descending I noticed that the grasses down the inner slope were washed flat and straggly by the heavy overflooding of the day before.

The marshman was standing in the porch of the cottage, looking at his ducklings which had hatched about a fortnight since. He wore his spectacles and had a book in his hands. We greeted each other, and I stopped to talk.

I always enjoyed talking with the marshman. His face pleased me. I liked his kind brown eyes, his grey hair, his small and intelligent sea-brown face. His dog had recently been kicked by a bullock, and had a broken leg which the marshman had set with a wooden splint. This knocked on the ground as the dog trotted about with apparent ease. The marshman was a skilful man: I remembered how he had saved the life of a sheep the year before, when it was staggering crazily, because, said the marshman, it had a worm in its brain. The marshman had held the sheep's head between his knees, cut a hole in its skull with a knife, and drawn out the tapeworm by suction through a quill cut from the pinion feather of a goose. It was an even chance, for most sheep so afflicted have to be destroyed. This ewe got well, and—but the story is about the mysterious loss of the marshman's ducklings, not of mutton.

In a soft voice he began telling me about the book in his hands, which he said was "wonderful and most interesting". It was thick, and heavy, and printed in small, close-set type. It was *The History of the Jews*, and the marshman had been reading it with the same care and patience with which, year after year, he had cut the reeds in the dykes, and scythed the thistles in the rank grass. For years he had been reading that book, and he had not yet reached the middle pages.

Would I like to take the book home with me and have a read of it? He was a bit busy just now and could easily spare it for a day or two. I was quite welcome to take it, if . . .

2

I was saved from a reply by the sudden change in the marshman's face. He was staring intently beyond the gate by which we stood. His spectacles were pushed back from his eyes. I looked in the direction of his stare, and saw the usual scene—fowls on the stony and feathery road, and a couple of pigs nosing among them; the down-hanging branches of the willow tree over the dyke; the green pointed leaves of the flag-iris rising thickly along both banks; the sky-gleams between them. On the water a brood of yellowish-white ducklings were paddling, watched anxiously from the road by the hen that had hatched them.

"The heller!"

At the muttered angry words the marshman's dog, which had assumed a stiff attitude from the moment of his master's fixed interest in something as yet unsmelled, unseen, and unheard by itself, whined and crouched and sprang over the gate. It had gone a few yards, sending the hens clucking and flying in all directions, when the marshman shouted. Seeing its master's arm flung to the left, the dog promptly turned in that direction. I saw its hackles rise. The narrow dyke, which brought fresh drinking water to the grazing marsh, was crossed under the willow tree by a clammer, or single heavy plank of elm-wood. As the dog ran on to the clammer I saw something at the farther end slide into the water. I had a fleeting impression of the vanishing hindquarters of a squat and slender dog, dark brown as a bulrush, and with the palms of its feet widely webbed as a duck's. It had a long tail, tapering to a point. The brown tail slid over the plank flatly yet swiftly, and disappeared without splash into the slight ripple made by the submerging animal.

" 'Tis that darned old mousy-coloured fitch," grumbled the marshman opening the gate. "It be after my ducklings. It took one just about this time yesterday. Yurr, Ship!"—to the dog. "Fetch un, Ship!" The dog sprang around barking raucously, and trotted along the plank again, nose between paws, and whining with excitement where the otter had stood. Then it looked at its master and barked at the water.

While it was barking the ducklings, about fifteen yards away, began to run on the water, beating their little flukey stumps of wings and stretching out their necks. *Queep! Queep! Queep!* they cried. The foster-hen on the bank was clucking and jerking her comb about in agitation.

"Ah, you heller, you!" cried the marshman, as a duckling was drawn under by invisible jaws. The other ducklings waddled out by the brimming edge of the road, and made for the hen in two files of uniform and tiny yellowish bodies aslant with straining to reach the cover of wings. Very red and jerky about the comb and cheek-pendules, with flickering eyes, this motherly fowl squatted on the stones and lowered her wings till they rested on her useless pinion shafts, and fluffed out her feathers to make room for the eight mites which, in spite of her constant calls and entreaties, would persist in walking on that cold and unwalkable place, which was only for sipping-from at the edge.

Peep peep peep, quip pip queep weep, whistled the ducklings drowsily, in their sweet and feeble voices.

The marshman came out of the cottage with a gun.

"The heller!" he said. "The withering beast, it ought to be kicked to flames!"

He waited five minutes, watching the water where the duckling had gone down.

Parallel lines of ripples, wavering with infirm and milk-white sky, rode along the brimming water. The tide was still rising. Twenty yards away the young strong leaves of the flag-irises began to quiver. We waited. The *peep-peeps* of the happy ducklings ceased.

Water began to run, in sudden starts, around the smoothed stones in the roadway. The tide was rising fast. A feather was carried twirling on a runnel that stopped by my left toe; and after a pause it ran on a few inches, leaving dry specks of dust and bud-sheaths tacked to the welt.

The outline of the dyke was lost in the overbrimming of the water. Grasses began to float and stray at its edges. The runnels curiously explored the least hollow; running forward, pausing, turning sideways or backwards, and blending, as though gladly, with one another.

3

"It be gone," said the marshman, lowering the gun, to my relief, for its double barrels had been near my cheek, and they were rusty, thin as an egg-shell at the muzzle, and loaded with an assortment of broken screw-heads, nuts, and odd bits of iron. He was as economical with his shooting as he was with his reading. Originally the gun had been a flintlock, owned by his great-grandfather; and his father had had it converted into a percussion cap. Its walnut stock was riddled with worm-holes; and even as I was examining it, I heard the sound like the ticking of a watch, which ceased after nine ticks. The death-watch beetle. It was doubtful which would go first—the stock "falling abroad" in its tunnelled brittleness, or the barrels bursting from frail old-age.

"It's a high spring tide," I said, stepping farther back. "I suppose the otter came up on it, and down the dyke?"

Then the marshman told me about the 'heller'. We stood with our backs to the deep and ancient thorn hedge that borders the road to the east, a hedge double-sheared by wind and man, six feet high and eight feet thick and so matted that a man could walk along it without his boots sinking. It was grey and gold with lichens. I had always admired the hedge by the marsh toll-gate. I leaned gingerly against it while the marshman told me that he had seen the otter on the two afternoons previously, and both times when the tide was nearly on the top of the flood. No, it did not come up the dyke; it was a bold beast, and came over the sea-wall, where the tide had poured over two afternoons ago. "My wife zeed'n running over the wall, like a little brown dog. I reckon myself th' heller comes from the duckponds over in Heanton marsh, and sleeps by day in th' daggers, or goin' on up to the pillhead, and over the basin of the weir into fresh water, after trout. Never before have I heard tell of an otter going time after time, and by day, too, after the same ducklings."

I was listening intently. Was that a low, flute-like whistle . . . ?

" 'Tis most unusual, zur, for an artter will always take fish when he can get fish, eels particularly, and there be plenty of eels all over the marsh. An artter loveth an eel; 'tis its most natural food, in a manner of speaking. 'Tis what is called an ambulance baste, the artter be, yes 'tis like a crab, that can live in both land and water, a proper ambulance baste it be. A most interestin' baste, for those that possess th' education vor to study up all that sort of thing. Now can 'ee tell me how an artter serves an eel different from another fish? Other fish, leastways those I've zin with my own eyes, are ate head downwards; but an eel be ate tail virst, and the head and shoulders be left. I've a' zin scores of eels, and all ate tail virst!"

While the old fellow was speaking, the water in irregular pourings and innocent swirls was stealing right across the road. It reached the hen, who, to judge from the downward pose of her head, regarded it as a nuisance. A runnel slipped stealthily between her cane-coloured feet, wetting the claws worn with faithful scratching for the young. She arose, and strutted away in the lee of the hedge, calling her brood; and *Wock! Wock! Wet!* she cried, for with tiny notes of glee the ducklings had headed straight for the wide water gleaming with the early sunset.

The marshman said, "Darn the flood!" for *The History of the Jews*, container of future years' laborious pleasure, lay in a plash by the gate ten strides away. He picked it up, regarding ruefully the dripping cover. He was saying that it wasn't no odds, a bit of damp on the outside, when I noticed a small travelling ripple in the shape of an arrow moving out from the plank now almost awash. It continued steadily for about three yards from the plank, and then the arrow-head ceased to push. Ripples spread out slowly, and beyond the ripples a line of bubbles like shot began to rise and lie still. The line, increasing steadily by lengths varying from two or three to a dozen inches, drew out towards the ducklings.

I took long strides forward beside the marshman. Our footfalls splashed in the shallow water. The dog trotted at his heels, quivering, its ears cocked. A swirl arose in the leat and rocked the ducklings; they cried and struck out for the grass, but one stayed still, trying to rise on weeny wings, and then it went under.

"The *heller*!" cried the marshman, raising his gun.

For about twenty seconds we waited.

A brown whiskered head, flat and seal-like, with short rough hairs and beady black eyes, looked out of the water. *Bang!* It dived at the flash, and although we peered and waited for at least a minute after the whining of a screw-head ricocheting away over the marsh had ceased, I saw only our spectral faces shaking the water.

4

The next afternoon I went down by the eastern sea-wall, and lay on the flat grassy ridge, with a view of the lower end of the Ram's-horn duckpond. Wildfowl were flying round the marsh and settling on the open water hidden between thick green reeds. Many scores had their nests in the preserve. Why did the otter, I wondered, come all the way to the dyke when it could take all the ducklings it wanted in the pond? Perhaps in my reasoning I was falling into the old error of ascribing to a wild beast something of human reasoning; for had I been an otter after ducklings I should certainly have stayed where they were most numerous.

The tide flowed past me, with its usual straggle of froth covering the flotsam of corks, bottles, clinker, spruce-bark from the Bideford shipyards, tins, cabbage leaves, and sticks. Two ketches rode up on the flood, the exhausts of their oil engines echoing with hollow thuds over mud and water. I wondered why they were wasting oil, when the current was so swift to carry them; but when they made fast to their mooring buoys, and the bows swung round, I realized the use of the engines—to keep them head-on in the fairway. Of course! Gulls screamed as they floated around the masts and cordage of the black craft, awaiting the dumping overboard of garbage. I waited for an hour, but saw nothing of the otter.

"Did ee see'n?" asked the marshman when I went back. His gun lay on the table, and Ship the dog was crouched on the threshold, nose on paws pointing to the clammer bridge over the dyke.

"He's took another duckling," growled the man.

The otter must have made an early crossing while I was lazing on the bank. Perhaps he had come through a culvert, squeezing past the sodden wooden trap; and then, either seeing or winding me, had crossed under water. The marshman, happening to come to the door, had seen the duckling going under, and although he had waited for ten minutes, nothing had come up.

"Ship here went nosing among the daggers, but couldn't even get wind of'n. I reckon that ambulance baste can lie on the bottom and go to sleep if it has a mind to."

By ambulance he meant amphibious, I imagined. An otter has no gills; it breathes in the ordinary way, being an animal that has learned to swim and hunt under water.

"Didn't you see even a bubble?"

"Not one!"

It seemed strange. Also, it had seemed strange that the engines of the ketches were 'wasting' oil. That had a perfectly ordinary explanation . . . when one realized it!

"And it took a duck in just the same way as before?"

"That's it! In a wink, that duck went down under."

"But didn't the ducklings see the otter?"

"Noomye! The poor li'l butie was took quick as a wink." He was much upset by it.

"Now I'll tell ee what I'll do," he said. "I'll till a gin for a rat, I will, and if I trap an artter, will, 'twill be a pity, as the artter-'untin' gentry would say; but there 'tis!"

Otters were not generally trapped in the country of the Taw and Torridge rivers, as most of the riparian owners subscribed to the otter-hounds. There were occasions, however, when a gin was tilled, or set, on a submerged rock where an otter was known to touch, or on a sunken post driven into the river-bed near its holt. About once in a season the pack drew the brackish waters of the Ram's-horn Duck-pond, but an otter was very rarely killed there, as there was impregnable holding among the thick reeds. I looked at the marshman's face, filled with grim thoughts about the heller (had he got the term from *The History of the Jews*?) and remembered how, only the year before, when an otter had been killed near Branton Church, he had confided to me that he didn't care much for "artter'untin'"; that it was "not much sport with all they girt dogs agin one small baste".

"I've got some old rabbit gins," said the marshman. "And I'll till them on the clammer, and get that heller, I will."

I went away to watch the mating flight of the golden plover over the marsh, and the sun had gone down behind the low line of the sandhills to the west, when I returned along the sea-wall. Three rabbit gins—rusty affairs of open iron teeth and flat steel springs ready to snap and hold anything that trod on them—lay on the plank. The marshman had bound lengths of twisted brass rabbit-wire around the plank and through the ends of the chains, so that, dragged into the dyke, the weight of the three gins would drown any struggling otter.

5

My road home lay along the edge of the dyke, which was immediately under the sea-wall. Old upturned boats, rusty anchors, rotting bollards of tree-trunks and other gear lay on the wall and its inner grassy slope. Near the pill-head the brown ribs of a ketch, almost broken up, lay above the wall. I came to the hump where the road goes over the culvert. Leaning on the stone parapet, I watched the fresh water of the river moving with dark eddies under the fender into the dyke, and the overflow tumbling into the concrete basin of the weir and sliding down the short length to the rising tide. It barely rippled. The air was still and clear, bright with eve-star and crescent moon.

The last cart had left the Great Field, the faint cries of lambs arose under the moon, men were all home to their cottages, or playing skittles in the village inns. Resting the weight of my body on the stone, I stared vaguely at the water, thinking how many strange impulses and feelings came helter-skelter out of a man, and how easy it was to judge him falsely by any one act or word. The marshman had pitied a hunted otter; he had raged against a hunting otter; he felt tenderly and protectively towards the ducklings; he would complacently stab their necks when the peas ripened, and sell them for as much money as he could get for them. In the future he would not think otter-hunting a cruel sport. And if the otter-hunters heard that he had trapped and drowned an otter, they would be sincerely upset that it had suffered such a cruel and, as it were, an unfair death. Perhaps the only difference between animal and man was that the animal had fewer notions . . .

I was musing in this idle manner, my thoughts slipping away as water, when I heard a sound somewhere behind me. It was a thin piercing whistle, the cry of an otter. Slowly I moved back my head, till only a part of my face would be visible in silhouette from the water below. I watched for a bubble, a sinuous shadow, an arrowy ripple, a swirl; I certainly did not expect to see a fat old dog-otter come drifting down on his back, swishing with his rudder and bringing it down with great thwacking splashes on the water while he chewed a half-pound trout held in his short paws. My breath ceased; my eyes held from blinking. I had a perfect view of his sturdy body, the yellowish-white patch of fur on his belly below his ribs, his sweeping whiskers, his dark eyes. Still chewing, he bumped head-on into the sill, kicked himself upright, walked on the concrete, and stood there crunching, while the five pools running from his legs and rudder ran into one. He did not chew, as I had read in books of otters chewing; he just stood there on his four legs, the tail-half of the trout sticking out of his mouth, and gulped down the bits. That trout disappeared in about ten seconds. Then the otter leaned down to the water and lapped as a cat does.

He was old, slow, coarse-haired, and about thirty pounds in weight —the biggest otter I had seen, with the broadest head.

After quenching his thirst he put his head and shoulders under water, holding himself from falling in by his stumpy webbed forefeet, and his rudder, eighteen inches long, pressing down straight behind. He was watching for fish. As though any fish remained in the water-flow after that dreaded apparition had come splashing under the culvert!

With the least ripple he slid into the water. I breathed and blinked with relief, but dared not move otherwise. A head looked up almost immediately, and two dark eyes stared at me. The otter sneezed, shook the water out of his small ears, and sank away under. I expected it to be my last sight of the beast, and leaning over to see if an arrowy ripple pointed upstream, I knocked a piece of loose stone off the parapet. To my amazement he came up near the sill again, with something in his mouth. He swung over on his back, and bit it in play. He climbed on to the sill and dropped it there, and slipped back into the water. It was the stone that had dropped from the parapet!

I kept still. The otter reappeared with something white in his mouth. He dropped it with a tinkle beside the stone, and the tinkle must have pleased him, for he picked up the china sherd—it looked like part of a teacup with the handle—and rolled over with it in his paws.

As in other Devon waters, the stream was a pitching place for cottage rubbish; and during the time I was standing by the parapet watching the otter at his play he had collected about a dozen objects —rusty salmon tins, bits of broken glass, sherds of clome pitchers and jamjars, and one-half of a sheep's jaw. He ranged them on the sill of the weir, tapping the more musical with a paw, as a cat does, until they fell into the water, when he would dive for and retrieve them.

6

At the end of about half an hour the sea was lapping over the top of the sill and pressing under the fender. Soon the dyke began to brim. The taste of salt-water must have made the otter hungry again, or perhaps he had been waiting for the tide, for he left his playthings and, dropping into the water, went down the dyke towards the marshman's cottage. I crept stealthily along the grassy border of the road, watching the arrowy ripple gleaming with the silver of the thin curved moon. The hillside under the ruined chapel above the village of Branton began to show yellow speckles of light in distant houses. The dyke being deserted (for the brood of ducklings with their hen had been shut up for the night) why then that sudden swirl and commotion in the water by the flag-irises, just where the ducklings had been taken before?

Bubbles broke on the water in strings—big bubbles. Then something heaved glimmering out of the leat, flapping and splashing violently. The noises ceased, and more bubbles came up; the water rocked. Suddenly the splashing increased, and seemed to be moving up and down the leat, breaking the surface of the water. Splashes wetted my face. A considerable struggle was going on there. After a minute there was a new noise—the noise of sappy stalks of the flags being broken. Slap, slap, slap, on the water. I saw streaks and spots of phosphorescence or moon-gleams by the end of the plank. The flapping went on in the meadow beyond the flags, with a sound of biting.

I stood without moving for some minutes, while the biting and squirming went on steadily. My shoes filled with water. The water had spread silently half across the road. Then the noises ceased. I heard a dull rap, as of something striking the heavy wooden plank under water; a strange noise of blowing, a jangle of iron and a heavy splash, and many bubbles and faint knocking sounds. The otter had stepped on the plank to drink, and was trapped.

At last the marshman, having closed *The History of the Jews*, placed his spectacles in their case, drawn on his boots, put on his coat, taken his gun off the nails on the ceiling beam, put it back for a fluke-spearing pronged fork in the corner, lit the hurricane lamp, said with grim triumph, "Now us will go vor to see something!" He was highly pleased that he had outwitted the otter.

"There be no hurry, midear," he said. "Give'n plenty of time vor to see the water for the last occasion in his skin."

We stood for a while by the clammer, under the dark and softly shivering leaves of the willow looming over us in the lamplight.

The water had receded from the plank when the last feeble tug came along the brass wire.

The marshman, watched by his dog hopping round and round on its wooden leg in immense excitement, pulled up the bundle of gins, and the sagging beast held to them by a forepaw. It was quite dead; but the marshman decided to leave it there all night, to make certain.

"I see in the paper," he said, "that a chap up to Lunnon be giving good money for the best artter skins"—tapping the spearing handle significantly with his hand.

When it had been dropped in the water again we went a few paces into the meadow with the lamp, and by its light we saw a conger eel, thick through as a man's arm, lying in the grass. The dark living sinuousness was gone from it; and stooping, we saw that it had been bitten through the tail. Suddenly I thought it must have come with the high spring-tide over the seawall; and soon afterwards, the keen-nosed otter, following eagerly the scent where it had squirmed and writhed its way in the grass. The conger had stayed in the dyke, hiding in a drain by the flag-irises, and coming out when the colder salt-water had drifted down.

The marshman carried it back to to his cottage, and cut it open, and then stared into my face with amazement and sadness, for within the great eel were the remains of his ducklings.

A Crown of Life

For five centuries Frogstreet farmhouse was thatched, the kitchen floor was cold and damp and uneven with slate slabs, and there was nothing to do on winter nights except to sit round the open hearth, on which all the cooking was done, and which smoked—nothing to do except go to bed, if you were one of the children, and listen to Father's voice mumbling through the floor, the whining of the new puppy shut up in the barn, cows belving for lost calves, the owls hooting in the trees, and the rain dripping from the thatch.

For five centuries the walls and the downstairs floors were damp and the rooms were dark. The yeomen Kiffts worked hard from before sunrise to after sunset during the four seasons; they possessed the lives of their sons, who worked, often beyond middle age, without pay, for their father; they shouted at and kicked their barking cattle-dogs as a matter of course; they thought nothing of beating, with their brass-buckled belts, their unmarried daughters if they stayed out late without permission; they went regularly to church on Sundays; and they died of rheumatism usually before the age of seventy. A small stream ran beside the wall, just below part of the kitchen floor, giving the place its name of Frogstreet.

2

When Clibbit Kifft inherited the property, it already had a mortgage on it, raised by his father because wheat no longer paid, owing to the importation of foreign corn; and Clibbit was forced to raise the second mortgage to pay death duties. Then he married the young woman he had been walking out with ever since his mother had had her second stroke and died. Clibbit Kifft had hated his father, believing that the old man's wickedness had killed his mother. Clibbit had loved his mother dearly.

Clibbit's wife was a large woman, retaining through life the fresh red cheeks and brown wondering eyes which made her prettiness when Clibbit had been courting her. She had been sorry for Clibbit, knowing how, when a boy, his father had thrashed and worked him. His long swinging arms were said to be so loose because of the number of times his father had caught hold of him by the arm and swung him round before hurling him on the kitchen floor. As a young girl, daughter of Vellacott farm, she had pitied the poor young man with the shy and awkward manner. After his mother's death, when they were walking out together, he had never seemed to want to take her in his arms, but always to be clasped and held like a child. He was often querulous and moody for no reason that she could see, liable to leave her suddenly and not come near her again for days.

They walked out during the fall and winter, and when the warmer days came they went among the furze brakes on the coombe side and she was tender to him, and during that spring he was almost happy, often making her laugh with the way he imitated and mocked his father's ways; but when one night she told him they must be wed, Clibbit got into a real rage and shouted just like his father, before breaking into tears with the thought of what his father would do to him now that he would have to find a cottage and work for wages—saying that Father wouldn't have no strange woman about the place.

Father told him to go and never show his face again; but the parson helped Clibbit, giving him two days' work in the rectory garden—that made three shillings a week coming in—and lent him seven shillings to buy a pig. The parson also gave him an old bed and a table with three legs which had been lying for years in the disused rectory stables. Clibbit rented a cottage for fifteen pence a week, and the banns had been read in church—none too soon, said the neighbours—when Clibbit's father died without making a will. Clibbit had been an only child, otherwise the farm would have been sold and lost to the family a generation before it actually passed into the hands of strangers.

3

When Clibbit's fourth child was coming, Clibbit was past thirty, and growing just like his father in every way, said the neighbours; with one exception: the old man had been a limmer, drunk or sober, while Clibbit was sweet as a nut when drunk.

Clibbit's wife and his small children lived in perpetual fear of him. She never knew what he would do next or how he might appear. He might be home on time for his supper, the last meal of the day and eaten about six o'clock, or he might come an hour or two late, and find his plateful put back in the oven. He might eat it in silence; but he was just as likely to mutter that he didn't want no supper, then take it out of the oven, give it a glance, and declare that it was zamzawed (dried up), or not cooked enough, and tip it on the floor for the dog. Whatever he did, his wife would say little, but look at him and then at the silent children with apprehension. This look, and the unnatural stillness of the children, set him off in a proper rage; and as the time for her fourth confinement came nearer so his moodiness and fits of violence increased.

One Sunday's dinner-time he seized the tablecloth and pulled it off the table and set all the things clattering on the floor. He kicked the loaf of bread through the window, where it was sniffed out by the sow and promptly eaten with grateful grunts. After that he neither ate nor spoke for three days, except to reply, once, to his wife's faltered, "Won't 'ee have your dinner, won't 'ee, surenuff? 'Tes no use denying your stummick further," that he couldn't "afford to ait no more meals, what with all the mortgage money vor to be paid next quarter day". On the fourth day of his fast he came home mazed drunk, said the neighbours, who behind window curtains watched him lurching down the street, followed by his Exmoor pony; and they listened at their thresholds for noises following the opening and banging-to of the farmhouse door. Clibbit had had only a half-quartern of whisky, and after eating his supper and saying it tasted proper he slouched about the kitchen, smilingly patting his children's heads, shaking his wife's hand with beaming solemnity before taking off his boots and leggings, and going up over—to sleep exhaustedly in his clothes.

So the years went by. One August his eldest son—who had just left school being fourteen years of age—was sent to the inn for two bottles of beer. Returning with these, the boy jumped down into the field which they were reaping, and the two bottles, one held in each hand, clashed together and were broken. Unfastening the leather belt with the big brass buckle which had been his father's and grandfather's girdle, Clibbit roared out a curse and ran after the boy, pursuing him across half the field, whirling belt in one hand and holding up his breeches with the other. He stopped only because his breeches were slipping down. The boy ran on, and when he disappeared over the skyline, nearly a mile away, he was still running. The village thought this a good tale, and it was laughed over many times during the next few months—the beer bottles knacking together and young Kifft rinning like a stag over the skyline.

The boy never came back, finding a home and work with his uncle at Vellacott Farm.

4

Clibbit Kifft's appearance was remarkable. Village boys called him Oodmall behind his back, but never to his face. They would sometimes dare to jeer when he had gone round the corner riding his short moor pony. The intense wild blueness of his eyes under shaggy brows was instantly noticeable because of the long nose with its crimson tip. He was tall and very thin, a bony animation of long arms and legs in ragged clothes. His ancient cloth cap was so torn by brambles, as he knelt to till his gins and snares for rabbits, that only the lining and half the peak and shreds of cloth were left. Likewise jacket and breeches; and his leather gaiters were almost scratched away by his work.

Passing through the village on the way to one of his fields, riding the shaggy pony bareback so that his great nailed boots on the long legs almost knocked on the road, his sharp-featured head glancing about him from side to side, he appeared to some onlookers to be gazing about him like an oodmall—woodpecker. The rims of his blue eyes were always inflamed and his voice was like the yaffle's. The Adam's apple in his scrawny neck was almost as big as his nose. "Clibbit's throat would cut easy," the hen dealer would remark at cottage doors after one of Clibbit's domestic rages.

The thatch of Frogstreet farmhouse was so old and rotten that docks, nettles, and grass grew out of the clumps of green moss on it. Oat sprays grew every summer, too, near the base of the chimney-stack. The green waving awns of June always pleased Clibbit. " 'Tes ol'-fashion like," he used to say to the rector in his yaffly voice. " 'Tes wonnerful old, thaccy wuts up auver. 'Twas me girt-girt-granfer, I reckon, laid thaccy wut reed up auver, 'cording to the records in the Bible box." Thatch was usually laid with wheat-reed, or unbruised wheaten stalks; oat or barley reed did not last so long as that of wheat. "Aiy, 'tes a wonnerful long time ago, when you come to think of it, Y'r riv'rence. 'Twas a master lot of smut that year, and the whate (wheat) crop was ruined, so they laid wut (oat) reed upalong. November, seventeen-seventy, George the Third's reign, I reckon, zur. A long time ago. Aiy. Wull, us'v all got to go some-time, beggin' riv'rence's pardon."

Everyone in the village liked the parson.

Rain went right through the remains of seven thatchings—the thatch was relaid four or five times every century, and the oat berry which sprouted and started a colony beside the chimneystack of Frogstreet farmhouse must have lain dormant in the roof for more than a hundred and sixty years.

Starlings, sparrows, and swifts made their homes under the eaves of Frogstreet, and every year a pair of martins built a mud nest over the front door, which opened on the road. In summer the stone of the threshold was continually being splashed by the clotted wreckage of flies, as the parent birds cleaned out their nest. Just like Oodmall, said the neighbours, "to be heedless of they dirty birds biding there"; but let it be remembered, now that all the life of that farmhouse is passed away, that Clibbit once said to the parson that the martins were God A'mighty's hens, which he liked to hear twittering there in the morning before he got out of bed.

When at last he was alone; when his three sons had run away, one after another, at school-leaving age; when his wife, whose cheeks were still fresh and eyes candid as a child's despite her experience, had left Frogstreet finally, taking away the four smaller children; when the cows and horses and sheep and the last pig were gone; when the various inspectors of the Royal Society for the Prevention of Cruelty to Children, and the Royal Society for the Prevention of Cruelty to Animals, had paid their last visits; when for years no one in the village except the parson said a good word for the farmer, the martins were still there. It is unlikely that they were the original pair: so many long flights to Africa and back would have worn out those tiny hearts. Let it be thought that, although the old birds were long since dead, the impulse and desire to fly home to the English

spring and the place of their birth was immortal. It lived on in the
younger birds, and when they too were fallen, in their nestlings.

The soft waking twitter-talk of house martins in their nests before
daybreak is one of the sweetest and happiest sounds in the world;
and, although the woodpecker head was often poked out of the window just by their nest, the martins of Frogstreet farm never had
the least fear of it.

5

"Aiy, Clibbit led bide they dirty birds," a village voice declaims,
"but what about the long black pig Clibbit shot?"

"A raving bliddy madman was Clibbit," declares the voice; "a
proper heller, that should have been stringed up long ago."

Yes, Clibbit shot a pig, a long black pig it was, that had been
reared on a bottle by his eldest daughter. A sow died of fever, and
the surviving seven of the farrow of little black pigs were placed in
a basket before the kitchen fire. One of the elderly female cats that
lived about the place attempted to adopt them, with an obvious lack
of success which amused Clibbit greatly. Six of the piglets were
fobbed off on Ship, the grey bitch who drove the cows to and from
milking; her litter of mongrel pups had recently been drowned. She
took to them as gladly as they took to her, and the old cat derived
pleasure from helping Ship wash them. The other piglet was bottle-
fed on cow's milk and afterwards grew to the habit of coming into
the kitchen to see the eldest daughter, who had fed it, and also to
rout for and crunch in its jaws charcoal in the hearth. Clibbit drove
it out with kicks and blows, and the pig learned to be absent whenever it heard his voice or footfalls; but, when, after listening and
staring and snuffing, it thought he was not about, it would walk in
and begin its eager search for charcoal. It so happened that one
evening Mrs. Kifft put back Clibbit's supper on the hearth, and
the animal had just finished a baked rabbit stuffed with sage and
onions, a dozen potatoes, and a score or so of carrots, when Clibbit
walked in. He swore and jerked his head about with rage, while the
frightened animal bolted behind his wife's skirts. "The withering
limmer!" roared Clibbit. "The flaming bliddy hog won't ait no
more zuppers nowhere, noomye! Why didden 'ee stap the bissley
bigger (beastly beggar) aiting vor my supper, you?"

"I didden hear nor see nought!" cried the wife.

"You vexatious li'l loobey, you!" screeched Clibbit. "D'ye mean vor say you didden hear no flaming bones crackin'?"

"I did hear something, surenuff, midear, now you do mention it, but I thought it was only th' ole pig, chimmering 'bout in they cinders, I did." She looked at him, her eyes wide with fright, and the look as usual set him dancing and swinging his arms with rage, while he ground his teeth and hit his head with his fists. Then, seizing the gun from the nails driven into the lime-washed beam across the kitchen ceiling, he whirled it round his head, took aim first at his wife, then at the baby happily gnawing a carrot in the decrepit perambulator in the corner, and finally pulled the trigger when the barrel happened to be pointing at the head of the pig. When the policeman, hastily summoned from sleep and wearing his helmet, with his tunic imperfectly buttoned over his nightshirt, knocked at Frogstreet door and entered to ask sternly what " 't was all 'bout", Clibbit replied that he knew of no law against killing a pig after sunset, and asked if he could sell him a nice li'l bit o' fresh meat.

6

Shortly after the incident of the pig shooting Clibbit was summoned to the Court of Summary Jurisdiction at South Dulton, the charge being cruelty to a cat, "in that he did cause it grievous bodily harm by compelling it to inhabit an improper place, to wit, a copper furnace of boiling water used in the process known as the washing of soiled domestic linen". Clibbit said he was sorry, and he looked it, and the chairman of magistrates, a prominent stag hunter, said he jolly well deserved to be pitched into boiling water himself just to see how he like it. Fined two pounds or a month's imprisonment.

While Clibbit, his small head jerking about like that of a woodpecker starved in frost, was trying to say that he didn't have the money, a voice at the back of the court said, "I should like to pay the fine on behalf of my friend, if he would permit me." It was the village parson.

A woman cried out that such brutes should not be given the option of a fine, but should be flogged, and then be shut away in solitary confinement.

"Order!" cried a voice, while the clerk prepared to read the next charge. Clibbit went out of court, wondering what he should say to his reverence; but the parson was gone. He saw the woman who had cried out; she was waiting for him among a group of friends with blank faces; and she said, "We're going to watch you, let me tell you, and you won't get off so easily next time with your revolting cruelty. We know all about you, so you needn't think we don't!" He did not know what to say, but stood there blinking awhile, smelling of mothball, and jerking his head about, unable to look at any face; then touching his 1894 bowler hat—for he wore his best clothes, which also had been his father's best clothes—he muttered, "Yes, ma'am", and shambled away to where his pony was tied up. He would have liked a drop of whisky, but didn't like to go into any of the pubs lest he be refused.

So he went home and ploughed the three-acre field called Booaze (Blue Haze) until it was dark, having had no food that day. The kitchen was dark, the family in bed. He lit a candle and took down the gun from the beam. He sat down in a chair, the gun across his knees, and tried to cry, but he could not. The poignant mood passed, and he put the gun back, thinking that he would sell the calf next market day and pay back parson.

Clibbit did not sell the calf, nor did he pay back the two pounds fine. He avoided the parson, or rather he avoided the awkward feelings of gratitude and obligation, almost resentment, within himself by keeping out of the rector's way. He was in debt already, for he could not work the farm single-handed, and the fields were poor, the successive corn crops taken off them during the Great War, the land's fertility, not having been put back in the form of bullocks' or sheeps' dung. Farmers at that time were undercut by the importation of cheap foreign food; as a slight relief, they were exempt from paying rates and taxes on their land and farm buildings; but despite this, many small farmers were being sold up, noticeably those who, before the final smash, spent many hours every day at the inns. Weeds grew in their fields unchecked. Ploughs rusted in patches of nettles. Grass grew over and buried the harrows. Sales by Auction increased at Michaelmas and Ladyday quarters; but Clibbit farmed on. He had no other life; and that life was mortgaged.

7

At last Mrs. Kifft made up her mind for good and all, she told the neighbours; her brother at Vellacott had lost his poor wife, and was agreeable to have her live there with the children. All the neighbours watched the departure. Clibbit, after a couple of calls at the inn, helped load the boxes and perambulator on the long-tailed cart.

"What, be goin' vor leave your old feyther?" he squeaked to the baby, also called Clibbit, as Mrs. Kifft turned to give a last sorrowing look at the room, and the broad bed, with its wire mattress like a chain harrow, where her children had been born. Clibbit bent down and wriggled a scarred fore-finger at the blue-eyed baby. He saw the tears in his wife's eyes, and spoke loudly to the baby. The baby smiled at Clibbit. "Proper, proper!" said Clibbit. "Be goin' vor leave Oodmall, hey? Aw, I ban't chiding 'ee, midear!" he said in a serious voice, gazing at the infant, whose eyes were suddenly round. " 'Tes proper, 'tes right, vor you to go away. I ban't no gude. You go away, li'l Clibbit, and don't trouble nought about I. Go along, missus, your carriage be waiting, midear." Blinking the tears from her eyes, the woman went downstairs with the baby, and out of the house, and Clibbit was left alone with his pony, his dog, a pig, and two cows.

That night he spent in the inn, smiling and nodding his head and praising his wife in a voice that after four glasses of whisky became soft under its perpetual roughness. The neighbours remained silent. Clibbit told them what a beautiful animal was Ship, the grey long-haired sheepdog that followed him everywhere. "A master dog, aiy!" Ship's head was patted; her tail trembled with gratitude on the stone floor. They said nothing to that, thinking that in the morning the dog's ribs were likely to be broken by one of Oodmall's boots. Ship had long ceased to howl when kicked or beaten by her master. Her eyes flinched white, she crouched from the blow, her eyes closed, and a sort of subdued whimper came from her throat. She never growled nor snarled at Clibbet. Nor did she growl at anything; she seemed to have none of the ordinary canine prejudices or rivalries. Ship was old then. She was a grey shadow slipping in and out of the farmyard doors with Clibbit, or lying in the lane outside, waiting to fetch the cows for milking and returning behind them afterwards. Strangers visiting the village in summer, and pausing to pat the old dog, were likely to wonder why there were so many bumps on her ribs; explanation of the broken ribs was always readily forth-coming from the neighbours.

That evening Clibbit was drunk, but not so happy that he could not find his way down the lane to Frogstreet. He sang in the kitchen, and danced a sort of jig on the slate floor; the first time he had danced and sung since his courting days. In the morning he awoke and got up before daybreak, lit the fire, boiled himself a cup of tea, and ate some bread, cheese, and onions. He milked and fed the two cows himself, watered and fed the pony, and gave the pig its barley meal. Afterwards he and Ship followed behind the cows to the rough pasture in the marshy field called Lovering's Mash; all day he ploughed with a borrowed pair of horses, and towards dusk of the wintry day he and Ship brought the cows back to be milked and stalled for the night.

After more bread and cheese, he went up to the inn, drank some whisky, and then smiles broke out of his angular, tufted face and to the neighbours he began to praise wife, li'l ol' pony, dog, and parson. When he had gone home the neighbours said he was a hypocrite.

8

Clibbit's lonely farming became the joke of the village. He was seen pouring away pails of sour milk into the stream which ran beside Frogstreet and through the garden. He tried to get a woman to look after the dairy, but no one would offer. A letter written by an anonymous neighbour brought a sanitary inspector to Frogstreet; one of the cows was found to be tubercular and ordered to be destroyed. Clibbit sold the other cow to a butcher. He sold his sow to the same butcher a month later. His fields were overgrown with docks, thistles, and sheep's sorrel. His plough stood in one field halfway down a furrow, its rusty share being bound by stroyle grass whose roots it had been cutting when the neighbour had come up and taken away the pair of horses. This neighbour, a hard-working chapel worshipper, intended to buy Frogstreet farm when it came into the market, as inevitably it must. He was the writer of the anonymous letter to the sanitary inspector, and saw to it that everyone knew the property was worth very little; meanwhile he waited to buy it. Clibbit still worked at his traps, always accompanied by old Ship, getting a few shillings a week for rabbits. The neighbours said he didn't eat enough to keep the flesh on a rat.

The pony, already blind from cataract in one eye, and more than twenty years old, developed fever in the feet, and hoping to cure it, for he was fond of it, Clibbit turned it out into Lovering's Mash. It was seen limping about, an inspector came out from town, and Clibbit was summoned to the Court of Summary Jurisdiction.

The stag-hunting chairman of the bench of magistrates, after hearing the evidence of the prosecution, and listening without apparent interest to Clibbit's stammered statement, remarked that he had seen the defendant before him on another occasion. The clerk whispered up to him. H'm, yes. For the callous neglect of the horse, which with the dog was man's best friend—a most un-British line of conduct, he would remark—defendant would be sent to prison for seven days without the option of a fine, and the pony destroyed by Order of the Court. A woman cried, "Bravo, English justice!" in a shrill triumphant voice; she was turned out of court. The clerk read the next charge, against a terrified and obese individual who had been summoned for riding a bicycle at night without sufficient illumination within the meaning of the Act—to wit, a lamp—who said he had forgotten to light the wick in his haste lest he be late for choir practice. He led the basses, he explained, nervously twisting his hat. Laughter. Clibbit, following a constable through a door, thought the laughter was against him. He had not eaten for three days.

That night, Ship broke out of the barn, wherein she had been locked, by biting and scratching a way under the rotten doors, and in the morning she was found sitting, whining almost inaudibly, outside the prison gates. The sergeant of police on duty, recognizing her, said he would report the stray for destruction, but a young constable, to whom as a small boy Clibbit had once given an apple, said he would look after it until the old Wood Awl came out.

When he came out, his hair cut and his nose not so red, Ship ran round and round him in circles, uttering hysterical noises and trembling violently. Clibbit patted Ship absent-mindedly, as though he did not realize why he or the dog was there, and then set out to walk home.

Next day he was seen about his incult fields, followed by Ship, and mooning about, sometimes stooping to pull a weed—a man with nothing to do.

It was a mild winter, and the frosts had not yet withered the watercress beside the stream running through the small orchard of Frogstreet.

Three weeks before Christmas, Clibbit picked a bunch of watercress and took it to Vellacott farm. "For the baby," he said. His brother-in-law told him to take himself off. "The less us sees of 'ee, the better us'll be plaised," he said. "You and your outrageous cruelty! And I'll tell 'ee this, too, midear: us be puttin' th' law on to 'ee, yesmye, us be suing of 'ee into town, in the court, for to divorce 'ee!"

Clibbit went away without a word. His body was found the next day lying in Lovering's Mash, gun beside him, and Ship wet and whimpering. Watercress was found in his pocket. The coroner's court found a verdict of *felo-de-se* after much discussion among the jury whether it should be *due to unsound mind* for the sake of the family.

The neighbours were now sorry for Oodmall, recalling that he had been a wonnerful generous chap sometimes, especially when drunk.

9

A week before Christmas the ringers began their practice, and the peeling changes of the Treble Hunt fell clanging out of the square Norman tower. It was freezing; smoke rose straight from chimneys. The first to come down the stone steps of the tower and out of the western door, carrying a lantern, were the colts, or youths still learning to ring; they saw something flitting grey between the elms which bordered the churchyard and the unconsecrated ground beyond. The colts gave a glance into the darkness; then they hurried down the path, laughing when they were outside the churchyard. But they did not linger there.

Others saw the shadow. The constable, followed and reassured by several men, went among the tombstones cautiously, flashing an electric torch on a heap of earth, still showing shovel marks, without flower or cross—grave of the suicide.

Frogstreet was dark and still, save for the everlasting murmur of flowing water; people hurried past it; and at midnight, when stars glittering were the only light in the valley, the greyness flitted across the yard and stopped, lifting up its head, and a long mournful cry rose into the night.

Towards dawn the cry rose again, as though from the base of the elms; and when daylight came the mound of earth was white with rime, and the long withered grasses were white also, except in one place beside the mound where they were pressed down and green.

The church choir, grouped forms and shadows and a bright new petrol-vapour lamp, went round the village, singing carols. Snow was falling when they walked laughing by the door and blank windows of Frogstreet, on the walls of which their shadows slanted and swerved. The girls laughed shrilly; Christmas was coming and life seemed full and good. Above the wall of the churchyard, raised high by the nameless dead of olden time, two red points glowed steadily. A girl ceased laughing, and put hand to mouth to stop a cry. In the light of the upheld lamp the red points shifted and changed to a soft lambency, and they saw the face of Ship looking down at them. "Oh, poor thing!" said the girl. She was kitchen-maid at the rectory. The cook told the rector.

The rector was an old man with a white beard, a soft and clear voice, and eyes that had often been very sad when he was young, but now were serene and sure. He had no enemies; he was the friend of all.

Late that night he went to the ground left unconsecrated by ecclesiastical law westwards of the elms and stood by the mound, listening to the sounds of the stream and feeling himself one with the trees and the grass and the life of the earth. This was his prayer; and while he prayed, so still within himself, he felt something warm gently touch his hand, and there, in silence, stood Ship beside him.

The dog followed him to the rectory, and touching the man's hand with its nose, returned to its vigil.

Every morning the rector arose with the sun and went into the churchyard and found Ship waiting for him, and his gift of a biscuit carried in his pocket. Then he entered the church and knelt before the altar, and was still within himself for the cure of souls.

10

On Christmas Eve the yews in the churchyard were black and motionless as dead Time. The ringers going up the path to the western door saw between the elms a glint and shuffle of light—the rays of their lantern in the icicles hanging from the coat of the dog.

And on Christmas morning the people went into the church while the sun was yet unrisen behind their fields, and knelt in their pews and were still within themselves while the rector's words and the spoken responses were outside the pure aloneness of each one.

With subdued quietness a few began to move down the aisle towards the chancel to kneel by the altar rail behind which the priest waited to minister to them. He moved towards them with the silver paten of bread fragments.

"Take and eat this in remembrance ..." he was saying, when those remaining in the pews began to notice a small chiming and clinking in the air about them, and as they looked up in wonderment, the movement of other heads drew sight to the figure of the old grey sheepdog walking up the aisle. With consternation they watched it moving slowly towards the light beginning to shine in the stained glass of the tall eastern windows above the altar. They watched it pause before the chancel step, as it stood, slightly swaying, as though summoning its last strength to raise one foot, and a second foot, and again one more foot, and then the last foot, and limp to the row of kneeling people beyond which the rector moved, murmuring the words spoken in olden time by the Friendless One who saw all life with clarity.

The verger hurried on tiptoe across the chancel, but at the look in the rector's eyes, and the slow movement of his head, he hesitated, then returned down the aisle again.

The dog's paw was raised to the rail as it sat there, with dim eyes, waiting; and at every laboured breath the icicles on its coat made their small chimmering noises.

When the last kneeling figure had returned to the pews, with the carved symbols of Crucifixion mutilated in Cromwell's time for religion's sake, the rector bent down beside the dog. They saw him take something from his pocket and hold it out to the dog; then they saw his expression change to one of concern as he knelt down to stroke the head which had slowly leaned sideways as sight unfocused from the dying eyes. They heard the voice saying, slowly and clearly, "Be thou faithful unto death; and I will give thee a crown of life", and to their eyes came tears, with a strange gladness within their hearts. The sun rose up over the moor, and shone through the eastern windows, where Christ the Sower was radiant.

The Maiden Salmon

Here lies the moor, wild with green bog and curlew's song in spring, grey with granite tors ceaselessly carved by the winds of centuries, the winds bringing Atlantic clouds which in the cold air over rock and valley fall as rain and fill many rivers flowing rapidly to the ocean again. In all the rivers, save those polluted by man with his mines and factories, salmon are born, and live their young lives awhile before migrating to the sea, to roam in deep waters where only death or dream has taken men; and after several years they return to their native rivers, in silver sea-dress, for the sake of love, to spawn; and nearly all of them die there.

One morning in the New Year a man was walking beside a thread of water which ran bright and clear under banks of carven peat. He walked on a path among rushes and granite boulders and soft green moss, a path used only by himself, by sheep, and wandering foxes. He walked alertly, hopefully, for the sun was shining and shadows of white billowy clouds were moving swiftly northwards over the moor. For weeks ice and snow had held down the life of earth and water; now the south wind was bringing hope and renewal with the sun.

Following his own path beside the runnel of water, he came into a wide valley made during hundreds of thousands of centuries by water hastening to the sea. Here under the hills ran the river from which the moor takes its name, one of the most famous salmon rivers of the south.

A score of paces before the junction of runner and river he stopped, and kneeling on a stone, examined something intently, his face near the water. When he looked up, his face was alight with joy: for one of the salmon eggs in the tray, made of stripped and charred withies of the dwarf willow, lying on the gravel, had hatched.

2

During the past summer this man, who was a poet and an ex-
soldier, had cut a channel through the turf, and dammed the runner
with boulders. A small pool was formed, and water flowed along its
new bed. He made a wooden fender, which could be lifted to
regulate the flow of water; and a box of fine granite gravel placed
inside the fender acted both as filter for silt and screen against any
fish or water-insect drifting down with the current. At the lower end
of the new channel he set a wooden box with a grill made of an
old pail, pierced with nail-holes, to stop entry from the river, knowing that eels and trout work upstream in search of food, especially
if that food be salmon-eggs. An eel quests for and works the food-
scents in a river as keenly as a hound after the quarry has been
found.

Then in October the rains fell, driving and drifting like smoke
across the moor; and when they ceased water cried night and day
against the earth, faintly in trickle and string and bubbly splash
through the peat hags of the higher ground, growing louder as it
fell in rillet and cascade and swilling glide over and on the granite
until it roared down the valleys, a dark-brown flood against which the
salmon bored and leapt, as they journeyed upwards to the spawning
redds at the river-head. The man watched them, identifying himself
with them. Water-bailiffs, paid by the Conservancy Board to frustrate
poachers with gaff, wire-noose, net, and bomb, soon ceased to be
suspicious of him, as day by day he stood by the fish-passes in the
weirs built along the lower beats of the river. To the watcher from
the moor the fish were noble travellers, returning to the perilous river
from the safety of Atlantic waters on the only true aristocratic impulse of life, the instinctive search for immortality through love..

Joyously the salmon were returning to the stream where during
the first two years of their lives they had worn the brown, red-spotted
dress of little trout—growing therein hardly as long as a man's
hand; now, as mature fish, they rolled and played joyously under the
weirs and waterfalls, strangely excited by the imminence of peril for
love's sake. These fish feared shallow water, yet they swam on, boring
a way up waterfall and torrent, often to be hurled back and pounded
against rocks which bruised their bodies and broke their tails; or
they clung with paired fins to certain jags which wore their scales
away until the flesh was exposed.

The poise of a salmon, the power of its accumulated sea-strength, lies along its tapered length. Its flexibility is its life; it dreads each upward leaping into the stupendous solid power of water roaring over a high precipitous weir; it noses the water; it slides up and drifts back, exploring with its sensitive flanks, again and again, until its own golden power of faith returns unto its being, and it hurls itself out of the foaming pool and bores its way into that which gives it immortality ... So the poet, lonely and proud in his own spirit, thought as he watched the autumn run of salmon ascending to the spawning redds on the moor. Weary beyond thoughts of crucifixion and resurrection, self-withdrawn in despair from the deathly ways of his fellow-men, living beyond hope of human companionship since the realization in his thirtieth year that he had been born to love God, he yet lived and was upheld with Faith; and in some way, which he could not (nor indeed did he wish to) formulate, salmon were of that Faith. All he dare think to himself was that a fish was anciently the symbol of baptism, of rebirth, of Heavenly Consciousness. And did not Jesus say that this was Love—Jesus, whose tears were clouds these many centuries? With such strange and incalculable feelings the hatching bed was made in the runner, high up on the moor; and a handful of salmon eggs from the spawning bed in the river transferred there, carried in damp moss.

The eggs were the colour of Californian grapes, a faint pinky brown. Lying still on the bank, he had watched the male fish taking the female's place over the eggs: a pale cloudiness floating away in the water. A farmer had seen the fish there, too, in water less than nine inches deep, so that their back fins and tails were in air. Next morning the redd, or spawning bed, was empty. A pitchfork had killed the fish, and lifted them out, to feed the farmer's pigs in the farm on the hillside, a small grey building standing gauntly within a rectangle of starved trees half ruined by wind.

Very carefully the poet had put the eggs in a hatching tray, and covered them with a hurdle made of willow and mountain ash wands to shut them from light and the scrutiny of birds. Then came frost and ice, and for weeks his own life was suspended with that life developing within the eggs. At last the warm south wind brought a thaw, and he waited in the sunshine for his own renewal.

3

Against the lower end of the wicker-basket he saw the broken egg-covering turning and bobbing in the limpid flow of water, scarcely an inch deep, which twirled through the spaces in the wickerwork. It was like a very small colourless grape-skin. There in the corner, hiding, was the baby salmon—an alevin, luminously opaque, no longer than his fingernail, a mite with the egg sac still dependent upon it, now its belly. He touched it with the tip of a curlew's feather, and it wriggled swiftly across the tray with extraordinary speed. He felt his life glow within him, as he covered the tray carefully to keep the light from its eyes, and rising, sang as he walked down the path to his hut.

The next morning other eggs had hatched. With the curlew's feather he lifted the skins from the water, and several eggs which were an opaque yellow, sign that they were dead. The alevins wriggled rapidly, always head to stream, under the eggs, to get away from the light. One wriggled more rapidly than the others, and he knew it for the alevin that had first hatched. Every egg was rolled over delicately with the tip of the feather and scrutinized for the slight furriness indicating the fungus of disease. The wicker tray, with its bars of withy almost touching, had been charred in the flames of his hearth so that any fungus on them would be killed, and any underwater growth prevented. Water wimpled clear over the un-hatched eggs and the semi-transparent alevins pressed between them.

Every morning he walked along the path by the runner, to watch over the alevins and remove the old egg-skins. After ten days all but six were hatched. These were still clear, they were infertile, and he lifted them up the side of the tray with the stiff edge of the feather and flipped them one by one over the lower screen. As the sixth egg struck the water there was a slight bulging rise, made by the head of a cannibal brown trout which for days had been waiting below the screen, drawn by the scent of salmon alevins. Seeing a blurred movement as the man stood upright, the trout sped away, making a ream or wavelet on the surface of the water.

At the beginning of the third week nearly half a hundred alevins were pressed together in one corner of the tray. The quickest of the alevins, browner than the others, was the one he always looked for; it was the first to be hatched, and already its sac was shrinking into its body, and in shape it was almost a little fish.

A water-snail wandered into the sanctuary, and although it was small its shell was several times the size of the holes in the screens. How came it there? He sought for holes, and found one under the entry screen. He had omitted to clear away grasses and rootlets which had collected there, and this had caused the water to rise higher and to fall through the holes, cutting a pit under the lower framing of the screen. This he blocked with a turf, which he firmly trod down. Afterwards he searched in the channel for any eel or trout that might have passed through.

Next morning, when he lifted the hurdle, he saw something that made him start with inward anguish, for against the side of the wicker-tray lay a small fish as long and broad as his thumb, with a squat ugly bull-like head, mottled and spotted with brown. It squatted there, holding to a blackened cross-stick with fins like yellow hands. And the right top corner of the tray, where the alevins had huddled together, was empty. The dwarf fish, eater of salmon fry, was alone in the tray.

The poet felt the doom of his previous life on the world's battle-fields, before he had sought purification by solitude upon the moor, coming upon him dreadfully; and he turned away with a gesture of weariness, and lay on the sward with one arm outflung, while the water seemed to be flowing away with his life, leaving it vain and purposeless as the sky which saw birth, growth, decay and death with equal vacancy. He lay there while the shadow of rushes in the south-running water slowly drew into the bank, leaving the stream sun-clear and glassy.

4

Footsteps brushing the heather made him look up, when the footsteps ceased. He looked into the clear eyes of a young girl regarding him with steadfast gravity. The sun was behind her, her outline arose slender and shining out of the moor. The flow of his life to the vacant sky ceased, and returned to him as she came slowly nearer, her eyes losing the firmness of their gaze as she approached, as though with doubt; yet their clarity remained. Lightly she came nearer, until she was leaning down over the narrow ribbon of water, staring at the tray with its misshapen occupant. Her clothes were poor and torn, her thin bare legs scratched with brambles, her mouth was large, her eyes were blue; probably she was, he thought, the daughter of the farmer to whom salmon were a means for cheaply feeding pigs and manuring vegetables; and his eyes lifted to the gaze of her blue eyes, childlike and calm with mental fearlessness, regarding him. They are gone, he heard her saying softly, and her eyes became wistful, and her gaze fell. A thought came to him, overlaying the thought of her candid eyes and brow, that by her remark she must have visited the hatchery, that she had put the mullhead in the tray —the ignorant and destructive ways of men were inescapable. Yes, he replied, and turned away from the sun.

She was gone without sound.

The water drew to itself a shadow from the bank, singing its song of bubble and swirl, green moss and white granite and gleam of sky, while a lark flew up and up into the blue, aspiring to the sun. The poet sat up, and looked sadly into the water, at the mullhead squatting there in the same place, replete, dull, gorged with its feast of the innocents. There was a glitter within the water as he shifted position. He peered down, and put his hand in the stream, to pick up a small piece of metal, star-shaped, that appeared to be, as he examined it . . . but was it possible? Gold? And how came it there? A gold star? Then he glanced down at the tray, where the dwarf had shifted when he had dipped his hand, and now was cowering in the corner; but it was not there he looked, but at a tiny fish which was poised, vibrating gently, behind the tail of the mullhead. He knew it for his own, and first-born, the alevin which now was a real fish, although scarcely more than an inch long, scaled, tapered for poise in water which flowed from the rock! The mullhead darted forward, and the little fish moved after it, keeping always behind its tail: the triumph of reason over massive strength, David defeating Goliath, life triumphing over death; and the gold in his hand was surely a symbol, a message of hope, like the morning star before sunrise?

He scooped the mullhead, against which he had had no feelings of anger or revenge, in his hand, and slipped it into the stream below the grill. There was a swirl in the water, and the olive-brown head of the cannibal trout showed in an instant; and then the stream flowed placidly once more.

5

Sweet summer lay over the moor, with cirrus clouds in the height of the sky. Bees climbed happily among the honey-bells of heather, and the murmur of water arose from among the feet of the hills. In the mellow evening light waterflies rose and fell over the river, dropping their eggs from delicate long whisks below their gauzy wings; to fall spent as the evening star glowed softly, the purpose of their lives fulfilled, to die as dreams of twilight and the everlasting compassion of death. The poet stood by the hatchery, while the rings of trout dimpled the river, and collected the tired flies, and let them drift, void of life, on the glimmering surface of the channel. Gracefully the samlet, with a slow sweep of tail, rose and lipped the water.

When the leaves of willow and mountain-ash began to turn yellow the samlet was as long as the man's little finger, a taper of golden brown spotted with black and red, and dark smudges, like thumb-marks, on its sides. It wore the workaday dress of a trout, like all young salmon while the Water Spirit prepares them for the deep waters of the Atlantic where they alone of fish are noble; but its mouth was smaller than a young trout of its own size, its head more shapely. When the poet leaned over the channel, the little fish with a double fanlike wave of its tail-fin would swim up from the resting-place on the white gravel and take food from his fingers. When he was gone it watched the water moving past for daphne, shrimp, and nymph of hatching waterfly, buoying itself in the gentle current; or it slept, resting on the bed of the channel, against the peaty side, while its golden-brown colour dulled and its scales took on the hue of the peat. There it passed most of the winter, its being suspended with the life of the stream.

In its second summer it grew longer than the man's middle finger, and it could leap easily thrice its length into the air after flies hovering there.

Again at the fall water ran everywhere down the moor-slopes, gleaming grey with a sky of low and swiftly passing clouds. On a certain day and night in November rain fell with a heavy steadiness that appeared to overcome all other elements, and the conquering roar of the spate filled the misty valley. The path by the runner was drowned, the runner itself was now a river tearing down past the hut on the knoll with the speed of wild moorland ponies. For seven days and nights the rain fell, ceasing only to assemble new darknesses of clouds, and the level of the spate rose and dropped back a dozen times a day. Once when he looked from the door of his hut, hazy with the smoke of a peat fire, the man heard a sound of whistling like curlews crying, and saw the brown whiskered heads of three otters riding down on the flood, as they passed in their play of hide-and-seek amidst the unfamiliar hurlyburlies of the torrent. Rocks weighing many tons were undercut and rolled down the valley with dull bumping sounds.

And then the rain ceased and the weak winter sun shone again, and within a few hours the water was running clear once more. The hatchery was gone, the old channel filled with rocks and gravel, the screens washed away. Where was the samlet now? he wondered forlornly; perhaps in the sea, carried there before its time, or champed in the jaws of one of the cannibal trout which dwelt in the deep weir pools down the valley.

Yet the poet had faith; and in his belief he set himself to clear the choked bed and to reset the dam of boulders across the runner by the channel inlet. A stone was placed where the top screen had stood, and water pouring over this carved a pool where the samlet had lurked before. In February, when the first flies began to hatch—small stone flies which as nymphs had built each around itself a shelter of stone specks cemented together, with a doorway for their heads—he saw one morning a slight bulge in the water, and there, poised between the two converging flumes of currents, maintaining its stance with the least muscular effort, was his samlet, thinner and darker with winter fasting, but there it was, his darling fish, returned to him after the winter drear.

So April came again, with the willow's hair drooping silver and green, and a solitary swallow playing in the light airs of the valley, while from afar came the voice of the cuckoo. Every day the poet came from his hut, where he was writing an epic of the moor's ancientness and wisdom, to visit the samlet. In the last week of April it began to leap into the air and play on its side when it saw him. It became strangely excited as April ended her days. The golden hue of its scales gleamed brighter; it was changing its shape, too, growing longer, slimmer. Now the red spots were vanishing, and the black spots were as though washed away by the stream, which was laving it with silver! No longer was it wearing its moorland dress of a trout, but before his eyes the Water Spirit was fashioning for it a sea-coat of newest silver. No longer was it a samlet, but a smolt, scaled with argent armour for its adventure down the river to the sea, and that journey to Greenland, far from the submarine ledges where the last of Europe breaks away into the realm of deep waters, where only death or dream has taken men.

Knowing the hour was come, he lifted the smolt from the water, fixed the star with silver wire to the little shortened rear fin on its back, and released it tenderly into the stream again. The next day the pool in the channel was empty.

6

Now every surviving Atlantic salmon, excepting an occasional straying fish, comes back to spawn in the river of its birth, from the northern feeding grounds of ocean. Scientists, who walk where poets fly, do not yet agree how each fish finds its particular way home. Some say they return by instinct. Of the Eastern Atlantic salmon, the short deep Tay fish returned to the Tay, the long lean Exe fish to the Exe, the heavy Wye thirty-pounder to that river which almost divides Wales. By instinct, say the scientists: every egg carries its potential sea-route. Innumerable generations passed up and down this river, the habit was laid deep, and eventually was put into the egg, like the habit feeding, breathing, swimming, and the deeper functions of gills, blood-course, and sight. This, they say, is instinct. By instinct the salmon returns. But the poet had seen eyed-ova of Tay salmon brought from Scotland to the extreme south-west of England, hatched in a Devon hatchery, planted as fry in a Devon river, and in time they returned, not to the Tay, but to the Devon river, short deep fish among the lean native salmon. There was, he knew, in the salmon a beautiful natural memory of place—pool, bend, fall, and quality of water—which to him was divine.

For nearly two years he lived and worked in his native cathedral city, inspired by thoughts and dreams of the fish which had gone down to the sea bearing the star of gold into the blue twilight of its ocean destiny. He was known to be queer from the shocks of battle he had sustained. His friends were sympathetic towards him; he realized that he had to make his own adjustment to living; but the passionate few alone saw beauty in his face, akin to that of mediaeval saints in old pictures, and recognized a rare quality in his poetry.

At the beginning of the second April after the smolt's departure the solitary young man was visited by a growing sensation of excitement and of the fateful imminence of an indefinable dread. After two years in the sea, he knew, the salmon would be between five and seven pounds in weight, and was likely to return to the river, a small spring fish. By the shape of the smolt he had known it was female. At that very moment his maiden salmon might be coming in from the Atlantic, travelling the route, with others of its generation, which would bring the schools east of the headland, along the shingle bank under the cliffs, and round the shore of the next headland to the estuary of the river.

The poet was almost to the climax of his epic, but he could write no further: he suffered mental anguish through doubt and confusion, which led to distrust of his inspiration, believing it to be self-delusion, his thoughts due to physical inactivity or frustration.

A line in his poem seemed to stand out of the page:

His tears are clouds since many centuries

and beyond that sorrowful truth he could find no pathway.

That night in sleep he dreamed of his salmon, which glowed with unearthly radiance in the night of his vision; and awakening, he dressed, packed his rucksack, took his staff, and set out on the road to the moor and the sea as the morning star was rising above the cathedral with its carved stonework figures obliterated by the rains and winds of seven centuries.

He walked throughout the day, resting at night at an inn, and the next morning went on his journey, arriving in the afternoon at the westward end of the shingle bank. Returning salmon were cruising through water a few feet from the shore, working round the coast, seeking the river. And along that shingle bank, at intervals, were fishermen with nets and boats, each waiting crew having a lookout man posted on the cliffs above the ruin of a fishing village washed away in one of the great storms which visit the coast of the English Channel once or twice every century.

7

For days the poet waited, concealing his anxiety; friendly with the fishermen, yet aloof.

Sometimes, as he stood by one or another of the watchers, he would hear a shout, see an arm pointing, cap in hand, in a certain direction. Men would appear out of the ruins of the village; they ran over the shingle; the small boat was launched; a net shaken over the stern while two men rowed vigorously in an arc towards where the watcher was pointing. A shadow-shape moving eastwards in the dim greenish water; a slim shape curving out of the sea less than an oar's length from the beach, falling back into its bubbled plunge and broken circle of whitish bubbles vanishing. The widening surge of ripples had hardly settled when the fish leapt again twenty yards farther on, to fall and smack the surface of the sea, thus hoping to rid itself of sea-lice clustered near the tail. Many times the poet hastened down to the shore to see a fish dragged in by the net; and he trudged from boat to boat, asking permission to look under the squares of canvas lying high up on the shingle, covering the day's catch of each crew.

On the seventh morning a new crew and boat appeared, rowed by an old man, his two sons, and his daughter. The poet watched her as they drew up the bow of the boat upon the edge of the shingle. The girl's thick fair hair, bleached by the sun, was clustered short on her shoulders. Her arms and legs were bare, golden-brown in the sun. She laughed with her brothers, tossing back her hair; she was strong in her sea-grace. The child he had seen by the hatchery four years before was now a woman. The poet stood there, still and silent, stirred by her beauty, his thoughts cloistered apart from that which was of the realm of dream. Then seeing him, the girl also stood still and silent for a moment, while he thought that never had he seen a brow so candid, or eyes so direct and clear, as though with the sky's clarity. A strange joy stirred in him.

A shout far away to the westward, another shout nearer, a third shout. There was excitement and movement among the boats on the beach. More shouting and waving arms from the cliff-watchers and crews alike: several fish had leapt at once. Again and again, leap along the shore.

One brother, wearing blue woollen jersey and sea-boots, remained on the shingle, holding the head-rope, while the boat leaped through the water, rowed by the girl and the other brother. Over the stern the father shook and loosened the folds of the net, which soon was hanging vertical in the water, between the row of corks on the head-rope and the leads on the heel-rope. The boat described an arc to the line of shore, thus cutting off and enclosing an area to imprison fish. One after another, "lepping like greyhounds", in the words of the old man above, large fish jumped over the curve of corks as the seine was drawn ashore. Grey mullet. They stopped rowing in disappointment. *'Twas zalmon I zeed, I tell 'ee!* roared the grey-beard, following his words with emphatic spittle. Then a salmon reamed along the water, and they bent to the oars again. The boat grated on the shingle, they jumped out and began hauling. The poet stood by, waiting with a feeling of his own life being drawn from him.

The net was hauled less slowly as the sea-drag lessened. The fishermen stared as they hauled hand-under-hand, heels dug into the shingle. The boat lifted and scraped gently at the water's edge. The last of the net, the long purse, came in rapidly. *A-aah!* One fish only. They were disappointed.

The poet's heart beat so that his body seemed hollow with noise, too weak to maintain itself standing. The solitary fish threshed the net in vain. A hand gripped it near the tail. It shook and curved, trying to escape. The poet saw a yellow sparkle in the sunlight, and his sight was instantly blackened.

The fish was carried up the shingle and dropped in a hollow amidst seaweed and the black horned shells of skate-eggs. There it writhed and writhed, seeking escape from the frightful elements of air and light. It was small-mouthed, silver-frosty, scarcely spotted— a maiden fish, said the fisherman, who did not notice the gold it bore on the small, pennon-like back fin.

It flapped and leapt and slapped down on the dry stones until blood broke out of the scales of the slender tail, and it weakened, fast losing its beauty, boring feebly, to lie still, dislustred; and after a while it leapt again, slapping away its life on the scalding shingle, seeking with the last of its strength to find the life which it had lost. The fisherman glanced casually at the figure of the man standing still by the fish, and then stooped to the re-piling of the net.

The poet stood beside the salmon, waiting during the agony and betrayal of the spirit's innocence by forces of life which he knew were irresistible and inevitable. And waiting there, he felt a strange joy arising through his pain, as he beheld the everlasting stream of time which flowed away from the world's end, to an immortal sea beyond the dusk of those great night suns called stars.

The salmon was scarcely breathing now. Slowly it lifted up, a curving sigh of farewell to its beauty; and it was ended.

The poet stood there, his eyes seeing not the steady glance of the girl beside him, nor anything mortal as he drowned in a sea deeper than the Atlantic.

8

Upon the shingle the breakers crashed, driven by the gale, to withdraw in white roar of foam. Far out beyond the estuary the sea was dark with peat water of the river in spate. Solid bends of swift water, brown but clear, hid the sills of weirs up the valley. On the hill above his hut stood the poet, watching the last of the sun sinking into the Atlantic, heedless of rain, lightning, wind. He watched dark clouds absorbing the last gleam and walked down to the lower ground, his head held high, his eyes steady and bright. His work was done, his life fulfilled, and now he might enter the everlasting stream of time beyond the end of the world. The river, faithful to the Spirit that breathed upon the face of its waters, creator of life through the symbol of baptism, should bear in the darkness his useless body to the sea's oblivion.

He entered his hut, and began to arrange papers, books, chair and cooking pots. The blankets were folded on the bed of ashpoles and bracken; the manuscript of his poem wrapped up, tied with string, addressed, left on the table. A note was written, giving these few belongings, and the use of the hut, to a younger poet whose work he had encouraged and helped into print. The fire on the hearth was sunken in grey ash and dull embers, a pale flame rising from the peat and sinking against the whitened stones of the hearth. Better to quench the fire before departing; but no, on this last night the virtue and service of fire should be treated with honour.

He sat before the wan flames hovering out of the peat, heather of olden time, that was yet sunshine and air and salt of the earth arising again in flame for the service of another form of life. The river's song arose in the night now glittering with stars, and he waited, serene and joyful in the ultimate triumph of poetry over the world. It became colder towards dawn, and he began to feel a return of doubt and terror; but he resisted the temptation to flinch. The flame was sinking, and soon he would be free to go.

And sitting there, his eyes closed, he rested in his spirit; and so fell asleep.

A pale visitant was now within the hut, revealing gradually table, walls, bed, floor, the poet's thin hands and knees and feet, the poet's face worn and tranquil, the eyes of which had dreamed beyond hope —the visitant revealed all as surfaces in one dimension: the visitant was Dawn.

Still in his dream, he saw himself getting on his feet and turning to the door. The door was opening of itself. A form appeared before him. Eyes of the sky's clarity looked into his eyes, and in her tender smile the sun's truth flowed to his being enfeebled by its long and lonely search in the moonlit land of truth. She was smiling, she came close to him, her eyes with the colour and truth of the sky. Her hand took his hand, and pressed it warmly. Her other hand was held open before him, with the golden star and silver link. His tears fell and he bowed his head, and she bent over him tenderly, and clasped him.

In the eastern sky the Morning Star, Eosphoros the Light-bringer, glowed with its white fires. Joyfully the song of water arose in the valley. The poet looked at his companion, and knew that his search was ended—for on that brow was the sunrise of a new world.

Where the Bright Waters Meet

I did not want to leave Devon, I did not want to go away in the least, yet I was here on the station platform, watching the 9.1 a.m. London train approaching on the single line of the track. A ticket was in my hand. Basil stood beside me. I felt vague resentment that I was going to London on a Monday morning. Basil had to go back because of his business. He had an office somewhere in Westminster, and sold, or tried to sell, plaster-of-paris to builders. He had inherited the business from an uncle, and disliked it. Occasionally he came down to Devon to spend the weekend with me, bringing his fly-rod.

The train came into the small station, which was built in a cutting. It was a delightful place, with its little goods-yard, rambler roses on the platform, and oil lamp with bulbous glass globe in iron frame on a wooden post.

Basil glanced round and smiled his whimsical smile, preparatory to saying goodbye and thanking me for a most enjoyable weekend. I knew exactly what he would say. Basil was always punctilious and charming; his hair was always well-brushed, with exactly the right amount of brilliantine; his clothes were always neat, almost fastidious. He had been much ragged as a Guardee, but had done well in the war. The death of his father following a financial crash had brought him into the uncle's business—there was a warehouse of sorts, and a shortly expiring lease of a small wharf somewhere in the lower reaches of the Thames. Basil mentioned it with reluctance, with a shrug of the shoulders, and a slight smile.

"Don't let's talk about it, it's so perfect here in Devon. May I fish the Tree Pool after tea? Or perhaps you—?"

"My dear fellow, I can fish any time. But be careful of Peter, won't you? No, do what you like. An otter or heron will get him if we don't. And if he goes away, he'll turn cannibal, of die of starvation, without the food he's used to. Get him if you can! *If you can.*"

Yes, it was foolish to be going to London on a Monday morning. I had no real business in London; it could all be done by letter, anyhow. Basil held out his hand.

"Well, I wish I weren't going, my dear chap! It's been most awfully kind of you to have had me. It's probably an outrageous request, but may I come again, and soon?"

"Do, Basil. But I'm coming with you to London."

"Are you, really?" He seemed surprised, even puzzled. "That's splendid."

We sat down opposite one another. There was no one else in our carriage. I felt worried by his surprise.

"But surely you remember we arranged at breakfast to go to town together, Basil? You said you'd take me over your wharf."

He frowned in his polite, puzzled way. Basil would never contradict or disagree with anyone; he carried the oblique method of conversation to the nth degree of perfection. "Of course, I'd love to take you over the wharf again, my dear fellow," he said blandly.

"Again? What do you mean? I've never seen your wharf, Basil! You said less than half an hour ago that you had to meet a man there at three o'clock this afternoon, and when I said how the idea of living in an old Thameside wharf fascinated me, to get away from the family and write, you know, you said, 'Why not come up with me and see it?' You remember, surely?"

"Of course I remember, my dear chap! But"—again the whimsical look of puzzlement, "I could have sworn we discussed it a month ago, and you'd seen the place then. Of course I'd be delighted to show you the wharf, such as it is."

The train was getting under way; we were passing the trees of the Deer Park on our right. Soon the tops of the firs and pines were slowly lowering themselves beside us. The cutting was dropping away; the viaduct over the valley was in front. We were now above the blue-green tops of the spruces. We sat on the right of the carriage, peering through the open window for a sight of the winding moorland stream with its fringe of alders and occasional great oaks, and of the thatched cottage far away at the end of the valley. The noises of wheels on rails were increasing to a thunderous hollow: we were upon the viaduct, Suddenly I remembered the Bentley: why were we not going to London in the car? It was a $4\frac{1}{2}$-litre supercharged model, and driving it was a pleasure. It was steady as a train at 80, 90, 100 m.p.h. Where was it? Had we left it outside the Ring of Bells the night before, when we had run up to the moor for a drink after dinner.

"Basil, where did we leave the car? I can't remember going home in it last night! We did go to the Ring of Bells, didn't we? Did we get very drunk, Basil? Am I still drunk? Is this a dream?"

"I've been wondering about that myself, my dear feller. Oh, look, there's the old grey heron, just alighting by the Tree Pool! I wonder if he'll get your big trout, Peter. Isn't the sun lovely on the trees! Look at the bullocks under that oak, beginning to swish their tails at the flies. Au revoir, river of bright water!" He sighed. "Why are we going to London on this heavenly day?"

We were now in the middle of the viaduct.

"Basil, I'm worried about the Bentley. And I can't remember walking to the station just now. How did we get there? Do you feel something queer—I say, who the devil are these two people down there, by the Tree Pool? Look, one of them is fishing! Damned poachers!"

"By Jove, yes! There's a spaniel with them, too. Calmly poaching! Probably they knew you were going to London."

"If only I could stop the train and get out! They may catch Peter."

We watched them in the distance. They were just visible beside the big hawthorn growing above the gravel ridge which floods had raised at the inner bend of the pool's tail. One of them was kneeling and casting; the other stood about a dozen yards behind him, out of the backward flight of the cast.

2

The viaduct of the Great Western Railway spanning the valley stands a hundred feet above meadowland and river. It rears itself on tall stone columns. I had often come here during the years of living in the thatched fishing cottage. One trespassed on railway property, of course, but that was part of its attraction. It was strange and fascinating to look down from that high place and see below one the slender tops of the spruce firs, where the wild pigeons had their nests. Jackdaws nested under the wooden sleepers bearing the weight of the shining railway lines; although they never appeared to have got used to the passing of trains, but flew out silent on black wings.

I became aware that the train was silent. It was at a standstill. Basil had opened the door, and had alighted. I followed him into the sunshine.

"We can go down through the trees, and then over the rushy ground without being seen until we're upon them," I heard myself saying, as we walked along the railway lines.

I moved in front of Basil. Rudeness, no doubt; but I was keen to get at those fellows below. I stepped rapidly from brown wooden sleeper to brown wooden sleeper, impatient at their short spacing, which curtailed a decent stride.

I scrambled down the steep slope by the first stone column, through the brambles and ash-plants growing in the rubble scree. A jump below, and I was in Farmer Coles's grazing, which was fenced with wire and posts from the Deer Park beyond. As I got under a loose strand of rusty wire I looked back for Basil, but I could not see him.

The two men fishing the Tree Pool were still in the same place when I peered from behind the oak growing on the bank above the gravel bed. Their forms were familiar, but I could not remember where I had seen them before. I was intensely interested in the way the leading man was fishing the tail of the pool. He was using my method of fishing in Devon streams, the unusual method of casting upstream with a single rough hackled fly on a fine tapered gut cast. Most fly fishermen fished with three wet flies downstream—tail, middle, and bob—and abandoned trouting when the water was low and bright; but this was the condition I loved, fishing upstream with a single dry fly.

One knew how a cat felt, stalking a mouse; every cast must be precise, the fly dropping lightly, its gamecock hackles glistening with the least touch of grease applied between finger and thumb, so that it rode high and airily on the slower water between stream and eddy where the fish lay. It was tiring work after prolonged writing at the desk, for one was taut and expectant, creeping catlike, all one's nervous energy in the eyes and wrist.

Now I knew that the man with the rod was drying his hackled fly by pressing it on a piece of *amadou*, that absorbent brownish substance made from a marine fungus. He was sitting on the edge of the gravel, among the young plants of docks and water celery. He lifted his rod, waving the fly backwards and forwards in the air as he pulled loops of line from the reel with his left hand. The fly sailed slowly, easily, to and fro over the water, until he had the length of line he required. I saw him tauten and the back of his head appeared to sink lower between his shoulders: he threw the fly forward with a deliberate slow intentness, while the movement of arm and shoulder, following the shooting of the line from a loop he had held in reserve, was perfect in its effect of slow-motion power.

I could sense the slow glide of the tapered and enamelled silken line through the agate and bronze rings. The line fell straight and aslant the direction of the stream, the lighter gut cast following after, and last to drop was the lure of silk and steel and feather. Almost as airily as thistledown it fell, to ride well-cocked on the water. From an underwater aspect the shining reddish hackles of the fly riding down imprisoned whirls of light; the shining skin of the water was crinkled but not broken. There it was, apparently a fat and juicy mouthful for any trout. I could feel the tenseness of the fisherman as I watched it, and when a blue-grey snout arose just where the water began to quicken into the tail of the pool, and sucked in the fly, and the fisherman gave a flick with his wrist that fixed the tiny barb into the corner of the bony mouth, I experienced an identical shock and excitement.

My tame trout, the three-pounder Loch Leven I had put into the Tree Pool a year previously, which had come by train in a carrier-tank from the fishery at Dulverton with a three-pounder brown trout, was hooked at last! I wanted to run forward, to demand furiously what they were doing there, but I remained watching. I noticed Basil kneeling on the gravel bank in front, and as the fish leapt he jumped up and ran forward. The man with the rod said to him excitedly, "You take the rod. I oughtn't to have done it". To my surprise I saw Basil take the rod, just before the fish dashed over the stickle below the pool's tail, and down the rough narrow water to the larger Viaduct Pool below. This was the trout's home, to which it had gone in its immense fear.

It fought as a hooked salmon behaves when it is red—that is, when it has been some time, perhaps four or five months, in fresh water, during which time it does not feed, but lives on its strength accumulated in sea-roving, waiting until the early winter when it will press up against floods to the top of its native river, where it will spawn, and perhaps die. A red salmon lacks the dash and surge of the clean-run fish. It bores, trying minute after minute to get to the bottom of the pool, there to avoid the terrible unknown enemy, usually invisible, which would drag it from the water. Gradually the unrelaxed pressure of the rod wears away its strength; it is confused, bewildered, beaten; it turns on its side, and is drawn to within reach of the gaff ... That was how the big trout fought the lightest of rods and gut casts. After twenty-two minutes he gave up, showed his bluish-grey length spotted black and brown, his yellow-grey belly, the slightly hooked tip of his underjaw, as the net lifted him out.

3

Should he be returned to the river? Consider: he had been put in thirteen months previously, weighing three pounds; now he was two pounds two ounces. The river could not feed this great stranger from the fish-hatchery; the smaller, wild brown trout, of an average weight of four ounces, got the natural food—the hatching nymphs, the fallen duns and spinners—before him. For three years in the hatchery he had been used to the twice-daily scattering of artificial food—a sort of crushed and soaked puppy-meal and dried meat fragments. For another year in the river he had been awaiting in the Viaduct Pool the same sort of food borne down in the rough stream, whereupon he would move up to the tail of the Tree Pool and cruise around until the expected spoonfuls were cast from the familiar figure in the alder tree above him. The figure usually climbed the tree about noon every day, except when it was frosty or the river in flood.

The spring balance told his weight at two pounds two ounces. What would happen if the unnatural food supply were stopped? He would starve to death. He was probably a cannibal already, although when feeding with the smaller wild trout, which after months of suspicion had accepted the unnatural food, he had never even threatened one. It was an Utopian life while it lasted; competition was unnecessary when the benevolent deity from the sky scattered spoonfuls of manna for them. Even the tiny fingerlings, the yearling trout and salmon-parr, hardly troubled to get out of his way, for while the daily shower lasted there was more than enough for all.

Two pounds two ounces; nineteen inches long; he had gone back a lot in condition. As for Paul, the big brownie which had been tipped from the tank with him a year before, a heron or otter had long ago had him. There were half-pounder Loch Leven trout in the pool, but they were quick and vital enough to feed in competition with the native fish; they were in marvellous condition, deep and fat like miniature Tay salmon, and their yellow-brown spots had changed to red—proof that they were nourished by natural food.

Poor Peter, there he lay, gasping on the stones, sometimes giving a desperate flap—a fish betrayed.

But if he were put back, he might go away, and, missing his food, become a cannibal, destroying hundreds of valuable yearlings.

The trout was grasped as firmly as possible across his lank and slippery middle by the left hand, while the right hand enwound with a handkerchief as protection from the prick of teeth, forced back the big upper jaw, until . . .

I tried to stop it; I ran to the edge of the water, crying out that he must not be killed, that the river and all it meant to my life would never be the same again if such a monstrous thing were done. He was my pet trout! He knew me; he would take food almost from my hand; he came up whenever I appeared on the bank of the Viaduct Pool, and waited there, expectant and confident. He must have trusted *me*, because if a stranger appeared on the bank he would remain at his resting-place under the ledge of rock at the pool's neck.

What words I shouted I don't know, but they were shouted in vain. Under the pressure the trout's neck cracked. He shuddered, and died.

I saw no more. In anguish I climbed the tree. The men were gone. A heron was standing on the sandy scour, where the visiting otters always scratched and rolled, ten yards above the neck of the Tree Pool. From my perch, where I had sat many hundreds of times before, I saw the stones of the river bed through the limpid water. I saw all the other fish I knew in their usual positions in the food-stream flowing into the pool. The sunlight made the brown and grey and blue stones, each with their clusters of caddis shell-cases, clear and beautiful. I felt all the past happiness of watching the stream return to me. And I looked round the trunk of the tree, and its shadow thrown across the shallow bed of the tail below, and there, in his position behind the mossy rock around which the faster water twirled, lay the big trout I called Peter.

4

He lay quite still, his belly resting on the gravel. His tail was set in a slight curve against the press of the current. There was a dark stain over the back of his head and shoulders. He breathed slowly, like a trout asleep. I could just discern the red of his near gill as it opened.

A hatch of fly was coming down. All the fish I knew were at their stations in the neck of the pool, in the stream itself swirling gently into the pool, and at the tail. Above the neck, where the heron stood, the water ran evenly round a bend, the bed of which was made of large stones grown with water moss. The stones were too heavy to be rolled by floods, and so they made a permanent hold for the water moss, which in turn was good holding for various crawling *larvae* or nymphs of the ephemeral flies. It was a hatch of the Iron Blue duns. The mature nymphs, their future wings formed and folded within their larval skins, were leaving the shelter of the moss where they had lived for the past year. What excitement as they ventured the stream, prepared to quit one element for another!

The run carried them into the pool, where the trout were waiting, the biggest fish in the best positions. I saw them, ranged alongside and behind one another, undulating their bodies and expelling water through their gill-covers as they drove forward gently against the current, thus keeping position, while balancing themselves with back, pectoral, and tail fins. The wimpling surface of the water was immediately disturbed by the rises. Those in the run were bulging rises, caused by the fish moving up to take the nymphs above them— for a feeding trout looks forward and upward. Those nymphs which were not taken passed into the broader, slower stream, and reaching the top of the water, struggled to break their confining skins at the thorax. There other trout rose to take them, sending out elliptical ripples which the flow smoothed away.

Those nymphs which passed the suction of opening mouths broke their shucks, and, standing up in them, unfolded their wings with miraculous speed, dried them quickly and arose into the warm air as duns. I watched some seeking shelter among the leaves of the alders, where they would wait and cast their drab wing-cases and body-covers; to fly up into the sky of late afternoon for their nuptial dances: to descend, and to drop their eggs upon the surface of the water: to sink exhausted into the stream again, and then—whither?

A hatch of fly, and the consequent rise of fish, was a sight I had never ceased to watch with thrilling excitement. The river was alive, its multitudinous life in balance under the sun! My nature drew life from the living water.

While I was watching dreamily, feeling myself suspended as a spirit of water, the heron peering from its stance on the scour lifted its long neck and held up its head anxiously. Soon I heard voices from the direction of the farm-road under the viaduct. The bird flew up, passing within six feet of where I sat immobile on my perch of branches. It was curious to watch it folding its spindly legs straight behind its tail and tucking its neck between its shoulders. It flew past me, in its alarm apparently failing to see me sitting there, less than a yard from it.

5

The voice came nearer. I recognized the man who lived in the lodge up the river, his son and wife, and Farmer Coles, the tenant of the rough grazing fields beyond the viaduct. They were dressed in their best clothes of dark material. The men wore bowler hats. I kept quite still as they approached. They were talking about the fish. They did not notice me, hidden by leaves and branches against the trunk of the alder.

"That's where it was," I heard Farmer Coles saying. "I seed'n often. Great big fish 'e was. There, behind that stone, only you can't see the stone now as the sun be shining on the water. I could've had'n out with a rabbit wire on an ash pole if I'd a mind to, many a time, but I like a bit of sport myself, and he seemed a nice sort o' feller once you got to the right side of 'n. Perhaps it would've saved a lot of trouble if I'd yanked'n out, tho'!"

They spoke for a minute or so, and then, declaring that it was nearly noon, and if they weren't early they wouldn't find standing room, they continued their way down the farm-road towards the Deer Park.

I felt that I could sit in the tree forever watching the fish in the water. I saw Basil walking slowly on the bank by the Viaduct Pool below me; and, getting down from the tree I went to him. He looked rather depressed, but smiled when he saw me.

"I say, old chap, has it occurred to you that something appears to have happened?"

"Well, now that you mention it, Basil, I must say I feel, well, rather—peculiar."

"You know the feeling one has before one realizes that one has 'flu? That exactly describes it. I think I'll go back to the house, if you don't mind, and rest in the shade."

We went home together, speaking occasionally, answering one another in monosyllables. The sunlight seemed harsh. It seemed to be beating like the clangs of great shining cymbals. Once or twice I felt a queerness in my progress, a distortion of the sense of balance. It was as though I were moving through flashing brass bars of dreadful sound. Through the plangent dissonance of life I noticed that many cars were drawn up outside the house.

"Something's happened, Basil. Keep by me. I feel so queer."

"So do I. God, my head aches."

He swayed. His face was very white. Vaguely I noticed two policemen standing by a six-wheeled lorry, on the body of which lay the remains of a smashed and burnt-out motorcar. I took Basil's arm, and we walked up the path by the hedge to the house.

It was packed with people. What were they doing there? It was an intolerable invasion of one's privacy. I remember complaining querulously to Basil, and that he did not seem to hear me.

Men and women, most of them strangers, were standing outside the open windows of the sitting-room. It looked like an auction. There must be some mistake. I tried to speak to one of the men crowding round the door, who were all peering one way. They were pressed too close together for me to get into my doorway. I thought of my wife, of my children. Where were they?

"Basil, what ever has happened?" I managed to say, through the hideous clanging sound of light.

Someone was speaking inside the room. I listened. It was the voice of the landlord of the Ring of Bells. He was describing a visit to his inn by two men in a motorcar.

"One on'm, the gennulman that writes books, had a master g'rt trout in a basket, sir. I heard tell of that fish—many had seen'n lying in the big pit below the viaduct. I gathered that the gennulmen who had the fishin', the writin' gennulman had caught his tame fish, and was very sorry he had done so. He said it was too thin, as far as I minds it."

"How much did he have to drink?"

" 'Twas a couple of whiskies, sir. It may have been three. I can't swear to it. Maybe it was four. The gennulman seemed very upset because he had caught his pet trout and killed it instead of puttin' it back in the river. But it was no case of drunkenness in my house, your honour. What happened afterwards was pure accident."

"That is for this court to decide. I want you to say only what you know, from your own observation. Were the whiskies, as you call them, were they half-quarterns, what is generally known as doubles?"

"Doubles, sir."

"You mentioned four. Are you certain of this number? You also mentioned a couple, and also three. Evidently you are uncertain. Did they offer you any drink, by any chance?"

"Yes, sir. I had one to drink the gennulmen's health with."

"I see."

Other voices. I recognized my solicitor speaking. Then Dr. Bennison. Basil seemed to be very ill now, as he clung to my arm. I felt wretchedly sick myself, with a most ghastly headache. My eyeballs seemed to be flaring. If only I could get in out of the harsh sunshine beating on my throbbing head. I think I was beginning to lose consciousness. Very remote sounded the voices. I heard, in a series of swaying recessions, the words—blazing headlights—seventy miles an hour, or maybe eighty—a terrible noise as the car crashed into the telegraph pole at the bend of the road, breaking it in two—the car turned over and over, and burst into flames—charred almost beyond recognition.

Basil heard, too. He smiled at me.

We sat by the river, in the shade of the beeches near the waterfall. We did not need to speak. It was so peaceful, watching the shallow stream rippling over the ford, where the white flowers of crow's-foot on long green bines were ever waving in the current seeking to drown those slender lengths. The grey wagtail flitted from stone to stone, the dipper sang its rillets of song. The bright waters flowed to the sea and the sky, I with them.

Acknowledgments

The stories taken from the collections THE OLD STAG and THE PEREGRINE'S SAGA are illustrated by the woodcuts of C. F. Tunnicliffe.

The stories taken from the TALES OF MOORLAND AND ESTUARY are illustrated by the drawings of Broom Lynne.